Megan of Merseyside

Rosie
Harris

Megan of Merseyside

WILLIAM HEINEMANN : LONDON

First published in the United Kingdom in 2006 by
William Heinemann

1 3 5 7 9 10 8 6 4 2

William Heinemann
The Random House Group Limited
20 Vauxhall Bridge Road, London, SW1V 2SA

Random House Australia (Pty) Limited
20 Alfred Street, Milsons Point, Sydney, New South Wales 2061, Australia

Random House New Zealand Limited
18 Poland Road, Glenfield,
Auckland 10, New Zealand

Random House (Pty) Limited
Isle of Houghton, Corner of Boundary Road & Carse O'Gowrie,
Houghton 2198, South Africa

The Random House Group Limited Reg. No. 954009

www.randomhouse.co.uk

A CIP catalogue record for this book
is available from the British Library

Papers used by Random House
are natural, recyclable products made from wood grown in
sustainable forests. The manufacturing processes conform to
the environmental regulations of the country of origin

ISBN 978 0 434 01343 2 (from Jan 2007)
ISBN 0 434 01343 9

Typeset in Palatino by Palimpsest Book Production Limited
Polmont, Stirlingshire
Printed and bound in the United Kingdom by
Mackays of Chatham plc, Chatham, Kent

For Rob and Andy Wotherspoon
And, of course, Edna, Alison and John

Acknowledgements

Once again many thanks to Georgina Hawtrey-Woore and all her colleagues. Also to Caroline Sheldon for her continued support.

Chapter One

Megan Williams knew that there was something troubling her dad the minute he came home from work. Even after he had washed away the slate dust from his hands and face Watkin Williams still looked grey and rather preoccupied.

'What's wrong, Dad?' she asked solicitously. 'Don't you feel too well?'

'Your dad's tired, that's all,' her mother said as she placed a steaming dish of potatoes in the centre of the table. 'He'll be all right once he's eaten.'

'No, Megan's right.' His frown deepened. 'There is something you should all know about. I'm changing my job!'

'Oh? Why is that, then?' Kathy Williams asked mildly.

Megan felt a chill run through her as she saw the way her father's mouth tightened and the fine lines around his dark eyes deepened.

'As you know, things have been very slow at Pengarw. There's been no overtime for months and now they're even starting to lay men off.'

'You mean they're talking of giving you the sack!' Megan exclaimed in a shocked voice.

'I'm afraid so.' Watkin sighed.

Kathy Williams frowned. 'A minute ago you said you were changing your job. Now you're

1

saying you've been laid off. So which is it?'

'One leads to the other,' he said tersely. 'It's the end of the road at the Pengarw Slate Quarry, so I decided to find something else before they decided to sack me.'

'You're a right one for making a fuss about nothing, and no mistake,' Kathy exclaimed. 'Things might only be slack for a month or so,' she added hopefully.

Nevertheless, her grey eyes clouded with sudden concern. Watkin had always been a conscientious worker and brought home a regular pay packet. Even though he handed over most of his wages for housekeeping, Kathy often found it hard to manage with their two girls, Megan and Lynn, both still at school, and she knew she'd never be able to make ends meet if he was on the dole.

'Don't worry. Something will turn up,' she murmured, as much to console herself as him.

'At my age it's no good sitting around just waiting for better times or hoping for another job to drop into my lap,' Watkin said sharply. 'There's precious little work going round here which is why I've already made up my mind about what I'm going to do. I waited until I'd sorted things out before worrying any of you about how serious things were.'

'Does that mean you've got another job?' Kathy asked.

Watkin nodded. 'Yes, I have. I'll still be driving a lorry, but it means moving back to Liverpool.'

Kathy's face lit up and her mood changed immediately from one of concern to one of jubilation. Megan couldn't ever remember seeing her so excited before.

'We're going to leave here and go back to live in Liverpool?' Kathy Williams stared at her husband in delight. 'Oh, Watkin, how wonderful!' Her plump, round face creased into a beaming smile. 'It's my dearest wish come true! Better than any holiday.' Impulsively, she hugged her husband and kissed him on the cheek.

'You think moving to Liverpool will be a holiday?' Megan stared at her mother in dismay. 'I think it sounds more like a life sentence,' she muttered unhappily.

She was deeply dismayed by the thought of leaving the slate-roofed stone cottage which clung like a limpet to the rock face at the top of the steep narrow road that led out of Beddgelert. It had been their home for the past five years and she felt distraught at the thought of moving away from the mountains that ringed the picturesque village like friendly giants. Their peaks rose proud against the skyline, pointing a warning when swirling grey clouds threatened rain or snow.

'Our Megan's got her rag up,' Lynn chortled, her grey eyes gleaming maliciously as she saw the consternation on her sister's face. 'It's because she doesn't want to be parted from her boyfriend, Ifan Jenkins,' taunted Lynn slyly.

'Don't talk so stupid!' Megan rounded angrily on the younger girl, her dark eyes fiery, her full mouth a tight line.

'Now, then, there's no need to carry on like that,'

Watkin reprimanded as Megan pushed her sister away.

He looked from one daughter to the other in bewilderment. 'It's not like you to get yourself so upset, Megan,' he said uneasily. 'Come on, now, let's get on with our meal before everything goes cold.'

'Going back to the 'Pool will be like a new lease of life,' Kathy interrupted ecstatically. 'I can't believe it! You say we'll be living right in the heart of the city. That means we'll be in the thick of things instead of being cut off from the real world and stuck out in the sticks like we are here.'

Her face was alight with happiness at the thought of big shops, noisy trams, crowds of people and the general bustle that the very name Liverpool conjured up for her.

Megan sensed that her own outburst had startled her father almost as much as his news had stunned all of them. If only he had warned them about what he was planning to do instead of springing it on them so suddenly. Surely he must have realised how upset she would be by such news?

She loved the grandeur and tranquillity of North Wales and had always thought he did as well. She was never happier than when the two of them were leaning on the bridge in Beddgelert, watching the crystal clear waters of the River Glaslyn flowing beneath the grey stone arches. Or when they wandered along the river bank, following the Glaslyn as it meandered its way down to Porthmadog and out into Cardigan Bay. As they walked he told her about Taliesin, The Lord Rhys, Llywelyn ap

Gruffudd, Owain Glyndwr and all the other Welsh heroes of the past. Wonderful magical stories, a tapestry of folklore and fact.

'In the end, it will be for the best, Megan,' he assured her earnestly.

She looked away quickly, afraid he might see the silent accusation in her eyes. She felt so betrayed. She was quite sure he'd hate leaving North Wales as much as she would. Most of all, though, she felt hurt that he'd not confided in her before making such a decision.

There was a lump in her throat as she looked around her, memorising every item in the stone-flagged room: the two well-used armchairs, one either side of the slate hearth, an oak settle piled with blue cushions, the Welsh dresser with its display of pretty dishes and ornaments. There was a fire in the black-leaded grate despite the August heat, and in front of the polished steel fender was the blue rag-rug she'd helped Granny Williams to make when they'd first come to live with her.

'We can always come back again, if it doesn't work out,' her father said placatingly, breaking into her reverie.

Megan nodded, but she knew they wouldn't. To return would be a sign of failure. Her father was too inflexible ever to admit defeat.

A small, wiry man, Watkin Williams had a will of iron. He always stuck by his convictions. If they were wrong then he bore the consequences in silence. Having resolved to leave Beddgelert nothing would bring him back again.

Most of the other men he worked alongside at

the Pengarw Slate Quarry had probably shrugged their shoulders when they'd heard rumours that they might be laid off. When it happened they'd sign on and draw their dole money and make the best of things, but Watkin's principles wouldn't allow him to do that.

He hadn't mentioned the matter to his family because he regarded it as his responsibility to support them by bringing home a wage packet each week.

It would have been a waste of time to talk to his wife about such matters. Easy-going, Kathy Williams always took the path of least resistance. Watkin was the one who made all the decisions. She was quite happy to put off anything she considered tedious. If the sun was shining she would cheerfully leave the washing or baking until the next day and take a picnic down to the beach at Porthmadog. Or she would potter around outside in the garden when she should have been making the beds or cleaning the house.

Watkin tolerated her short-comings without a murmur. If she overcooked the weekend joint, they simply poured thick gravy over it; if she burned the apple-pie then they covered it with custard.

For all her happy-go-lucky ways, though, they were a united family. Kathy inevitably agreed with whatever her husband said whether she believed he was right or not. And because of this, Watkin always tried to do his very best for her and his two daughters and ensure they were all happy and content.

Megan, slim, dark haired and dark eyed, was nearest in looks and temperament to Watkin. They thought alike over most things and, like him, Megan was both determined and tenacious.

Lynn was a replica of her mother. She much preferred to be out with her friends, playing ball or riding a bike, to doing her homework. Megan was the studious one; Lynn rarely took anything seriously.

Suddenly, Megan felt she couldn't stand the atmosphere any longer. With a cry that seemed to tear itself from deep inside her, she ran from the house, down the slate-edged gravel path and through the white picket gate.

'Megan . . . come back here, girl!'

She heard her father calling after her as she crossed the road, but she took no notice. Climbing over the low stone wall, she ran headlong through the lush summer undergrowth and began scrambling up over the short slippery grass that covered the grey rock face of Moel Hebog. She was hot and breathless by the time she reached a scrub-screened hideout halfway up the mountainside.

Her mind swirled with memories as she struggled to reconcile herself to the future. Disbelief that her father could have taken such a momentous decision without a word to any of them mingled with despair at the thought of all she would be leaving behind.

As she made her way up the mountainside she feasted her eyes on the grandeur of the countryside she loved so deeply. The patchwork of fields and forest with the river, a glistening silver thread, snaking along until it became one with the sparkling sea.

Her father had first brought her to this spot when they'd been visiting his mam, shortly before he'd gone into the army. She'd been seven and it had been a birthday outing, a long-standing promise. Together they had climbed up Moel Hebog, the Hill of the Hawk, and he had showed her this very special cave concealed by an overhanging rock. According to legend, he told her, it was where Owain Glyndwr had hidden when pursued by the English during his rebellion against Henry V.

Now she felt a greater empathy with Glyndwr than ever before. When they moved to Liverpool she, too, would be losing what she thought of as her real homeland.

Her father had been born in the tiny stone cottage where they were living now. After the war started in 1914, and they'd heard frightening stories about what might happen in the cities, her father had thought they would be safer here with his widowed mother than in Liverpool.

Old Mrs Williams had been seriously ill by the time the war ended in 1918 so when Watkin had been demobbed there was no question of returning to Liverpool. He had found work at the Pengarw Slate Quarry and they'd gone on living there even after his mother had died.

Now, if they moved back to Liverpool, she'd even be separated from Jennie Jones and Gwyneth Evans, who had been her friends since the day she'd first arrived in Beddgelert. Sending letters to each other wouldn't be the same.

She wondered whether Ifan Jenkins would keep in touch. They'd been going out together for almost a year now. Not that there was anything serious between them, Megan reflected. Ifan hadn't exactly swept her off her feet. A few clumsy kisses was as far as she'd ever let him go, but she'd probably miss him.

Why had her father chosen to go back to Liverpool? she wondered. Surely he could have found work somewhere else nearby. She shuddered. Why was he prepared to leave the peace of the mountains that he loved so much for Liverpool? Was it because it had been her mother's home and, knowing how much she hated the countryside, he felt he owed it to her to return there?

After all these years? Surely not!

They were like a divided camp, thought Megan. Her mother and Lynn were always yearning to be back in the midst of the noise and bustle of city life while she and her father were perfectly content where they were.

After a long day delivering the heavy lorry loads of slate, the tranquillity of the River Glaslyn drew him like a magnet. She knew he'd miss their walks along its banks and nearby meadows as well as climbing the steep, rutted footpaths of Moel Hebog, with the wind at their back pushing them up the steep incline like a friendly hand.

She stood up, brushing the short wiry grass from her cotton skirt. It had been childish to run away like that. She'd better go back home and talk to him. After all, she was fifteen now so she'd have to find work in Liverpool, too. It was her future as much as his that was at stake.

* * *

9

'Leave her be, Watkin. She'll come back when she's hungry,' called out Kathy Williams as her husband rushed out of the house after Megan.

He ignored her shout, his booted feet scrunching on the gravel path as he strode towards the roadway.

Placidly, Kathy continued to dish out their meal.

'Come on, Lynn. There's no point in this being ruined,' she reasoned, ladling out a helping of lamb stew and passing it across the table to her youngest daughter.

'Thanks, Mam.' Lynn smiled as she helped herself to potatoes.

Before she sat down to eat her own meal, Kathy placed the casserole and the dish of potatoes back in the oven for Megan and Watkin when they returned.

'I don't know why you're bothering to keep it warm for them, Mam,' protested Lynn. 'They both knew you were ready to dish up.'

'Perhaps it's because I'm so happy!' Kathy beamed, her plump cheeks creasing into a smile. 'I still can't believe we're going back to Liverpool. It's something I've dreamed of for years, but I never thought it could possibly happen.'

The lethargy that had gradually turned her from an active, laughing young woman who loved to dance and enjoy herself into a plodding housewife seemed to slip from her shoulders like a discarded old coat.

She wondered if Liverpool had changed very much since the war had ended. It was ten years since she'd lived there so it was bound to have done so, she told herself. She'd noticed new shops and buildings when she'd been back on a visit shortly before her own mother had died four years ago. Lynn had been about nine then.

She sighed and let her thoughts drift back even further, to her own childhood. She'd been born and brought up in Anfield, a leafy suburb of Liverpool. She could still remember the excitement she'd always felt whenever they went into the city centre.

So many people had thronged the pavements in Lime Street, London Road and Church Street that she'd always clung tightly to her mother's hand. She'd loved the brightly lit stores like Hendersons, C&A, Lewis's, and George Henry Lees. In her mind's eye she could still see their windows with life-like models wearing wonderful clothes. She could also remember the smart shops in Bold Street where everything was so expensive it took your breath away when you looked in the windows. And there had always been the tantalising smell of coffee as you walked past Coopers or the Kardomah.

She'd been eighteen when the new king paid a visit to Liverpool in 1904. It had been a glorious July day and along with a million others she'd stood for hours waiting to see Edward VII and Queen Alexandra. It had been such a fleeting glimpse that she'd been bitterly disappointed.

The grand parade in honour of their arrival had been wonderful, though. Horses, their coats gleaming and polished brasses jingling, had pulled decorated carts and floats. There'd been any number of bands playing and men in uniform had marched along behind them carrying all sorts of Union banners, followed by people in fancy dress. If she closed her eyes and concentrated she could remember every detail.

She thought nostalgically about her first boat trip to the Isle of Man. She'd stood on the top deck as they left Liverpool, thinking how impressive it all seemed. The Mersey had been like a busy roadway with fussy little tug boats hooting and snorting as they made their way up and down the river, out to the Bar, and then back again, guiding the liners and big ships.

In front of the Liver Building, immense ocean-going liners had been berthed, dwarfing all the other boats on the river. She'd tried to imagine what it would be like to go on one of them, sailing over the ocean for weeks and weeks as they made their way to Africa or Australia.

Once the Isle of Man boat had crossed the Bar, the Irish Sea had seemed like a watery desert, so vast that it frightened her. As they sailed on into its choppy waters their boat had started to pitch and roll. One minute it seemed as if they would plunge into the water and the next minute hit the sky. She'd felt so ill that she never wanted to put to sea ever again.

All that waiting and being sea-sick for just twelve hours ashore! Douglas hadn't been any better than New Brighton. The boat trip to go there only took about twenty minutes and there was no rough sea or rolling waves to make you dizzy and sick.

She loved New Brighton, with its golden sands, donkey rides, and every kind of amusement. Bowls, a miniature putting course, tennis and swimming. You could walk the length of the pier or, if it was warm and sunny, sit on the promenade eating an ice cream and giggling at some of the outfits worn by people sauntering up and down the Ham and Egg Parade.

It was lively at night, too. There were concert halls, cinemas, theatres and pubs. There was dancing to big bands at the imposing, red-brick Tower Ballroom with its magnificent tower that dominated the New Brighton skyline.

She brought her thoughts back to the present. It was years since she'd let herself think about those days and when she'd been a young wife and the mother of two small girls and a husband who any day would be going away to fight for his country.

And now they were going to move back to Liverpool! She couldn't believe it was happening. Even the fact that they'd be living in a flat failed to dampen her spirits. As long as it was in Liverpool, she didn't mind what it was like.

Lynn would love Liverpool, there was no doubt at all about that. She'd be in her element at a big school and make a lot of new friends. She'd soon be old enough to go dancing and to the pictures on her own. Yes, Lynn would love every minute of it.

Megan didn't seem very pleased at the idea, but she'd soon come round and realise it was the best thing that could have happened. She'd never be able to find a worthwhile job here in Beddgelert.

Moving to Liverpool would get her away from that hulking Ifan Jenkins, Kathy thought with satisfaction. Nothing wrong with the lad, but he was so awkward and ungainly. He worked for his father and he'd be middle-aged before he had a chance to take over the farm or even have a say in how it was run.

Anyway, she couldn't see Megan making a very good farmer's wife, not with all that mud and mess; she was much too pernickety. Megan would be able to meet a very different type of boy in Liverpool. With any luck, a white-collar worker who'd be able to match up to that sharp brain of hers.

Yes, Kathy mused as she mopped up the last of the thick tasty gravy from her plate with a piece of bread, it was going to be a fresh start for all of them.

Chapter Two

Megan dreaded the ordeal that lay ahead. She felt numb. It was almost as if she'd swallowed a lump of ice and the painfully cold tentacles were spreading right through her body.

She leaned against the rails at Liverpool Pier Head, one hand shielding her eyes against the sudden glare of the early morning September sun as it was reflected on the river, wishing herself miles away.

Ships and boats of all shapes and sizes dotted the Mersey. She watched two small tugs skilfully guide a massive blue-funnelled vessel into dock and a larger single tug noisily chugging a tanker up the deep, narrow channel out to the Bar. Once there the tanker would make its way out from Liverpool Bay, across the Irish Sea, and sail on to the Atlantic, bound for such remote places that she couldn't even imagine what they were like.

A ferry boat manoeuvred alongside the landing stage, disgorging a shoal of people. They hurried up the floating roadway, disappearing onto buses or along one of roads that led to the heart of the city. Megan envied them; they were all so full of purpose and determination, their day already planned.

None of them cast a second glance at the slim

girl wearing a belted navy raincoat, a scarf tied over her dark hair to protect it from the blustery wind, who was standing by the railings, mesmerised by what was happening around her.

Behind Megan, the imposing, grey granite buildings, reaching skywards like enormous temples, formed a scenic backcloth to the waterfront. The magnificent gilt Liver birds, perched on top of the tallest building, were like silent sentinels guarding the busy Mersey.

Seagulls massed on the many ledges, their bright, beady eyes watching every movement. Wheeling and diving, they swooped down, scavenging the waterfront. Their harsh, raucous screams sent a shudder through Megan and she ached to be back in the wooded mountainside around Beddgelert.

The thought of going for an interview made her feel nervous and awkward. She knew that once she entered the room she would either dry up or her mind would go blank. Either that or she would speak so fast that they wouldn't be able to understand what she was saying.

It was all very well her father telling her to 'take a deep breath and count to three before you start to speak'. Whenever she'd done that the person interviewing her seemed to think she wasn't going to answer or that she hadn't understood the question. Often they began asking her the same question all over again, which only added to her confusion.

Most of the people who'd interviewed her so far since she'd arrived in Liverpool had seemed so stern and unfriendly that she'd wanted to slink out of the room and vanish. It was as if they resented her taking up their time, and it made her feel as if they were doing her a favour by even seeing her.

At that moment she would have gladly swapped places with her friends back in Beddgelert. She'd thought that the jobs they'd be doing after they left school would be dull and monotonous, but now she envied them the cosiness of their daily routine. They didn't have to try to convince complete strangers about how proficient they were. Or worry about whether they were going to be able to cope with the work if they were lucky enough to get the job.

Jennie, in her white overall, serving behind the counter of her father's shop, enveloped in an aroma of freshly baked bread and cakes, would be greeted each day by a constant stream of familiar faces. Gwyneth, too, would see the same people each day as she handed out newspapers and cigarettes or served sweets to the local children.

With a deep sigh, Megan checked the time. There was still twenty minutes before she was due at the Walker's Shipping Company's offices.

It was the fifth job she had been after in the three weeks since she had come to live in Liverpool and each time it had been a dismal failure. At the end of each of the interviews they'd said, 'We'll let you know', but she'd not heard a word from any of them.

This time it would be different, she told herself optimistically. Her father had heard about the vacancy from his co-driver, Robert Field, even before it was advertised in the *Liverpool Echo*, and she was determined not to let him down.

The chiming of the clock on the Liver Building brought her back to the present with a jolt. Turning her back on the Mersey, she began to make her way up the steep road between the warehouses and offices.

As she turned into Old Hall Street she caught a glimpse of her reflection in one of the plate-glass windows. Hastily she removed the chiffon scarf that she'd tied over her head before leaving home to make sure her hair stayed in place because Lynn had insisted on styling it into a face-framing bob to try to make her look more 'with-it'.

'I've combed on plenty of sugar water to make certain it stays in place,' Lynn had explained with a grin as she'd stepped back to admire her handiwork.

Megan knew that having a new hairstyle should have made her feel more confident, but it didn't. As she stood outside the revolving doors, etched in gold with the name Walker's Shipping Company, she still had to take a long, deep breath to try to calm the panic she felt building up inside her. Her legs seemed to turn to water as she tried to summon up the courage to go inside.

'Give it a good hard push. Or let me do it for you. It can be a bit stiff sometimes.'

Megan jumped at the sound of a man's voice in her ear.

Turning sharply, she found herself staring up into a pair of brilliant blue eyes belonging to a good-looking young man in his early twenties. He had black wavy hair, thick dark brows, a bold nose and firm chin with a cleft right in the centre of it. He was dressed in a well-cut grey suit, pale-blue shirt and was wearing a grey and blue striped tie.

'You were going in?' he questioned.

Megan nodded, wishing she wasn't so tongue-tied, longing to be able to say something smart and witty.

He grinned as though amused by her reticence and she noticed how white and even his teeth were.

'Indeed, yes . . . I have an appointment at half-past ten,' she blurted out.

'Really! And have you come all the way from Wales for this interview?' The blue eyes twinkled and his eyebrows shot up questioningly.

'There's clever of you to know that I'm from Wales.' She grinned shyly.

'But you are living here in Liverpool now?'

'Yes,' she admitted with a hint of a sigh.

'And you've come after the junior clerk's job?'

'That's right! I've got an appointment with a Miss Pearce . . . and I'm terribly nervous.'

'I don't think you need to be, she won't eat you,' he reassured her.

'I know that, but it's tremendously important to me that I get the job, see.' She bit her lip, wondering whatever had come over her that she should confide in a complete stranger.

'Stop looking so anxious.' He grinned. 'I'm sure you'll be fine.'

'You really think so?' she asked, frowning.

'Well, let's say you deserve to get the job.' He smiled encouragingly.

'The trouble is I've no previous experience and there's bound to be plenty of local girls after it who have. There always are.'

'As far as I know, it hasn't even been advertised yet, and you know what they say about being the early bird,' he said solemnly.

She stared at him for a moment in silence, then managed a weak smile.

'Come on,' he guided her through the swing doors, 'I'll show you where to go.'

'Thanks. I hope it's not taking you out of your way.'

'No. I work here.'

'Are you in the office?' she asked as they made their way up a flight of stairs and along a corridor at the top.

'Sometimes, but mostly I'm down at the docks.'

'What do you have to do there?'

'Check the bills of lading, sort out problems with customs, that kind of thing.'

'It all sounds very complicated.' Megan sighed. 'I suppose that's why when they advertise they always say that they want people with experience.'

'It's surprising how quickly you get into the routine and know what to do,' he told her cheerfully.

'Was this your first job? Did you start here straight from school?' Megan asked.

'My family have always been in shipping,' he said evasively as he escorted her through the maze of corridors. 'I grew up listening to people talking about it so I knew quite a lot before I actually started work.'

'That probably did help,' Megan admitted. 'I've never worked in an office or known anyone who did.'

She was tempted to tell him that her father also worked for Walker's as a lorry driver, but she thought better of it.

'So where were you living before you came to Liverpool?'

'Beddgelert in North Wales. It was beautiful there, magnificent mountains and quite near the sea.'

'And no office blocks.' He laughed.

'The only offices were at the slate quarry. It wouldn't have been too bad working there, mind. More homely, see. And I would have known most of the people, anyway.'

'You'll soon make friends once you start work.'

'I hope so. I feel like a fish out of water. You're the first person, outside my family, that is, that I've really spoken to since we moved to Liverpool. Back home everyone had time to talk to each other, but here everybody seems to be so busy. They haven't even got time to say good morning!'

'Here we are, then.'

They came to an abrupt halt outside a dark oak door marked GENERAL OFFICE. Megan stared at it fearfully, feeling her mouth go dry.

'Tell the receptionist who you are and she'll phone through and let Miss Pearce know you've arrived.'

'Thank you. I'll do that.' She hesitated nervously. He frowned. 'If you want to tidy up first, the

21

ladies room is the last door on the right at the end of this corridor.'

'Thank you.' Megan smiled gratefully.

'Good luck with the interview.'

She smiled at him shyly. 'Thank you. I feel a lot better about it after talking to you.'

'Then I shall expect to find you working here next time I come into the office.' He grinned, his vivid blue gaze mesmerising her.

Before she could answer he had disappeared down the passageway and she was left standing outside the general office. Heart thudding anxiously, she hesitated for a brief moment and then scurried along the corridor to the ladies room.

Colour rushed to her cheeks the moment she caught sight of herself in the cloakroom mirror. No wonder he had suggested she might want to tidy up before her interview. The carefully constructed hairdo now looked a complete mess. The strong wind had played havoc with it since she'd removed her headscarf.

In desperation, she wrestled with the tangled mess, trying to restore it to the smooth face-framing style Lynn had created. It was hopeless. Frustrated, she combed it back behind her ears, wishing she'd never let Lynn touch it.

It was a wonder that such a good-looking young man had spoken to her at all, looking like she did, Megan thought grimly. She wished she knew his name. It would be the first thing Lynn would want to know when she told her about meeting him. She could imagine the look of disgust on her sister's face when she said she didn't know.

22

She sighed, remembering how handsome he'd been. He was very different from Ifan Jenkins. Certainly the sort of chap Lynn would go overboard for, all right.

Lynn thought that Ifan, with his massive shoulders and heavy build, was a joke. It was something they constantly argued about.

'I don't know why you bother with him, Megan. He's a real clod-hopper,' Lynn told her time and time again.

'He can't help being a bit clumsy. He's big framed,' she always claimed in his defence. Lynn was right, but Ifan was good-hearted and she didn't like her sister criticising him.

'And fat with it. He eats like a pig.'

'He needs lots of food to keep his strength up. He's out working on his father's farm before six every morning.'

'I know.'

'And then he has another stint to do when he gets home after school.'

'What sort of life is that?' Lynn would jeer. 'He's nothing more than a labourer.'

'He'll own the farm one day.'

'Scratching for a living, chasing sheep all over the mountains, milking cows night and morning and mucking out the pigs. That's no future.'

'It's not all work. He goes hunting and shooting with his father and sometimes they go fishing.'

That didn't impress Lynn in the slightest. 'How can you like someone who enjoys killing animals?' she would sniff contemptuously.

'I suppose you'd prefer a chap who dressed up

23

in a smart suit and a white shirt to go to work and still looked clean and smart when he came home at six each night.'

'Of course! Especially if he brings home a fat wage packet at the end of the week.'

It's a pity Lynn isn't the one who has come for this interview, Megan thought ruefully. Nothing ever disconcerted her. She'd be so much more confident than I am. If she didn't know the answer to any of the questions they asked then she'd bluff her way.

'And that's exactly what I had better do if I'm going to make sure of getting this job,' Megan muttered aloud as she made a last critical scrutiny in the mirror to check that her lipstick hadn't smudged and that her nose wasn't shiny.

She passed the comb through her hair again, wondering if she should have left it like Lynn had styled it for her. She supposed it had looked more sophisticated framing her face, but she felt more comfortable with it neatly tucked behind her ears in the way she always wore it.

She frowned at her reflection. There was still something not quite right about her appearance. Perhaps it would be better if she took off her raincoat and carried it. It was her school one and didn't really go with the smart image she was trying to create.

She took a deep breath; what was she worrying about? It was only another interview and it would probably come to nothing anyway.

That was the whole problem, of course. This time it did matter, quite a lot. Her father was counting on her making a good impression.

Still, she told herself, if a complete stranger thought she was right for the job when her hair was all windblown and she'd been looking a complete mess, then surely, now that she'd smartened herself up, she stood a pretty good chance of being successful.

Head high, ignoring the butterflies inside her, Megan made her way back to the general office, hoping she looked more confident than she felt.

All she had to do was convince Miss Pearce that she could cope with the work, she told herself firmly.

From what the young man had told her it seemed she might be the first applicant. If she put her mind to it, concentrated really hard, answered the questions in a clear voice and didn't get flustered, there was no reason why she shouldn't be successful. And then he would find her working there next time he came into the office. She felt a frisson of excitement at the thought.

Chapter Three

The waiting seemed interminable. As the days slowly passed and there was no news from Walker's, Megan's hopes dwindled. She had been on cloud nine when she'd walked down Old Hall Street after her interview. Her mind had been full of dreams, thinking what it would be like to set out for work each morning, to be part of the teaming throng that made up the city's life.

The interview had gone so well. Valerie Pearce was a rather plain, stocky woman in her early thirties, with tightly marcelled fair hair and hazel eyes behind horn-rimmed glasses. In her trim navy suit and high-necked white blouse, she had looked rather prim; yet Megan had felt at ease with her, happy to answer her barrage of questions.

For her part, Valerie Pearce liked the quiet, serious young girl with the wide-set, intelligent brown eyes. Her neat appearance and the absence of heavy make-up or jewellery had impressed her. She'd even liked her soft, lilting accent, which made a pleasant change from the Merseyside voices she heard most days.

Walker's was a staid, family firm, and the last thing they wanted was one of the new-style flappers, with their short flouncy clothes and doll-like hairstyles. Girls who thought more about what they looked like than about their work, and distracted the men. She would have liked to have given Megan the job right away, but knew she was expected to talk the matter over with Mr Walker before making a decision.

Megan wanted the job so badly it hurt. In the days that followed she found it was hard to keep her mind on anything else. Lynn was at school so most days she went window-shopping with her mother.

As they looked at the fashionable clothes in Owen Owens, C&A, and Lewis's, Megan ached for her first pay packet. It would be wonderful to be able to buy some of them, she thought wistfully.

'To help pass the time, why don't you try your hand at decorating that dingy little bedroom you and Lynn are sharing?' her father suggested.

'I've never done anything like that before,' Megan demurred.

'There's a first time for everything and I'm sure you could manage to paint the woodwork and put some emulsion on the walls.'

It was hard work and took much longer than they had expected, but they were all thrilled by the results.

The pale pink walls and fresh white gloss woodwork transformed the tiny room, making it seem larger as well as much more light and airy.

'It looks good,' her mother agreed. 'How about having a go at decorating the living room? I'll give you a hand, if you like.'

They started on it right after breakfast the next morning. It took them several days but once again they were all pleased by the results.

For the first time since they had moved into the flat it began to feel like a home, although it would never be as cosy as their cottage in Beddgelert, Megan mused as she soaked in a hot bath to get rid of the aches and pains and soak away the paint stains from her hands and arms. Although she'd tried to work carefully, she'd even got paint in her hair.

She ran some more hot water into the bath and slid down until it covered her shoulders. Then she closed her eyes and gave herself up to dreaming about the young man she'd met when she went for her interview.

She wished she'd asked him his name. He wasn't a John or a Jim, or a Bill or Bob, she felt quite sure about that.

If she knew his name then she could ask her father if he'd ever met him. If he knew him then perhaps he could ask him if the job at Walker's had been filled yet. It was the uncertainty of not knowing that she couldn't stand.

She sighed dreamily, remembering the young man's vivid blue eyes, strong nose and firm jaw. He'd had such an unforgettable face. There couldn't be all that many chaps working at the docks who looked like him. He'd stand out from the crowd, she reflected, remembering the smart cut of his grey suit that seemed to mould itself to his broad shoulders and long, lean legs. If she got the job at Walker's, and they met again, she wondered if he would remember her.

The sound of her mother calling her roused her

out of her reverie. She hooked out the plug with her toe, and reached for a towel. She'd ask her father tonight if he knew him. So far, the only person he'd ever mentioned was his co-driver, Robert Field.

'Didn't you hear me shouting you?' her mother grumbled as Megan emerged from the bathroom.

'I was just coming. What's up?'

'There's a letter come for you. It's got Walker's name on the envelope. Come on, hurry up and open it, let's hear what they've got to say.'

Wrapping herself in the towel, Megan followed her mother into the living room. Heart in mouth, she opened the letter and drew out the single sheet of headed notepaper. The words danced in front of her eyes.

'Well . . . have you got it?'

'I . . . I don't know. I think I might have!' She smiled hopefully. 'They want to see me again.'

At the second interview, having first checked on one or two of the details Megan had supplied during their first meeting, Valerie Pearce confirmed that the position was hers.

'Oh! That's wonderful,' Megan exclaimed with a smile of relief.

'There is one stipulation. Since you can't type we shall expect you to attend night school and take shorthand and typing classes. Walker's will pay all your fees,' Miss Pearce assured her. 'Is that understood?'

Megan was almost too excited to concentrate as Valerie Pearce went into details of the work she would be doing when she started. Foremost in her mind was the fact that at last she had a job.

'Right. Now, can you start next Monday?'

'Yes, of course.' Eyes shining, Megan nodded enthusiastically.

'Good. I'll see you Monday at nine o'clock, then,' Miss Pearce confirmed.

Megan came away from Walker's in a daze. She could hardly believe her luck. She was to be paid ten shillings a week with the promise of a rise in three months' time.

There were ten pay days before Christmas so that meant she'd be able to buy everyone a Christmas present as well as some new clothes for herself, she told herself gleefully.

She wasn't sure about going to night school on her own, and wondered if she could persuade Lynn to join as well.

'No! I go to school all day that's quite enough for me,' Lynn told her emphatically. 'I can't wait to leave and get a job so that I can earn some money.'

'You'd stand a much better chance if you were able to do shorthand and typing,' Megan pointed out.

Lynn pulled a face. 'I don't want to be stuck in an office even if you do! I want to be where there's plenty going on, where I'll meet people and have fun.'

'An office job is much better than serving behind a counter.'

'Who said anything about working in a shop?' Lynn retorted indignantly.

'Well, if you change your mind, let me know,'

Megan told her resignedly. 'I've promised to go and enrol tomorrow.'

Even Lynn's open jealousy about her starting work didn't stop Megan feeling excited. She spent all day on Sunday getting ready. She washed her hair, sponged and pressed her skirt and polished her shoes. She went to bed early, wanting to be on her own so that she could think about all the things that might happen the next day. Before she fell asleep she even rehearsed what she would say to the blue-eyed young man in case she was lucky enough to bump into him.

Megan found her first few days working at Walker's utterly bewildering.

'We're a relatively small company so that, although everyone has their own specific job, the work is very integrated which means that it's important that we all cooperate with each other,' Miss Pearce explained to Megan after she'd allocated her a desk in the general office. 'Come along, I'll introduce you to the other people working here.'

Olive Jervis, the receptionist, was a smartly dressed blonde of twenty-five. She smiled coolly, looking up from the switchboard only long enough to cast a supercilious glance over Megan's neat but nondescript blouse and skirt.

At a high desk near the main window, Mr Newbold, a spare, balding man in his mid-forties, sat hunched over enormous ledgers. He gave a thin smile of acknowledgement as Valerie Pearce told Megan she could ask him for help if ever she had any problems with her work.

In the far corner of the general office, Mavis Parker, a plump, youngish woman with a frizz of sandy-coloured hair, was typing at tremendous speed. She barely paused when Megan was introduced to her.

Megan's heart beat faster when Valerie Pearce took her into an adjoining room and said, 'This is where the shipping clerks work. They spend most of their day down at the docks, so leave anything for their attention in that green tray and they'll deal with it next time they're in the office.'

Megan wondered whether she should ask what their names were and tell Miss Pearce that she had already met one of them, but the moment passed before she could pluck up the courage to do so.

Finally, she was taken to meet the managing director, Martin Walker. He was a portly man with prominent features, shrewd blue eyes and greying hair. Megan found his curt manner very intimidating.

His imposing office had an enormous mahogany desk, and two walls housed floor-to-ceiling bookcases and glass cabinets containing models of all kinds of ships, from sailing vessels to modern cargo boats and liners. A smaller connecting room, adjacent to his office and also furnished with a mahogany desk and matching filing cabinets, was where Valerie Pearce worked.

For the first few days there were times when Megan thought she would never fit in. Mr Newbold and Mavis Parker were so engrossed in what they were doing that she was reluctant to interrupt either of them to ask them to help her. As she made mistake after mistake she waited nervously for someone to tell her she would have to leave.

By the end of the week, however, she was beginning to master the sequence of sorting and filing the invoices and bills of lading. When Valerie Pearce handed over her wage packet and remarked how well she seemed to be settling in, Megan felt almost light-headed with relief.

As she made her way home she tried to think what she should do to celebrate her first pay day. She had agreed to give her mother six shillings a week and intended to save a regular amount each week for new clothes, but the rest was for spending. She decided to start by taking Lynn to the pictures.

'Pictures?' Lynn screwed up her nose and shook her head. 'We ought to do something more exciting than that!'

'Like what?'

Lynn's grey eyes suddenly sparkled. 'I know, let's go dancing.'

'I'm not all that keen on dancing.' Megan frowned.

'Oh, come on, don't be such a spoil sport,' Lynn protested. 'You said you wanted to celebrate by taking me out and that's what I'd really like to do.'

'I would much sooner go to the pictures.'

'We'll do that another night. There's nothing any good on at the moment, anyway,' Lynn told her airily. 'Please, our Meg, I really want to go to the Tower Ballroom at New Brighton. Remember how Mam used to talk about the wonderful dances there were there? You'll like it. We'll have fun.'

The moment Megan mentioned their plan to her mother she looked doubtful. 'You'd better see what your dad has to say about that,' she said cautiously. 'I don't think he will agree to you going on your own.'

'Well, we haven't had time to pick up any blokes now, have we?' Lynn pouted.

'Lynn!' Her mother looked shocked. 'You'd better not let your dad hear you talking like that or he most certainly won't let you go to the New Brighton Tower Ballroom.'

'When he told us that we'd be moving back to Liverpool you said I'd love it because I'd be able to go to dances, like you used to do when you were my age,' Lynn reminded her mother.

'Yes, I know, but things have changed quite a bit since then,' Kathy told her.

'You mean you've become more stuffy,' Lynn said cheekily. 'We wanted to do something really special to celebrate Megan getting her first wage packet.'

'Well, you ask your dad if it's all right. I won't say a word, but I don't think he will agree to the two of you going off like that.'

'Not after you've had a chance to tell him you don't want us to go,' Lynn muttered.

'It's all right, Mam, we'll go to the pictures. That's what I suggested in the first place,' Megan said quickly as she saw the hurt look on her mother's face.

'You can go to the pictures if you want to,' Lynn stormed, 'but I'm not!'

Before Megan could answer she'd flounced out of the room, banging the door noisily behind her.

'Take no notice, luv,' Kathy murmured. 'She'll come round when your dad has had a word with her.'

'I suppose there is a chance that he might say we can go, of course,' Megan said tentatively.

'Oh no, so don't build-up your hopes,' Kathy said emphatically. 'Let the two of you go across the river to New Brighton and not come home until after midnight? Are you mad? Think of the danger. All sorts of unpleasant characters are out and about at that time of night. Drunk most of them, too. Anything could happen to you, you might even be accosted.'

'What about if you two came with us?' Megan suggested hopefully. 'I wanted to take Lynn out somewhere special to celebrate my first pay day.'

'I know luv, but it looks as though it will have to be the pictures. Your dad wouldn't go to a place like that, he never liked dancing.'

'What about you coming with us?'

Kathy shook her head. 'Your dad still wouldn't think it was safe and he wouldn't like the idea of me going dancing, I'm afraid!'

Kathy was right. Watkin was most emphatic that they musn't go. 'Heaven alone knows what might happen to you,' he pointed out. 'Lynn hasn't even left school yet, and you've only been at work for a week, Megan. Wait until you're older, until you both have young men to accompany you and take care of you.'

'Well, can we go to a dance if it's in Liverpool?' Lynn pressed. 'There's a jazz club . . .'

'No!' Watkin Williams' roar silenced even Lynn.

'You know nothing at all about what goes on in Liverpool. It's a big city not a village where everyone knows everybody else. You don't start going to those sort of places under any circumstances. Have I made myself clear?'

'Is it all right if I take Lynn to the pictures, then, Dad?' Megan asked.

Her father frowned.

'Please. As a special treat to celebrate my first wage packet,' she explained.

'Well, all right. As long as you go early and you are back home before nine o'clock.'

'Perhaps you could go to the Saturday matinee,' Kathy said tentatively.

Reluctantly, Lynn agreed to find out what was on and they both promised they'd be back home by nine at the latest. The moment they were out of the house, Lynn had other ideas, though.

'Can we take a peep in at the Stork Club for a minute?' she begged. 'It's a jazz club. Some of the girls at school told me about it. They let girls in free, and . . .'

Megan looked at the earnest, round face, the pleading grey eyes and felt tempted. Perhaps Lynn was right. It would be a new experience . . . something to look back on and remember as the way she had celebrated her very first pay packet.

Chapter Four

As they made their way towards Queen Square, Megan stared in awe at the Stork Hotel.

'We can't go in there, Lynn!' she exclaimed, aghast. 'It's much too posh, we aren't dressed right for a place like that.'

'Don't be daft, Megan, we're not going into the Stork Hotel itself. The Stork Club is in an annexe. Come on!'

Grabbing hold of Megan's hand she half dragged her towards a two-storey building at the side of the hotel.

As they reached the door that led into a carpeted entrance hall, Megan pulled back. Lynn squeezed her hand more tightly and before she could protest Megan found herself inside a room that was crowded with girls and young men.

At the far end of the room there was a highly polished counter where a red-haired girl was taking people's coats and hanging them on the rows of rails behind her.

Lynn pulled off her coat and then grabbed at Megan's. 'Come on, get it off, we leave them here,' she said excitedly.

Lynn handed over their coats then led the way up some stairs and through a pair of huge double doors. These opened into a large high-ceilinged room that was packed with people. They were greeted by a blast of noise and cigarette smoke.

Megan stared round. She'd never been in such a large room in her life before. There seemed to be no windows but a warm light came from three massive chandeliers. The centre one looked like a huge ball and seemed to be a mixture of coloured lights that cast a rainbow of colour over the room. The polished parquet floor shone like glass and the dark red walls were lavishly decorated with painted gilt swags.

At the far end of the long room was a raised stage and on this, seated on gilt chairs, the band was getting ready to play.

'Like it?'

Lynn's voice was tense, but her eyes were shining with excitement,

'I don't know,' Megan said hesitantly. 'I've never been anywhere quite like this before.'

'Sensational, isn't it!'

'What do you mean?' Megan frowned.

'Brilliant, you know!' Lynn laughed. 'It makes you feel all of a doodah!'

'If that's supposed to mean that it's rather noisy, then I agree with you,' Megan told her as the band suddenly let forth at full strength.

'Jazz has to be loud!' Lynn laughed as her body began to sway in time to the beat. 'Come on, let's move onto the floor and dance.'

The next moment, Lynn had vanished into the crowd already circling the dance floor and Megan found herself desperately trying to see where she'd gone.

Megan felt uneasy. There was no doubt she would remember this outing, she thought wryly. It was certainly a momentous way of celebrating her first pay!

She waited a few minutes, expecting Lynn to come back. When she didn't, Megan decided she'd better try to find her. It would be so easy to lose sight of her altogether in this large throng, she thought worriedly.

Megan pushed her way through the wildly gyrating dancers on the crowded floor, frantically searching for Lynn. The lights were now dimmed and there were so many people, and such a fug of cigarette smoke, that she couldn't even see across the room.

The noise coming from the stage where the jazz band was playing was absolutely deafening.

There seemed to be hundreds of people in the room. Most of the men wore lounge suits with slicked-down hair and shiny shoes. Women, mainly young girls, were in short slinky dresses, some so short that they were above the knee, while others wore skirts with elaborate handkerchief or scalloped hemlines.

Megan concentrated anxiously, hoping to be able to spot Lynn. Since her sister was only wearing an ordinary cotton dress, she would stand out from the others in their fashionable floaty fabrics.

She felt fear gripping her like a cold hand when there was still no sign of her. She dreaded to think what her father's reaction would be if she returned home without Lynn, or worse still if she came to some harm.

When he learned that they had gone to a jazz club instead of going to the pictures as she'd promised they would, he'd be terribly angry. He'd condemn the place as a 'den of iniquity' and say that she should have known better than to have ever put a foot inside such a place.

She took a deep breath, trying not to panic, but she felt suffocated in the hot, perfumed atmosphere. The entire place seemed to be under the spell of the saxophonist as he blasted out wild compelling sounds that stirred the blood.

In her eyes, the gyrating dancers were like zombies as they responded to the wild beat, and Megan wondered if they were intoxicated by drink, or even drugs.

She gave a shriek of protest as a man grabbed her around the waist and whirled her round. She struggled to free herself but found him clutching her even more tightly as he swayed in time to the music.

The noise was so deafening that Megan found she was unable to make him hear what she was saying when she asked him to let her go. Instead, she found herself being twirled and twisted out of his arms into those of another man.

As the blare of music seemed to increase she lost all track of time and she felt so terribly frightened because she still couldn't see Lynn anywhere.

On the verge of hysteria, her eyes smarting from the smoke, Megan pushed away the man who was now holding her in a tight clinch and elbowed her way through the melee of dancers back to the cloakroom.

If Lynn's coat was still hanging there, she told herself, then at least she would know that Lynn hadn't left the club. If she was still among the dancers then she'd be able to find her if she took her time and looked carefully enough.

'Yeah, everyone's coat's still here, luv,' the red-headed girl told her. 'No one would leave yet,' she laughed, 'things are just hottin' up. Who yer looking for?'

'My sister,' Megan said worriedly. 'We came together, but now I can't find her.'

'What's her name, then?'

'Lynn . . . Lynn Williams, but I don't think you'd know her. We haven't been living in Liverpool very long.'

'Yer mean the Welsh kid. Course I know her, luv. She's a right little jazz fiend and no maybe. She comes in here nearly every lunchtime with a gang of other kids from school.'

Megan shook her head. 'I don't think so. This is the very first time we've ever been here.'

'Look, luv, don't you worry about her.' The girl laughed, ignoring her protestations. 'She'll be in there with a crowd of her school cronies. They come most days, regular as clockwork. I know them all by name! You've not been here yourself before, though, have you?'

'No, it's my first visit.'

'So you're not still at school like your sister, then?'

Megan shook her head. 'I'm at work.'

'It's easy to tell you're not a jazz fan.' The girl laughed. She shrugged. 'I know it's not everyone's sort of music, but I love it. I could listen to King Oliver and his band for ever. The music simply pours out of them,' she murmured dreamily.

By the time Megan managed to track Lynn down she was feeling utterly dazed by the continuous noise. Her throat and chest felt sore from the pungent cigarette smoke and her head was thumping in time to the frenzied beat of the music.

She'd never seen any dancing like it in her life before. Some of the men were lithely gyrating and their women partners were sinking sensuously to their knees and then rising again, flexing their entire bodies as they did so.

Nor had she even heard of some of the dances when they were announced, because they had names like The Shimmy and the Grizzly Bear. She'd heard of the Charleston and Boogie-Woogie, but she'd never seen them danced before and the steps seemed to be so intricate that she knew they were completely beyond her.

When she finally spotted Lynn she was with a crowd of girls all about her own age. They were all dancing and twirling as if demented. As she made her way over to them several young men grabbed her and tried to partner her, but she pushed them all away, intent on reaching Lynn and telling her it was time for them to leave.

Lynn shook her head. 'We've only just got here,' she protested. 'Come and join in, you'll soon get the hang of things.'

'It's been a really thrilling outing, Megan,' Lynn enthused when they eventually left. 'Thanks for taking me.'

'You didn't tell me you'd been there before,' Megan said accusingly as they walked home. 'I was told that you often go there with a crowd of your school friends,' Megan persisted when Lynn didn't answer. 'Even the red-headed girl who took our coats seemed to know who you were.'

Lynn shrugged. 'I've been along once or twice. So what, everyone goes there,' she added defensively. 'I'm surprised you haven't seen the girls from the shops and offices queuing up every midday since you're working quite close by.'

'I don't have time to walk round the streets during my lunch hour,' Megan told her. 'I eat my sandwiches and then get on with my work.'

She felt herself colouring and wondered what Lynn would say if she knew that the real reason she stayed at her desk all through the lunch hour was in case the young man with blue eyes came into the office. She'd only seen him once since she'd started working there and that had been a fleeting glimpse of him leaving the building.

'Proper Miss Goody-Goody, aren't you? I sometimes wonder if you ever have any fun at all except going to night school,' Lynn snapped.

Megan refused to commit herself. The night's adventure was still too raw. Now that they were safely away from the Stork Club she didn't mind admitting to herself that she had been really frightened.

Even when they reached home the cacophony of trombones, cornets and trumpets all vying with each other still rang in her head. The thought of Lynn going to a club of that sort on her own worried

Megan. She knew her dad would be furious and she wondered what she ought to do about it.

She hated telling tales but she didn't want Lynn ending up in any trouble. She knew she was dance mad; she even put records on their wind-up gramophone and danced round the room at home when their dad wasn't there. Sometimes their mam would dance with her and she'd shown them both a lot of dance steps that she'd known when she was a girl. Lynn had mastered them with no trouble at all. Megan preferred to simply listen to the tunes because she always felt as if she had two left feet.

Chapter Five

By the end of the second week at Walker's, Megan found she had caught up with the backlog of paper that had mounted up on her desk. Now that she understood what was expected of her, and why it was necessary to process the various documents in a certain way, she was beginning to find the work interesting.

Another reason for her state of euphoria was that the young man she had almost given up hope of ever meeting again had breezed into the office one morning like a breath of fresh air.

She wasn't the only one to appreciate his arrival. Everyone else seemed to suddenly come alive as they chorused, 'Good morning, Mr Miles!'

Olive Jervis's supercilious manner vanished as she greeted him warmly and Mavis Parker, eager to exchange a few words with him, even stopped frantically pounding her typewriter for a few minutes.

Valerie Pearce was in the general office at the time and Megan noticed how she looked astonished when Miles congratulated her on getting the job. Megan found herself blushing because she was so pleased that he had remembered their meeting.

'Did you realise that was Mr Walker's son who

came and spoke to you, Megan?' Miss Pearce questioned officiously after Miles had gone.

'No . . . I had no idea!'

'So how do you know him?' Miss Pearce frowned.

'I met him at the door the day I came for my interview. He told me that he worked here and showed me where to find your office.'

'I'm surprised you didn't realise who he was when you heard his name was Walker,' persisted Valerie Pearce, seeing the bewildered look on Megan's face.

'I didn't know that was his name,' Megan told her. 'Everyone refers to him as Mr Miles so I thought that was his surname.'

'He's called "Mr Miles" to avoid confusion with his father. It would be very difficult if we had two Mr Walkers in the office,' Miss Pearce explained. 'At the moment Mr Miles is still learning the business. He's gaining experience by finding out what goes on down at the docks. Some day, he will take over here, a point you shouldn't forget.'

In spite of Valerie Pearce's obvious disapproval, Megan was intrigued by Miles. She eagerly looked forward to his next visit to the office and the opportunity to exchange a few words with him again.

When she did she asked him why he hadn't told her that his name was Walker and that he was the boss's son. He laughed.

'It doesn't make any difference, does it? I only work here, the same as you do. The only thing is, you have a much cushier job than mine,' he teased. 'You aren't trudging around the docks in all kinds of weather.'

But it did matter. Miss Pearce made it quite clear that she didn't approve of him stopping to chat to Megan whenever he came into the office. Since Miss Pearce was so rarely in the general office, either Mavis or Olive must have reported the fact to her.

'Simply ignore them,' advised Miles when Megan told him.

'I daren't! I might get the sack and I don't want that to happen.'

'In that case, if I can't talk to you in the office then we'll have to meet after you finish work.' He grinned.

For a moment, Megan couldn't believe she had heard aright. Ever since she had first met Miles, even before she knew he was the boss's son, she had fantasised about how wonderful it would be to go out with him.

The new clothes she had bought, the lipstick and eye make-up, had all been chosen with him in mind. She spent hours in front of a mirror experimenting with them. She even listened when Lynn insisted she really needed to do something about her hair.

'That straight style makes you look as if you are still at school,' Lynn told her. 'Stop pushing it back behind your ears. Try bringing it forward onto your cheeks at least!'

'It won't stay like that.'

'It will if you do it properly.'

'It's all very well for you,' grumbled Megan. 'Your hair is different. You can do anything you like with it.'

'Well, try fastening it into place with two or three hair grips before you go to bed,' Lynn suggested.

'I've tried doing that, but they've always fallen out before morning.'

'Why don't you have a marcel wave, then?' Lynn suggested.

'I can't afford one! Not yet anyway because there's so many other things I need to buy.'

'Mam will lend you the money if you ask her.'

'Yes, perhaps I will after Christmas.'

'Please yourself.' Lynn shrugged. 'I know I would rather borrow it than go round looking like you do.'

Now, with Miles standing there beside her desk, waiting for her to answer, Megan wished she had taken Lynn's advice. It might have helped her to feel more sure of herself if she'd had a smart haircut.

'I'd like to, but I have to go to shorthand and typing classes three nights a week,' she heard herself telling him apologetically.

'That still leaves four nights free, doesn't it?'

'Well, yes. I suppose it does!' As she looked up into his brilliant blue eyes she felt as if she was drowning. Even her legs seemed to go weak. More than anything in the world she wanted to go out with him.

Megan felt sick with disappointment as Miles turned and walked away. She couldn't believe what was happening. The chance of a date with Miles Walker, something she'd dreamed about for weeks, and she'd bungled it!

For a long time after Miles had left the office

she sat there staring into space, wondering how she should handle it. She even planned what excuse she could make at home if he ever asked her again.

Her father had stopped them both from going out in the evenings ever since he had found out that Lynn was still sneaking off to the Stork Club after he'd told them not to go there. Megan being allowed to attend night school was the one exception.

'I want both of you to keep right away from that place,' he ordered, 'or you'll be getting a bad reputation.'

Lynn protested defiantly. 'Why must we? It's only a jazz club . . .'

'I mean it!' He cut her short, his eyes dark with anger. 'You are both to stay away from the Stork Club, now is that understood?'

Megan had tried to comfort Lynn when she found her huddled on her bed crying.

'You don't understand,' Lynn sobbed. 'It's all your fault, you've spoiled everything for me. I've got a date there with this boy, Flash.'

'You'll just have to tell him that you can't see him.'

'I especially want to see him because he's really into jazz. He's a smashing dancer and he picked me out because he said no one else partners him like I do.'

'You heard what our dad said about going to the Stork,' Megan reminded her.

'I know, but I could still manage to get out to meet him if you helped me.' She wiped the back

49

of her hand across her eyes. 'If I said I was coming to night school with you . . .'

'No! I'm not scheming like that,' Megan told her emphatically. 'I know you too well. You wouldn't come back on time and I would be the one left to make excuses.'

Despite Lynn's pleading, Megan remained adamant. As it was, she suspected that Lynn was still going to the midday sessions at the Stork Club. She was only a kid still and she could so easily be led astray by someone like this Flash, she decided.

Megan's glum mood when she arrived home after her gauche mistake with Miles brought a barrage of prying questions from Lynn, but Megan refused to confide in her even though Lynn kept on pestering her until Megan felt she would scream.

It was three days before she saw Miles again and he didn't even bother to smile or speak to her. She felt terribly upset; she was positive it was because she hadn't accepted his invitation to go out with him.

By Saturday, she could hardly bring herself to go to work she felt so miserable. Much as she longed to see Miles, and knew he usually came into the office on Saturday mornings, she couldn't bear the thought that he might ignore her again.

'It's only for a few hours, luv,' her mother sympathised when she complained of not feeling well. 'Try taking a couple of aspirins, that should help.'

When she left the office at midday, and saw

Miles waiting at the corner of Old Hall Street, Megan's heart missed a beat. For a moment she was tempted to turn and walk the other way. Then commonsense prevailed. She would have to face him sooner or later so she might as well get it over with now.

'Hello, Megan. Sorry I had to ignore you the other day. My father has been lecturing me about being too friendly with the office staff, so I decided I'd better be a bit more careful,' he explained with a grin.

'Oh, I thought it was because I didn't accept your invitation to go out with you.'

'You little goose.' He laughed. 'So when are we going to have a night out together, then? What about Monday?'

Megan's face flamed. 'I go to night school on a Monday night.'

'Give it a miss. Go on,' he urged, 'it won't hurt to skip one lesson.'

Megan hesitated. She had dreamed of going out with Miles ever since their first meeting but Monday was out of the question. This particular Monday evening there was an end of term test and such a lot depended on her marks.

'I really am sorry, Miles, but it's impossible. You see . . .'

'Oh come off it! Of course you can if you really want to,' he said impatiently.

'No, really I can't. I am free tonight,' she added hopefully.

'Well I'm not,' he told her curtly. He looked at his watch. 'I must be off,' he said abruptly. 'See you around sometime!' He raised his hand in a brief wave and was gone.

Megan stood staring after him, her eyes blurred by tears, a lump in her throat. If only he had given her a chance to tell him why she couldn't skip night school on this particular Monday, she was sure he would have understood.

She brooded about it all over the weekend, explaining her moodiness away by saying she was worried about the forthcoming tests.

'You'll do fine,' her mother consoled her. 'Anyway, what does it matter if you don't?'

'It's important that I get good marks because they'll send an end of term report to Miss Pearce and she will probably show it to Mr Walker.'

'Well, you can't be expected to know very much yet, you've only been going to these classes for a couple of months,' her mother pointed out. 'It must take years to learn shorthand. All those silly squiggles! I don't know how you can ever remember what they are supposed to mean.'

Chapter Six

The opportunity to sort things out with Miles came much sooner than Megan expected. When he came into the office on Monday morning to pick up some documents that he needed to take with him down to the docks, Mr Newbold sent him across to her desk for them.

Finding Miles standing so close to her, Megan's mind almost went blank. She didn't even hear what he had asked for, not until he had repeated it a second time.

'Yes, of course. They're here, somewhere.' In her confusion, she knocked over a pile of invoices and they scattered around his feet like falling leaves.

Miles gathered them up and placed them back on her desk. Deftly, he sorted out the papers he needed and made to leave.

Panic stricken because she hadn't explained her reason for not going out with him, Megan grabbed at his arm. At that moment, Valerie Pearce walked into the general office.

'Sorry! Have I taken the wrong ones?' Miles leaned over the desk as though checking the papers he was holding against some of the others lying on Megan's desk.

'I'll be in touch, so don't try to say anything to

me now,' he warned in a low voice as he straightened up.

'Is there a problem of some kind?' Miss Pearce asked, bustling over and looking from one to the other with a puzzled frown.

'Everything is in order now,' Miles told her blandly. 'Megan was trying to stop me from walking off with the wrong set of documents.'

'I see. Are you quite sure it is all sorted out correctly now?'

'Yes, thank you, Miss Pearce, I've got the right ones here.' He waved the sheaf of papers, then left the office whistling.

In the build-up to Christmas, Megan's hopes that Miles would contact her as he had promised to do began to fade. He seemed to be coming into the office very early in the morning, before she started work.

Several times she was tempted to leave a message in his tray, hidden among the bills of lading or custom documents. The only thing that stopped her doing so was that she was scared it might get into the wrong hands.

It would be disastrous if Bob Donovan, the other shipping clerk, picked it up and read it. Or, even worse, what would happen if Mr Newbold or Miss Pearce came across it?

If she hadn't heard from Miles by the time they closed for the bank holiday, then perhaps she'd leave a Christmas card on his desk, she decided. Surely no one would think that there was anything wrong in her doing that?

Her spirits sank when, on Christmas Eve, Miss Pearce announced they would be closing the office early, at one o'clock. She said that it was in order to give everyone the afternoon off so that they would have time to finish any last minute Christmas shopping.

Despondently, Megan resigned herself to the fact that her last chance of seeing or hearing from Miles was gone. She didn't even have the heart to take the risk of leaving a Christmas card on his desk for him.

At midday, Mr Walker came into the general office to wish everyone a happy Christmas. With a stiff smile and a curt handshake, he presented each of them with a bottle of sherry.

Megan found herself trembling as her turn came because Miles, looking suave and handsome, had joined his father. Simply knowing that he was in the same room made her pulse quicken.

She tried to concentrate her attention on Mr Walker, and to smile and thank him properly for her present.

When Miles also shook her hand she found herself blushing furiously. As their eyes met she felt transfixed by his blue gaze; so much so that she was unable to reply when he wished her a very happy Christmas.

'I'm looking forward to seeing you in the New Year,' he added quietly before he let go of her hand. He said it so softly that she wondered if she'd imagined it.

His words floated inside her head, though, for the rest of the day. Although she knew she was probably making too much of it his words filled her with hope.

She had been dreading Christmas, knowing it would be so very different from previous ones spent with friends and neighbours in their snug little cottage in Beddgelert. Now that no longer seemed to matter. She would be able to dream her way through the holiday knowing she had something special to look forward to afterwards.

Along with the rest of the family she even promised her father that she'd make his co-driver, Robert Field, who had been invited to spend Christmas Day with them, feel welcome. Privately, though, Megan agreed with Lynn that he sounded rather a bore. They had already decided that he would be at least as old as their father, possibly grey haired and certainly pompous.

He seemed to be the only person her father had made friends with and it annoyed both her and Lynn the way their dad always seemed to be quoting this man's opinion on every subject under the sun.

Meeting Robert Field for the first time on Christmas Day, they were both surprised at how wrong they'd been. It came as a shock to find he was only in his late twenties and really quite presentable in his charcoal-grey suit, light-blue shirt and grey tie.

Tall and broad framed, he had the well-developed muscles of a man used to doing manual work, but he certainly wasn't a rough workman. He was quietly spoken, he had a warm, friendly smile and was quite good-looking. His thick, light-brown hair, brushed back from his brow, gave his face a lean, strong look.

Robert had brought them all gifts. For Kathy, there was an elaborate box of toiletries, malt whisky for Watkin, a lead-crystal paperweight for Megan and a jazz record for Lynn.

Megan stood holding her present, viewing the intricate blue, white, pink and purple pattern through the multifaceted sides and thinking she had never owned anything quite so lovely before.

If only it had been a present from Miles, she mused!

The moment the thought came to her she looked up guiltily, conscious that Robert was watching her, his light-blue eyes speculative.

'It's lovely,' she exclaimed quickly. 'Thank you very much.'

His face relaxed into a smile. 'I'm glad you like it. I thought you might find it useful since you work in an office . . .'

'Oh, I wouldn't dream of taking this in to work!' she interrupted quickly. 'No, it will have a treasured place here . . .' She stopped, blushing furiously, hoping he wouldn't read more into her words than she had intended.

When her mother called out from the kitchen that she needed someone to help her, Megan quickly made her escape.

The rest of the day passed pleasantly enough. They sat down to turkey with all the usual accompaniments, followed by a traditional plum pudding, which Robert ceremoniously lit. Afterwards they were all replete and so relaxed that they even enjoyed listening to Lynn's new jazz record.

Later, after mince pies and Christmas cake, they played cards until it was time for bed.

'It's much too late for Robert to go home,' Watkin pronounced. 'Fetch some blankets, Kathy, and make him up a bed on the couch.'

Boxing Day dawned crisp and clear. There was frost glistening on the rooftops, and the sun was shining from a blue sky. After a rather late breakfast, Robert suggested that they should all go to New Brighton and take a walk along the promenade.

Lynn and Megan enjoyed the crossing. Although they had been living in Liverpool now for over three months it was the first time they had been on one of the ferry boats.

'It must be wonderful living over on this side of the Mersey,' Megan remarked as they walked briskly along the promenade towards Wallasey Village. 'Those houses high up on our left must have views right out to sea.'

'Yes, they can probably even see right over to the Welsh mountains when the weather is as clear as it is today,' agreed her father.

'Mr Walker lives in one of those houses,' Robert told them.

'Really!' Megan looked startled. 'Do you know which one it is?'

'It's that big white place right at the edge of the headland. Can you see it? It looks like a miniature castle.'

Megan couldn't tear her gaze away from the magnificent building. With its crenellated walls

and round tower at one corner, it looked like something out of a fairy tale.

The thought that Miles was so near was disturbing. She felt the blood rushing to her face when
Robert said conversationally, 'The Walkers also
have another place over in Wales, so I expect they're
spending Christmas over there.'

Suddenly the walk had lost its appeal for Megan.
She wanted to know where in Wales the Walkers'
place was, but she didn't like to ask. She felt that
if it was anywhere near their old home then that
would be another link between herself and Miles.

She shivered and clutched her coat more tightly
round her. She longed for the Christmas holiday
to be over so that she could be back at work and
see Miles again.

When Robert asked, 'Are you feeling cold,
Megan? This wind is a mean one, shall we turn
back?' she was the first to agree.

Chapter Seven

Megan's pleasure in returning to work on the Monday after Christmas was something of an anti-climax. Very few boats had entered or left the port over the holiday period. As a result, there were no bills of lading to process so she found herself at a loose end.

Even more disconcerting was that she wouldn't be seeing Miles. Along with Bob Donovan, the other shipping clerk, and Mr Newbold, they had been given some extra days off and so they wouldn't be back at work until the New Year.

The only people in the general office were Mavis Parker and Olive Jervis, and after a brief, dis-interested greeting they completely ignored her.

Mavis spent most of her time perched on the end of Olive's desk, near the switchboard. The two of them were sharing details of how they had spent Christmas and what presents they had received. Whenever they heard the tap of Valerie Pearce's heels, Mavis would scuttle back to her own desk and hammer away on the typewriter at her usual frantic speed.

Confident that she could now type reasonably well, Megan rather shyly suggested to Mavis that perhaps she could help by typing up some of the invoices.

'What's going on, you after my job, or something, kiddo?' Mavis asked as she and Olive exchanged amused glances.

'No, of course not! I haven't any work to do and you seem to be snowed under,' explained Megan, indicating the huge pile of work stacked up on Mavis's desk.

'Well, OK then. I suppose it will be all right. Have a go if you want to, but don't go making any mistakes or messing them up, mind.'

'Robert Field came to your place on Christmas Day, didn't he?' commented Mavis when Megan returned a batch of neatly typed invoices.

'Yes, he did. My father is his co-driver, and he invited him,' explained Megan. She felt uncomfortable and wondered how on earth they could have known about Robert spending Christmas with them.

When they'd lived in Beddgelert, it had been understandable that in such a small village everyone knew everybody else's business, but here, in a city the size of Liverpool, it was uncanny.

'You'll soon learn that you can't have any secrets in this place,' teased Olive, leaving her desk and coming over to join them.

'Is your dad a member of this new *Plaid Cymru* outfit that's started up in Wales?' probed Mavis, her green eyes hard and sharp.

'Why do you want to know about something like that?' Megan hedged as she saw Mavis and Olive exchange knowing glances.

'The police were here making enquiries about him a couple of weeks back . . . after that fire at the Top Ten Jazz Club.'

Megan looked bemused. 'I don't understand what you're talking about.'

'You must have read about the fire. It was on the front page of the *Liverpool Echo*,' Mavis reminded her.

'The police think it was a torch job,' explained Olive. 'The club only opened at the beginning of December and two weeks later it was burned to the ground.'

'And they thought it might be *Plaid Cymru* who'd done it,' added Mavis. 'They're pretty ruthless at burning places down so as to get attention, aren't they!'

'I don't know what you are talking about and I don't know what on earth it has to do with my father,' defended Megan hotly.

'Nothing, possibly,' Olive shrugged. 'The police were making enquiries, though, and Watkin Williams was one of the people they wanted to question. Didn't he tell you?'

'No!'

'I thought that must be why your dad asked Robert Field to your place for Christmas, because he was grateful to him. It was Robert who spoke up and cleared his name,' Mavis added cattily.

'What do you mean?'

'Robert Field told the police that your father was with him when it happened. He gave him an alibi, if you see what I mean.'

The news disturbed Megan. She could think of nothing else all morning and at lunchtime she went to see if Lynn was at the Stork Club to find out what she knew about it.

Tentatively, she explained to the doorman that she had a message for her sister and she thought she might be in there.

'You mean you want to go in and join her?'

Megan shook her head. 'I have to be back at work in twenty minutes,' she explained.

'But you wanted to have a word with her?'

'Yes.' Megan gave a small smile.

He frowned heavily and for a minute Megan thought he was going to turn her away.

'You better go in and see if she's in there, then!'

The Stork Club was packed and just as smoky and noisy as Megan remembered it from her previous visit. The only difference was that instead of the music being supplied by a live band, it was coming from gramophone records.

Megan found Lynn, with about ten other girls, moving in time to the music that was blaring out.

'Whatever are you doing here, Megan? Have you come to spy on me?' Lynn gasped as her sister grabbed her by the arm and pulled her to one side.

'No! I want to ask you something.' She paused and looked round hesitantly and then lowered her voice. 'Did you know that Dad was questioned after the Top Ten Jazz Club burned down a couple of weeks ago?'

'Yes, of course I did!'

'And you never told me!'

'The police came one night when you were out at night school.'

'And you mean that none of you thought to tell me about it when I got home!' Megan repeated in astonishment.

'Our mam was upset and said she didn't want to talk about it.'

'That's not the point! I should have been told,' Megan fumed.

'Don't shout at me,' Lynn scowled. 'I was probably in bed when you got home.'

'You could have told me next day.'

Lynn shrugged. 'What are you getting so upset about? Everything was all right. The police went away when he told them that he wasn't even near there and that Robert Field could vouch for him and prove that he had nothing at all to do with it.'

'And no one said a word to me about what had happened! Can you imagine how I felt today when someone at work asked me about it?'

Lynn pulled a face. 'Keep your hair on. It's no big deal.'

'You don't understand, do you! I felt awful not knowing anything about it. I think they thought I was trying to cover up.'

'So what!' Lynn said dismissively. 'It's all over and forgotten now.'

'Maybe it is, but I still want to know why the police picked on our dad,' Megan insisted in a bewildered voice.

Lynn shrugged her shoulders. 'That's the way of it when you're a stranger.'

'Who told you that?'

'Flash did. He said that Dad's new round here and when the police heard that he had come from Wales then it made him a number one suspect when something like that happened.'

'Flash says?' Megan frowned. 'Does that mean you are still meeting him?'

'Of course I am. I'd have a job not to since he's a regular here.' Colour flooded Lynn's round cheeks and she avoided Megan's eyes.

'You watch your step with this chap Flash,' Megan warned. 'I bet he doesn't know that you are still only a schoolgirl.'

'I shan't be for much longer,' Lynn told her, tossing her head defiantly.

'Oh yes you will be, for quite some time yet,' Megan assured her. 'If you pass your exams this summer then you can go on to technical college . . .'

'You can forget that right away,' her sister exploded hotly. 'And don't go putting any of those stupid ideas in our mam's head either. I'm leaving school at Easter.'

'You can't do that!'

'Oh yes I most certainly can. In fact, it might even be earlier. I'm going to ask if I can leave on my birthday.'

Long after she was back at her desk, Megan was haunted by their conversation. Although she was only two years older than Lynn, Megan had always been made to feel responsible for her younger sister and the habit was hard to break.

When Lynn had first started school, she had been expected to make sure that no one bullied her. With her fair, wavy hair, enormous grey eyes and round, pretty face there had been very little likelihood of that ever happening.

Even at five, Lynn had been gregarious. Making

the most of her wide, cheeky grin and dare-devil nature she easily made friends.

In fact, Megan recalled, she'd been the one who had been bullied at school, often by Lynn and her playmates. And if she ever complained about it her mother refused to listen.

'Picking on Lynn because you are jealous of her is a waste of time as far as I am concerned,' Kathy would scold. 'You'll do a lot better if instead of burying your nose in a book you go out and play with your sister and her friends.'

That hadn't been easy because Lynn and her friends didn't want her around. Now, though, with Lynn's birthday only six weeks away, Megan felt she ought to try to talk to her and make her see sense.

The trouble was, Lynn hated taking advice. It wouldn't be easy convincing her that she might be ruining her future prospects if she left school too early and without any qualifications.

It was not only a matter of her leaving school, either. It worried her that Lynn was still visiting the Stork Club even though they'd both been told not to do so. Equally worrying was the fact that she was still meeting this boy called Flash.

None of them had met him, and Lynn didn't even seem to know his proper name or where he lived. He was obviously a reckless sort of character to have earned a nickname like Flash.

She didn't like telling tales about her sister, but she felt her mother and father ought to know in case Lynn landed herself in some sort of trouble.

Chapter Eight

Watkin Williams was extremely concerned when Megan told him that Lynn was planning to leave school as soon as she possibly could.

'Don't you worry about it, I'll have a quiet word with her,' he promised.

Lynn was almost a replica of what Kathy had been like when he had first met her and it seemed to him that history was repeating itself.

He would never forget the first time he had met Kathy. It had been a bitterly cold, wet November night. The crowd of sailors he had come ashore with had decided to go into a pub called the Angel. Kathy's smile had been so warm and friendly when she came over to take their order that he had fallen for her on the spot.

When the others decided to leave, he had stayed on, smoking a cigarette, waiting for her to come and clear the table so that he could talk to her.

By the time the Angel closed he had won her interest and knew he was madly in love with her. The thought of sailing on the morning's tide, and perhaps never seeing her again, filled him with despair.

He had taken her to the State Restaurant for a meal, the only place that was still open. When that closed, they sheltered against a corner of the building, his greatcoat shielding her from the cold drizzle as they made love.

His ship had sailed before dawn but, when he returned to Liverpool six months later, the moment they disembarked he'd gone straight to the Angel to look her up.

A hatchet-faced woman behind the tea urn had laughed at him when he'd asked for Kathy Miller. 'Some sod put her in the club the end of last year and then sailed off. Don't know where she is now.'

All the time he had been away at sea he'd thought constantly about the pretty fair-haired girl who'd won his heart. He'd been strictly brought up and now he was aghast at what had resulted from his unforgivable, rash action.

Anxious to make amends, he was determined to find her. He'd asked around for several days and then, surprisingly, he had bumped into her in the busy shopping centre. The fair, wavy hair, the deep-set grey eyes, the round, pretty face were just as he remembered them. Instead of looking slim with delicate curves, however, she was now heavily pregnant.

She recognised him immediately and he thought she was going to faint she went so white as she murmured his name. They were married as soon as he could get a licence. Ten weeks later Megan had been born.

He'd been bewitched from the moment he set eyes on the baby. Megan had his dark hair, and dark eyes. As she grew older they shared so many similar interests that it was like reliving his own childhood all over again.

Lynn, who had been born two years later, took after Kathy, something that became even more apparent as Lynn grew older. They were like two peas from the same pod. As well as looks, she had her mother's impulsive nature, love of noise and crowds, and her habit of sulking if she couldn't have her own way. Like her mother, she was also prone to inconsequential chatter, a habit that irritated both him and Megan.

Neither Kathy nor Lynn had been really settled in Beddgelert. He'd persuaded Kathy that they should go to live there with his mother after the war had started in 1914, but right from the start she'd been alienated by what she called the desolation and wildness.

It bewildered him when she claimed that the towering mountains were overpowering and threatening. Whenever he scaled their rugged sides, and rested in one of the shadowy groves, he found the utter silence peaceful and soothing.

To him the mountains were like sentinels guarding his home. Earth mothers, holding the sheep safe in their green, velvet-soft aprons.

Kathy hated the sheep. She complained that their plaintive bleating made her feel so irritable that she wanted to scream. She refused to walk where they were grazing in case they butted her.

In winter, when the narrow roads around Beddgelert were icy or blocked by snow, she stayed indoors, huddled over the fire, and he and the girls had to do all the shopping.

Only in summer, when the sun was shining and it was hot enough to lie on the sands at

Porthmadog, did Kathy seem in the least bit happy. Then she was never at home. She would pack up a picnic and take Megan and Lynn to the beach, arriving back only minutes before he got home from work.

He never complained. It was enough for him that Kathy was happy.

Now, when Megan told him about Lynn's friendship with a boy called Flash, all this came rushing back and all his old anxieties surfaced. He tackled Lynn about it in front of Kathy, hoping she would add her weight to his rebukes.

Lynn stared at him insolently, tossing back her mane of fair hair. 'Our Megan's been tittle-tattling about me again.' She pouted, her big grey eyes filling with tears as she looked at her mother for support.

'She didn't need to, I've got eyes in my head,' her father told her sharply. 'I've noticed the change in you since we've been in Liverpool. You even dress differently. You go to extremes and wear your skirts inches above your knees trying to look like these young flappers. It's a wonder you don't find yourself mistaken for a "totty". You mend your ways, girl. I shan't tell you again,' he threatened.

Her defiant attitude angered Watkin. Usually, he ignored her sulks and moods, but this was more serious. The time had come to take a firm stand, he decided grimly.

The following day, when Robert Field suggested to him at work that they might all like to go to a New Year's Eve dance at the Tower Ballroom in

New Brighton, Watkin turned down the idea.

He didn't care for dancing himself, he explained, and Kathy had gone down with a heavy cold after their walk on Boxing Day. He went on to tell him about Lynn and that he deemed it a good way of punishing her.

'That means Megan is being made to suffer as well,' Robert pointed out. 'Why not let me take her on her own? I'm sure she would enjoy it.'

'Perhaps you're right,' agreed Watkin. 'Mind you have her back home before midnight, though.'

'On New Year's Eve! Surely she can stay and see the New Year in,' protested Robert. 'We'll leave right afterwards,' he added quickly. 'They're running extra boats and buses so there won't be any problem about getting back here.'

Megan was rather taken aback when her father told her what had been arranged. 'It sounds too grand for me,' she demurred. 'I've nothing suitable to wear.'

'Then you'd better go out and buy yourself something,' he told her in a conspiratorial whisper and slipped a crumpled five pound note into her hand.

'Thanks, Dad!' Her dark eyes widened with delight. Then her face clouded. 'Won't our Lynn be awfully upset if I go and she has to stay at home?'

'Her turn will come when she's old enough. You are out working now, so it's time you started having a life of your own.'

'Whose idea was it . . . this dance, I mean?' Megan persisted, frowning.

'Don't worry, I haven't been doing any match-making,' he assured her. 'Robert wanted all of us to go but when I refused he suggested you might like to go with him. He's a nice fellow, Megan, so go and enjoy yourself. Give 1925 a good start. Now run along and buy that dress before all the shops are shut.'

The Tower Ballroom was quite the grandest place Megan had ever been in. It stood about a hundred yards from New Brighton Pier and Megan felt quite nervous as she walked off the boat with Robert and saw what an imposing building it was.

Once inside the ballroom her excitement increased. The shining parquet floor was already crowded. On a raised stage at one end of the room a five-piece orchestra was playing popular dance tunes which she enjoyed, and coloured beams of light from a revolving central chandelier played on those who were dancing.

Megan was glad she'd done as her father had suggested and bought something new to wear. She felt very elegant and glamorous in her sleek full-length, deep-blue evening dress, with its floating panel of light-blue chiffon.

Although Robert had told Lynn that he didn't like jazz very much, he was quite an expert when it came to the more traditional dances like the Fox Trot and the Waltz.

By the time the interval came, she felt quite exhausted. When Robert led her across to one of the small tables on the edge of the dance floor and told her to sit there while he went to fetch some refreshments, Megan was more than happy to comply.

With a sigh of relief she sat down and slipped her aching feet out of her shoes.

'Someone been dancing on your toes?'

Megan's heart flipped at the sound of a familiar voice. She looked up, startled. Miles Walker, looking incredibly handsome in flawlessly cut evening wear, with a frilled white dress shirt, was standing there.

'Whatever are you doing here?' she gasped.

'I could ask you the same thing,' he countered, his vivid blue eyes studying her with amusement.

Before she could answer, Robert returned with their drinks. For a moment the two men stared at each other in silence, then with a brief nod Miles nonchalantly walked away.

Megan felt deflated. She scanned the crowded ballroom, trying to spot him, wondering who he was with, desperately willing him to come back and ask her to dance.

Up until that moment, she had been having a wonderful time, but now she found herself comparing the two men. Miles, darkly handsome, dominant and dashing; Robert so solid and reliable.

She had to admit that she felt very comfortable and relaxed in Robert's company, but Miles was a challenge. His brilliant blue eyes mesmerised her, arousing feelings that were new and strange to her.

Commonsense told her that Robert was by far the more dependable of the two men, but she was drawn to Miles. He excited her even though she suspected he was selfish and egotistical. She already knew he was quite prepared to do an about-face if it suited his purpose, as he had the day when he'd ignored her in the office.

At the stroke of midnight, the lights dimmed and a piper circled the ballroom while outside bells, bugles and sirens, from ships lying at anchor in the Mersey, sounded their noisy greeting to the New Year in a wild cacophony of sound.

When Robert kissed her on the cheek and wished her a happy New Year, Megan closed her eyes and thought of Miles.

As her warm, sweet breath cascaded over him, Robert held her more tightly. He felt stunned by the overpowering reactions she created in him.

The magical moment ended abruptly. Someone tapped him on the shoulder and before he knew what was happening he was pushed aside and Megan was swept out of his arms.

The vast crowd had become delirious. Megan found herself whirled from one to the other as complete strangers hugged and kissed and wished each other a happy New Year.

'I wonder what 1925 has in store for *us*.'

Unbelievably, she found herself in Miles' arms. His intense blue eyes were unfathomable as she looked up at him.

The noise, the cigarette smoke, and even the crowd all faded into the background as she slid her hand around Miles' neck. With her fingers entwined in his crisp dark hair, she pulled his face closer clinging to him, waiting for him to kiss her.

74

His lips trailed across her cheek, then hovered tantalisingly above her eager mouth for an intolerably tormenting moment before they met hers.

As he kissed her, his lips hot, hard and demanding, she felt an uprush of emotion. She closed her eyes, savouring every second. Then he was gone, swallowed up in the melee, leaving her dizzy with desire.

Chapter Nine

Like her mother, Lynn loved everything about Liverpool. She found the huge buildings were far more inspiring than towering mountains; the murky grey Mersey more fascinating than the crystal clear Glaslyn. The noisy, never-ending stream of traffic, mingled with the wild cries of seagulls when rough seas drove them inland, excited her, made her feel alive.

Most of all, she enjoyed being a part of the thrusting, jostling crowds. The city never seemed to sleep. After dark, when everywhere was lit up by the street lights and shop window displays, it was sheer magic.

Ever since she had been very young, and her mother had told her stories about the great bustling seaport that had been her home, Lynn had dreamed of coming back there to live.

One of Lynn's most vivid memories was the occasion when she had been about nine and Kathy had brought her on a visit to Liverpool to see her grandmother. The busy streets with their huge, clanging trams, the crowds and all the wonderful shops had made a lasting impression.

Inside the semi-detached house where old Mrs Miller lived, everything had been neat and orderly with starched lace curtains at all the windows. The bedroom had smelled of lavender and moth balls.

Lynn remembered how every piece of furniture had gleamed and there had been little crocheted mats under all the ornaments so that they wouldn't scratch the polished surfaces. As well as a rug in front of each armchair, to protect the patterned carpet from people's feet, there were also embroidered covers on the back and arms of the chairs. Lynn remembered lifting one of them to peek underneath and had been startled to find the colours were so much brighter that without them the chairs would have looked like patchwork.

Everyone had shushed her to silence when she had asked where Grandad Miller was. Afterwards, her mother had explained that he'd gone to heaven a long long time ago. A few weeks after they returned home to Wales, she was told that Grandma Miller had gone to join him.

After that, whenever possible, Lynn would cajole her mother into talking about her childhood in Liverpool. She never tired of hearing about the days when Kathy had lived in Anfield and she would listen with rapt attention, seeing it all as clearly as if she was living there herself.

'It was lovely out there, away from the docks, yet you could be right in the centre of the city in next to no time,' Kathy would say dreamily.

Sometimes, Lynn would try to hurry her past these details of her early years, eager to hear what happened after her mother had left school.

'Those were the days, I can tell you,' Kathy would say and sigh ecstatically. 'Nights out, going dancing, and taking trips over to New Brighton on the ferry boat with Ruby Adams. She was my best friend at school and we started work together serving in a grocer's shop.'

Lynn's eyes would shine with delight when they reached this part of the story. 'Go on, Mam,' she would beg, 'tell me about when you met Dad.'

'Well, I was almost seventeen by then and Ruby and me were having some real fun. We knew it couldn't last for ever so we decided to make the most of it while we could. For a start we decided to change our jobs and become barmaids.'

Although she had heard it a dozen times before, Lynn never tired of listening to the account of how her parents had first met. Kathy's face would soften, her eyes grow dreamy and there would be a pause before she started speaking again as if she was inwardly reliving the occasion.

'One day Watkin came into the Angel, the pub where we worked, with a bunch of young sailors. They were only in Liverpool for one night as they were due to sail on the morning tide.'

'Go on, Mam,' Lynn would beg, hanging on her every word. 'Tell me how old he was and what he was like. Did you both fall in love at first sight?'

'Well, he was different from the others who came in with him. He was older for a start and he had an air of authority about him. The others didn't stay long, they wanted a bit more excitement than the Angel had to offer. As soon as they had finished their pints they were off. Watkin went on sitting there, smoking a cigarette, and I could feel his dark eyes following my every movement.

When I went over to clear his table he asked me what time I finished.'

'And he was waiting for you and you went to the State Restaurant and had a crazy night out before he sailed away next morning. I know that bit,' Lynn said impatiently. 'Tell me about after that, when he came back to Liverpool again.'

'I'd given up working at the Angel by then and when he asked after me they couldn't even tell him where I lived.'

'And you met by chance, as if fate had decreed it,' Lynn breathed rapturously. 'It's so romantic!'

'I was walking down Lord Street,' her mother went on, 'and there he was coming the other way. We just stopped and stared at each other. We couldn't believe our eyes, either of us. Then we were hugging and kissing each other and before I knew what was happening he'd asked me to marry him.'

'Exactly like a fairy tale,' Lynn said with a sigh.

'Yes, it was,' agreed her mother. 'I'd never thought to see him again, I can tell you.'

'Had you thought about him a lot?' Lynn pressed.

'I certainly had . . . night and day,' her mother assured her.

'Fancy loving someone that much,' murmured Lynn dreamily.

'He was never out of my mind,' repeated her mother with a deep sigh.

'You should have waited and not had a baby right away.' Lynn frowned. 'Then I might have been the eldest or perhaps your only daughter,' she added mischievously.

Kathy was not to be drawn.

From that point it was a closed book. No matter how skilfully she framed her questions, Lynn never managed to find out anything at all about the early days of her parents' marriage. Kathy always changed the subject.

Now that they were back in Liverpool, Kathy would often point out places she had known as a girl, or the changes that had taken place in the city centre since those days.

The shops, though, Kathy was the first to admit, were the biggest attraction for her. There were so many new ones and she was never happier than when they were going round them. C&A in Church Street was her favourite.

Lynn preferred Woollies or one of the markets, because the clothes they sold were so cheap compared to Hendersons or Lewis's. Even so, she would have spent a fortune in them if she'd had it.

As it was, she usually managed to wheedle money out of her mother to buy something new, as long as she promised not to let her father or Megan know. When they reached home she would hide away whatever she had bought, ready to wear the next time she went to the Stork Club.

Lynn loved the atmosphere there. Unlike Megan she felt carried away by the jazz beat and then everything else was obliterated from her mind.

No two visits were ever the same. She reached dizzy heights of happiness on the occasions when Flash was there. Her heart would thunder crazily and she'd be as talkative and exhilarated as if the air was filled with contagious excitement.

Kathy felt vaguely uneasy when Lynn talked incessantly about Flash, remembering what had happened to her when she'd been not much older than Lynn.

'Watch your step with this boy,' she warned. 'You are still at school and we don't want any problems.'

'I only go dancing with him,' Lynn protested hotly. 'You can't get into much trouble doing that in the Stork Club because it's far too crowded!' she added with a cheeky grin.

'You'd like him, Mam, you really would!' Lynn told her enthusiastically. 'He's absolutely great!' she added dreamily. 'He's ever so good-looking. Tall, with black wavy hair and blue eyes and he dresses really smart . . .'

'You'd better not let your father hear you going on like you do about this boy,' interrupted her mother. 'He's already said you're not to go to the Stork Club and if he found out you were defying him by nipping in there in your lunch hour then he might very well put his foot down and stop you going out of the house altogether.'

'Oh Mam, he wouldn't!'

The dismay in Lynn's wide grey eyes brought a reassuring smile from her mother. 'Then watch your step. You are a bit young to be going out with boys, you know,' she reminded her.

Lynn scowled. 'He doesn't say anything about our Megan going out with fellas, though, does he! He even let her go to that New Year's Eve dance at the Tower Ballroom with Robert Field. Yet he wouldn't allow me out of the house at all that night!'

'Megan is two years older than you, Lynn.'

'Yeah, and she's sensible and wouldn't do anything stupid. I know! I bet she's never even kissed Robert. He's crazy about her, too. I wish he'd take me out.'

'Lynn! He's much too old for you. In my opinion he's too old for Megan,' she added sharply.

'I don't get it! Dad's older than you are!'

'Yes, maybe, but I don't want either of you to get married too young. Grow up and have some fun first.'

'That's what I want to do but everyone is trying to stop me.' Lynn pouted.

'No we're not, luv. We're just trying to protect you. There's some wild ones about these days and naturally I'm worried about you and this boy when he has a name like Flash. Whatever is his proper name?'

Lynn frowned. 'I don't know! I've never asked him. Everybody at the Stork Club refers to him as Flash. He's perfectly respectable, though, Mam!'

'Perhaps you should bring him home, then, and let me meet him and judge for myself.'

Lynn giggled. 'He'd run a mile and probably never speak to me again if I suggested that to him. It's not like in your day, Mam. Boys don't expect to be taken home to meet a girl's family until they're going steady.'

'Well, watch what you get up to with him, we don't want any problems,' warned her mother ominously.

'You're more likely to get those from Megan than from me,' retorted Lynn with a mischievous grin.

'She's got two men on a string! Robert Field and someone called Mr Miles.'

'Who?' Kathy looked surprised. 'She's never mentioned him to me. Who is he?'

'A chap she knows at work. I bet he's old enough to be her dad, too!'

Kathy frowned. If this chap worked at Walker's then perhaps Watkin knew him. She would try to remember to ask him.

She hated admitting it, even to herself, but in some ways coming back to Liverpool was proving to be a bit of a headache. It had been so much easier bringing up the girls when they'd lived in Beddgelert, she reflected. There, she had known where they were every minute of the day and the temptations they'd faced had been pretty limited.

She'd dreamed about coming back to Liverpool for far too long, she supposed, but everywhere she looked there were changes going on. The new cathedral was still being built, but there was also talk about building another one for the Catholics on the site where the workhouse stood. Plans were underway, too, for a tunnel that would take motor-cars and lorries right underneath the Mersey to Wallasey and Birkenhead on the other side.

It was no longer the Liverpool that she had grown up in, she thought sadly.

Chapter Ten

'I wonder what 1925 holds in store for *us!*'

The words Miles had whispered in her ear at the Tower Ballroom haunted Megan and in the days that followed she put a hundred and one interpretations on what he might have meant.

Seeing him had made it the most confused evening of her life. Being there at the same time as Miles, dancing to the same band, had made New Year's Eve all the more memorable.

There had been times since, though, when she wondered if it had all been a dream. In bed at night she went over every tiny detail: the way the lights had been lowered on the dot of midnight, the band playing *Auld Lang Syne*, and the wild pandemonium as complete strangers hugged and kissed each other. Being swept away from Robert and finding herself with people she had never seen before had been scary. And then to find herself in Miles' arms, looking up into the handsome face that was always in her thoughts, had been unreal.

Her heart had pounded wildly. She remembered closing her eyes as she felt the heat of his muscular body pressed against her. She'd felt convinced it must be a dream, and yet she'd desperately wanted to hold on to it a little longer.

It hadn't been a dream, though. She had felt his

breath warm on her cheek and when she had opened her eyes he had been smiling down at her. The next thing she'd known was that his mouth was covering hers in a lingering kiss that sent her pulses racing.

And it was then he had whispered those magic words.

Before she could say a word he'd gone, swallowed up in the surging crowd. Robert was back at her side, struggling to hold on to her arm as people pumped his free hand and slapped his back, and others tried to kiss her on the cheek or pull her away from him.

She hadn't told Robert that she had seen Miles.

She wasn't quite sure why she didn't mention it, except that there had been a sense of hostility between them when they had met earlier in the evening. Some inner caution warned her that to do so might spoil Robert's enjoyment and, after all, if it hadn't been for him she would not have been there at all.

By the time the *Royal Daffodil* ferry boat sailed from New Brighton pier back to Liverpool, it had been packed with revellers returning home from the Tower Ballroom. Robert had found seats for them inside and he'd taken her silence for tiredness. She hadn't been tired at all, only lost in thought, reliving the excitement of the evening, especially meeting Miles and mulling over what he had said.

She couldn't be sure whether Miles had intended it as a private, personal message or whether it was merely a casual comment made on the spur of the moment.

On the first day back at work in the New Year,

Megan felt uneasy about what she should say to Miles.

Then, as the days went by and she didn't see him, she even began to wonder if he was deliberately avoiding her since he hadn't come in to the office at all.

Her world seemed flat without him. In the end, she plucked up the courage to ask Bob Donovan, the other shipping clerk, if he knew where Miles was.

'He's off sick. Gone down with flu. Is it anything I can handle?' he asked.

'No, no it's quite all right.' She flushed with embarrassment, wishing she hadn't been so impatient.

Another week went by before Miles returned to work and during his absence Megan's thoughts strayed constantly to the Walkers' place perched high on the headland at New Brighton.

She tried to imagine what Miles' room was like in such an enormous house. She decided it would probably be a huge room looking out over the sea.

There was bound to be a desk in there, she mused, and perhaps an armchair. On the wall would be photographs of his school group, or cricketing team. And he probably had a gramophone and perhaps even one of the new wireless sets to listen to as well.

By the time Miles did return to work they were so busy that when he breezed into the office there was no chance for them to speak to each other.

Megan began to think that his remark on New Year's Eve had meant nothing after all. Her spirits sank and even her father commented on how list-less she had become.

'Are you finding it too much having to go to night school three times a week?' he asked sym-pathetically.

'No! If I didn't go there then I'd just be sitting at home here every evening, wouldn't I?'

'Not necessarily. You could be out enjoying your-self, going to the pictures or out dancing with Robert.' Her father smiled.

'He certainly asks you often enough,' her mother chipped in.

Megan coloured, knowing this was true. Ever since he had taken her to the Tower Ballroom, Robert had been trying to persuade her to go out with him again, but she always found an excuse to turn him down.

She knew her family all liked Robert and couldn't understand her reason for doing it. Lynn was always going on about how good-looking he was with his thick fair hair and smoke-blue eyes and how she'd jump at the chance of going out with him if she'd been Megan.

What none of them knew was that when she compared him to Miles all these attributes faded into nothing. Miles was far better looking, his strong features so much more handsome. His bril-liant blue eyes had such sparkle and verve that Robert's seemed dull in comparison.

She didn't dislike Robert, but he always took everything so seriously. He was always discussing politics with her father.

'Our Lynn seems to enjoy herself well enough

now that we've said she can go dancing, so why don't you go out with her now and again?' Kathy suggested.

'Go with her to the Stork Club! No thanks! You can cut the atmosphere in there with a knife. It gets so crowded that you can't breathe let alone dance.'

'Megan's right. I should never have let you talk me into letting Lynn go there,' stated Watkin emphatically. 'It's a wonder to me that the authorities don't close the place down.'

'It's not all that bad,' retorted Kathy mildly.

'I hear there was practically a riot in the place the other week,' commented Watkin. 'I would have thought Lynn could find something better to do with her time than listen to jazz bands playing and dancing around,' he argued sourly.

'Leave her alone, Watkin, the girl's only having a bit of fun and it keeps her happy going there. I'd be doing the same thing if I was her age.'

'Why don't you let her go out with Robert?' suggested Megan. 'He'd take her to the Philharmonic, or somewhere like that, to hear some proper music.'

'Lynn would go out with him like a shot if he asked her, even though he's a lot older than her,' retorted her mother sharply. 'The trouble is he seems dead set on you, and most of the time you ignore him. You want to remember he owns his house in New Brighton. A far better place than what we're living in here.'

'That'll do,' growled Watkin. 'Stop match-making. If Megan doesn't want to go out with Robert then that's her decision, though I agree with you she could do a lot worse for herself.'

Or a lot better, mused Megan as she remained silent, thinking of Miles. She was relieved that her father had brought the discussion to an end. She'd been afraid her mother might pursue the matter and want to know why she didn't like Robert Field. How could she explain that, although he was pleasant enough as a friend, he had none of the dashing qualities she admired in Miles? It was like comparing a block of unpolished wood with a shining veneered surface.

Robert was kindly and capable but he couldn't begin to compete with Miles. Miles intrigued her. He was a challenge. She was well aware that he could break her heart if she wasn't careful, but she was attracted to him like a cat to cream. She knew he could be quick-tempered and off-hand, but one flash of his winning smile could start her heart thumping and her spirits soaring. Robert's slow smile, on the other hand, was reassuring; rather like being wrapped in a soft blanket.

Next day, her reticence was rewarded.

It was bitterly cold, the sky grey and leaden. The tall buildings leading up from the Pier Head formed a wind tunnel, trapping the intermittent gusts that came straight off the Mersey, turning them into a full-scale gale.

Nevertheless, her need to be out of doors was overpowering. In her lunch break Megan tied on a headscarf, determined to take a walk down to the waterfront.

As she turned into Chapel Street, head down as she battled against the buffeting wind, she bumped into someone hurrying in the opposite direction. When she looked up, an apology on her lips, she was stunned to find it was Miles.

'Where are you dashing off too like a headless chicken?' he asked in surprise.

'To the Pier Head for a breath of fresh air,' she mumbled, colouring up.

'You'll find plenty of that down there,' he laughed. 'It's blowing a gale. Why don't you change your mind and walk up to Exchange Station with me?'

Her pleasure at being asked was so great that she could only nod her agreement. As they walked back up Chapel Street she let Miles do most of the talking.

'I'm on my way to Manchester,' he told her. 'One of the boats that should have come into Princess Dock has berthed there by mistake and they started unloading before they realised that the consignment was intended for Liverpool.'

'So that means you'll be working very late tonight?'

'It certainly does! You people in the office don't know how lucky you are finishing work promptly at half-past five every afternoon. What do you do with yourself for the rest of the evening?'

'I go to night school three times a week,' Megan reminded him.

'Don't you ever go to the pictures with your boyfriend?'

'I haven't got a boyfriend.' She flushed uncomfortably as he raised his eyebrows questioningly. 'Sometimes I go out with my younger sister,' she added quickly.

'You were dancing with that chap Robert Field on New Year's Eve. I thought he was your boyfriend.'

'No!' Megan shook her head emphatically. 'He's a friend of my father's . . . that's how I came to be there with him.'

'Really!' His blue eyes twinkled wickedly. 'So he's not your choice. In fact, you are heart whole and fancy free with nothing to do in the evenings.'

'I told you, I've got night school and then I have my homework to do.'

'And Friday night you stay in to wash your hair.' He grinned. 'It's a pity because I would still like to take you out, but it looks as if you're too busy to spare the time.'

Megan bit her lip, aware that he was teasing her.

'What about it then? Shall we say next Tuesday night?'

'I'd love to, but it's one of the evenings I go to night school,' Megan told him, her voice heavy with disappointment. 'I haven't any classes on Monday . . .'

'Right, let's make it Monday, then.' He took a quick look at his watch. 'I must dash or I shall miss my train. Next Monday, then. Seven o'clock.'

It wasn't until after Miles had vanished into the Exchange Station that Megan realised he hadn't said where they were to meet. Even that didn't matter. Her head was in the clouds as she made her way back to the office. She was going out with Miles Walker. Her dreams were coming true at least. 1925 *was* going to be special.

Megan hugged her secret to herself for the rest of the week, counting not only the days until she would meet Miles but even the hours. She planned every item of what she would wear, then changed her mind and started all over again.

Snow, ice and freezing fog made getting about something of a nightmare but Megan scarcely noticed. She was cocooned in a blanket of happiness that kept her oblivious to what was going on around her.

There were moments when she wondered how she was ever going to get through the weekend without blurting out her wonderful news, she felt so keyed up.

The only thing that stopped her was the fact that she didn't know where she was expected to meet Miles on Monday night, and if she mentioned her date to Lynn then she would be bound to ask.

By midday on Monday, she was convinced he'd forgotten their date, or else that he'd been stringing her along. She stayed at her desk right through the lunch hour, hoping against hope that at any minute he'd drop by to confirm that he was taking her out that night.

It was late afternoon when Miles finally breezed into the office. He deposited a pile of shipping documents on her desk and when he left again, without a word, Megan felt sick with disappointment.

As she blinked away the threatening tears, her heart quickened. Lying on the top of the pile was a scrap of paper with 'Tatler, Church Street. 7 p.m.' scrawled on it.

The rest of the afternoon passed in a dream. In

a whirlwind of excitement she rushed home to get ready. When she told them that she was going to the pictures with a friend, Lynn immediately wanted to know who the friend was.

'Someone from the office,' Megan told her and kept her fingers crossed that her sister wouldn't ask any more questions.

'Can I come with you?' Lynn asked.

'No, you can't,' her father said sharply. 'You have homework to do. You'd better put your back into it my girl or you'll not be passing your exams.'

'I don't want to pass any exams,' Lynn said with a pout. 'I want to leave school and get a job so that I have some money of my own.'

'The sort of money you could earn serving behind a shop counter wouldn't keep you in stockings,' her father told her scornfully. 'Get some qualifications behind you and then you'll be able to earn a worthwhile salary.'

While they were arguing, Megan slipped away to get ready. She was still frantically debating what to wear when Lynn burst into the bedroom they shared.

'Say I'm coming with you, Megan,' she begged. 'I won't really tag along! I want to get out so that I can meet some friends. Mam knows . . . she says it's all right,' she added hopefully, her grey eyes pleading.

'No!' Megan's chin was set stubbornly. 'If I did that I would have to arrange to meet you afterwards so that we come home together.'

'No, you won't. Mam said she'll give each of us a key and persuade Dad to have an early night.

As long as we both come in quietly he'll never know. Be a sport, Meg. Go on! I'll let you use my new red lipstick.'

Lynn's wheedling voice and plaintive face overcame Megan's resistance. How could she refuse when she was going to have such a wonderful evening herself, she thought guiltily.

'All right, then. One thing, though, Lynn. Although we leave the house together we go our separate ways at the end of the road. I'm not having you spying on me.'

'What makes you think I'd waste my evening by following you,' Lynn said scornfully.

'I don't know. You haven't said where you're going.'

'Only to the Stork Club to see if Flash is there. I haven't seen him for ages. Someone said he'd been down with this flu bug that's going round.'

When they parted company at the end of the road, Megan took a devious route to Church Street, constantly stopping to look in shop windows so that she could check if Lynn was following her. She dallied so much that she had to run the last few hundred yards and arrived at the Tatler out of breath.

She scanned the crowded foyer for Miles, worried in case he had arrived early and thought she wasn't coming. Then he was at her side, and she hardly recognised him he was dressed so differently from when she saw him in the office. Instead of the smart suit and discreet tie, he was wearing a tweed sports jacket and grey flannel trousers.

They stumbled into the darkness of the back

94

row. Megan struggled out of her coat, clutching it on her lap as she sank into the plush seat.

As the big picture started, Miles slipped an arm round her shoulders. After that, she had very little idea of what was on the screen, aware only of his closeness. She could feel his breath fanning her cheek and the sharp clean smell of his newly shaved face, that was almost touching hers, made her senses reel.

After a while, the weight of his arm across her shoulders became increasingly uncomfortable. She moved cautiously, not wanting him to think she was rejecting him.

As she leaned forward slightly, his arm slid down until his hand rested on her waist. Involuntarily, she stiffened, pulling away. His hand tightened, drawing her body closer until she was resting against him.

When the interval came, and the lights went up, he withdrew his arm, flexed his shoulders and stood up.

'Sit tight, I'll be back in a minute.'

As Miles edged his way along the row, she felt a wave of panic at being left on her own. The lights were just dimming when he returned with a box of chocolates.

As she tried to open it, she was loudly shushed by the people sitting near them. Miles took the box from her, ripped away the rustling wrappings and placed the box in her lap. Putting his arm around her again, he turned his attention back to the screen, helping himself to the chocolates from time to time.

After they came out of the pictures he took her to a milk bar near Lime Street Station. As they sipped milkshakes, Megan felt she'd never before experienced such a wonderful evening.

She would have liked it to last for ever, but suddenly Miles said abruptly, 'Come on, I'll see you to the end of your road. Don't breathe a word to anyone in the office that I've taken you out . . . understand?' he warned, tucking her hand into the crook of his arm as they emerged into the street.

'Are you trying to tell me that I'm not good enough for you?' she asked, drawing away from him.

'Come here.' Before she could stop him, Miles had pulled her into the shelter of a shop doorway and his mouth was on hers, hot and hungry. 'Now do you know how I feel about you?' he asked softly as he released her.

'I'm not sure!' she gasped, shaken and trembling.

'I want to see you again,' he assured her, 'but you musn't mention it to anyone, because of my father. He's so old-fashioned in his ways. He believes that unless the boss keeps his distance from the workers it destroys discipline.'

'Indeed! Then why did you take me to the pictures if you knew your father would disapprove?' Megan asked, puzzled.

'Perhaps I don't think the way my father does,' he murmured, pulling her back into his arms, his lips nuzzling her neck. 'It's best if it stays our secret, though, Megan. I don't want you to mention to anyone that we're seeing each other . . . especially to anybody at the office. Understand?'

Chapter Eleven

'Oh no! There must be some mistake!'

White faced, her grey eyes bleak and her lower lip trembling, Lynn looked up from the letter she had just opened and stared helplessly round the breakfast table.

'Let me see that,' demanded her father, holding out his hand for the letter.

With a smothered sob, Lynn flung it across the table. 'Don't start lecturing me,' she snuffled. 'I knew I wouldn't get through those stupid exams. You should have let me leave at Easter like I wanted to do. I hate school and I'm not going back.'

'You *are* going back, my girl. This isn't the end, far from it,' Watkin declared waving the sheet of paper in the air. 'You can sit those exams again.'

'But, Dad . . .'

'It's no surprise to me that you've failed,' he went on relentlessly. 'All this gallivanting about and going to the Stork Club when you should be studying. From now on you'll stay in at night and at the weekend as well. Disgraceful, I call it. You've every opportunity to get on and what do you do? You cavort around with those jazz-mad imbeciles that you call friends. Wastrels they are! Every one of them! I don't know what the world is coming to. When I was your age . . .'

'All right, Watkin, all right. We know you've never had the chances our Lynn has had,' Kathy interrupted shrilly. 'We know all about that, but things are different now. The world is changing . . .'

'I can see that for myself,' he snapped. 'And not for the better, either.'

'Well, that's neither here nor there and nothing at all to do with our Lynn. It's happening and we have to live with it. No need to go shouting your head off at the girl, now, is there? She's upset enough as it is.'

'I'm fed up with school and I'm never going back,' Lynn blubbered. 'Let our Megan take all the exams she likes. I want to live!' Dramatically she pushed back her chair, tossed her head and stalked from the room.

'Come back here, girl, and finish your breakfast,' roared Watkin, his face set and angry as the door crashed shut behind her.

'Let her be, luv,' Kathy begged as he stood up to go after her. 'Sit down and have another cup of tea,' she murmured placatingly, refilling his cup.

'I'll not have her behaving like that,' Watkin muttered crossly.

'Leave her alone and she'll soon calm down. Talk to her again when she's in a more reasonable mood.'

'You're not to let her take the day off school, mind,' he warned.

'Come on, drink your tea and get off to work. We'll sort it all out tonight.'

When he arrived at Albert Dock, where he and Robert Field were to collect a load from one of the

98

bonded warehouses, Watkin Williams was far from happy. It was hard, heavy work, but he hardly noticed because he was so upset over Lynn.

When the lorry was loaded, and they took a well-earned break before setting off to the Midlands to deliver their consignment, he confided his disappointment to Robert.

'I shouldn't worry about it too much. Lynn's a good-looker and has a winning way with her. She won't starve. Probably get married in next to no time.'

'There's rubbish you're talking, Robert Field,' Watkin said bitterly. 'She has the chance of a fine education and all you can think of is that she will be getting married. I want her brain sharpened first so that she can do something useful with her life. Get married, yes. I want grandchildren the same as the next man, but I want her to have a rewarding life as well.'

'For some, getting married is reward enough,' Robert stated mildly. 'It wouldn't be for your Megan, I can see that, but young Lynn is a different type of girl altogether.'

'Well, you're right on that score! They are as different as chalk and cheese, I'll grant you that,' Watkin agreed as he stirred his tea angrily.

'Come on!' Robert Field drained his mug and stood up. 'Let's get on the road or we'll be working overtime and we don't get extra pay for doing that, remember!'

While Robert was at the wheel, Watkin brooded over Lynn's future, planning how he could persuade her to adopt a more serious attitude to life.

In some ways he blamed himself for what was happening. Uprooting her from Wales only a few months before taking her exams was bound to have upset her concentration. She wasn't the studious type like Megan.

His heart filled with pride when he thought of his eldest daughter. He knew how hard it had been for her to leave Wales, to exchange the tranquillity of the mountains for the bustle of city life, yet she was making the best of it.

He had never once heard Megan grumble. And the way she had settled at Walker's delighted him. There was only one thing that disappointed him: the fact that she didn't seem to like Robert Field.

He studied his companion's profile. It was a strong, clean-shaven face, with a firm set to the jaw. The widely spaced, light-blue eyes, fair hair brushed back to reveal a deep brow, and strong, straight nose gave him a Nordic look. There was such power in the brawny forearms and square, capable hands resting on the wheel. Watkin could imagine him at the oars of a Viking ship, looking as calm and determined as he did now driving a lorry.

Yes, Watkin reflected, Robert would make an admirable son-in-law. Give it time and perhaps Megan would soften, he thought hopefully. At present, though, she only seemed to be interested in carving out a career and he would never want to force either of his daughters into a relationship they didn't want.

When he returned home that night he found the house in uproar. Kathy was in tears and a grim-faced Megan was trying to reason with her.

'Is there something wrong?'

'It's Lynn,' sobbed Kathy. 'She's not come home from school.'

'She's probably with her friends and forgotten about the time.' He frowned, checking his watch.

'She'd let me know,' Kathy told him, shaking her head.

'Maybe she forgot to tell you.'

'No, she wouldn't forget. Even if she's only going to look round the shops, she always pops home first to let me know where she will be.'

'Then perhaps some of her friends know where she went when she came out of school,' Watkin persisted, turning to Megan.

'All her close friends left school at Christmas,' whined Kathy, her tears flowing anew.

Megan and her father exchanged anxious looks. Uppermost in both their minds was the likelihood that Lynn hadn't come home at four o' clock because she hadn't been to school at all.

'I'll just check with one or two people who might have seen her,' Megan said, slipping on her coat. 'I won't be long.'

She made her way to Queen Square, knowing that if Lynn was anywhere it would be at the Stork Club.

'Looking for your sister again, are you?' the doorman commented. 'Well, now you've no call to go in because she's not here.'

'Have you any idea where I might find her?' asked Megan anxiously.

'Heavens, yes! I can tell you that in a minute.

A working girl is our Lynn!' His eyebrows shot up in surprise. 'Are you telling me you didn't know?'

'Working? Lynn hasn't left school, yet.'

'Well, she has now! Sure, it's a fine little number she's got herself and happy as a lark she is to be there. Saw her myself only an hour ago. Chipper as can be! A smile on that pretty face of hers and a ready answer to all the banter she gets from the customers. She makes a little cracker of a waitress and no mistake.'

'Waitress!'

'That she is! Working at the Copper Kettle. Hasn't she told you?'

'Not a word! Mam is out of her mind with worry because she didn't come home from school at her usual time.'

'Oh, she's a bad one!' His eyes twinkled. 'I bet she wanted to make sure she liked working there before she told you. Do you know how to find it?'

'I'm not sure. Is it the one in Slater Street?'

'That's right. You can't miss it. There's a big copper kettle in the window. Nip up Church Street, into Bold Street and it's the first road on your right. Now, have you got all that?'

'I think so. And thanks for all your help.' Megan smiled gratefully.

'Off you go, then, and remember – don't be too hard on that little sister of yours,' he warned. 'Grand girl she is, to be sure.'

Megan found the Copper Kettle without any difficulty. Sure enough it was easy to spot with its shinning copper kettle in the window. Inside it

was packed, but Megan couldn't see Lynn anywhere.

'I'm looking for my sister, Lynn Williams. Do
you know if she's here?' she asked a couple of
young girls about Lynn's age who were sitting at
one of the tables.

'She was here a minute ago. That chap over
there, Alan, he's the owner so ask him,' one of
them told her. She pointed to a stocky, bearded
man with curly black hair who was loading a tray
with steaming cups of coffee and plates of toasted
bread thick with jam that were being passed to
him through a hatchway.

As she made to move towards him, the girl
grabbed her by the arm. 'Hey, kiddo, are you
related to Alan?'

'No? Why do you ask.'

'You have the same surname and your Lynn
sounds Welsh sometimes so I thought perhaps
that's how she managed to get a job here. Alan!'
The girl raised her voice to a shrill scream so that
it could be heard above the general babble.

'Coming! Have patience or else come to the
counter and collect it yourself,' he said in a good-
natured reproof as he brought the loaded tray over
and dumped it on the table.

'Someone here looking for Lynn,' the girl told him.

'Oh? Nothing wrong is there?' he asked, his
dark eyes scanning Megan.

'Lynn is my sister, I was told she was working
here.'

'That's right. She started today.'

'She never said a word about it at home. We

were worried when she didn't come home from school at the usual time,' Megan explained.

'There's a bad one she is.' He laughed. 'Mind, she didn't know herself when she left home this morning that she'd end up the day working here, though.'

'What do you mean?'

He shrugged. 'She walked in and asked for a job saying that since she spends so much time here she may as well get paid for it.' He grinned, widely. 'Short handed I was, see, so naturally when she said she could start work right away I agreed to give her a trial.'

'Can I have a quick word with her, please?'

'She's finished for the night. She left about twenty minutes ago.'

Megan didn't hurry when she left the café. She knew Lynn would be in trouble when she got home and she didn't want to be dragged into it. There would be heated arguments between them all and she didn't intend to take sides. It was Lynn's future and something she had to sort out for herself, Megan decided.

She had problems of her own. Her relationship with Miles was not going smoothly. She knew she was head over heels in love with him, but she was not at all sure what his feelings were for her.

He had sworn her to secrecy about their meetings, saying that if his father found out he would sack her. That was the last thing she wanted to happen, but she found it increasingly difficult to speak to Miles in a calm, impersonal voice when he came in to the office.

He seemed to have no difficulty in remaining aloof as he handed over the bills of lading, or checked queries on the documents. He was so formal that she found it unbearable.

What hurt most of all was the way he laughed and joked with the other two in the office, yet remained off-hand with her.

She knew Mavis and Olive whispered about it behind her back and their snide remarks were beginning to make her feel very uncomfortable.

When she had plucked up the courage to mention it to Miles, pointing out that by behaving towards her as he did he only drew attention to what was going on between them, he'd been annoyed.

His blue eyes had narrowed and so too had his mouth, his lips thinning into a hard line. The next time he had come in to the office he had ignored her completely. Megan had felt so upset that she had been on the verge of tears. When Mavis asked her what was the matter, her excuse that she had a bad headache hadn't sounded very convincing.

She had been at Walker's for over eight months now and was confident that she was doing her job efficiently. She seemed to be well liked by both Mr Walker and Miss Pearce, so why couldn't Miles openly acknowledge their friendship? she thought bitterly.

Megan stopped and stared unseeingly at one of the shop windows. On their very first date, she recalled, Miles had warned her that his father would object to their friendship because he didn't believe the boss should be too friendly with employees. Miles wasn't her boss . . . at least, not yet. He was an employee the same as she was.

If only Miles felt the same way about her as Robert Field did, she thought wistfully. Robert was for ever asking her to go out with him. She liked him well enough, but she felt he was too old, and not her type because he was much too serious.

Miles was nearer her own age and when they were on their own the repartee between them was spiced with humour. He knew how to spark off her reactions, and she found him to be a constant challenge.

When she was with Robert she felt that he was bending over backwards all the time to agree with her, as if afraid he might upset her if he voiced an opinion that differed from hers.

A brilliant shaft of lightning, followed by a clap of thunder, made her jump. As huge raindrops splashed down she dashed into a covered alleyway for shelter.

It was then she became aware that she was not alone. The uneasy feeling she'd had ever since she'd left the café that someone was dogging her footsteps was confirmed.

Trembling, she looked round at the thin, lanky young man with greasy shoulder-length hair. 'Are you following me?' she demanded.

'I've been walking behind you since you left the Copper Kettle, if that's what you mean.'

'Why?'

'Why not?' He grinned widely. 'I heard you tell Alan Williams that you were Lynn's sister and I'm a mate of hers.'

'Are you Flash?' She looked at him suspiciously. Lynn hadn't mentioned anything about him wearing glasses.

'No, kiddo. I'm not Flash.' He grinned, showing big, irregular teeth.

'So how do you know Lynn?'

'I've met up with her at the Stork Club. Right little smasher she is!'

Megan bit her lip and said nothing.

'I'll take you for a bevvy, if you like,' he offered, 'and we can get to know each other.'

'No, thank you.' She hoped he wouldn't hear the squeak of fear in her voice. At the back of her mind was a prickly foreboding. She regretted having taken shelter in the alleyway; it was so deserted.

'Let's go for a nosh, then. They do a smashing bowl of scouse at the Sweatrag in Scottie Road. Come on, we can cut through the jowlers and be there in next to no time.'

As he grabbed hold of her arm, Megan felt petrified. She pulled away and let out a scream as her stomach knotted with fear.

'What's wrong? You'll have the Scuffers on our necks carrying on like that,' he scowled, letting go of her.

'Don't you touch me or I really will scream,' she warned, breathing hard and hoping he wouldn't notice that she was trembling.

'Yeah, I reckon you would an' all.' He grinned, a note of respect creeping into his voice. He shrugged his thin shoulders. 'Well, please yourself, kiddo. Some other time, perhaps!'

When Megan said nothing, he pulled up his

collar against the heavy rain that was now sheeting down. 'See you around, then. Tell that sister of yours to bring you along to the Stork sometime,' he called over his shoulder as he loped off out of sight.

Megan waited until he had disappeared from sight then she took to her heels and didn't pause until she reached home. As she went indoors she was shaking and her breath was catching audibly in her throat. She felt bewildered and exhausted by what had happened.

As she opened the door to the cramped little flat she thought longingly of their cosy cottage, ringed by mountains, and wished with all her heart that she was back in Beddgelert.

Chapter Twelve

'You must come, Megan; it's your birthday treat!'

Megan tried to avoid her sister's pleading grey eyes because it seemed churlish to refuse. Yet the Stork Club, where she might again bump into that awful man who'd followed her from the Copper Kettle, was the last place she wanted to go to on her birthday.

Given the choice she would have been fulfilling her dream of having dinner somewhere with Miles Walker. That was wishful thinking, though! Miles hadn't sent her a card or even popped into the office to wish her a happy birthday.

Since late spring, when the nights had started to lengthen, they had met less and less frequently.

'Its too risky, someone might see us,' he would say evasively.

He would smother her protests with passionate kisses and, as his mouth took possession of hers, and she gave herself up to the magic of the moment, her resentment and powers of reasoning dissolved. It was only later, when she was alone, that all the niggling doubts would come back.

Why was Miles still so insistent that no one must know they were seeing each other? They'd been meeting at least once a week to go to the pictures for over six months now, yet she still knew

practically nothing about how Miles spent his
leisure time when they were not together.

She thought about it constantly, but no matter
how much she questioned him she never received
a satisfactory answer.

'What do you do at the weekends?' she pressed.
'I'm sure you don't just sit at home!'

'No, I'm out and about. I play cricket quite a
lot.'

'Where? Can I come and watch?' she asked
eagerly.

'Sorry, it's a private club.'

'Surely you can take a guest along occasionally.'

'Since my father is the president that's quite out
of the question because he'd recognise you!'

She sighed. 'You must do plenty of other things,'
she persisted.

'Yes, family dinner parties.' He yawned widely.
'You have no idea how incredibly boring they can
be! I get fed up of listening to dry as dust opin-
ions about how the country is going to the dogs
and how things should be run.'

'Surely that doesn't take up the entire evening.'

He shrugged. 'Sometimes if they leave early I
go for a spin along the prom on my bike. It's
practically deserted late at night and I can put
my foot down and watch the speedo clocking up.
It's terrific!'

That part she believed. It was what he did on
all the other evenings that she wanted to know
about.

'Don't you ever go dancing or any place where
we could meet?' she persisted.

'I go to jazz clubs sometimes.' He laughed as he saw the look of distaste on her face. 'Don't you like jazz?'

'It's OK, I suppose,' she said evasively. 'I'd possibly like it better if I went with the right person!'

She waited for him to suggest they went there together. When he didn't she felt both hurt and bewildered.

Commonsense warned her that he must know plenty of girls and she began to suspect he might be two-timing her. If only he would tell her the truth, she thought unhappily.

As she sat in front of her bedroom mirror, putting on her make-up, Megan wondered if Miles really did find her attractive. Her face wasn't too bad, she decided, turning this way and that to study it. Her nose and chin were neat, she had well defined cheekbones, good skin and her teeth were white and even.

In fact, she decided with some satisfaction as she ran a comb through her hair, when she smiled the rest of her face seemed to come alive, as though her dark brown eyes were smiling, too.

She moved back from the mirror, twisting round to study the rest of her appearance. Her figure was far better than Lynn's! Yet Lynn was the one who had the boys flocking round her like starlings round a bird table.

She knew that if Lynn was in her shoes she would have told Miles Walker that either they met openly or she would stop seeing him. She wished she had the nerve to do the same, but she wasn't sure their friendship meant as much to Miles as it did to her.

She was afraid that if she took such a step it might well mean the end of their friendship altogether.

Even that might be better than the hole-and-corner way they were behaving at present, she thought miserably. It hurt terribly when he came into the office and hardly spoke to her or pretended not to see her.

As Megan and Lynn made their way to the Stork Club, they found the streets were packed with Liverpool-Irish who earlier in the day had marched through the city centre to mark Orangeman's Day. Now, most of them were drunk and they were accosting passers-by. By the time the girls reached Queen Square, they were almost out of breath from trying to avoid the unwelcome attentions.

'Take no notice of them, they're only Paddies, they won't hurt us,' Lynn whispered, tightly clutching Megan's arm.

'Most of them are so drunk that they'll be fighting each other before very long.' Megan shuddered.

'The police will have seen them off by the time we come home, and the doorman won't let any strangers in the Stork,' Lynn told her.

'I wouldn't be too sure about that,' Megan warned.

In that, Megan proved to be right. Even Lynn had to admit she had never seen the place so crowded.

'See if you can grab a table while I go and look for Flash,' she told Megan.

'You'll never find anyone in this mob,' Megan said in a disgruntled voice. 'For goodness' sake let's stay together.'

She was too late. Lynn had already gone, swallowed up by the crowd. Megan looked round nervously at the jostling mass hoping she might see someone she knew, but wherever she looked they were all complete strangers.

The music had not yet started, but the noise was deafening as they shouted to friends or talked to each other at the top of their voices to make themselves heard.

The heat, combined with cheap perfume, was overpowering. The atmosphere was tense. As the band began to tune up the noise became even more ear shattering. Megan found it hard to believe that Miles liked such places. She wondered if he would be here tonight. If he was she resolved she would ignore him. Afterwards she'd tell him that she'd done so because she didn't want any of her friends to see them together.

Lynn returned, her mouth pulled down at the corners in disappointment. 'I can't find Flash anywhere,' she grumbled.

'We are very early, the place has only just opened,' Megan pointed out. 'Give him time.'

'He always comes in early. He only stays for about an hour and then just vanishes,' Lynn said petulantly.

Megan looked at her, puzzled, but said nothing. What was wrong with Liverpool boys? she wondered. They all seemed to behave as if they were living double lives. Flash sounded no better than Miles and yet both she and Lynn were infatuated by them.

'I'll go and get us some drinks,' announced Lynn

restlessly, 'he may have arrived by now and be at the bar.'

As Lynn disappeared again, Megan looked round nervously, wishing herself anywhere but here. The sound of the saxophone was reverberating through her head and she didn't think she could stand it for much longer. If Flash wasn't there perhaps she could persuade Lynn to change her mind and they could go to the pictures instead, she thought hopefully.

There was so much jostling as people tried to locate their friends that Megan found herself pushed right up against the stage. As she looked up her gaze locked with that of the drummer and she felt a blind whirling panic as she recognised him. It was the chap who had followed her from the Copper Kettle the night she'd been there looking for Lynn. She averted her gaze quickly, hoping he hadn't recognised her.

'Hi there, kiddo! You've come looking for me, then.' Without pausing in his beat, he bent forward, his face contorted by a self-satisfied smirk.

Megan shrank back, embarrassed.

'Don't run away, I'll see you later,' he called out, loud enough for her to hear above the music.

Quickly she elbowed her way through the crowd, determined to find Lynn and tell her she was leaving. As she reached the bar, a scuffle broke out. Raised voices, flying bottles, girls screaming and men shouting and swearing, rapidly turned the place into a battlefield.

Her heart pounding with fright, Megan climbed onto a chair to try to see if she could spot Lynn.

At that moment the crowd surged wildly, sending the chair crashing.

She screamed as she felt herself falling.

'You're OK, I've got you.'

A pair of strong hands grasped her round the waist and steadied her. The voice was so familiar that she turned her head sharply and found herself looking up at Robert Field.

'What are you doing here?'

'I could ask you the same question,' he said drily. 'I thought you said you didn't like the Stork!'

'I don't!' She grimaced. 'I came with Lynn, but I can't see her anywhere now.'

'Stay put while I find her. Then I think we should all get out. There's going to be real trouble here tonight.'

By the time Robert returned, with a very dishevelled Lynn, the fracas had built up into an ugly scene.

'Come on.' Robert grabbed their arms and began to steer them towards the door. As they drew abreast of it they were blocked by the formidable bulk of a uniformed policeman.

'Looks as though there's going to be a spot of bother here tonight so we're leaving,' Robert told him disarmingly.

The policeman gave him a penetrating stare, then with a curt nod let them pass.

'What do we do now?' Lynn asked with a pout once they were outside. 'The evening's ruined and it was meant to be Megan's birthday treat!'

'We could go to the Philharmonic,' Robert suggested.

'Huh! I would sooner go home and play my gramophone, thank you very much,' Lynn told him scathingly.

'Go on then, and I'll take Megan to the Phil,' he teased.

'Don't be daft! We could go to the pictures, though,' she suggested.

'All right. That's if there's anything good on.'

'Could we go to see *The Gold Rush*, the new Charlie Chaplin picture?'

'Hold on! Megan might not fancy seeing that. She might prefer to see *The Sheik*. Rudolph Valentino is in that.'

'You mean *you* would!' Lynn grinned cheekily.

'Well, which is it to be?' Robert looked questioningly at Megan.

After the fracas at the Stork Club, Megan would have much preferred to go home, but she realised Lynn would be upset if they did.

'*The Gold Rush*, I think,' she murmured, and was rewarded by a whoop of delight from Lynn.

Robert sat between them and Megan tried to pretend that it was Miles, not Robert, sitting there.

When they left the cinema the streets were still full of noisy revellers and she was glad Robert was with them, especially when Lynn insisted they should go to one of the brightly lit milk bars before they went home.

'You managed to find the girls, then.' Mrs Williams winked at Robert conspiratorially when they arrived back.

In the kitchen, as she made a hot drink for them

all, Megan felt annoyed that it had all been planned behind her back.

It was a long time before Megan got to sleep that night and when she finally drifted off her mind was a dense tangle of disquieting thoughts as for the hundredth time she compared Robert and Miles.

She woke early next morning. There was a Sunday hush over the house and the road outside. She managed to get dressed without disturbing Lynn, and she left a note propped up on the mantelpiece to say she had gone out for the day.

Liverpool was shuttered, the pavements deserted. Even the lorries that were usually unloading at the warehouses were absent. It was so early that the trams hadn't started running. Boys delivering newspapers, and a few people hurrying off to early morning Mass, were the only signs of life.

A hazy sun promised heat later in the day. Feeling as if she was on holiday, now that she was out of their stuffy flat, Megan walked towards the Pier Head.

She found the New Brighton ferry didn't start sailing until mid-morning so she went on the *Royal Iris* to Seacombe, hoping that she could get a tram from there to New Brighton. The boat was almost empty. As they pulled away, she went up on the top deck and walked round, fascinated by the view of Liverpool from the river.

She leaned her arms on the rails as she studied it all, happily accepting that it was all part of her new life. The Liver Building with its clock face and huge gilt Liver birds dominated the waterfront, towering over the Docks and Harbour Board offices and the massive Cunard Building. On either side were the long lines of warehouses with boats at anchor, waiting for Monday morning.

As the *Royal Iris* bumped to a stop against the landing stage at Seacombe, and the gangplank was lowered, Megan felt a heady sensation of freedom as she made her way up the floating roadway to the waiting trams.

The New Brighton one pulled away almost immediately. A panorama of shops, Wallasey Town Hall, and road after road of imposing houses running down to the river flashed past.

At the New Brighton terminus, a milk bar was just opening up. Suddenly hungry, she went in for a hot drink and something to eat. When she came out again the sun was breaking through, turning the grey Mersey to liquid gold, the tide-damp sand into dappled silver.

Megan set off at a brisk pace along the promenade, past the domed Winter Gardens Pavilion and the ribbon of small hotels towards Wallasey Village.

When she reached the point where the Mersey widened and became one with the sea, she paused. There, ahead of her, high on the sandstone cliff, were the imposing houses she'd first seen when she'd walked along the promenade on Boxing Day.

She stood transfixed, staring at the turreted one that was right at the tip of the headland . . . the one where Miles Walker lived.

'Out and about early after your late night.'

Robert's voice brought her out of her reverie.

Megan swung round, staring at him in disbelief.

'What . . . what are you doing here?' she gasped, flushing with embarrassment.

'I live here, remember? And,' he added, 'I always take a walk along the prom on a Sunday morning.'

Megan bit her lip and looked uncomfortable.

'Fancy a guided tour? I'll include those houses up there in Warren Drive. You are wasting your time, though,' he added gravely. 'Miles Walker is a heartbreaker. It would be best to forget him.'

Anger and misery choked her as she realised Robert had guessed her feelings for Miles. Tears blurred her eyes and she blinked them away quickly. The joy she'd felt when she'd set out, the elation she'd experienced when she'd boarded the tram at Seacombe Ferry, knowing that it was not just taking her to New Brighton but towards where Miles lived, had turned to ashes. The day that had promised to be so fulfilling was completely ruined.

'Take a look over there!' Robert told her, pointing to where purple shadows, almost like clouds, were massed on the skyline. 'Those mountains are on the other side of the river Dee.'

'Does that mean they're in Wales?'

Robert Field nodded. 'Why don't you let me take you over there for the day,' he suggested. 'It would be the next best thing to actually being in Beddgelert.'

Chapter Thirteen

Kathy Williams was uneasy. She was filled with a vague disquieting feeling as if her dreams were unravelling like an old jumper.

All the time she had been living in Beddgelert she had hankered to be in Liverpool. Now that she was back in the city where she had grown up, it was something of a let down.

The moment Watkin had told her they were moving to Liverpool she had looked forward to being in touch again with all her old friends. Remembering the fun and escapades she and Ruby Adams had enjoyed after they'd both left school and started work, she'd imagined they'd be able to have more great times together. Like all the other people she had once known, though, Ruby had married and moved away.

That wasn't the only reason for Kathy's disenchantment with her new life. She had grumbled about the many short-comings of their cottage in Beddgelert but that had been a palace compared to the dreary, poky little flat they were living in now, she thought ruefully.

Looking back, the only thing she had really disliked about Beddgelert was the fact that nothing ever seemed to happen there. You saw the same people, day in, day out; except in summer when holiday-makers visited the area.

In those days she had longed for the big shops or a market to browse around looking for bargains. Yet now that the big stores were only a few streets away, they had lost their attraction. The initial thrill of looking at wonderful clothes, or exciting things for the home, quickly faded when you were doing it on your own. Unless you intended to buy something, and you couldn't do that all the time.

Before Lynn had started work she had occasionally met her from school and they would window-shop on the way home. Lynn liked nothing better than to go in the big stores and try on everything from shoes to hats if they took her fancy. The two of them used to have a good laugh because Lynn always had such outrageous comments to make about the new fashions.

For all that, Lynn would have bought most of them if she'd had the money, Kathy thought as she made herself a cup of tea. Little spendthrift was Lynn. Now that she was working, most of her wages were earmarked before she got them. And if they weren't spent on clothes then the money went on gramophone records or visits to the Stork Club.

Not like Megan, Kathy mused. She was cautious with her money. She had inherited Watkin's thrifty nature and no mistake. When Megan bought something new it was carefully chosen to fit into her existing wardrobe, as well as being practical enough for work.

Except the time when she'd bought a full-length blue evening dress, the night she'd gone to the

New Year's Eve dance at the Tower Ballroom. That must have taken every penny of her savings, reflected Kathy. Either that or Watkin had given her something towards it.

Lynn had said she looked like a duchess in it and wondered who she was trying to impress.

It certainly couldn't have been Robert Field, sighed Kathy as she refilled her cup, even though he'd been the one who had taken her.

This was something else that was continually bothering her, Kathy thought tetchily. Keeping tabs on Lynn and Megan was much harder here in Liverpool than it had been in Beddgelert. There they had spent most of their time together and she had been able to rely on Megan to keep an eye on Lynn. Not any longer, though. Now it was as if there was some sort of feud going on between the two of them.

When Lynn had still been at school it hadn't been too bad. Now that she was working at the Copper Kettle, though, she had no idea how she spent her spare time, or who she was with when she wasn't at the café. She left home before Megan in the morning and often it was nine o'clock at night before she came home again. Kathy frowned, remembering how insolent Lynn had been when she'd tried to talk to her about it.

'I'm working, Mam. It's not like being at school, you know.'

'I know that but you don't have to do a twelve-hour day! It's probably illegal at your age, anyway.'

'I've come home once or twice when I've had a midday break but you're never here, so I may as well stay on at the café. At least I can have a proper cooked meal there.'

'You don't have to work until nine o'clock at night, though, surely.'

'I don't always! When I finish early I go to the Stork.'

'Your dad doesn't like you going there . . .'

'So what! I shan't tell him so he's not likely to find out . . . Unless you keep going on about it,' Lynn retorted.

'Are you still meeting this boy Flash when you go there?'

'Sometimes.'

'Are you seeing any other lads?'

The moment she began asking these sort of questions Lynn would flounce off to her bedroom and slam the door shut. Her life was a closed book, but Kathy knew from her moods that everything wasn't going the way Lynn wanted it to.

She had asked her time and again to bring this boy Flash home so that they could get to know him, but Lynn would only scowl or pull a face and change the subject.

Megan didn't seem to have made any friends either. Robert Field was always offering to take her out but she rarely accepted. On the few occasions she did go somewhere with him, she would persuade Lynn to go along as well.

Kathy couldn't understand it. True, he was a few years older than Megan, but what did that matter? He was nice looking, quiet, well spoken, owned his own house and had a good job so what more could Megan possibly want?

123

The only thing that seemed to interest Megan, though, was working for her secretarial diploma. She'd become quite fanatical about it.

Kathy didn't see the sense in it. Being a secretary was all very well but where did it really get you in the end? You were still waiting hand and foot on some man so why not have the security of marriage.

It was less of a worry than Lynn going to the Stork Club night after night, of course. Jazz music seemed to attract some strange types in there, if the accounts she had read in the *Liverpool Echo* were true. She couldn't help feeling anxious about Lynn mixing with people like that.

At one time, Watkin had been very strict with the girls, but since Lynn had started work at the Copper Kettle he'd washed his hands of her.

'You agreed she could leave school and go to work there knowing it was against my wishes, so you can worry about her,' he'd pronounced. 'Don't ever forget, though, that I wanted her to stay on at school.'

She'd protested that Lynn had found herself a job without a word to any of them.

'If you'd supported me then she would have had no choice but to jack it in,' he'd argued grimly. 'Instead, you said leave her alone so from now on that's what I'm going to do.'

And he had. He turned a deaf ear when she expressed concern about the long hours Lynn worked at the café. And he ignored the arguments that flared up when she remonstrated with Lynn for coming home so late at night.

The family unity they'd known when they lived in Beddgelert seemed to have gone for ever. They rarely sat down to their evening meal together. Either Lynn was working, or Watkin was doing overtime. And three evenings a week, Megan had to have her meal early so that she could get to night school on time.

Sunday was the only occasion they ate together and more often than not there was an argument and the mealtime ended in discord.

The trouble was that Watkin, Megan and Lynn were all so wrapped up in their own lives that they hadn't time for each other. Nor did any of them have much time for her, Kathy thought despondently.

Was it any wonder that most of the time she felt lonely and neglected? she thought as she rinsed her cup and saucer. She knew so few people. In Beddgelert, whenever she had walked into the village she had met someone she knew. If she wanted to, she could stop and have a chat with them. Here, she could go out every day and not see the same person twice. She'd even taken to shopping in Paddy's market for fruit and vegetables, because the stallholders there seemed to be more friendly than any of the shop assistants in Scotland Road.

'Find yourself a hobby, or get involved in something, then you'll soon get to know more people,' Watkin told her whenever she'd complained she was on her own too much.

It wasn't that easy. She went to the pictures two or three times a week. The seats were half price for matinees. At first, she felt guilty when she came out. It seemed all wrong to be sitting in there in the dark when outside the sun was shining. Then as the days grew shorter and colder, she enjoyed the warm darkness, happy to lose herself in the celluloid world of make-believe. She even began to resent having to hurry home afterwards in order to have a meal ready for her family when they came in from work.

Megan was the only one who seemed concerned about what was happening to her and the way she was spending her time.

'Sitting in the cinema every afternoon is making you put on weight,' Megan had remonstrated. 'You need more exercise.'

'Keeping this place clean and doing all the shopping is exercise enough for me.'

'Why don't you go over to New Brighton when it's a nice day and take a walk along the prom?' she'd suggested, and occasionally at the weekends they went out together. Once they'd gone on the bus to Southport; another time they'd taken the train to Chester. The two of them had spent a wonderful day there. They'd visited the cathedral, and walked round the walls as well as looking at all the shops.

Megan was so caring that it reminded Kathy of what Watkin had been like when they'd first been married. It was bred in her, mused Kathy. She'd been Watkin's daughter from the very first day she'd been born.

She'd been a good baby. She'd rarely cried and had grown into an obedient child. Her dark, soulful eyes, framed by long lashes and thick dark brows, had sometimes seemed too large for her elfin face.

Lynn had been the exact opposite. A fretful, demanding baby, she'd grown into a self-willed little girl who always liked to be the centre of attention. She'd been so pretty, Kathy had melted whenever she looked at her. And Lynn had played on this.

'You're spoiling that little one, you know,' Watkin had warned her over and over again. 'You give in to her far too much.'

Although she knew he was right it made no difference. It had filled her with an incredible feeling of satisfaction to bring a smile to Lynn's face. Lynn hadn't changed; she could still twist most people round her little finger.

As they had grown older, Megan and Lynn had spent less and less time playing together. Lynn was always out with a crowd, often getting into mischief. Megan was more solitary and she had grown closer to Watkin. The two of them would often take a picnic and go off for the day, climbing Moel Hebog or wandering along the banks of the River Glaslyn.

Kathy had never been able to see the sense of doing that. The grass was the same there as it was anywhere else so what was the point of struggling to climb to the top of a mountain? There wasn't even a decent road to walk up. The rough footpaths were full of jagged stones and you had to watch your step all the time or you could twist your ankle.

There was nothing to see when you'd scrambled to the top, except more sheep and more mountains and away in the distance a glimpse of the sea.

If she wanted to look at the sea, she had taken herself off to one of the sandy beaches at Porthmadog. There she could stretch out and soak up the sun while the girls amused themselves building sand castles or going for a paddle.

Looking back to those times, she reflected that they had been some of the happiest days of her life, only she hadn't realised it at the time.

If Watkin hadn't been so afraid of losing his job at Pengarw they might still be there. The possibility haunted her. It was such a pity he'd acted so impulsively. Sometimes she just didn't understand how his mind worked.

She didn't understand how Megan's mind worked, either! The way Megan avoided Robert Field and turned down his invitations to go out left her speechless. She just couldn't stop thinking about it. At one time she'd been convinced that Megan must be seeing someone else, but she so seldom went out on her own that it didn't seem possible.

Lynn had said she was sweet on someone at work called Mr Miles, but when she had mentioned the name to Watkin he had become quite incensed. His face had been mottled with suppressed anger.

'Don't talk so daft, woman!' he'd said scornfully. 'Our Megan getting involved with Mr Miles . . . there's a load of old rubbish! Whoever told you that?'

He hadn't even answered when she had asked who Mr Miles was. Instead, he'd put on his coat and slammed out of the flat, leaving her to fret over it on her own.

She'd pushed the incident to the back of her mind. There was no point in worrying when she didn't know the full story.

Lately, she'd started treating herself to the occasional glass of sherry. She didn't let the others into her little secret because she was pretty sure they wouldn't approve. She didn't see any harm in it, though. She found having a little drink now and again bucked her up no end and made even the cramped little flat seem more bearable.

When they'd first come back to Liverpool, Watkin had been full of promises about moving into a bigger place, but nothing had ever come of it.

The idea had kept her spirits up for quite a while. She had even started to save a few shillings out of her housekeeping money each week ready to buy things for their new home. When Watkin seemed to lose interest in moving, though, she'd decided to spend the money on herself. That was when she'd started treating herself to the occasional bottle of sherry.

Chapter Fourteen

Megan was so engrossed in her work that the days flew by. She scarcely noticed that summer was over and that the few drab trees she passed each morning on her way to work had begun to shed their grime-encrusted leaves. Grey skies and keener winds were the only outward signals that it would soon be winter.

In Beddgelert, as autumn advanced, it was as if an artist had run riot with his palette. The entire countryside donned a mantle of rich colour. Mountainsides flamed as bracken changed from green to gold and then to a burning red. The conifers cresting the skyline swayed like a rolling sea as the October winds sliced across them or gusts of ice-cold rain drenched their dark green branches. As the days grew shorter and colder, the sheep grazed their way down to the lower slopes, as if aware that soon they would need to seek shelter from snow and bitter winds.

Once, the changing seasons had been an integral part of Megan's way of life. Now she had other things to fill her mind. After she'd gained her secretarial diploma with high marks Miss Pearce had given her the opportunity to use her newly acquired skills.

Delighted that her work was no longer confined

to the routine checking of shipping documents, Megan looked forward eagerly to each new challenge. She worked conscientiously, determined not to make mistakes.

Her efforts were rewarded when Valerie Pearce praised her and confided that, as she would be leaving the following spring to get married, there was a very good chance of Megan being considered as her replacement.

Megan stared at her in astonishment. 'You mean become Mr Walker's secretary?' she gasped.

'That is what I hope!' Valerie Pearce smiled. 'Providing Mr Walker doesn't think you are too young and inexperienced for such responsibility.'

'Oh!' Megan's feeling of elation rapidly subsided.

'I thought it might be a good idea for you to act as *my* secretary for a few months,' Valerie Pearce added quickly as she saw disappointment darken Megan's eyes.

'To give me some idea of what is involved?'

'That's right! It will be good practice and prepare you for my job when the time comes.'

When Megan told her family that evening, her father's delight equalled her own.

'We'll celebrate by having the best Christmas ever,' he promised. 'With all the overtime I've been doing lately we will certainly be able to afford it,' he enthused.

'Don't count on me being around much of the time,' Lynn told him. 'I might be working.'

'They're not going to open the Copper Kettle on Christmas Day, surely?' her father exclaimed angrily. 'You spend far too much of your time there as it is.'

131

'You've always said if a job's worth doing then it's worth doing well,' she told him pertly, shrugging her shoulders.

'Job!' he repeated angrily. 'I don't consider that a job, not for one minute. I thought that by now you would be tired of the place and fed up with handing out bacon butties and mugs of tea and found yourself some proper work.'

'I did think of going to work at the Stork in the New Year, looking after the cloakroom.'

'Stop teasing, Lynn. They've already got someone doing that job,' Megan pointed out.

'Yeah, but she's joining one of the bands as a singer so they're looking for someone to take her place.'

'Take no notice, Dad, she's just kidding,' Megan said quickly as she saw her father's dark eyes blaze and knew his anger was rising.

Afterwards, when they were alone in the bedroom they shared, Megan tried to persuade Lynn that it really was time she looked for a better job.

'Look, just because you're angling for promotion there's no need to come all holier than thou with me,' Lynn retorted. 'I like what I'm doing, thank you very much,' she added, moving across to the mirror and starting to style her hair.

'If you enjoy being a waitress then why not try for a job in one of the restaurants? You'd earn more money, for a start!'

As their eyes met in the mirror, Lynn pulled a face and gave an exaggerated shrug.

'Promise me you'll think about it, Lynn,' Megan pleaded.

'Perhaps,' Lynn told her laconically. 'Do you like my hair cut as short as this?'

'No, I don't! It makes you look like a boy,' Megan told her critically.

'It's no worse than the way you do yours,' Lynn argued. 'You're still wearing it tucked back behind your ears like you did when you were a kid at school,' she added deprecatingly.

'I like it this way,' Megan told her firmly. 'At least it's tidy! Yours looks like a bird's nest most of the time, especially when you go out in the wind.'

'Yeah, and yours stays all neat and prissy, like those prim little dresses you wear. Talking of clothes, Meg, what I would really like for Christmas,' Lynn said in a wheedling voice, gazing starry eyed at her sister, 'is a fur coat.'

'Then you'd better get a job where you earn more money so that you can save up for it,' Megan told her cuttingly. 'Do you know how much they cost?'

'How about you, Mam and Dad buying it between you?' Lynn suggested, hopefully.

'I don't know. I might get you one for your birthday in February. I should know by then whether I'm going to get my promotion. If I do become Mr Walker's secretary I'll probably get a pay rise and then I might be able to afford to buy you one,' Megan told her.

'Fur coats might be out of fashion next year!' Lynn said sulkily. 'Anyway, the winter will be almost over by then.'

'Well, in that case, the prices may have come down or I might be able to buy it in the sales.'

'Trust you to think of picking one up cheap,'

Lynn said with a curl of her lip. 'I'm going to ask our mam if I can have one for Christmas. If she agrees, will you put some money towards it? It's what I want more than anything in the world, and I know you haven't done your Christmas shopping yet,' she persisted.

'How do you know? Have you been rummaging in my cupboard again? You've not been borrowing anything of mine, I hope.'

'I wouldn't be seen dead in any of your clothes,' retorted Lynn scathingly. 'Ta anyway, I'll tell Mam you said OK about the fur coat.'

Megan shrugged helplessly. It wasn't what she had said at all, but she knew it was pointless to argue with her. Perhaps a warm coat would be a good present for Lynn, though, since her skirts were always so short, but she wasn't sure about it being a fur one.

When she mentioned to her mother the idea of them clubbing together to buy a coat for Lynn, Megan found that her sister had already been dropping hints.

'Don't worry about it, luv. I've already picked one out. It's exactly what she wants!'

'They're awfully expensive . . .'

'I asked the shop to put it to one side and I've been paying off a few pounds each week,' Kathy told her proudly.

'Do you want me to put some money to it?'

'That's up to you,' her mother answered. 'The only trouble is, it means she will only get one present and you know how Lynn likes to have lots of parcels to open. She's still only a kid, remember.'

She smiled fondly. 'Why don't you buy her something else.'

'Can you suggest anything?'

'Well, yes. I'll let you into a secret.' Her mother lowered her voice to a whisper. 'Robert is buying our Lynn a new gramophone that has one of those horn things. I think they call them loudspeakers. Why don't you buy her some records.'

'Robert's buying us presents again this year!' Megan exclaimed in dismay. 'Whatever for?'

'Well, I suppose he thinks it's a nice thing to do since he's coming here for his Christmas dinner.'

'We invited him last year! I was looking forward to us having this Christmas on our own . . . It's not the same with a stranger here,' muttered Megan resentfully.

'It's probably so that he can be with you that he's so keen on coming.' Kathy smiled. 'Mind you, I don't know why he bothers since you practically ignore him,' she added tartly.

'I do not! I'm perfectly civil to him!'

'Until he asks you to go out somewhere with him and then you snap his head off.'

'He shouldn't keep asking,' retorted Megan, her colour rising. 'I've told him enough times that I don't want to go out with him.'

'Why ever not? He's not bad looking. He owns his own house and he earns as much money as your dad. Think how well off you'd be married to someone like that.'

'Stop matchmaking, Mam! I've told you, I don't think of Robert Field in that way.'

'You don't think of him at all, that's the trouble.'

'He's all right . . . as a friend of the family.'

'If our Lynn was a couple of years older, and he showed the interest in her that he does in you, she'd go out with him.'

'From the way she ogles him whenever he comes here she'd jump at the chance right now,' Megan said drily. 'You'd better watch where you hang the mistletoe.'

Discovering that Robert was going to spend Christmas Day with them irritated Megan. She knew it was selfish of her, but she had been looking forward to the four of them spending the day on their own like they'd done when they'd lived in Beddgelert.

Memories of those days came flooding back. The cosy living room decorated with sprigs of holly, cotton-wool snow, painted fir cones and the home-made paperchains that she and Lynn spent hours making. She remembered how they always dug up a fir tree on Christmas Eve, standing it in a big bucket complete with its earth ball so that it could be replanted a week or so later.

They'd always saved the biggest logs for Christmas so that the house had not only been warm but had a special welcoming glow about it. Neighbours would pop in during the morning for a glass of home-made wine and a mince pie, but no one had stayed the whole day!

Christmas dinner on their own had been the high spot. They began planning for it in November, when they all stirred the pudding and made a wish. Early in December, they ordered the turkey from Ifan's farm. Collecting it a couple of days before Christmas was all part of the ritual.

It went into the oven early on Christmas morning and her father would baste it every hour or so. When it came to the table it would be a deep golden colour. Megan could remember so clearly the way her father would make a great show of sharpening the carving knife and they would all hold their breath as he carved the first slice of creamy white flesh, sampling it, and then ceremoniously declaring it the 'best turkey ever'.

Robert being with them last Christmas, their first in Liverpool, had spoiled all that. The fuss over carving the turkey had seemed childish; she had felt embarrassed.

'Make the best of it, girl,' Watkin Williams told her when she complained to him that she preferred them to be on their own. 'I know how you feel. Family man I am myself, but I can understand the need for others to socialise. Your mam's been shut away in North Wales for so long she's like a bird that's been set free. Only wish we had a better home so that we could make a real splash. Perhaps next year . . .' His voice trailed off but there was a gleam in his eye that prompted Megan to probe.

'You mean you're thinking of moving back to Beddgelert?'

'No, not back to Wales, but to something a bit better than where we are living now. We need a bigger place with three bedrooms so that you and Lynn can have a room each. You'd like that, wouldn't you?'

'Very much, but it's not all that bad having to share,' she added loyally.

'Oh, come on, now. I've heard the two of you bickering. Always helping herself to your things, now, isn't she? Well, if you had your own room you could lock the door,' he laughed.

'If I get my promotion, and a pay rise, I'll be able to help with the rent,' promised Megan.

'We'll see. You'll have plenty of other expenses to take up any extra money you get.'

'Well, I might have to dress more smartly. I'd also like to have a holiday in Beddgelert as soon as I've saved up some money,' she admitted.

On Christmas morning, Robert arrived while they were still at breakfast. Megan thought it inconsiderate of him to come so early but her father seemed so pleased to see him that she kept her thoughts to herself.

Lynn, wearing an emerald-green dress, her short hair gleaming, greeted him with a squeal of delight when he handed her an enormous parcel.

Her excitement mounted when she tore away the decorative paper and discovered what it was. Impulsively, she flung her arms around Robert, hugging and kissing him. Overcome with embarrassment, he backed off.

Megan felt that her present of two jazz records was something of a let down, even though Lynn enthused over them and immediately placed one of them on her new gramophone.

'This is from me and your dad,' said her mother, beaming, handing over another bulky package.

The brown beaver-lamb fur coat brought renewed gasps of pleasure from Lynn.

'We know it's what you want, so try it on, luv, I'm dying to see you in it.'

It fitted Lynn perfectly. Smiling, she pirouetted round the room, her grey eyes shining. 'This is the best Christmas ever.' She sighed dramatically. 'What have you got, Megan?'

Megan looked taken aback. Apart from a make-up box from Lynn she hadn't been given any presents at all.

'Your present is outside,' her father said. He looked over at Robert as he spoke, his eyebrows raised enquiringly. 'Put your coats on all of you,' he added as Robert nodded.

'I've already got mine on,' Lynn announced, giggling and turning up the collar of her new fur coat.

Mystified, they followed Watkin. It was an ice-cold day with a translucent blue-grey sky and a cutting wind. Lynn shivered then slipped her arm through Robert's and snuggled up against him.

'You should be warm enough inside that.' He smiled, disengaging his arm and moving away.

'Is it round the corner, Robert?' Watkin asked.

'Yes. Wait here and I'll fetch it. No point in us all trailing round there.'

Sheltering in the doorway, shivering as the biting wind stung their faces, Lynn and Megan exchanged puzzled looks.

In seconds, Robert was back, driving a black T-Ford motorcar. He pulled up, jumped out, and handed the keys to Watkin.

'There you are, Megan.' Her father held them out to her. 'From your mam and me. Happy Christmas.'

'The car . . . You mean, it's for me?' Megan asked, bewildered.

'That's right. Do you like it?'

'It's terrific! I don't know what to say!' She gasped as she hugged them both. 'It's a wonderful present.' She walked round the car, touching the bodywork then standing back to admire it. The T-Ford was about three years old, but it had obviously been well looked after. The paintwork gleamed, there were no dents or scratches, and the interior was immaculate.

'Go on, then, sit in it, luv,' urged her mother, giving her a little push.

Nervously, Megan took her place behind the steering wheel, tentatively touching the various controls.

'It's absolutely wonderful,' she breathed. 'Where am I going to keep it, though? It won't be safe left out in the roadway all the time.'

'Don't worry about that,' her father assured her. 'I've rented a garage in the next street.'

'Are we going for a spin in it before we all freeze to death?' Lynn asked impatiently, her teeth chattering.

'Not with me driving, we're not.' Megan laughed.

'I know that! Dad could drive . . . or Robert.'

'Be a squeeze getting five of us in,' her father warned.

'It won't matter. I want to see what it's like to ride in, and I bet Megan does, too. Megan and me

140

and our mam can fit into the back seat and you and Robert in front.'

'Yes, I suppose we can do that,' Watkin agreed. Laughing, they all piled in and with Robert at the wheel drove through the centre of Liverpool, along Tithebarn Street and back to Scotland Road.

'Shall I garage it?' questioned Robert as they stopped outside the house.

'I suppose you'd better. Go with him, Megan, and then you'll know where it is being kept.'

'My car really is wonderful,' she enthused when she returned home. 'Now I know why you've been doing so much overtime, Dad. I only wish I could start learning to drive it right away. I wonder how long it will take me to do so?'

'No time at all once Robert starts giving you lessons.'

'Robert!' Megan frowned. 'I thought you would be the one to teach me, Dad?' she added quickly. 'You're on the spot, Robert wouldn't want to come all the way over from Wallasey . . .' Her voice trailed away. She knew she was putting it badly but suddenly her joy was being diluted and she felt threatened.

'It's not a good thing to be taught by a close relative,' her father told her gravely. 'It usually ends up in heated arguments! Robert will come here straight from work, have his meal with us and then take you out for an hour's driving practice. That way you'll be proficient in next to no time.'

'Here's your Christmas present from me,' Robert said, handing over two parcels.

'Go on, let's see what you've got,' urged Lynn, excitedly.

Inside the larger one was a pair of leather driving gloves.

'Try them on,' encouraged Robert. 'If they're the wrong size I can change them for you.'

'Open your other present,' pleaded Lynn.

Megan's colour rose as she removed the wrapping paper from a long slim box and saw that it carried the name of one of the most expensive jewellers in Bold Street.

'Whew!' Lynn let out a long slow whistle as Megan lifted the lid of the box to reveal a gold St Christopher medallion lying on a bed of cream satin.

Megan stared down at it, her heart thudding. From the thickness of the gold chain, and the delicate filigree work around the outside of the engraved charm, she knew it must have cost an awful lot of money.

'It's beautiful, Robert!' she said in a stunned whisper, 'but I don't feel I can accept such an expensive gift.'

'Well, I can't wear it,' he told her abruptly.

'Why don't you put it on, luv, and let us see what it looks like,' prompted her mother.

With trembling fingers Megan tried to fasten it round her neck.

'Here, let me.'

A nervous flutter rippled through her as Robert's hands touched hers. She was conscious of his breath warm on her neck as he deftly fastened the catch.

'Look in the mirror, Megan,' breathed Lynn, her eyes wide with envy.

'It's supposed to protect you from accidents, isn't it?' Kathy asked.

'That's right!' agreed Watkin. 'Very appropriate, I'd say.'

The colour deepened in Megan's cheeks. She still felt uncomfortable about accepting such a gift.

'It's lovely, Robert. Thank you.' She smiled at him cautiously.

'Happy Christmas, Megan,' he murmured softly.

As his lips brushed against hers, she remained motionless; her heart was pounding so loudly that she was sure he must hear it. With an effort, she forced herself to look up at him and the burning intensity in his light-blue eyes startled her.

Chapter Fifteen

Megan stared in awe at the gilded, deckle-edged card, turning it over in a bemused way before passing it across the breakfast table so that Lynn and her mother could look at it.

It was the first wedding invitation she had ever received and she felt strangely excited. For the past month, ever since Valerie Pearce had announced the date of her wedding, there had been talk of little else at work, but Megan had never expected to be invited.

'So the wedding is to be at St Hilary's Church. That's in Wallasey, isn't it?' Lynn commented.

'That's right, and the reception is at the bride's home in Rolleston Drive,' added her mother. 'It sounds rather grand, luv!'

'That's what I thought,' Megan agreed. 'I suppose I'll have to buy something new to wear.'

'Yeah, go on, treat yourself. You can afford it now you've had a rise,' Lynn told her.

'It should be quite warm by the end of April so I could buy something that I could wear for best all through the summer.'

'And you must have a hat,' insisted her mother.

'Yeah, a little straw cloche, shaped so that it frames your face and has a tiny curved brim,' prompted Lynn.

'It depends on what sort of dress she picks,' argued Kathy. 'Have you anything in mind, Megan?'

'Not really. Do you want to come shopping with me and help to chose it?'

'Oh yes!' Kathy's eyes lit up. 'We could make a day of it. What about next Saturday?'

'I can't, I'm working,' Lynn said, 'but somebody ought to go with you or you'll end up looking a complete frump.'

'Thank you very much!' Angrily, Megan snatched back the invitation and slid it into its envelope.

'I didn't mean it quite like that,' Lynn muttered. 'I only meant that other people can see what something looks like on you better than you can yourself. You know what it's like, the assistant wants to make a sale and will tell you it looks good even if it doesn't fit properly.'

'Well, there's no hurry, the wedding is over a month away so I could leave it until you have a Saturday off.'

The shopping trip turned out to be a tremendous success. Megan and Kathy had been window-shopping the previous Saturday afternoon and decided on the sort of outfit that was most suitable. The pretty blue and white floral dress had a straight skirt that was draped round the hips and gathered into a decorative buckle. Lynn helped her to choose a white hat and accessories to go with it.

As she set out for the wedding, although she was confident she looked her best, Megan still felt nervous. She had driven her T-Ford a number of times on her own, but it would be the first time she'd taken it onto a ferry boat and she felt scared about doing so.

'I could drive it onto the boat for you, if you like,' her dad offered.

Wallasey sparkled in spring sunshine as she reached the Cheshire side of the Mersey, and she arrived at St Hilary's Church with plenty of time to spare. As the church filled up she took a seat in a pew near the back.

Her heart raced when Miles and his parents arrived. He looked so handsome in a light grey morning suit with draped lapels, a white fancy-weave shirt, grey and white striped tie and a grey top hat. Mr Walker was also wearing a grey morning suit, but his was in a darker shade.

It was the first time Megan had seen Mrs Walker. She was of average height but very slim. Her elegantly styled navy silk dress had a matching wrap-over coat and looked very expensive. With it she wore a white and navy hat.

As the Walkers were ushered into one of the front pews, Miles looked round the church, nodding and smiling to various people. As he looked in her direction, Megan smiled eagerly as their gaze momentarily locked. When there was no answering smile and his eyes remained blank as he refused to recognise her, she felt her colour rising, flooding her face and neck in embarrassment.

Megan's joy in the day vanished. She felt numb.

Only two nights ago, she'd lain in his arms in the gathering dusk of the early spring evening, his kisses arousing tremors of physical craving in both of them. He had been so passionate that she had felt her last shreds of resistance melting. Her own desire had been so great that she'd almost given in to his demands.

Was that why Miles was ignoring her? she wondered. How could she agree they should go all the way, though, when she was not really certain of his feelings. If he loved her, as he claimed, why did their meetings have to be so secretive? And why did he cut her dead when he came into the office?

When they were alone, he was a different person. Then he was warm and full of fun. His overpowering, irresistible vitality seemed to make the air around them crackle with excitement and her heart would thunder crazily.

He knew exactly the right moment to become serious. His vivid blue gaze would linger on her face before his firm lips took possession of her mouth. As he cradled the swelling fullness of her breasts, an inner glow seemed to radiate through her, leaving her weak with desire.

A lump rose in her throat at the memory. Why didn't he admit openly that they were in love? He couldn't be that scared of his father!

Megan tried to dismiss the jumble of conflicting thoughts from her mind and centre her attention on what was happening. There was a hushed expectancy as the strains from the organ changed, signalling the bride's arrival.

Valerie Pearce looked radiant as she entered the church and made her way down the aisle on the arm of her elderly father.

At work she was always so restrained in her

manner and in the way she dressed. Now, in her cream wedding dress of embroidered tulle and lace, she looked poised and beautiful.

The bridegroom half turned and his face became wreathed in smiles as Valerie approached. Megan thought how wonderful it would be if she was the bride and it was Miles waiting there at the altar for her.

During the reception at the bride's home, the reason for the unsatisfactory state of affairs between her and Miles came to her with blinding clarity. Miles was ashamed of her background! She couldn't understand why she hadn't realised it before. She had only to look round the beautifully appointed house and compare it with her own home to be aware of the gulf that divided them. The Walkers' magnificent home in Warren Drive was probably even more luxuriously furnished.

She was so engrossed in studying the contents of the room, so intent on remembering every detail, that she was taken by surprise when Mr Walker came over and spoke to her.

'Hello, Megan, are you enjoying yourself?'

'Yes, very much . . . thank you,' she stammered, slightly flustered.

'Good! Come with me, I'd like you to meet Mrs Walker,' he told her.

His wife smiled non-committally as she shook hands with Megan. Her eyes, the same brilliant blue as Miles', were sharp and critical.

'I had no idea you were quite so young,' Mrs Walker pronounced in a disapproving voice. 'You musn't let my husband work you too hard. My son tells me he can be quite a slave-driver.'

'Nonsense!' Mr Walker laughed heartily. 'We're like one big happy family, aren't we, Megan? The length of time Valerie has worked for us proves that,' he went on without waiting for a response. 'Megan has fitted in excellently,' he added. 'She's going to make a first-rate secretary.'

Megan smiled gratefully at Mr Walker. His words of praise helped to restore her self-confidence. As she looked up and saw the warmth in his eyes she wondered if he knew about her friendship with Miles and that he was trying to tell her that he approved.

As Miles sauntered over to join them her heart thudded as she waited for him to greet her. Instead he gave her a warning look, as if willing her to be careful what she said.

For one wild moment, she was tempted to tell them about their relationship. To disclose that they had been going out together for almost a year even though, at this moment, he was acting as though he barely knew her.

The opportunity passed. The best man announced that the newly-weds were about to leave, and the Walkers moved away to join the crowd wishing Valerie and her new husband good luck.

As everyone gathered outside, crowding round the happy couple to wave them off on their honeymoon, Megan made her escape. She felt out of place. She might be as well-dressed as anybody else there, but she was an outsider. Their jokes and repartee were all above her head.

What made her even more uncomfortable was

that she didn't know how to handle Miles' hostility. Surely, by persistently avoiding her in such an obvious way, he was only drawing attention to the fact that they were more than just working colleagues?

Tears blinded her as she unlocked her car door. For several minutes she simply sat behind the wheel trying to regain her composure. The hurt deep inside her was like a physical pain as she remembered the intimate caresses she and Miles had shared.

She knew that if she had any pride at all she wouldn't speak to him ever again. She also knew that he had only to smile at her to set her heart racing. And if he suggested they should meet then she would be waiting for him whenever and wherever he said.

As she drove away along Rolleston Drive in the direction of New Brighton she was fired by a sudden desire to drive by the Walkers' house. She headed for Warren Drive and parked outside the wrought iron gates. From there she could see the magnificent turreted house at the end of the gravelled driveway.

Knowing the Walkers might return at any moment, she stayed for only a few minutes then she drove off, taking the first road that led down to the sea-front. King's Parade promenade was almost deserted so she parked, switched off the engine and sat gazing out to sea, thinking over the events of the afternoon.

In her heart she could understand the dilemma that faced Miles. With his background he was bound to find it difficult to explain to his family and friends that the girl he was in love with lived in a poky flat in the Scottie Road area.

Mrs Walker would certainly take it very badly! Especially since her son's future father-in-law worked for their company as a lorry driver!

Having analysed the problem, Megan began scheming for the future. When she finally headed for home her mind was made up. Regardless of what happened between her and Miles, it was important that her family moved to the Cheshire side of the Mersey.

Persuading her father to do so would be no problem, she reasoned. Several times he had mentioned finding a house over there. It might be difficult convincing Lynn because she spent so much time at the Copper Kettle, or the Stork Club, that she wouldn't like the idea of moving out of Liverpool. Unless I can persuade her to change her job, Megan reasoned.

She wouldn't say a word about it to Miles, she decided. From now on she intended to treat him merely as an office colleague. There would be no more secretive meetings. If he couldn't accept her for what she was then she didn't want to have anything to do with him.

Back at work on the following Monday, Megan was grimly determined to keep the promises that she'd made to herself. As it happened she found it surprisingly easy. Miles, she learned, had gone to London on a three-month business course.

She heard the news with mixed feelings. She felt angry that he hadn't mentioned it to her, but relieved that she wouldn't have to put her strength of will to the test.

Over the next couple of months Megan subtly campaigned in favour of them going to live on the other side of the Mersey. Whenever it was a nice weekend she persuaded her mother, and Lynn as well if she wasn't working, to pay a visit to New Brighton. Lynn usually turned up her nose at the idea of going to listen to the band playing in Vale Park, but she was always eager to go to the fun fair at New Brighton or to see a show at the Pavilion Theatre.

Megan made the most of the situation by taking them there in her car. When they reached the other side she would take a different route each time, commenting on how nice the houses were until even Lynn began to agree with her and to grumble about how drab their place was in Liverpool.

After that it was plain sailing.

'Don't you think it would be quite nice to live over this side?' Megan commented one Sunday as she and her mother left Vale Park where they had been listening to a band concert and joined the crowds strolling along the promenade.

'Places over here are too expensive for us,' Kathy Williams said with a sigh.

'Oh, I don't know. Perhaps we should make some enquiries, we might be able to afford it,' Megan said tentatively. 'I've had a pay rise, remember, and Dad's earning good money. I know he would like to move. He said so once when we were talking,' she added diffidently.

'He did? He's never said a word to me.'

'That's because he thinks you prefer living in Liverpool because it was once your home.'

'I do like Liverpool, luv, but it's not the same as I remembered it,' her mother admitted. 'None of the people I used to know seem to live here now! I've never really thought about moving, though. And then there's our Lynn. I don't know how she would feel about leaving Liverpool.'

'If the rest of us decided to live in Wallasey then she'd have to come with us, wouldn't she,' Megan pointed out.

'I suppose so. It's the odd hours she works. I'd be so worried about her if she had to come home on the ferry boat late at night.'

'She might find a job in New Brighton. And that would get her away from the crowd she mixes with at present.'

'Well, that's true. It worries your dad her being so involved with these jazz people.'

'There's nothing wrong with jazz,' Megan commented, 'it's the crowd that get into the Stork Club. Some of them even take drugs.'

Kathy Williams looked shocked. 'I suppose that's why the police are always turning up there.'

'I expect it is. They've made several arrests. Sooner or later our Lynn is bound to be taken in for questioning.'

Kathy looked worried. 'Perhaps you're right, Megan. It might be for the best if we moved out of Liverpool,' she agreed.

Megan wasted no time in letting her father know how things stood.

'Why don't we look for a place to rent in Wallasey and then tell Mam?' she suggested.

'You mean take her to see it after we've decided what we want and save all the arguments.' He laughed.

'Something like that.' Megan smiled.

'You're on!' agreed her father. 'We'll ask Robert to help.'

'Must we?' Megan said with a frown. She felt apprehensive because she had no wish to encourage his interest in their affairs.

'Robert has lived in New Brighton all his life, remember, so he'll know the most suitable areas for us to start looking,' persisted her father.

'I suppose you're right,' Megan admitted reluctantly. 'As long as we make sure that we don't rent a house too close to where he lives,' she warned.

Chapter Sixteen

The Williams family move to Wallasey was a tremendous success. From the first moment she saw the house to rent in Belgrave Street, Kathy was won over to the idea. They would be living close to Central Park and yet within easy walking distance of Liscard shopping centre. Belgrave Street was on a bus route so she could be walking along the promenade at New Brighton, or shopping in Liverpool's Church Street, within half an hour.

The semi-detached house had been newly decorated throughout so they were able to move in without any delay. For Watkin, having a garden again was almost like turning the clock back to Beddgelert days.

Lynn seemed to enjoy the adventure of travelling by tram and boat to Liverpool. 'It's great being able to walk around on the top deck and get a good blow,' she enthused. 'You meet all sorts of interesting fellas,' she added with a broad grin.

Megan was delighted that the move had gone so smoothly. She knew they had Robert to thank. He had checked out a great many houses on their behalf until he had found something suitable.

She'd felt guilty about turning down so many of them, but she considered them to be much too near to where he lived. She didn't want to find herself bumping into him every time she went shopping or out for a walk.

Megan knew it amused Lynn the way she avoided Robert whenever he called, but she was determined not to become too friendly with him. It was difficult. He was always suggesting somewhere he wanted to take her and she didn't want to hurt his feelings.

'Why don't you go, Megan,' Lynn teased. 'He won't try anything on, he's much too respectable. You could have him eating out of your hand if you wanted. I wish he'd ask me out, I'd go like a shot.'

'Don't talk rubbish! Do you know how old he is?'

'He's thirty. That's not old! I like older men, they have more style.' She sighed dramatically. 'I sometimes wish Flash was older and thinking of settling down.'

'Stop being silly, Lynn. You've only just left school so there's no question of you getting married for years.'

'I'd get married tomorrow if the right fella asked me,' Lynn told her.

'Why do you want to throw away your life like that? If you'd had any sense you would have stayed on at school and passed some exams and got a decent job . . .'

Lynn wasn't listening. She was scanning the pages of the *Liverpool Echo*, and her face was wreathed in smiles when she looked up.

'Listen to this,' she exclaimed excitedly. 'The King Oliver's Jazz Band are going to be on at the Tower Ballroom.'

'So what is so marvellous about that?'

'You know nothing, our Megan, do you?' retorted Lynn scathingly. 'They're the tops and they play all the new dances like the Shimmy and the Charleston. How about us going to the Tower on Friday night?'

'No thanks! It will probably get very rough. Remember the night when we went to the Stork . . .'

'You're always bringing that up,' grumbled Lynn. 'Oh, come on, Meg. This is happening right here on our doorstep. I'm not asking you to go over to Liverpool. Please! Just this once. Mam's bound to create if I say I'm going on my own because it doesn't finish until midnight.'

Lynn could be persuasive when she chose and eventually Megan gave in. A night out would be something to look forward to. Although her job was going well there hadn't been much excitement in her life since Miles went away on his course.

Not seeing him, or even hearing from him, although she understood from the office grapevine that he had been home on a number of weekends, only intensified her feelings. In bed at night, she agonised over her memories, wondering if things would have been different between them if only she had given in to his demands.

Her face flamed as she remembered an evening before Valerie Pearce's wedding when, instead of taking her to the pictures, Miles had driven to a secluded part of Leasowe foreshore. Snuggled up under a plaid car rug, they'd kissed and caressed, exchanging whispered endearments, lost in a heaven of their own making.

He'd grumbled when she adamantly refused his ultimate caress and pulled away from him, re-arranging her clothes, her face burning, her passion quelled as though she had been doused in cold water.

Angrily, he had struggled into his jacket, searching in the pocket for the car keys. Wheels spinning, he had zoomed out onto the main road. When they had parted he had not even said good-night. And, although her throat had ached with bottled-up tears, Megan had refused to let him see how desperately hurt and unhappy she was.

At the time she'd felt she was right to refuse him. Now, after weeks and weeks of silent separation, she wasn't sure. Perhaps Lynn was right and she was fuddy-duddy in her outlook. Miles had certainly seemed to think so. A night out with Lynn and her friends might help to put the incident in its right perspective, she thought wryly.

Lynn was right. It was a gala occasion. New Brighton was packed. Extra ferry boats had been organised to bring the hundreds of fans over from Liverpool.

'Why don't you leave your car in Robert's drive?' Lynn suggested. 'It would be much safer there.'

'That would be an open invitation for him to come along with us,' Megan replied with a grimace as she parked in a side road.

'It might be a chance for him to let his hair down. You might learn to like him if he wasn't quite so stuffy,' teased Lynn mischievously.

'Don't start,' warned Megan. 'I want to enjoy myself tonight.'

'Does that mean you are going to come backstage with me at the interval?' Lynn asked, raising her carefully pencilled brows.

Megan hesitated for a fraction before agreeing. 'Of course. That's what is going to make the evening special, isn't it,' she said lightly. 'Maybe I'll meet this Flash character you are always going on about.'

Lynn pulled a face. 'Flash won't be there, worse luck. He's working away and only gets home every other weekend.'

'They're a great crowd, aren't they,' Lynn commented triumphantly on the way home.

'Playing the same tunes night after night seems an odd way to earn a living,' opined Megan.

'What an existence, though! It seems they never know where they'll be appearing next. London, Liverpool, Manchester, Sheffield, you name it and they've played there.'

'Someone said they're planning to make some more records.'

'I told you, they're a winning band. Sometimes the whole group are in the Copper Kettle, huddled in a corner, plotting and planning their next tour. That's when they're not getting high!'

'High?'

'Oh, Megan, you are dumb!' Lynn rolled her eyes in feigned despair.

'You mean they're using drugs!'

'Well,' Lynn pulled a face, 'I suppose you could

say that, but only in a mild way. Flash says they could get equally pepped up on champagne.'

'Flash seems to know an awful lot about it,' Megan said suspiciously. 'Is he into drugs?'

Lynn shrugged. 'Possibly,' she said evasively.

'I hope you're not indulging!'

The alarm in Megan's tone brought a flush of anger to Lynn's cheeks.

'Of course I'm not! Do you think I'm daft?' she exploded.

'Well, you seem to know a lot about it,' argued Megan stubbornly.

'I told you, they all come into the Copper Kettle and talk about these things.'

'It's a good thing you didn't tell me all this before we went to The Tower,' Megan said crossly. 'If you had, then I certainly wouldn't have gone with you.'

'Oh, for heaven's sake, Megan, stop being such a back number.'

'And what's that supposed to mean?'

'Well, listen to you. You sound about ninety. We're living in the 1920s, everything's changing! You've got to move with the times. Drugs are part of it!'

'So you *are* dabbling in drugs,' censured Megan.

'I never said so . . .'

'Then why are you acting so guilty?'

'I don't know what you mean,' retorted Lynn huffily, turning away and staring out of the window into the darkness.

'Oh, yes you do. There's something going on,' persisted Megan.

Lynn refused to reply. As they turned into Belgrave Street and pulled into their own driveway Lynn made to get out of the car but Megan stopped her.

'You're not . . . not sleeping with Flash, are you?' she asked worriedly.

'What's it to do with you if I am?' Lynn retorted with a toss of her head.

'Oh, Lynn . . . Are you letting him . . .' Megan's voice trailed away as she stared in horror at her sister. 'Oh, Lynn, you've not long left school . . .'

'What difference does that make? We know what we're doing, I'm not going to get pregnant or anything stupid like that!'

'How can you be sure? Fancy trusting him.' Megan stared at her younger sister in dismay. 'Oh Lynn! Whatever would Mam say if she knew!'

'Who is going to tell her, or Dad? No one knows except you!'

Long after she was in bed that night, Megan lay staring into the darkness, wondering if Lynn really was telling the truth or simply boasting. She found it hard to believe that she would take such a momentous step.

The thought troubled Megan even while she slept. She awoke late, feeling cross and disgruntled and decidedly out of sorts.

'What's got into you, girl?' Kathy asked in surprise when Megan complained that the tea was too strong and the toast not browned enough. 'Not like you to find fault!'

'Nothing's the matter with me.'

'I'd say that late nights don't agree with you,'

her mother told her. 'Our Lynn's chirpy enough, though. What's happened, have you fallen out with your boyfriend?'

'Our Meg hasn't got a boyfriend.' Lynn sniggered. 'She's too prim and proper for that sort of thing,' she added meaningfully.

Aware that her mother was watching her closely, Megan pushed aside her unfinished breakfast and went back up to her room before deciding to go out. A brisk walk to clear her head was what she needed.

Chapter Seventeen

1927 was the worst winter for over a hundred years. From January until mid-March everyone shivered; even the English Channel froze over in places. Snow and ice piled up from one end of Britain to the other. As fast as the roads were cleared, fresh falls of snow created further chaos. The death from cold of many elderly people made headline news.

The roads were so dangerous, with frozen sludge and black ice, that Megan was afraid to drive her car, so she crossed to Liverpool on the ferry each morning. Only the hardy few still took their constitutional on the top deck. The rest, Megan and Lynn among them, huddled inside the lower deck saloon, grateful for the shelter and even prepared to put up with an atmosphere that was blue and choking with tobacco smoke.

'We'd be worse off if we were still living in Beddgelert,' Lynn reminded her.

'It's said in the newspaper that most of Wales is cut off completely.'

'It's a different kind of cold there.' Megan shivered, pulling her woollen scarf higher under her chin. 'This wind is raw and damp because it's coming straight off the Mersey.'

'Yeah.' Lynn shuddered, 'They were saying

yesterday in the Copper Kettle that it was so cold that a lorry load of beer that was being delivered to a pub in Whitechapel exploded in its bottles!'

For those working at the docks, it was sheer hell trying to handle crates and cargo that were slippery with ice. Freezing winds buffeted the men unrelentingly as they worked on the quayside. Their hands were cut and sore, their faces chapped and raw.

Driving was hazardous. Each time her father and Robert Field set out Megan was on tenterhooks until she knew they were safe. They had been stranded so many times that her mother was rapidly becoming a nervous wreck with the worry of it all.

It seemed spring would never arrive. In mid-March, fresh falls of snow and bad weather brought further appalling road conditions. Yet again unable to use her car, Megan travelled to Liverpool by ferry. Buffeted by icy winds as she struggled up the floating roadway after a rough crossing she sometimes wished they had never moved across to Wallasey.

It had all been pointless anyway, she thought morosely. Her hopes that, once they were living in a nice house in respectable surroundings, Miles would openly acknowledge their friendship hadn't materialised.

Sometimes she found the strain almost unbearable. He hadn't been near the office, or contacted her at all, since he'd been away on his course. Yet she knew he had often come home for the weekend because she had heard Mr Walker mention the fact when he'd been talking on the phone.

She kept meaning to ask him how Miles was, but at the last minute her courage always failed her. She became so quiet and withdrawn that even Mr Walker noticed.

'Are you worrying about your father driving in this atrocious weather, Megan?' he asked one day at the end of a dictating session. 'You seem to be extremely preoccupied lately.' He frowned.

She looked at him, startled. 'I'm sorry. Have I overlooked something?'

'No, everything is fine, Megan. I am more than pleased with your work, but you do seem to be rather tense.'

'I'm all right, thank you.'

She wondered what his reaction would be if she told him that she was frantic for news of Miles. Would he understand and tell her what she longed to hear, or would he be taken aback by her audacity?

'It is worrying when the weather conditions are so bad but the worst is over now,' she said quickly as she became aware that he was waiting for her explanation.

'Since it is almost April let us hope you are right.' He smiled. 'Perhaps what you need is a holiday. You haven't had any time off since you started working here, have you, Megan?'

'No. I wasn't due for any holidays last year.'

'I shall be away myself for about a week at Easter, so you can take a couple of extra days off then, if you wish.'

The more Megan thought about taking a holiday the more she liked the idea. It would be wonderful to visit Beddgelert and see all her old friends.

She decided to write to Jennie and Gwyneth right away to see if she could stay with either of them for a few days.

She pictured the look of surprise there would be on Ifan Jenkins' face when she drove up in her own car. Jennie replied by return of post. Excitedly, Megan told her mother about what she was planning to do.

'Drive all that way!' Kathy Williams exclaimed, worriedly. 'Do you think you should . . . The weather may turn bad again.'

'Nonsense! After such a terrible winter we'll probably have a run of good weather now.'

'It's such a long journey, though . . .'

'Stop fussing, Mam! Dad goes a hundred miles some days,' Megan interrupted.

'He's not on his own, though. If anything should go wrong then Robert is there to help sort things out.'

'You're not suggesting I should ask Robert to go with me, I hope,' Megan shot back, pulling a long face.

'I'd feel a lot happier if you did.' Her mother smiled. 'I still don't know why you dislike him so much.'

'I don't dislike him, I don't want to go out with him, that's all.'

'Well, it's your choice, of course, but he won't wait for ever, you know,' she said with a sigh.

'What do you mean?'

'A man of his age must be keen or he would have taken up with someone else long before this. It's you he wants. It's written all over his face. He's a different person when you're around. Surely you must have noticed?'

'Stop it, Mam! You're talking a whole load of nonsense,' Megan said crossly.

'No, I'm not! He never takes his eyes off you when he's here. And look at the way he's always giving you presents. Hardly a week goes by without your dad bringing home something Robert has sent for you. Books, ornaments, scarves, flowers . . . It's never ending.'

'And I wish he would stop it.' Megan frowned. 'I don't want half the stuff, anyway.'

'That's as maybe, but it proves how much he thinks about you. Doesn't that mean anything at all to you?'

'Not really . . . I've never given it much thought,' she added evasively.

'Our Lynn's right,' said her mother. 'You are naive! If you can't see that he's trying to win you over then you must be blind. You could do a lot worse, you know. He's good-looking, has his own house and a well-paid job and he thinks the world of you.'

Megan clamped her hands over her ears to shut out Kathy's diatribe. She didn't want to listen to her mother going on and on about Robert or about his feelings for her.

Perhaps if she knew about Miles she'd understand why I'm not interested in Robert Field no matter how hard he tries, Megan thought ruefully. Yet what was the point of talking about it when there wasn't really anything to tell.

She'd be more than ever convinced that I was

naive if I told her that there hadn't been a single word from Miles since he'd returned from London. Or if I told her how he ignores me when he sees me at work and used to only meet me after dark in some out of the way place, Megan thought dispiritedly.

Determinedly, she put the matter from her mind and concentrated on planning her forthcoming holiday. The more she thought about it the better she liked the idea of getting right away from Merseyside, even if it was only for a few days.

She had so much to tell her old friends. Although they'd all promised to write to each other, they hadn't done so, except for cards at Christmas and the one she'd sent to let them know her new address when they moved to Wallasey.

She wouldn't mention Miles, she decided. Not at first, anyway. She'd tell them about the problems Lynn seemed to have pinning Flash down to any commitment first and see what they said about that.

It was much the same situation, she thought unhappily. She had lost count of the number of times Lynn had asked her to go to the Stork Club or the Copper Kettle to meet Flash, and each time it had been a wasted journey.

'You shouldn't tell him I'm coming to meet him. He's probably shy.'

'Tell him he's going to meet you, you must be kidding. That's the last thing I'd do! He doesn't even know I've got a sister. I don't intend to let on who you are. I'll just say you're a friend.'

'Why?' laughed Megan. 'Are you ashamed of me or something?'

Lynn shook her head. 'He'll probably think you're quite la-di-da when he hears you talk. He's posh himself in a way, mind, but it might put him off, though, if he knew we were related.'

'Or he might be afraid you are getting too serious.'

Lynn shrugged and pulled a face and Megan suspected that she'd caught her sister on a raw spot.

'What does he do for a living?' she asked casually.

'I don't know, he never talks about it. Something down at the docks, I think. His time seems to be his own, I never know when he's going to pop into the café. Lately it's mostly been at the weekends.' She sighed dramatically. 'That's half the excitement . . . Seeing him when I least expect to do so.'

'Why don't you bring him home and let us all meet him?'

'Megan! He's not the type to sit around drinking tea and making polite conversation. He's a bundle of laughs, always doing outrageous things.'

'You mean when he's high! I thought you promised me you would keep away from drugs,' scolded Megan sternly.

'I'm not the one on them, idiot,' snapped Lynn angrily. 'The only trips I take are carrying trays backwards and forwards. I don't need pepping up.' She grinned, her grey eyes flashing. 'I get all the excitement I can take from the people I meet at work every day.'

'I wish I could believe you,' Megan muttered.

'It's dangerous, Lynn. Once you get hooked you can't break the habit and you need more and more and more of it.'

'Rubbish!'

Their arguments always stopped at this point because Lynn would change the subject.

We're a funny family, Megan thought ruefully. Dad and his concern over work, Mam with her shopping trips, and Lynn with her crush on Flash.

There would certainly be plenty to tell Gwyneth and Jennie! She could imagine their faces when she told them about what went on at the Copper Kettle and the Stork Club and that she'd been to dances at the Tower Ballroom. The three of them would probably sit up half the night talking.

As she tidied her desk before leaving for the night she found herself thinking that the visit to Beddgelert in a few days' time could be a turning point for her. It would clear the cobwebs from her mind. When she came back it would be like starting afresh.

I might even change my job, she told herself, and look for something more challenging since there are plenty of opportunities in Liverpool.

Her reverie was disrupted by sounds from the general office. Her heart beat faster as she recognised Miles' voice. Emotions she had almost convinced herself were dead came bubbling back to life.

Desperately, she tried to ignore them, but the familiar voice and deep laugh stirred too many memories for her to do so.

Instinctively, she smoothed her hair into place.

On the one hand she wanted to escape before there was any chance of them meeting. On the other she was delighting in the fact that she was wearing a smart red suit and a crisp white blouse.

As the door opened and Miles came through into her office her breath caught in her throat. It was months since she had seen him and he seemed to be even more attractive than she had remembered.

Dressed in grey trousers, a tweed jacket and a blue shirt that matched the intense blue of his eyes, his masculine appeal was devastating. His wide smile and casual greeting, as though they had only seen each other a day or so ago, left her speechless.

'I hear you're off to North Wales for Easter.' He grinned, his blue gaze hypnotising her. 'We're going to our place in Mostyn over the holiday,' he told her. He lowered his voice. 'That's only about twenty miles from Beddgelert so why don't we meet up?'

'See each other . . .' She stared at him, bemused, colour staining her cheeks.

The desperate hours of heartache; the sleepless, tearful nights; the harrowing doubts; the hopes that had buoyed up her spirits and the misery of rejection that had so often sent them crashing, churned inside her.

Had she been wrong? Perhaps the months of separation had been as poignant for him as they had been for her. Dare she believe that now, at long last, he intended to bring their friendship into the open?

'I'd like that, Miles,' she told him eagerly. 'Which day would you like me to come over to Mostyn?'

'Are you mad!' His raised eyebrows ridiculed her assumption.

Too late she realised she'd mistaken his meaning. Her anger flared. How dare he treat her in such a cavalier fashion. Once she might have felt flattered that he wanted to see her and agreed to whatever arrangements he might make. Now she felt enraged.

'I . . . I'm not prepared to go on meeting you secretly,' she told him vehemently. 'I . . . I'm sure your father knows about us . . .'

'What have you been saying to him?' The cold rasp in his voice, and the look of anger on his face, alarmed her.

Before she could answer, Miles grabbed her arm. 'Come on . . . what have you said?' He bristled, his face only a few inches from her own, his mouth a hard ugly line.

'Let go! You're hurting me, Miles.'

Savagely, he pushed her away, turned on his heel and strode off, slamming the door behind him.

Her feelings were in turmoil. She wanted to call him back, assure him that she hadn't said a word to his father. Trembling, she sat down at her desk, holding her head in her hands, trying to control the ache in her heart and the shivering in her limbs.

All the time he had been away, Miles hadn't even sent her a postcard, hadn't phoned her once. And now he calmly walked back into her life and expected to renew their friendship as though he'd never been absent. It was a game she wasn't prepared to play. In his absence she'd had to learn to control her emotions, conceal her heartache and present an efficient face to the world. It had made her less vulnerable and more aware of her own value.

She had no idea of how long she sat there, deep in thought. She was still trying to analyse her feelings when Olive popped her head round the door to say she was going home. She stared at Megan with unconcealed curiosity. 'Is something wrong or are you working late?'

'Why, what time is it?' Megan glanced towards the window; the sky had darkened and grey clouds had built up as if a storm was imminent.

Megan shook her head then looked at her watch. It was almost six o'clock. She'd been sitting there for well over an hour.

Savagely, she rubbed the back of her hand across her eyes. She'd meant every word of it when she'd told Miles she wasn't prepared to go on meeting him in secret. Why did they need such a subterfuge? she asked herself as she covered up her typewriter and picked up her handbag.

As she was leaving the office the phone rang. She hesitated. Should she let it ring or ought she to answer it? she wondered. It might be Mr Walker phoning from Manchester . . . or even Miles ringing to apologise.

Chapter Eighteen

At first, Megan thought the phone call might be a hoax. Replacing the receiver she sat staring at the pad in front of her, rereading the message she had taken down. It had been rather like taking dictation. Although she had written down the words, and checked they were correct by repeating them back, she had been completely detached from their meaning.

Now, reading them over for a second time, the full impact of the message was like a physical blow.

Inform Mr Martin Walker that his son, Miles Walker, has been involved in a road accident and has been taken to Liverpool General Hospital.

It must surely be a hoax, Megan decided. The caller had claimed to be from the police, but he hadn't given his name or rank, or even left a phone number.

Not that she had asked, she thought, uneasily.

She read the message through again and a shudder went through her. It must be true, no one would joke about something like that, she told herself.

Not unless it had been Miles!

Had he deliberately disguised his voice to try to frighten her . . . some sort of sick retaliation because of their quarrel? Was he trying to make her feel guilty . . . ?

She knew she was wasting time trying to work it out, but she felt so undecided about what to do. She didn't want to contact Mr Walker and have him come hurrying back from Manchester on a wild goose chase. Perhaps if she phoned the hospital they could confirm if it was true.

As she waited for the receptionist to check the admission register she tried to convince herself that was a hopeful sign and that Miles wasn't there; that it had been a hoax after all.

When the girl eventually confirmed that a Miles Walker had been admitted, Megan found herself shaking so violently that it was only after she had put the phone down that she realised she hadn't asked for any details. She had no idea whether Miles was seriously hurt or not.

Pulling herself together she decided to ring the hospital again, then changed her mind and replaced the receiver.

That was only wasting time, she told herself. It would be better if she tried to contact Mr Walker right away since it would take him at least an hour to get back from Manchester.

He'd left a series of telephone numbers where he could be located. It took three calls before she tracked him down. Even then she couldn't speak to him because he was in a meeting.

Reluctant to leave a message in case it didn't reach him, she asked the receptionist to get Mr Walker to phone her the moment he was free.

'They may not be out before I go home . . .'

'Then in that case you'd better get this message to him right away,' Megan told her and repeated word for word the police phone call. 'It's very urgent,' she emphasised. 'And I would like him to phone me here at the office to let me know he's on his way back to Liverpool,' she added before she rang off.

As she waited for the return call, Megan's concern about Miles made her feel sick. She really wanted to ring the hospital again but was afraid that if she did Mr Walker might try to phone her and not be able to get through.

She felt so helpless. All she could think about was the blind rage Miles had been in when he had slammed out of the office and wonder if that had contributed to the accident in some way.

An image of Miles lying in the roadway, covered in blood after an accident on his motorbike, blotted everything else from her mind. She didn't know what to do. One thing was certain, she couldn't set off for Beddgelert until she knew what had happened.

On impulse she decided to go to the hospital. She felt sure Mr Walker would get the full message and go straight to the hospital rather than try to call her first.

Outside, rain was sheeting down, the sky grey and overcast. Feeling in no state to drive, she tied a scarf over her hair, turned up the collar of her coat and went in search of a taxi.

Her anxiety mounted when she arrived at the hospital and was told that Miles was in the operating theatre. No one was prepared to give her any details about the accident. Time dragged. She waited so long in reception that her concern began to be replaced by vexation. Rather irritably she went over to the desk to ask once to make sure they hadn't forgotten about her.

It was a different receptionist and she was much more helpful. 'The road accident casualty? I'll enquire for you.'

'He's out of theatre and in Stanley Ward. I'm not sure if you will be able to see him. You'll have to check with the ward sister. Usually they only let in close relatives,' she warned as she told her where to go.

'I shall have to ask Sister if you can see him . . . it's relatives only,' the nurse on duty told her.

Again Megan found she was kept waiting and fresh doubts about why she was at the hospital at all assailed her. Since Miles had made it quite plain that he had no intention of telling his parents about their friendship, she had resolved to put him out of her mind, she reminded herself.

Coming here to see him is only looking for trouble, she thought ruefully. I'm letting my heart rule my head again. Yet when the sister asked who she was, Megan explained that she was a special friend and begged to be allowed to see him, to set her mind at rest.

'Very well, for a few minutes, then. He's in the side room, halfway down the ward on your right.'

Megan's knees were shaking by the time she reached the screened-off alcove. She could see Miles, lying propped up by pillows, his face ashen, one heavily bandaged arm supported above his

177

head. A drip feed tube was attached to his other arm and there was a cage supporting the bed-clothes over the lower part of the bed.

Her heart thundering, Megan whispered his name as she moved towards the bed. His eyelids flickered and he gave a faint groan as he turned his head restlessly on the pillows.

'Oh, Miles . . .' Her words choked as she stretched out her hand to touch him.

'Miss Williams! This is a surprise, how kind of you to come . . . It really wasn't necessary.'

The icy, imperious voice startled Megan. She had been so taken aback at the gravity of Miles' condition that she had not even been aware that there was anyone else in the room. She stared in confusion at his mother who was sitting in a chair on the far side of the bed.

'Shouldn't you be in the office, Miss Williams, taking care of things there?'

Ann Walker looked elegant and well turned out in her tailored brown and cream check suit that toned perfectly with her cream silk blouse. The pearl designer pin in her lapel matched her neck-lace and earrings added an overall air of elegance. The sharpness of her voice, with its querulous undertones, added to the image of superiority.

'I . . . I was anxious to see how Miles was,' Megan stuttered, chilled by the coldness in Mrs Walker's blue eyes.

'I do hope you have contacted my husband and let him know what has happened. I expected him to be here long before now!'

'Mr Walker's in Manchester. I tried to contact

him but he was in a meeting. I have left messages . . .' she added hurriedly, almost apologetically.

'Indeed! Well, I think you should run along back
to the office and keep on phoning until you do get
hold of him,' interrupted Mrs Walker. 'Messages
don't always get passed on, you know . . . especially if there is no one in the office to deal with
them,' she added pointedly. 'Even at this moment
he may be trying to ring you to find out more
details.'

The sting in Mrs Walker's words was not lost
on Megan and, although she knew she had been
dismissed, she stayed by the bedside staring down
at Miles. If only he would open his eyes for one
brief moment so that she could be sure he was going
to regain consciousness, she thought desperately.

Megan stretched out her hand to touch his, then
withdrew it abruptly, aware that Mrs Walker was
watching her and she found her scrutiny disquieting. She now knew why Miles had been so insistent about keeping their friendship secret. He had
said it was because his father wouldn't understand,
but she thought it was much more likely that his
mother would be the one who would object.

Megan had found her intimidating when they
had first met at Valerie Pearce's wedding. Now, as
they faced each other across the hospital bed, she
could sense Mrs Walker's disapproval as if it was
a tangible barrier between them. She knew she
should leave, but she desperately wanted to stay,
to be there when Miles regained consciousness.

'Was there anything else, Miss Williams?'

179

Megan looked up at her, startled, and Ann Walker noticed the film of tears that misted the girl's dark brown eyes and sparkled on her lashes like tiny stars.

'I . . . I just wondered if there were any appointments Miles might want me to cancel . . .' Megan's voice trailed off uncertainly.

'Really, Miss Williams! Work is the last thing my son wants to be troubled with at the moment. Can't you see the state he is in?' Mrs Walker bristled. 'Kindly go back to the office and do whatever you have to do. My husband will attend to anything connected with my son's work commitments in due course.'

As she reached the door, Megan looked back at Miles' recumbent figure despairingly. If only Miles would open his eyes, even for a brief second. If only she knew if their quarrel had anything to do with his accident.

Ann Walker was relieved to see Megan leave. In her estimation, the girl was much too young to be a secretary. She would have to be replaced. She'd tell her husband to hire someone older, someone who would mother Miles not flirt with him. The moment she had realised that the girl who'd replaced Valerie Pearce as her husband's secretary was young, inexperienced, and brought up in some remote part of Wales, she had been expecting trouble.

With that sort of background she was bound to imagine herself in love with Miles, Ann Walker thought cynically.

With his good looks and natural charm, Miles

had always had a devastating effect on girls. They had always fluttered round him. Even on his first day at school. She had left him awash with tears at being parted from her. When she returned to collect him he had been waiting at the gate surrounded by little girls. Several of them had insisted on kissing him goodbye and assuring him they'd see him there next day.

As Miles grew older, and even more attractive, girls came along to watch him play football or cricket. On sports day they cheered him to victory in the races and queued up to partner him at tennis.

In his teens, when he had decided to go to art school, she had been delighted that he had found a new interest. Until she learned that he had been playing truant in order to go to the Stork Club and then she'd started worrying about him again.

'Martin, I think it is time you took Miles into the firm,' she told her husband without preamble.

'I've been telling you for ages that it was a waste of time sending him to art college,' he stated pompously. 'He's not learning anything that is going to help him to earn a living.'

'Then take him to the office with you tomorrow and start teaching him the business,' she snapped.

'He won't like it! He'll have to start right at the bottom and learn the job properly. I don't intend showing any favouritism. For the first few weeks he'll be making the tea and running messages,' he warned.

'I don't wish to know the details, simply do it!'

'It won't be easy,' he repeated speculatively. 'He's been spoiled ever since he was a nipper and now you want me to make a man of him overnight.'

Those had been Martin Walker's only words of reproach. She hadn't questioned his methods, although she had witnessed a marked change in Miles.

During working hours, Miles conformed to the standards demanded by his father. In a very short time he graduated from being a mere office dogs-body to undertaking more responsible work.

He seemed to enjoy the work when he was sent to the docks to deal with the transference of cargo from boats to their own warehouses or lorries. His ready charm made him popular with the customs officials, the skippers of the cargo boats and the captains of freight boats.

'I do wish he'd stop going to the Stork Club,' Ann Walker said with a sigh. 'The types he mixes with there are not a good influence!'

'He'll grow out of it, just give him time,' her husband assured her. 'We can hardly dictate who his friends are, not at his age.'

They'd both breathed a sigh of relief, though, when Miles started dating Carol Brocklehurst. Taking out a girl from their own circle must surely be a sign that he was settling down at last, they thought.

Carol, a stunning red-head, only a year younger than Miles, was the daughter of one of their closest friends. She was a tall, willowy girl with a perfect oval face and a quiet self-assured manner, and Ann Walker was convinced she would make him the ideal wife.

Both sets of parents watched with delight when

Miles began taking her to the Royal Court Theatre and to symphony concerts at the Philharmonic. It seemed like the perfect match.

Now, as she thought about Megan, recalling the neat hairstyle and discreet make-up, and critically assessing the good quality red suit and neat white blouse, Ann Walker felt uneasy. She wasn't the right type for Miles, of course, but neither was she one of the little floosies who made up the Stork crowd, so it might be difficult to discourage her from taking an interest in Miles.

Chapter Nineteen

Megan didn't even notice that the rain had stopped. As she left the hospital, she automatically turned up her collar and huddled inside her raincoat. The cold shivers rippling down her spine were more from shock than the weather.

Her brain was racing as she tried to reason out how Miles had come to be involved in an accident. Had he been so immersed in black thoughts when he left the office that he had walked into the path of an oncoming vehicle? She felt a desperate need to know the answer, but she had no idea of how to find out.

As she skirted the puddles that shone like pools of molten silver on the forecourt she heard someone call her name. Her breath caught in her throat. She turned quickly, half hoping that someone had come after her to tell her that Miles had regained consciousness . . . that he was asking for her!

Her hopes faded and she felt a sense of irritation when she saw it was Robert Field.

'Megan . . . I'm so glad I've found you! How did you know about it?' he asked, bewilderment shadowing his light blue eyes.

'The police phoned the office. Mr Walker is in Manchester so I came to see if there was anything I could do. Oh Robert.' She flung herself against his broad chest. 'He looks terrible! His face is so white and he's attached to all these tubes and pulleys . . .' She shivered violently, unable to go on.

'Hush, hush!' Robert held her close, stroking her hair, trying his best to calm her. When her breathing steadied and her sobs subsided he gently raised her face so that he was looking down into her eyes.

'Who are you talking about, Megan?'

'Miles, of course! He's been badly hurt in a road accident. Isn't that why you were looking for me?'

'No, I knew nothing about that . . . What happened?'

'I'm not sure!' Tears rolled unchecked down her cheeks. 'Can you find out? I need to know.' She scrubbed a hand across her eyes, squaring her shoulders in an attempt to pull herself together. 'Why were you trying to find me?' she asked in a puzzled voice.

Robert hesitated, reluctant to deliver what he knew was going to be another blow when she was already so upset. He looked down into her tear-stained face, searching for the right words in order to break the news as gently as possible.

His expression made her uneasy. He stood there, a solid rock of a man with an unfathomable look in his light blue eyes.

'It's about Lynn. She was involved in a road accident,' he said in a low voice. He placed a protective arm across Megan's shoulders. 'Your parents are with her. They asked me to come and fetch you.'

Wide eyed, Megan stared at Robert in silent disbelief. She found it difficult to take in what he was saying. She felt as if she was caught up in a nightmare. It was as if the horror of Miles' accident was happening all over again only this time it was Lynn who had been hurt. It didn't make sense.

She closed her eyes trying to shut out the picture that was taking over in her mind. She couldn't bear to think of Lynn lying in a hospital bed, attached to all the paraphernalia of drips and tubes, like Miles had been.

Lynn was always so active, so vibrant. Lynn couldn't sit still for ten minutes. She had to be doing something, even if it was only tapping her foot or drumming with her fingers to the music inside her head. Lynn so gregarious, fun loving and daring, and who always had to be the centre of attention. Although they often argued, she loved her sister.

'I must see her!' Sobbing, Megan pulled away from Robert and turned back towards the hospital.

Robert strode after her, grabbing her arm and pulling her to a stop. He spun her round until she was facing him, pinning her arms to her side as she tried to fight him away.

'Calm down, Megan. It's no good going in there in that state, they wouldn't let you near Lynn in case you upset her. Take a deep breath, get a hold on yourself.'

His heart ached for her as she stared up into his face, her eyes filled with tears. She looks like a terrified child, he thought tenderly. His arms tightened around her and the shudder that ran through her had the impact of an electric shock to his own body. He held her closer, murmuring soothing words to calm her, stroking her hair until her sobs subsided.

Gradually she relaxed against him, her head resting on his chest.

'Robert, we're wasting time. I must go to Lynn.' She pulled away wearily, as if her limbs were leaden.

They walked in silence, side by side, back into the hospital. Robert led her past the reception desk, taking her straight to one of the side wards.

As they reached the doorway, Megan paused. The shaking was back, turning her legs to water. The colour drained from her face and Robert thought she was going to faint. Then with a tremendous effort she steadied herself, took a deep breath and, with her hands clenched into tight fists at her side, walked into the room.

The nightmare feeling of déjà-vu became even more vivid as she approached the bed.

Lynn's fair hair was a tangled mass against the pillows. Her eyes were closed, her lips a pale gash in her bloodless face. Her breathing was shallow and laboured.

Watkin Williams moved a few paces away from the bed as Megan approached it. He placed a restraining hand on her arm as she bent over and whispered Lynn's name.

'She's been unconscious ever since they brought her in . . . She won't know you are here,' he murmured.

'I think she does,' protested Megan. 'Her eyelids moved when I took her hand and said her name.'

'She shouldn't be disturbed. Perhaps if you came back later . . .'

'I want to stay,' Megan begged.

'I think not.' Gently, Robert led her away from the bedside.

'Come back later, *cariad*,' pleaded Watkin, laying a hand gently on her arm. 'Your mother and me will sit with her.'

Kathy said nothing. Her face was puffy from crying. She sat staring at Lynn as if waiting for a miracle.

As she walked out of the hospital for the second time within an hour, Megan suddenly remembered that she ought to get back to the office. She needed to try to contact Mr Walker and make sure he knew about Miles.

'Robert, do you know how Lynn was injured?' she asked, suddenly struck by the coincidence of the two accidents taking place almost simultaneously.

'Lynn was thrown from the back of a motor-bike,' he told her tersely. 'It seems the bike skidded on the wet road. That's all I know. Oh, and that it was somewhere near Whitechapel.'

'Isn't it odd that she was in an accident at almost the same time as Miles. Do you think it could have been the same accident?' She frowned.

Robert didn't answer, but his mouth tightened and a nerve at the side of his jaw twitched. He hoped she wouldn't ask any more questions. He didn't want to be the one to tell her the truth. Although in a way it was none of his business, in his heart he knew he should have spoken out a long time ago.

'Who was on the motorbike with Lynn?'

He forced himself to meet her puzzled gaze. It

was the question he had dreaded. Now she had voiced it he knew he could no longer avoid the issue, yet the last thing he wanted to do was upset her even more.

His feelings for Megan went deep but he knew she didn't feel the same way. Although she was always sweet and friendly, she treated him as if he was an elder brother, nothing more, Robert thought sadly.

'You do know, don't you, Robert?' she persisted. 'Was this boy Flash that Lynn is always talking about involved?'

'Yes,' he said slowly. 'She was with Flash.' He took a deep breath. 'You . . . you've never met him, have you?'

'No!' She shook her head, a faint smile lifting the corners of her mouth. 'I was supposed to be meeting him on my birthday, the night the Stork Club was raided by the police and you arrived in the nick of time and got us both out.'

'I remember!'

'Several times after that, Lynn tried to fix up a meeting but something always went wrong, and he never turned up.'

'You do realise that Flash isn't his real name?' His anxious gaze searched her face.

'Lynn always called him that.' Megan frowned.

'But you must have known it was just a nick-name,' Robert persisted.

'Of course, but I don't think she knew his real name.'

'She didn't?'

'Robert, what's all the mystery?'

'It seems that neither of you knew that Flash and Miles Walker were one and the same person?'

Robert silently cursed himself for his tactlessness as the colour drained from Megan's face. Her eyes became saucer-wide pools of pain as she stared at him in disbelief.

'It can't be true!' She shook her head as if refusing to accept Robert's statement.

'Lynn said that Flash always wore flannels and a tweed jacket. Miles dresses in a smart suit with a collar and tie,' she said in a strangled voice, desperate to prove Robert wrong.

Even as she spoke she recalled that Miles wasn't always dressed like that. Often when they met late in the evening he wore a tweed jacket and flannels. She tried to quell the horror rising inside her: that's what Miles had been wearing when he'd called in the office . . . just before the accident.

'I think I can explain what has been happening,' Robert told her. 'Miles kept a motorbike down at the warehouse. He also had a change of casual clothes there. Whenever he intended going to the Stork Club he would change from his office suit into them.'

'You've known all along . . . so why didn't you tell me?' she gasped accusingly. 'Does Mr Walker know about this?'

'I shouldn't think so. I only found out about the clothes and motorbike by chance. I promised Miles I would say nothing. At the time it didn't seem to matter.'

'You're making this up,' she accused, two spots

of colour staining her cheeks. 'You've got it in for Miles. Once before you told me that I was wasting my time with him.'

'I knew Miles was a two-timer and I didn't want to see you getting hurt,' he told her sharply.

'Why didn't you tell me the whole story, then?'

'I couldn't! Not without betraying Miles' confidence.'

'Yet you're doing that now,' she said scornfully.

'This is an emergency,' he reasoned quietly.

He braced himself to look at her. A peculiar stiffness seemed to freeze her features and the pain in her voice distressed him. Her face was drawn and white, her eyes staring at him reproachfully.

'If I had told you all this before the accident would you have believed me?' he asked gently.

'No, probably not. I'm not sure I do even now, but at least I could have checked it out with Lynn,' she said dully. 'Please don't say anything about it to my parents,' she warned him.

'I hate to see you hurt like this, Megan, but I can't make a promise like that. It's bound to come out! You must realise that.'

'I don't see why it should.' She bit down on her lower lip. 'I doubt if Miles will say anything and . . . and I certainly won't,' she added firmly.

'There's been a serious accident, Megan, the police will be involved. They'll dig until they've got all the facts. You can't hide something like that from experienced detectives.'

'I must get back to the office and make sure Mr Walker's been informed about the accident,' she said abruptly.

'Shall I come with you?'

'No! I would prefer to be on my own.' She struggled to keep her feelings of frustration and despair in check, knowing that once she gave way to tears she wouldn't be able to stop crying. She longed to prove Robert wrong, but deep down inside she knew instinctively that he was right and that she had lost the battle even before it had begun.

How could Miles have played such a trick on them both? It was a question she would be asking herself for ever. How could she and Lynn have both been so besotted by the same person? It didn't make sense.

Her mind became a jumble of inconsequential thoughts. She began comparing what Lynn had told her about Flash with things she knew about Miles. So many of them linked like interlocking pieces of a complex jigsaw. The blue eyes, the darkly handsome looks, mannerisms, even fragments of conversation that Lynn had reported to her began to be identifiable with Miles.

She tried to tell herself that she was only thinking this way because Robert had sowed the seed of suspicion in her mind. Yet the similarities between Flash and Miles continued to pyramid until it became agonisingly clear that Robert was probably right and that they were one and the same person.

'Where are you parked? Let me walk that far with you at least,' Robert said, bringing her back to the present.

'I came by taxi.'

'Then I may as well give you a lift,' he insisted.

'You needn't trouble.'

'Come on. I have to go past the office on my way to the docks.'

They drove in silence. When Robert drew up in Old Hall Street she got out of his car without a word. She stopped with a feeling of panic when she saw he was following her.

'I need to have a word with Mr Newbold,' Robert said abruptly.

'Surely it can wait. He's probably left the office by now.'

'Then I'll leave a note on his desk,' he insisted stubbornly. 'Mr Newbold will have to arrange for some extra help so that your father can have some time off work.'

'You will be careful what you tell people,' she said uneasily as they walked into the office. 'People don't know about Miles and me . . . no one does.'

As the tears that she'd held in check began to roll down her cheeks, Robert gave her his handkerchief. He felt unable to console her in case he said something that made matters worse so he waited in silence until her sobs subsided.

'I'll be all right now.' She scrubbed at her eyes. 'I've made an awful mess of your hanky,' she murmured with a ghost of a smile. 'You'd better let me wash it.'

He nodded without speaking. He would have treasured it as it was, soaked by her tears. He wished he'd not been the one to disclose the silly jape Miles had perpetrated. Lynn would probably have laughed it off, but with Megan such things went so much deeper.

Chapter Twenty

April slid into May, then became June and still Lynn remained unconscious. The strain on all of them was tremendous. Kathy lost weight and looked drawn and tired. What had once been a series of double chins had now become slack jowls. A dejected, shapeless figure, she lost all interest in her appearance and would go days without having a wash or even combing her hair.

It made Megan sad to see her mother setting off for the hospital wearing an old cardigan over a washed-out cotton dress simply because she couldn't take the trouble to get changed.

'What does it matter, Lynn can't see me,' she would exclaim bitterly when Megan pleaded with her to smarten up, or at least run a comb through her hair and use some make-up before she went out of the house.

'You wouldn't want Lynn to see you like that if she did wake up while you were sitting there, now, would you?' Megan chivvied her.

Watkin, too, looked haggard. Not only was he concerned about Lynn's recovery, but he had been deeply shocked by the revelation that she had been riding pillion on the back of Miles Walker's motorbike when the accident happened.

When Martin Walker had demanded to know

about the relationship between Miles and Lynn, Watkin had been flummoxed.

'She's never mentioned your son's name. Lynn never kept anything secret, she was a proper little chatterbox,' he added, shaking his head in bewilderment.

'Did she ever talk about anyone called Flash?'

'Oh, yes! She was always going on about Flash.' He frowned, running his splayed fingers through his hair. 'What has that got to do with it?'

'Apparently, she knew my son as Flash,' snapped Martin Walker.

'Miles was Flash!'

The incredulity in Watkin Williams' voice seemed to irritate the other man. Frowning, he leaned back in his chair, fiddling with the gold watch chain that spanned his paunch, staring hard at Watkin.

'Maybe she preferred to call him that because she knew who he really was and she was afraid to tell you,' accused Mr Walker.

Watkin looked bemused. 'I don't follow.' He frowned.

The two men's gaze locked. Martin Walker was the first to look away.

'If your daughter realised that he was your employer's son then she would know she was overstepping the mark,' he said tetchily.

'That wouldn't have worried our Lynn,' Watkin said quietly. 'She was ready to be friends with everyone.'

'It mightn't worry her, but it certainly doesn't meet with my approval,' Mr Walker exploded. 'I object most strongly to my son fraternising with the daughter of one of my lorry drivers,' he added caustically.

'I see!' Watkin's face hardened at Mr Walker's words. Anger blazed in his dark eyes but only the clenching and unclenching of his fists revealed the tension he was under.

'Don't worry any more about it, Williams,' Mr Walker said magnanimously. 'I'll have a word with Miles when he comes out of hospital. It's about time he stopped patronising the Stork Club. It's just a phase left over from his art college days. I never did approve of the friends he made while he was there; always persuading him to skive off lectures. You should warn your daughter to stay clear of the place. For boys like Miles, picking up young girls is all part of growing up.'

'You may tell your son whatever you wish,' Watkin growled, struggling to hold his temper in check. 'There will be no need for me to tell my daughter anything . . .'

'Well, please yourself. I'm just giving you a friendly warning,' interrupted Martin Walker. 'I've always told Miles that if he gets a girl in trouble I don't want to know about it. And he shouldn't feel guilty about it, either. It's as much her fault as his and it's her responsibility to look after herself, not his . . .'

He stopped, startled and apprehensive as Watkin stood up and, placing both hands on the desk, leaned forward until their faces were only inches apart.

'My daughter still hasn't regained consciousness!' muttered Watkin, his voice bitter. 'Perhaps you should tell your son that!'

'What on earth are you talking about, Williams?'

'My Lynn's been unconscious ever since the accident.'

'Good God! I had no idea she was that seriously hurt! Why didn't you say so when you first came into my office,' blustered Martin Walker. 'Good heavens, this is terrible.' He pulled out a large white handkerchief and began mopping his brow.

'The doctors don't hold out much hope,' Watkin went on, 'and they warned me that even if she does regain consciousness she will probably be brain damaged.' He turned away, shoulders bowed, and walked towards the door.

'Look, Williams . . . if there is anything I can do . . . If you need more time off . . .' Mr Walker's voice trailed away uncertainly.

Watkin and Kathy were both at her bedside when the end came. Although he felt a sense of relief, Watkin was beside himself with grief.

Kathy accepted the news with the same numb blankness that she had shown all through the vigil. It was almost as if her mind refused to take in what had happened.

Watkin signed all the relevant papers, but it was Megan who read them through and Megan, helped by Robert Field, who organised the simple funeral.

It was a glorious morning in late June when, sombre-faced, they sat in the black limousine that followed the hearse from Belgrave Street, along Manor Road to Rake Lane Cemetry. If only they'd stayed in Beddgelert, Megan thought wistfully, this tragedy might never have happened.

It was hard to believe that Lynn was gone for ever. She could never remember a time when Lynn had not been part of her life. All their petty quarrels were forgotten. She could only remember Lynn's vivaciousness and her wide, cheeky smile.

Lynn had loved life so much, enjoyed every second. To have died so young and under such tragic circumstances was such a waste, Megan thought sadly.

When the short service ended and they emerged from the cool darkness of the chapel into the brilliant sunlight once again, Megan was astonished by the mountain of flowers banked up outside.

Sprays, crosses, and wreaths bearing fond messages of farewell, confirmed how popular Lynn had been. One wreath of pure white flowers seemed to stand out from all the others. Curious to see who it was from, Megan bent down to read the card and was taken aback when she read the words *Walker's Shipping Company*. As far as she knew there had been no collection which meant the wreath could only have been sent by Mr Walker himself.

As she stood up, Megan saw her father was watching her closely, his mouth grim, his eyes hostile, and a ripple of unease ran through her. She turned away quickly, wondering what he was thinking.

In their initial reports of the accident, the local newspapers had made quite a feature of the fact that Flash was also Miles Walker and that Lynn's father was employed by Walker's.

Eager to make as much as they could of such a story, reporters had called at the house, wanting to interview members of the family. Robert had dealt with them, politely but firmly, and sent them on their way.

Now Megan was worried in case it was all revived with the news of Lynn's death. Her parents had been through enough; further speculation and scandal would be intolerable.

'I shouldn't think there's much chance of them showing any further interest,' Robert assured her when she voiced her concern to him. 'The accident is yesterday's news. If Lynn had died right away then they might have built it up. Now she's merely another statistic,' he added bitterly.

The accident had brought them closer together. Robert was such a tower of strength that she automatically turned to him with her problems. Nothing was ever too much trouble for him and, because he was less emotionally influenced by what had happened, he was able to see things more logically.

He had also been a stalwart support to her father through the crisis. Often when her father left the house in the morning he looked like a man sleep-walking, and certainly in no fit state to be behind the wheel of a lorry. Megan suspected that it had been Robert who had undertaken most of the driving over the past months.

The days when she and her father had been close and confided in each other were no more. Sometimes he was so wrapped up in his own thoughts that he didn't even reply when she spoke to him. He rarely mentioned Lynn and Megan hesitated to do so in case it distressed him further.

The person most severely affected by all that had happened was Kathy Williams. Drained of colour and vitality, she looked an old woman. Megan was so worried about her that she sought advice from the doctor. He prescribed a tonic and suggested that Kathy might benefit from a holiday.

'Your mother needs a complete change so that she can distance herself from what has happened,' he told Megan. 'She won't improve while she's clinging to her memories, reliving the accident and your sister's last days.'

'Perhaps if I took Mam on a visit to Beddgelert it might do her good,' Megan suggested after she had told her father what the doctor had said.

'Nonsense! She hated the place as you well know,' he said wearily. 'It was the reason we came here to live!'

Megan was about to argue that what he said was only partially true. It hadn't been the sole reason for their move but she realised it wasn't the time to point that out.

'Why don't you take Mam away for a holiday, then, just the two of you?' she suggested.

'Holiday!' His scornful tone made it sound sinful.

'Think of it as a cure for her,' Megan persisted. 'Go over to the Isle of Man, or to London. Mam used to love shops so perhaps London is the answer.'

'All that would be doing is changing one city for another,' he muttered scathingly.

Megan persisted so consistently that finally Watkin agreed to talk it over with his wife, but Kathy turned all his suggestions down and steadfastly refused to consider a holiday.

'I want to stay here with Lynn,' she said firmly. 'As long as I am in this house she's close to me. Whenever I can touch her things I can feel her here beside me.'

'That's morbid, our mam, and you know it,' Megan told her exasperatedly. 'It would do you both good to get away for a few days,' she pleaded. 'While you're gone I'll turn out Lynn's room and get rid of her things . . .'

For the first time since the accident, her mother seemed to come alive. Eyes blazing, her voice strident, she turned on Megan, upbraiding her for her lack of feeling.

'You never did have any time for Lynn,' she railed. 'Now you want to wipe out all my memories of her. I won't let you do it, though. You're not to touch a single thing of hers, not one! Her room is to stay as it is . . . exactly as she left it. You're not to go in there. Do you understand?'

The row ended with Megan being the one in tears. Not even Watkin could calm Kathy down. She was incensed by the idea of Megan tidying away Lynn's belongings.

From then on Lynn's room and everything in it became like a shrine that Kathy dusted and polished every day.

Megan felt mortified, even when Robert pointed out that the altercation had been beneficial.

'Now she is back in the real world she will come

to terms with her grief and gradually accept the fact that Lynn is gone,' he reassured Megan.

They were sitting in Robert's car on New Brighton promenade, watching the brilliance of an August sunset. It had been a baking hot day and they were enjoying the cool breeze that swept in from the Irish Sea.

'That's not your only problem, though, is it, Megan?' he said gently, reaching out and taking her hand.

'No!' She sighed and shot a quick sideways glance at him and was relieved to find he was staring out to sea.

'What else is wrong?'

'Mr Walker's attitude. He seems distant. I think that perhaps he blames me for the accident!'

'That's ridiculous.' Robert frowned. 'How could it have had anything to do with you?'

Megan remained silent, searching for the right words to explain the predicament she found herself in.

'Do you mean because Lynn was your sister he might be thinking you were the one who introduced her to Miles?'

'No, it was something that happened immediately before the accident.' She hesitated, wondering if she should tell Robert, yet knowing she had to confide in someone since it had prayed on her mind ever since.

'Go on.' Robert didn't look round, but his hand squeezed hers reassuringly.

'You remember the day it happened . . . You met me coming out of the hospital. I didn't know anything about Lynn then, only that Miles had been in an accident. The reason I was so upset was because less than an hour before it happened Miles and I had a terrible row. He'd slammed out of the office in a violent temper. When the phone call came to say he had been in an accident I felt I was to blame. That was why I went to the hospital.'

'Go on.'

'When I saw Miles lying there, all wired up to tubes and drips and things, and a cage over the lower part of the bed, I went to pieces. I didn't realise there was anyone else in the room.'

The hand covering hers tightened but he said nothing.

Megan took a deep breath. 'Mrs Walker was sitting on the far side of the bed, hidden by all the pulleys and things so I didn't notice she was there. She made some very cutting remarks and more or less ordered me to leave.'

'And you think Mrs Walker may have mentioned your visit to see Miles to her husband?'

'Well, he's certainly very off-hand with me these days.'

'He could be feeling uncomfortable knowing that Miles was responsible for your sister's death,' Robert told her quietly.

She gave him a startled look. 'I hadn't thought of that!' She gave a relieved smile. 'Thanks, Robert! You've been such a tower of strength over these last few weeks,' she added gratefully.

'Glad to have been of service,' he told her with a humourless smile, releasing her hand.

'It's going to take time for us all to forget what

has happened,' said Megan. 'I miss Lynn so very much. It feels as if nothing will ever be quite the same again.'

'And how about things between you and Miles?' demanded Robert abruptly.

'I haven't spoken to him since the accident.'

'On purpose?'

'We seem to have been avoiding each other.' She shrugged despairingly. 'I don't know what to say and I don't suppose he does, either.'

'Give it time!' He stared ahead into the golden sunset, a glazed look of hopelessness in his eyes. Miles Walker had so much to answer for, he thought bitterly.

'Oh Robert, I'm so miserable!'

Suddenly her defences crumbled. She had refused to give way to tears but now they rolled unchecked down her cheeks, her shoulders heaving as huge sobs engulfed her.

Robert gathered her into his arms as if she was a small child. Rocking her, crooning words of comfort, gently stroking her dark hair.

He wanted to cry with her. Not because of Miles, or Lynn, but because she was so blind to the love he had to offer her. He was ready to protect her from the world, if only she would give him the chance.

He was still cradling her in his arms when the sun dipped into the sea and twilight gave way to velvety darkness. Stars sprinkled the skyline. Out at the Bar a ship that had been lying at anchor, waiting for the tide to turn, embarked on a new journey.

Megan had dried her tears but was still leaning against him, her head resting on his chest so intimately that he was finding her presence disturbing. Her perfume, the softness of her body pressing against him, were rousing his senses to a pitch where self-control was becoming increasingly difficult.

'I love you, Megan. I want you so much, my darling.' He breathed the words into the scented sweetness of her hair, longing to say them louder, but he knew it was not the right time to do so.

He must go on being patient. At the moment, if he declared his feelings, she would probably run like a scared rabbit.

Chapter Twenty-one

Megan found it was impossible to cut Miles out of her thoughts. Lynn's death had made her feel much more vulnerable. The hard outer shell she had intended to build as a barrier between them, so that she could concentrate on her career and forget all about him, simply crumbled away.

Remembering every detail of her bitter quarrel with Miles, she dreaded the thought of their first meeting when he came back to work again. Yet she was impatient for him to return to the office because there were so many questions to be answered.

His relationship with Lynn puzzled her. She was determined to find out whether he had known that they were sisters and had been deliberately two-timing them both.

Simon Gregson, a thin, sallow man in his early thirties, with short spiky hair and light-hazel eyes behind pebble glasses, had been taken on to assist Bob Donovan at the dockside. Whenever he came into the office to report to Stanley Newbold, Megan's spirits would sink, knowing it meant that Miles had still not returned to work.

It was January 1928 before Miles returned to work and when he did his position in the firm changed. Now that he had managerial qualifications he no longer worked on the dockside but in the office as assistant to his father.

Megan found it embarrassing the first time she was called in to take dictation and found them closeted together. She had expected Miles to look thin and haggard. Instead, he was deeply tanned, and when she learned that he had been recuperating in the south of Spain she felt annoyed and angry.

While she had spent sleepless nights worrying about his injuries he had been sunning himself on a beach, she thought bitterly.

His manner was even more brusque than before and he was adept at avoiding her. Whether this was because of guilt over the accident, or because he had been two-timing her, Megan couldn't be sure.

As the weeks passed and he made no attempt to clear the air she despaired of how to handle things and turned to Robert for advice.

It was a Sunday afternoon in late March and they were sitting in Robert's car at New Brighton. The weather was unexpectedly warm and King's Parade promenade was packed with people enjoying the sunshine.

Everyone looked so contented and happy as they strolled along, laughing and chatting, couples holding hands, others with dogs or children, that it made her feel isolated. The need to share her problem was suddenly overwhelming.

Robert listened gravely as she spewed out her fears, doubts and worries into untidy little heaps as though she was emptying a dirty clothes basket ready for the wash. When she had finished, she felt drained.

'Let's walk along the shore,' he suggested, heading towards a flight of concrete steps. 'It might be cooler there.'

The receding tide had left the sand damp and dappled and for a while they walked in silence towards the sandhills at Leasowe.

'Why have you suddenly decided to tell me all this?' Robert asked as they turned and began to walk back to where his car was parked.

'I hoped it might help clear my mind,' she answered. 'I'm so confused! I thought if I told you I might see my way out of the mess I seem to be in.'

'You mean over Miles?'

'That's right. I should be hating him for double-crossing Lynn and me, as well as over the accident, and yet I can't.'

'Are you telling me that your feelings for him are still the same?' he asked incredulously.

'I still love him,' she whispered, miserably.

'You must be crazy, Megan! I warned you once before that you were wasting your time. He will never marry you, you know that. But perhaps that doesn't matter,' he added scathingly.

'Oh, it does! I wouldn't settle for anything else,' she added, blushing furiously as she realised how naive she sounded.

'Then forget him!'

'I can't! I've tried to do so, but it's impossible.'

'Rubbish!'

'You don't really understand, do you, Robert?'

He didn't answer. He knew only too well how impossible it was to put someone from your mind. He had been trying to do so ever since the first moment he had met Megan. Night and day, her sweetness invaded his mind, tormenting him with desire. He wanted to hold her, to taste the soft fullness of her lips, to see love for him shining from her dark eyes.

Megan was so different from her sister. Lynn had probably been street-wise from the cradle. She had loved to charm, to lead a man on, to tease with a lift of her eyebrows. He had liked Lynn, enjoyed her company and been able to laugh off her flirtatious invitations.

Megan was from a different mould and watching her succumb to Miles Walker's charms had not been easy, knowing Miles' reputation as he did.

Miles' exploits at art school and his behaviour at the Stork Club were common knowledge among the men who worked on the docks as well as some of the employees at Walker's.

His immediate reaction when he had heard about the accident had been one of guilt. If he had spoken out about the motorbike and the clothes hidden at the back of one of the warehouses, then it might never have happened. The knowledge still nagged him even though he realised it was too late to change events.

Robert's mouth tightened. 'You'd better talk to Miles about this,' he told her uneasily, knowing he was being evasive. 'You certainly can't spend the rest of your life moping after him . . . not if he doesn't want you,' he added harshly.

He looked away, unable to bear the pain that shadowed her face as she struggled to control her feelings. He stuffed his hands deep in his pockets as he heard her sharp intake of breath. He wanted to hold her, to protect her from Miles Walker and from herself.

His blood raced with desire. To remain silent and watch her torment herself over her feelings for Miles was sheer hell. Yet he was afraid to speak out and tell her what was in his mind in case she turned from him completely. As things stood, he thought glumly, at least she confided in him.

I shouldn't have asked him, I've only made him angry, Megan thought miserably as she struggled to keep up with Robert's strides. No one, not even Robert, seemed to understand how she felt. He was right, of course, the time had come to stop prevaricating and face up to Miles.

When she walked into Miles' office first thing the next morning, he tried to hide his surprise. He eyed her uneasily as she closed the door and walked towards his desk.

'I have an appointment in half an hour,' he pronounced, glancing at his watch.

'It's not until eleven o'clock. I checked,' she told him unsmilingly. 'I want to clear the air, Miles.'

She had gone over what she was going to say so many times that the words came out in a well-rehearsed rush. 'About us . . . Lynn . . . the future . . .' Her nerve deserted her; she stumbled over the words, her voice breaking.

As he came round to her side of the desk and placed his hands on her shoulders, her resolve to be firm weakened and she felt the mounting pressure of tears.

His hands dropped to his sides. Swiftly he moved over to the door and locked it. 'Come on, then, tell me what's on your mind,' he invited.

'You . . . you never told me you knew my sister . . .'

He frowned. 'It was hardly likely that I would connect a fair-haired, round-faced giggler like Lynn with someone as dark and solemn as you, Megan.'

'Her name was Williams . . . the same as mine.'

'I didn't know that for ages. To me she was just Lynn. The only thing that could possibly have linked you was that you both had Welsh accents. It was only when she told me where her sister worked that it dawned on me that you were related.'

'Yet you said nothing to either of us,' accused Megan.

'Dating both of you seemed a bit of a laugh at the time.' He shrugged helplessly. 'Lynn knew me as Flash, and she never asked any questions about where I worked, so I never told her,' he admitted. 'She was good fun. Neither of us took the other seriously,' he protested.

'She was crazy about you!'

'As far as I was concerned she was just another Judy who was free and easy with her favours.'

'How dare you! She wasn't like that!' defended Megan angrily. 'Properly brought up was our Lynn. We both were!'

'Which only proves how little you knew your sister, then,' Miles said disparagingly. 'She was the opposite to you, a little raver, in fact. That's why, when I realised you were sisters, I could never understand why you were so prudish.'

Megan was so angry she found it impossible to reply. A panorama of events that had happened since she'd first met Miles flashed through her mind. She felt sickened by her own gullibility. Their secretive meetings; his evasive manner when he didn't turn up; his insistence after their first couple of meetings that they musn't be seen together in case his father found out and sacked her.

She had thought that was the reason he'd avoided taking her to the Stork Club or the Copper Kettle. Instead, it was because he didn't want Lynn to see them together!

Some of the things Lynn had said about Flash skimmed through her mind. If only she'd listened. Had she done so it would have been obvious that Flash and Miles were one and the same.

But would it? It was so easy to draw conclusions when you knew the answer, she reflected miserably. She had long suspected that Miles might have another girlfriend, but it would never have dawned on her that it could be her own sister.

Hearing Lynn described so scathingly as a 'raver' and a 'free and easy Judy' was devastating. Lynn hadn't been like that at all. She had the chameleon-like ability to adapt to her surroundings and could charm the birds off the trees if the occasion demanded. And Miles had taken advantage of the fact that she was just a precocious youngster.

'How did you come to be with her that day . . .

on your motorbike . . . You'd only just left me?'

'I'd gone to the Stork Club after that stupid row with you. Lynn was there. We hadn't seen each other for ages. She teased me about having a secret lover hidden away somewhere. I almost told her about the row I'd just had with you . . . I didn't, though. We were laughing and joking when all of a sudden she started panicking about being late getting back to work so I gave her a lift.'

'And you were showing off!'

'No. We were going pretty fast . . . The roads were wet . . . We skidded. You know the rest. It was an accident, a dreadful accident, but it wasn't my fault.'

The note of impatience in his voice made her uneasy.

'In that case, why have you been avoiding me ever since you came back to work?'

'I would have thought that was obvious! With everyone holding me responsible for what happened I thought you probably did as well.'

'I've never accused you. I've never had the chance,' she said bitterly. 'You've avoided me ever since you came out of hospital. Have you never wondered how I felt? Didn't you think you owed me some sort of explanation?'

He placed a hand placatingly on her arm. 'Don't forget I was injured too, Megan!'

She felt herself weakening as memories of him lying unconscious in the hospital bed attached to tubes and drips came flooding back. She struggled against the overpowering feeling of surrender that threatened to engulf her, determined to be strong and find out exactly what his intentions towards her were.

'Leave me alone, Miles.' Determinedly she pushed his hand away, refusing to be fobbed off by his persuasive charm. 'I must settle things between us. I can't go on living with this uncertainty . . .'

'Uncertainty! That's no way to describe my feelings for you,' he exclaimed. 'You know how I feel about you! I thought I was being considerate by keeping away from you. I knew how much you must be grieving about your sister and I didn't want to do anything that might make things worse for you.'

There was no guile at all in the blue eyes that looked deeply into hers and Megan felt ashamed that she should have so misunderstood his intentions.

'I'm sorry,' she whispered. 'It's just that I love you so much, Miles.'

'I know.' Tenderly, he gathered her into his arms. 'And you know how I feel . . .' His words faded as his mouth covered hers in a long, lingering kiss.

'I'm going to let you into a family secret,' he murmured as he released her. 'My father has promised to make me a director of the company. Until that's settled I daren't risk doing anything that might make him change his mind!'

'Surely that doesn't mean you can't be seen speaking to me? Or is that why you've been so . . . so . . . off-hand!'

His mouth captured hers, silencing her questions, stirring her emotions, proving beyond doubt that his feelings for her burned like a raging fire, stronger than it had ever been.

'Come on, I don't have to spell it out for you,' Miles whispered huskily. 'Play it my way. I know what I'm doing.' He kissed her again, an eager, hungry kiss that set her pulses racing, her whole body aflame.

'You will remember that what I've just told you must remain a secret?' he whispered as he lifted his mouth from hers. His face hovered so tanta-lisingly close that she found herself reaching up to pull his head down until their lips met again.

'Now, if I'm to keep that appointment I must fly. Not a word to anyone,' he warned. 'For the moment, if I sometimes seem "off-hand" as you put it, play along with me. Remember it's only a precautionary measure until I'm made a director.'

Chapter Twenty-two

It was like taking a step back in time, Megan reflected as she recalled her excitement a year earlier when she'd first planned to go on holiday to Beddgelert. Then, the prospect of driving to Wales alone had delighted her. Now, the fact that she was not telling her parents the complete truth about where she would be staying perturbed her. She wasn't given to lying and the subterfuge worried her.

'I ought to tell them, they're worried as it is about me going on my own,' she had argued with Miles. 'They won't tell anyone else.'

'No!' Miles remained adamant. He still refused to let her tell her parents, or anyone else, about their unofficial engagement and he certainly didn't want it leaked that they were planning on spending a weekend together in Mostyn.

Megan was also faced with the problem of explaining to Jennie why she would be leaving Beddgelert first thing on Thursday morning. She had told her she would be staying for a week so Jennie was bound to think it odd that she wanted to go home early, even if she made the excuse that she was worried about leaving her mother on her own for too long.

She brought her car round to the front door and as her father stowed her suitcase into it she felt guilty that she was going off enjoying herself when her mother still looked so pale and washed out.

'It's you and Mam who should be going on holiday, not me,' she told him.

'I know that as well as you do, girl,' said Watkin with a sigh. 'Your mam doesn't want to leave the house. She still hasn't got over Lynn's death. I sometimes wonder if she ever will. She seems afraid to face the world.'

Megan was well aware that her mother spent several hours each day dusting and tidying the room that had been Lynn's while the rest of the house was neglected. No one else was allowed in Lynn's room.

Megan had taken over the housekeeping while Lynn had been in hospital, and had carried on doing so afterwards, but she now felt it was time her mother took charge again. Even though she was going to be away for a week, she'd not stocked up with groceries hoping that forcing her mother to go shopping would help her to re-adjust. As far as the housework was concerned, it wouldn't matter if that was left for a week. Her father would tidy round each day and she could give the place a thorough clean when she got back.

As she crossed the bridge at Queen's Ferry that took her over the border into Wales, she felt a sense of freedom. It was a crystal clear spring day with the sun bathing the hillsides in a rich golden light. Her spirits rose at the sight of the towering mountains. She had missed them so much. As she neared her destination, it seemed that the air was sweeter and the colours more pronounced.

She stopped at Betws-y-coed and went in search of a café. The holiday season had barely started so very few of them were open. She remembered the last time she had been there was with Lynn and her mother. She could almost sense their presence as she recalled how the three of them had strolled along the main street without a care in the world.

Snowdon was outlined majestically against the blue sky as she drove towards Capel Curig, its topmost peak wreathed in feathery, scudding clouds. Then she was on the last stretch of her journey, down into Beddgelert.

Snowdon was forgotten as Moel Hebog came into view. It was her first glimpse of it for three years and there was a sudden tightness in her throat. In a state of euphoria, she drove over the stone bridge that would take her up the hill and right past the cottage where she had lived as a child.

It felt like coming home.

Jennie greeted her with hugs and kisses. She seemed to Megan's eyes to be bigger than ever, taller as well as plumper. She'd had her gingerish-brown hair shingled and it was now a fuzz that emphasised her round face.

'There's posh you look, Megan! And your own car! *Duw* I thought that was just a story to make me feel jealous. Not that I was, mind you, since I can't drive anyway.'

They laughed together, bubbling over with snippets of news, as Jennie carried Megan's suitcase up to the bedroom under the cottage eaves where she was to sleep.

'There's an old owl comes onto the sill each night. I hope its noisy hooting won't frighten you, *cariad*,' Jennie warned her. 'My da talks about shooting it, but Mam says leave it be because it's lucky. You know what she's like! Nearly as superstitious as Gwyneth.'

'How is Gwyneth?'

'She's fine, ever so pleased about you coming. I think she's a bit put out, mind, at you staying here with me. She said we ought to split your visit so that you spent three nights at my place and three nights with her.'

'Look, Jennie, I may as well tell you right away, I . . . I won't be staying the whole week,' Megan said awkwardly.

'No? And why is that, then?'

'I . . . I promised to look in on someone on the way back. I said I'd be there sometime Thursday afternoon. I hope that's not putting you out . . .'

Jennie's plump face clouded. 'No, no of course not. I had counted on you being here all week, though. Got something special planned for Friday night, see.'

'Oh!' Megan flinched from her friend's gaze. 'I'm sorry about that.'

'Perhaps we can change things round a bit.' Jennie smiled generously. 'Come on, we'd better get downstairs. Mam has made a batch of bakestones. She said you've probably not had any since you've been in England.'

'You make it sound like a foreign country,' laughed Megan.

'Well, that's because it is, in a way. I expect

you'll find it quiet here after Liverpool. Not much happens. Except to Gwyneth, of course.'

'Oh?'

'Well, now, don't think I'm trying to steal her thunder,' Jennie said, her soft dark eyes full of concern, 'but I must warn you that Gwyneth is engaged.'

'Terrific. Anyone I know?'

'Well, yes . . . that's why I'm telling you.' Jennie bit her lower lip, avoiding Megan's eyes. 'She's engaged to Ifan Jenkins. We didn't want you to get a shock, like, seeing as how you were once sweet on him.'

'That was a long time ago,' Megan said softly. 'Thank you for telling me, though.'

It was the first of many indications of the way they had grown apart. She quickly found that many of the things Jennie and Gwyneth had planned to do, and which she would have found exciting at one time, now seemed tame and no longer of any interest to her.

I've changed, she thought, remembering the countless times since she'd moved to Liverpool when she had longed for the tranquillity of Beddgelert. Now, after her initial delight at seeing familiar faces and places, she found it much too quiet.

Stepping back in time made her restless. At least that was what she told herself, but deep inside she knew it was because she couldn't wait for the second part of her holiday to begin.

Jennie and Gwyneth were a good audience. They listened wide eyed to Megan's account of her new life. They sympathised about the awful place in

Liverpool and seemed delighted by her account of the pleasant house they'd moved to in Wallasey. They sighed with envy when she told them about the wonderful shops in Liverpool and the delights of living so near to New Brighton and being able to go dancing at the famous Tower Ballroom.

She had written to let them know about the accident, but at first they seemed almost afraid to mention Lynn's name. Once Megan began to talk about her, however, they were avid for every detail, especially about the Stork Club, and they envied Lynn's job at the Copper Kettle.

They talked of nothing else until Megan thought she would scream. By Tuesday night she was so restless that she found herself counting the hours to when it would be time to leave.

On Thursday morning she was dressed, packed and ready to get on the road when Jennie went off to work. She was not due to meet Miles until early evening so she drove to all the places around Beddgelert that she had known as a child. It felt like a pilgrimage; almost as if she wouldn't be coming back.

The sun was shining and, against the light blue sky, Moel Hebog had never looked more impressive. She climbed the rough track that had been her favourite walk with her father. Breathless, she sat down. The thin white scudding clouds that had floated around the peak began to darken; a cutting cold wind brought mist and rain. Shivering, she abandoned her walk and hurried back to her car.

The barren mountains on her left were almost

obscured by the low cloud and heavy drizzle as she drove along the winding road towards Capel Curig. She had forgotten how desolate the area could be when the clouds loomed up from the west bringing driving rain in their wake, and how eerie it felt when low mists obscured Snowdon from view.

The need to get away, to put it all behind her, was so great that she didn't stop until she reached Prestatyn. Then, realising that she was far too early, she parked near the prom and sorted out her suitcase, leaving in it only the things she would need over the next couple of days, bundling up the rest and stowing them in the boot.

As she handled the tissue-wrapped, filmy nightdress and silky lingerie she had bought especially for the occasion she felt like a bride going on honeymoon.

It was still only mid-afternoon so to pass the time she went into a café. She was too nervous to eat, but she drank two cups of coffee and then decided to walk along the shore.

The tide was so far out that it was just a grey strip on the horizon. The thin cutting wind was not confined to the mountains, it was here as well, robbing the sun of its heat.

She trudged along, studying her footprints in the damp sand, keeping her mind a blank, refusing to acknowledge that what she was about to do was wrong for so many reasons.

She had come to terms with the moral issue. She'd convinced herself that if Miles hadn't insisted their engagement must be kept secret until his father had signed the papers confirming his directorship, they could have announced it long before now.

What still worried her, though, was what her parents were going to think about it all. Her mother still held Miles responsible for Lynn's death and became enraged whenever his name was mentioned. No matter how hard she tried to explain to her how the accident had happened, her mother refused to listen.

In the end she'd given up trying, but she hadn't stopped seeing Miles. It was as if his life was fused with hers. Sometimes she felt so mortified by his treatment that she hated him. When he ignored her, she felt as hurt as if he had stabbed her with a knife.

She was so immersed in her thoughts that it wasn't until the sun began to dip that she became aware of how far she had walked. In a panic, she began to retrace her steps. The sun, now a fiery ball of red, was almost swallowed up by the blue-grey sea, and the skyline was a great smudge of reds and purples.

She drove recklessly from Prestatyn towards Mostyn, following the directions Miles had given her. She knew she was going to be late and was worried in case Miles might think she had changed her mind. What on earth would she do if he had given up waiting and gone back to Wallasey? she wondered.

She reached Mostyn and still hadn't seen a signpost to Tynmorfa, the road leading to the Walkers' house. Panic stricken she turned and drove more slowly back along the road to Prestatyn.

When she finally spotted it she couldn't believe that the narrow sandy lane on the outskirts of the town could possibly be the right one. There was no one around she could ask so she decided the only thing to do was take a chance and see where it led.

With the sea on her right and high sandbanks on the other side she crawled along. The light was fading, and she had almost given up hope when the bungalow belonging to Rhys and Sybil Jones, the couple who looked after the Walkers' place, loomed up out of the dusk.

Her heart raced as she accelerated past it and drove towards the Walkers' house which she could now see in the distance. As her wheels scrunched on the gravel drive, the porch light went on and she could see Miles waiting on the doorstep. When she braked to a stop he came towards her, a black Doberman frantically barking at his side.

'Where the hell did you get to?' he snapped as she wound down the window.

'I'm sorry if I'm late, but I spent too long in Prestatyn. I went for a walk on the shore. I've absolutely crawled all the way from the main road because I couldn't believe that this really was the right place,' she gabbled nervously.

'I did warn you that it was along an unmade lane. Never mind, you're here now. Park a bit closer to the house and come on in. Don't take any notice of Jason,' he added, pulling the dog to one side as she stepped from the car. 'He isn't nearly as savage as he sounds.'

As Miles took her case she patted the dog's

smooth, black coat and let him nuzzle her hand. Then she followed Miles into the house.

'I'm starving,' he said, dumping her case in the hallway and tossing her coat over a chair.

He led the way through to a large kitchen fitted out with oak cupboards and units. In the centre, a round oak table was laid ready for two people.

'Hope you like these,' he said as he took two jacket potatoes from the oven and placed one on each plate. 'Sit down. Help yourself to salad and cheese.'

It wasn't the most romantic start to the evening, Megan decided, but she had to admit the hot meal was very welcome. And it certainly helped to dispel the tension she'd felt building up ever since she had left Beddgelert.

'We can leave these for Sybil Jones to do in the morning,' Miles told her as he stacked their used dishes onto the draining board.

He picked up a tray. 'Come on, we'll take this through into the sitting room.'

He produced a bottle of whisky and insisted that Megan should have some of it with her coffee. The fiery liquid seared her throat and brought tears to her eyes, but it also dispersed the very last traces of the apprehension that had filled her mind ever since she'd left Beddgelert.

'Shoes off, feet up,' Miles instructed, indicating the comfortable settee drawn up in front of the log fire. Tiny bursts of desire bubbled up inside her as he slipped his arm around her, cuddling her close as they watched the flickering firelight. Her rapid breathing betrayed her turbulent emotions when

225

his hands slid down from her shoulders to fondle her breasts and then moved sensuously over the outline of her hip as she lay pressed against him.

Megan shivered expectantly as Miles suddenly stood up and began leading her upstairs to his bedroom.

She had no idea where he'd put her suitcase. All the finery she had packed for their first night was no longer of any importance. All that did matter was that they were alone together.

Their undressing became feverish, clothes discarded like fallen leaves, piled indiscriminately. The passion that now burned between them overcame Megan's modesty.

She had often dreamed of them being naked together; now she gloried in it. With a feeling of ecstasy she ran her hands over his smooth, tanned flesh.

She shuddered and gave a moan of joy as his lips encompassed one of her erect nipples. As her body arched, his responded. A hot hardness pressing against her thighs sent a shiver of burning anticipation through her. There was no holding back now; she wanted him: she was ready to give herself utterly and completely.

As their bodies melded, strange heats and a stab of searing pain flared inside her, leaving her dazed by their intensity. Moments later, she knew a fulfilment that made the waiting all the more worthwhile.

Utterly spent, his groan of exhaustion was sweet music to Megan's ears. She cradled his head on her breast as they both drifted into a contented sleep.

She woke to the harsh screech of gulls, just as dawn was fingering the curtains, aware that she was quite naked.

Had it been a dream?

She turned and saw Miles' dark head on the pillow beside her and the memory of all that had happened the night before came flooding back.

She stretched out a hand and traced the firm outline of his profile. The square chin, the broad, tanned brow. She ran her fingers through his dark wavy hair and then drew back, startled, when she saw he was watching her through half-closed lids.

Before she could speak he grabbed her, pulling her body across his. His blue eyes gleamed as his hands cupped her buttocks, pressing her against him, his need urgent.

'Quick,' he breathed. 'Before Mrs Jones catches us!'

They made love again before breakfast. She wondered how he was going to explain her being there to the housekeeper, but when Sybil Jones arrived she accepted Megan's presence without question. Megan felt relieved and wondered if perhaps Miles had told her in confidence about their engagement.

'I'll leave a chicken casserole in the oven for your evening meal. And you can have fresh fruit or biscuits and cheese to follow, if that's all right.'

'That will do fine,' Miles told her.

The rest of their time together was like an extended dream. They visited Conway, explored the Castle and walked the length of the medieval walls before returning to Mostyn, to their casserole and another night of erotic love-making.

Miles was already dressed when she woke next morning. As they ate breakfast he seemed uneasy.

Jason's frenzied barking sent him rushing to the window.

'It's only Rhys Jones,' he revealed in relief.

'Who did you think it might be?'

'My parents are coming for the weekend. They don't usually arrive before midday, but they could be here early, you can never tell.'

The spell was broken.

Miles' goodbye kiss was a perfunctory peck on her cheek. His anxiety for her to be on her way was so obvious that Megan felt shocked. Too choked to say anything, she made her way to her car feeling belittled and bitterly hurt.

Chapter Twenty-three

Megan had been away for four days before Kathy Williams accepted the fact that unless she went and did some shopping there would be nothing to put on the table when Watkin came home from work that night.

The previous evening she'd served up beans on toast and expected Watkin to complain, but he said nothing at all, simply cleared his plate in silence then commented, 'You'd better do some shopping or we'll have no food in the house over the weekend!'

'Megan can do it when she gets home,' Kathy replied sullenly.

'Don't talk daft!' growled Watkin. 'We don't know what time she'll be back and after driving all the way from North Wales she won't want to go out shopping for food, now will she?'

'I don't want to go out shopping for food, either,' Kathy retorted. 'Why couldn't she have seen to things before she went gadding off on holiday?'

'Come on, be fair now. Megan's not responsible for running the house, now is she?'

'Who is then?'

'You are, of course,' he told her gently.

Kathy looked at him blankly, then her face clouded and tears glistened. 'It mattered when I had little Lynn to look after. She needed me.' She gave a sigh that ended in a shudder.

'You've still got me and Megan to look after,' Watkin told her, his voice a little unsteady.

'Megan!' She stiffened. 'Megan's not here! Anyway, she doesn't need me to look after her.'

'The girl needed a break, Kathy,' Watkin told her reproachfully. 'She's waited a long time for this little holiday so don't begrudge her the chance to see her friends at Beddgelert.'

'She should be here when I need her,' argued Kathy dully.

'She's been at your beck and call for months now, *cariad*. High time you started to fend for yourself.'

'That's right, take her part . . . but then you always did. Never put yourself out for our Lynn, though, did you?'

'I treated both of them the same.'

'Nonsense! Did you buy our Lynn a motorcar the same as you did Megan? No!' She rushed on, not giving him a chance to reply, 'If Lynn had had a car like our Megan then she wouldn't have needed to cadge a lift on a motorbike and she'd still be alive.'

'You're talking utter rubbish,' growled Watkin.

'I'm not and you know it,' argued Kathy, her eyes glittering, her mouth tight. 'You always treated Megan differently to our Lynn. Even when we lived in Beddgelert you'd go off up that old mountain with Megan, but never once did you take little Lynn along with you.'

'And with good reason! Lynn hated walking, that's why.'

'Lynn was a good little walker. She'd walk round the shops with me all day . . .'

'She hated walking along country lanes. She didn't enjoy watching the fish swimming in the Glaslyn, or the eagles soaring on the up-currents around Moel Hebog.'

'Lynn had more go in her than Megan, that's why. She didn't spend her time mooning around, she lived life to the full . . . what she had of it,' choked out Kathy, dabbing her eyes.

'Look, *cariad*,' Watkin said placing a hand on his wife's shoulder, 'you've got to try and come to terms with what's happened. Go and do some shopping, go for a walk, meet people . . . see something of what goes on outside these four walls.'

'It's easy for you to talk,' Kathy replied, sniffing and shrugging his hand away. 'You have your precious work to occupy your mind. I'm left here on my own all day, surrounded by memories. Sometimes it's as if Lynn's right here; her voice is all around me . . . I couldn't forget about her if I wanted to.'

After Watkin left for work Kathy stood staring out of the window. She knew he was right. She'd have to make herself go out. Perhaps she'd walk to the shops in Liscard.

She turned from the window and buried her face in her hands. It was no good. She wasn't ready to face people yet. She couldn't stand the thought of people asking her how she was, knowing they were remembering the accident and trying to avoid mentioning Lynn's name. Yet she couldn't stay in the house for ever.

A walk in Central Park might be the answer, she decided. If she met anyone she knew she'd keep on walking and not give them the chance to ask questions about Lynn.

Three times Kathy put on her coat. Once she even opened the front door and stepped outside. Then her courage deserted her and she rushed back indoors.

There was nothing at all for Watkin's supper when he came home from work. 'I did try,' she told him. 'Tomorrow . . . I promise I'll go to the shops.'

'Fish and chips for us both tonight, is it *cariad*?' he said with forced cheerfulness. 'Put the kettle on and cut some bread and butter, while I go and fetch them.'

'There's no bread left, Watkin.'

'I'll get some extra chips and a portion of peas.'

Breakfast for them both next morning was a cup of black tea.

'Could you pick up some bread and a pint of milk and a pound of sausages on your way home?' Kathy asked.

'No! Remember your promise last night? Today you definitely go to the shops, so no more excuses. I'll expect to find a meal waiting when I get in tonight.'

'I sometimes wonder if I'm handling this situation in the right way,' Watkin confided to Robert later on that morning as they travelled towards Manchester with a heavily loaded lorry.

'In what way?'

'Forcing Kathy to go out.'

'Well, she's got to face the world sometime,' Robert commented, frowning.

'I know that but forcing her makes me seem so heartless, somehow. She's so wrapped up in her memories that half the time she doesn't even know what time of day it is.'

'What does Megan have to say about it? She's the one who has been doing the shopping, cleaning and most of the cooking, ever since the accident.'

'Megan thinks that it's high time her mam took over again. That's why she didn't stock up before she went on holiday. She thought that once the cupboard was bare her mam would pull herself together and go shopping.'

'Maybe she will. Perhaps today will be the turning point. If you say there's no bread or anything else in the house she won't be able to get herself a meal, will she?'

'I hope you're right. The trouble is, food doesn't seem to worry her . . .'

'When did you say Megan would be back from North Wales?' Robert asked. He kept his eyes glued to the road ahead but Watkin was aware of the way his partner's jaw tightened.

'Sometime tomorrow . . . She didn't say what time, only that she'd come back on Saturday because she wanted a day at home to get herself organised before going back to work on Monday.'

'A bit tough on her if the first thing she has to do when she gets back is to go shopping for food, isn't it?' questioned Robert.

'That's what I said to Kathy,' agreed Watkin. 'She doesn't see it like that . . . she thinks Megan should have stayed at home and looked after things.' He sighed. 'Where will it all end?'

Robert frowned heavily. It worried him to learn that Megan was being put on by her mother. He'd always noticed that Kathy favoured Lynn over Megan, but he realised that was often the way in families. Kathy and Lynn shared a similar outlook on life, a love of clothes, but Megan was quieter, deeper, more thoughtful and preferred reading to dancing. Not that Megan was dull. Far from it, he thought, remembering with keen pleasure the arguments and discussions they'd had over everything from religion to politics. He'd gone out of his way to win her affection and it both puzzled and grieved him that he had been so unsuccessful.

'I wonder if I ought to pick up some bread and stuff,' muttered Watkin uneasily as he climbed back into the cab and took the wheel for the return journey after they'd unloaded.

'If you give in now Kathy will never go out of the house or get back into the swing of things,' warned Robert.

'But it's Saturday tomorrow . . .'

'Well, if she hasn't been shopping today you can do it tomorrow afternoon. Maybe that would be best all round. If you take Kathy with you, that might give her the confidence to go out on her own next week.'

Megan was still feeling despondent over the way she and Miles had parted when she reached home. Kathy and Watkin were eating their midday meal when she walked in.

'So you're back,' commented Kathy harshly. 'I thought you'd be making the most of it and staying another night.'

'I told you I'd be home on Saturday,' murmured Megan as she kissed her mother on the cheek.

'You also told us you were going to Beddgelert,' snapped Kathy.

'Kathy! That will do. Listen to what Megan has to say before making any judgement.'

'Judgement! What are you both on about?'

'Sit down, girl, and get your breath back.'

'No! Let's have it out now,' Kathy interrupted, her eyes hard and accusing. 'It's no good you denying it, Megan,' she said harshly. 'Beryl Parsons from next door saw you . . . in Conway . . . with Miles Walker!' Her voice broke as tears cascaded down her cheeks. 'How could you, Megan? How could you go away with him after he caused our Lynn's death?'

'No, Mam!' Megan knelt beside her mother's chair, clasping her round the waist, one hand stroking her bowed head. 'That's not true . . .'

'He was riding the motorbike she was on, wasn't he?'

'Well, yes, she was on the pillion, but the accident wasn't Miles' fault. It had been raining and the roads were slippery. He braked and skidded . . . you must try and understand . . .'

'What is there to understand? It was his bike . . . he killed her! Nothing you or anyone else says will alter the facts.'

'Mam! She was at the Stork Club and had to get back to work and Miles offered her a lift.'

'How could you even speak to him after what happened?' persisted her mother.

'I love him, Mam,' Megan told her quietly.

'Love him!' Kathy almost choked with anger. 'He was two-timing you with your own sister! And then to go away with him!'

'Is it true, Megan? Have you been away with Miles Walker?' asked Watkin in a shocked voice.

'Of course she has. Didn't I tell you?' shrieked Kathy. 'Look at her face, there's guilt written all over it.'

'So you never went to Beddgelert.'

'Yes, I did . . .'

'And then sneaked off to be with Miles Walker! Fooled us into believing you were going to see your friend Jennie and instead you spent the time with that blackguard.'

'I did stay with Jennie.'

'For how long? One night, two nights . . .'

'I was there until Thursday.'

'And then sneaked off to meet him! You'd got it all planned out! Beddgelert indeed! You certainly pulled the wool over our eyes, all right.'

'You've got it all wrong, Mam.'

'If Mrs Parsons from next door hadn't spotted you in Conway you'd never have told us a word about it, would you?'

Megan shrugged helplessly, biting back the hot words of protest, knowing that she could never make either of them understand.

The dismay on her father's face hurt far more than her mother's accusations. She hated to see him so upset. She wished she'd told him what her plans were before she'd set out, but would he have understood or would he have tried to dissuade her? At that moment she wished she had told him and that he had stopped her and saved her from such a sense of disillusionment.

While she had been with Miles at Tynmorfa everything had seemed so blissful. The hurried way in which he had urged her to leave, however, had soured things and turned what had been a momentous occasion into something underhand and sordid.

It had worried her all the way home. Why was Miles still so reluctant to tell his father that they were seeing each other? Why did their engagement have to be kept a secret? Miles had let her down; he hadn't even bought her a ring.

She was tired of all the pretence, of hiding the truth from her parents and, above all, from Robert when he had been such a good friend to her, though, by mutual consent, they no longer mentioned Miles.

Miles' explanation that he wanted to be sure of being made a director before telling his father that they were going to be married didn't ring true, she decided.

Chapter Twenty-four

Megan listened in stunned silence, a thousand questions buzzing through her head, as Miles told her that his father had suffered a heart attack.

'Take charge of the office until I get there,' he told her, and she was aware of a new edge of authority in his voice.

'If people ask where he is, what shall I tell them?'

'The truth, of course, Miss Williams,' he replied sharply. 'I'll be in later in the morning to deal with things myself,' he added, then rang off abruptly.

It was only when she had replaced the receiver that Megan realised he had addressed her as Miss Williams. Her lips tightened. Was this something else Miles would be using as an excuse to put off telling his family about their engagement? she wondered. It was now over two months since their weekend at Tynmorfa and he still hadn't come out into the open about their relationship.

'We agreed to wait until I had been made a director,' he prevaricated each time she mentioned it.

'Does that matter?' she protested.

'Of course it does! I can't afford to support a wife until that happens.'

Megan bit her lip. She wanted to say they would

have her salary as well to live on, but she was very much afraid that she would not be able to count on it for much longer.

Telling Miles that she was pregnant was something else that had to be confronted as soon as possible, but she didn't feel she could tell him now, not when he was faced with this new problem. She didn't want him to feel she was trying to blackmail him into marrying her.

The next few weeks were chaotic. Miles was duly appointed director, but he spent very little time in the office. There were constant visits to the solicitors to sign papers and documents, interspersed with visits to the private nursing home where Mr Walker was recuperating.

Although Martin Walker had been warned that he must rest, he insisted on being consulted about everything that was going on. Megan visited each day, taking along letters and ledgers. She sometimes thought it would have been easier if she'd taken her typewriter as well and dealt with correspondence on the spot.

The effects of the miners' strike a couple of years earlier was affecting the shipments they handled. Like a stone dropped into a pool, the ripples had spread. Trade slumped and their figures had never looked worse.

Convinced that the reason schedules were being lost was due to Miles' lack of experience, Martin Walker insisted on coming into the office for a few hours each day. Weak and tetchy, he imposed a greater strain on the staff than if he had followed his doctor's advice and stayed away.

In face of this, Megan's own problems seemed insurmountable. Her initial fears that she might be pregnant had been confirmed. She knew she couldn't keep the fact hidden for much longer. She felt desperate knowing that Miles had still not mentioned their engagement to his father.

'I'll tell him as soon as I can,' he promised.

'Why not now?' she persisted.

'And take the risk of my father having another heart attack! What difference are another few weeks going to make?'

Megan didn't answer. She knew she really ought to tell him that she was pregnant but she couldn't bring herself to do so.

'Come on, cheer up. I'll take you out on Saturday night. We'll have a meal in Chester and afterwards we can go to the Odeon.'

Megan was not so easily persuaded. To his surprise, she refused.

'I thought you'd be pleased,' he said with a scowl.

'I might have been if it had been somewhere local.'

'I thought you liked Chester?'

'Come off it, Miles. You picked Chester because it's far enough away that no one is likely to see us together.'

She walked away, her head held high, her eyes blurred with tears. She desperately wanted to go with him but she was no longer prepared to accept things on his terms. Why was he so scared of them being seen together?

*   *   *

'How about coming with us to The Nelson, Megan?' Robert said when as usual he called at their house on Saturday evening to go for a drink with her father.

Megan was about to refuse then changed her mind. Going out for an hour might help to take her mind off her problems.

'All right, if Mam comes along as well,' she agreed with a ghost of a smile.

Her mother looked up at her, startled. She had not had an evening out since Lynn's death and before that her idea of an outing was to go to the pictures.

'Yes, come on, Kathy, it will do you good,' enthused Watkin. He knew it would have been useless for him to have made such a suggestion, but he was delighted that Megan had done so.

'I don't know . . .' Kathy hesitated, looking from one to the other as they waited for her answer.

'If you don't come then neither will Megan,' reasoned Robert, with a conspiratorial wink at Megan.

'Off upstairs and get ready both of you,' urged Watkin. 'Hurry up, we're wasting good drinking time.'

They were all seated in the lounge of The Nelson in Grove Road, happy and relaxed, when Robert dropped his bombshell. They had been discussing the many changes that had taken place at Walker's in recent months and speculating about what the outcome might have been had Mr Walker not made such a rapid recovery from his heart attack.

'I suppose the next big event will be the wedding,' Robert remarked.

Megan felt the colour flooding her face and wondered how on earth he had found out. His next words, however, left her stunned.

'Money marrying money there, all right,' Robert went on.

'Who are we talking about?' asked her father.

'Young Miles, of course. He's marrying Brocklehurst's daughter. With their fleet tied in with Walker's, Miles will probably be a millionaire before he's forty.'

'I didn't know Brocklehurst had a daughter,' Watkin Williams said, taking a long drink from his glass.

'Red-headed girl. A couple of years older than Miles, I'd say. Still, he needs someone to keep him in line.'

'And she's welcome to him, the double-crossing killer,' declared Kathy Williams bitterly. 'Perhaps now you'll believe what a blackguard he is and stay away from him in the future,' she added, glaring at Megan.

For a moment there was an uneasy silence. Quickly Robert began to talk of other things to try to cover Kathy's outburst. It was too late; the evening was ruined for both Megan and Kathy.

Hours later, as she tossed and turned in bed, fighting her outrage at Miles' deception, Megan tried to convince herself that it was just dockside gossip. She refused to believe that he had invited her to Tynmorfa and made love to her when all the time he was planning to marry someone else.

It must be a mistake! Robert must have got it all wrong.

She spent Sunday in an agony of despair. Several times she was tempted to phone Miles. Only the thought that Mr Walker might answer the phone, and that he would probably recognise her voice, stopped her from doing so.

On Monday morning, Megan was on tenter-hooks waiting for Miles. The moment he arrived she went straight into his office.

'I can only spare you a few minutes, Megan. My father is waiting to speak to me.'

'What I have to tell you will only take a few minutes and then you can be the one to explain the situation to your father,' she said in a stran-gled voice.

'Something wrong?' His eyebrows furrowed. 'Don't tell me you are leaving us for a better job?'

'I shall be leaving, but whether the job is a better one or not depends on you.'

'I don't follow!' His frown deepened. 'Come on, straight talking, Megan. I'm in a hurry.'

'All right.' She took a deep breath. 'I'm preg-nant . . . so when are we getting married?'

For a moment she thought he didn't under-stand what she had said. His blue eyes had a strange blankness as he stared at her. Then a nerve at the side of his jaw began to twitch as his mouth tightened. Dull red colour spread up from his neck.

'I don't believe you . . . you've heard that I'm to marry Carol Brocklehurst and you are trying this on,' he blustered.

For a moment her nerve deserted her. She had steeled herself to face him with the news. She had been prepared for dismay, concern, apologies even, but not an outright admission that he was planning to marry someone else.

The lacerating things her mother had said about Miles came rushing back. Her mother was right, he was a two-timer. He had not only been dating both Lynn and her, but Carol Brocklehurst, and probably other girls as well.

Scenes she had witnessed at The Stork Club on the few occasions she had visited it, crowded her mind. The impetuous flirtations, the wild dancing, the torrid atmosphere. He had probably flirted with any number of girls there, but they had most likely laughed it off, knowing that it was just the wild mood of the moment, engendered by the crazy jazz music.

Simple, country-bred girl that she was, she had thought Miles had meant the words of endearment he had whispered when she was in his arms. She'd felt flattered when he told her how much he needed her. When he had promised marriage she had believed him. She would never have agreed to spend two nights with him at Tynmorfa otherwise!

For her that had been the ultimate commitment. For him it had been merely a passing fling.

Remembering the aplomb with which Mrs Jones had accepted her presence probably meant that it wasn't the first time Miles had taken a girl there, she thought miserably. How they must have laughed when he had packed her off early on the Saturday morning before his parents arrived for the weekend, she thought bitterly.

'I'm telling the truth, Miles. You can probably work out when it happened,' she added, biting down on her lower lip.

'When you were on holiday in North Wales, I would say,' he commented flippantly. 'So why are you telling me?'

For a moment she felt taken aback, shocked that he could jest about something so serious, but one look at his face put her on her guard.

'It happened when I stayed with you at Tynmorfa,' she said vehemently.

'Can you prove it wasn't one of the other boyfriends you slept with while you were visiting Beddgelert?'

Anger seethed through her like a forest fire. 'How dare you? If you don't tell your father then I shall . . . and I shall be telling him that you asked me to marry you,' she exploded, her dark eyes misting with emotion.

'Do you really think you could convince him?' sneered Miles, his lip curling, danger flags in his eyes. 'My father wouldn't believe you for one minute!'

His contemptuous laugh echoed in her ears as she fled from his office. Too distraught for tears, she sat down in the swivel chair in her own office, but turned away from her typewriter. She couldn't work. Her brain was like a gigantic generating box sending out shock waves of anger and self-recrimination because she'd been so easily manipulated.

She couldn't believe Miles was acting so despicably. Never, as long as she lived, would she forget the supercilious look in his eyes or the scorn in his voice.

She paced the room, wondering what to do. She must talk about it to someone.

She had considered herself so clever, so capable of managing her own life. She'd thought that the steady progress in her career put her above her mother's homilies. Yet her mother had seen through Miles from the start.

She recalled how wide eyed with envy Jennie and Gwyneth had been when she'd told them about her new life, and wondered what they would think if they knew the truth.

Miles had even double-crossed Carol Brocklehurst! For one fleeting moment she actually felt sorry for the girl. What sort of life could she expect to have unless he changed his ways?

As her anger abated, it was replaced by a feeling of fear and despondency as she wondered how she was going to sort things out. She couldn't turn to her parents so there was only one other person left . . . Robert.

Even that wasn't going to be easy, she thought, as the dilemma of how to go about telling him went round and round in her mind.

When her father mentioned that he had invited Robert for Sunday lunch, Megan wondered if fate was on her side.

She felt edgy throughout the meal wondering how she was going to manage to get Robert on his own.

'You are very quiet today,' Robert commented as he helped her to clear the table.

'I . . . I have a headache,' she told him with a frown. 'I think there's a thunder storm brewing up. I thought of going for walk.'

'Want me to come along?'

'I'd like that.'

When she saw the warmth in his eyes, panic swept through her. Would he turn against her when he knew? It was a chance she had to take, she decided, since there was no one else to advise her.

'Right. Shall we go to New Brighton and walk along the prom?' he suggested.

It was hot and muggy. A wind was whipping up a scummy froth on the grey water. Clouds raced across the leaden sky. They trudged along King's Parade propelled forward by the wind. 'Hang on or you'll be blown away!' Robert laughed, pulling her hand through his arm.

She found the closeness of his body against her own was comforting.

'Something wrong, isn't there?' he remarked after they had walked for a few minutes without speaking.

'Come on Megan,' he murmured softly when she remained silent. 'I know you too well not to know when something is troubling you. How can I help?'

'I don't know if you can,' she mumbled.

'Try me. Look, let's sit in one of the shelters out of the wind.'

He listened in silence. She sensed him stiffen when she told him about the time spent at Tynmorfa with Miles, but apart from that he gave no sign that he was in any way affected by her story.

247

'And now you can't decide what to do,' he said quietly when she had finished.

'I know what I must do,' she said and her voice thickened. 'I . . . I've got to get rid of the baby while I still can, so that means as quickly as possible.'

'Only if you want to do so,' he said quietly.

'What do you mean? Of course I must. Think what it would do to my mother if she knew.' She turned to face him, then looked away quickly, disturbed by the look in his light blue eyes. It wasn't condemnation. She wasn't sure what it was.

'You could keep the baby if you were married.'

'Miles is marrying Carol Brocklehurst, you already know that. He's marrying money so there's no possibility of him changing his mind,' she added bitterly.

'I wasn't thinking of Miles,' he said in a flat voice. 'I was thinking you could marry me.'

'Marry you!' Her eyes widened in astonishment. She knew Robert was fond of her, that was why she had felt she could confide in him. Marrying him, though, that was something she'd never even considered and she had difficulty in taking his suggestion seriously.

'You can forget I said that if it upsets you,' he said stiffly as he saw her stunned reaction.

'Robert, I'm sorry. I . . . I was taken by surprise. If I had time to think about it . . .' She shrugged helplessly. 'Have you realised what you are saying . . . and that you would be taking on another man's child?'

'If it made you happy I could come to terms

248

with the situation,' he told her, his gaze sharp and direct.

'How could you when the father is a man you despise?'

'Forget it!' He laughed harshly. 'I can see it's not the solution you were looking for. I have no idea how you go about getting an abortion, but I can probably find out . . . if you are quite sure that is what you want.'

'It's the only way, Robert. Surely you can see that? And I've got to do it without my parents knowing.'

'It might be expensive. Is Miles going to pay?'

'Robert!'

His callousness shocked her as much as he intended. Her rejection, even though he had expected it, left him bitter. As he saw the distress in her eyes, though, Robert felt contrite. He didn't want to hurt Megan, only to punish Miles Walker.

'Don't worry, I can lend you the money if necessary. The thing is to get something organised. Leave it with me. I'll find out what has to be done. Come on.' He stood up. 'We'd better be getting back or your mother will start worrying.'

This time he did not take her arm.

The week that followed seemed endless. She hardly slept at all. There were days when she felt indifferent to everything around her, submerged in apathy, aware only of her own predicament.

She had almost given up hope of any help from Robert when unexpectedly he came into the office. 'Everything is fixed for next Friday. You'll have to take the day off but you should be OK for work by Monday. The details are all in there.' His face was expressionless as he handed her an envelope.

He was gone before she could reply.

She sat staring at the envelope for a long time, then slipped it unopened into her handbag.

'Jennie's again! It's only a couple of months since you went to see her . . . or so you said,' Kathy Williams exclaimed when Megan told her she was going away for the weekend.

'You must be mad, driving all that way for a weekend. You sure you're not off for another fling with that Miles Walker?' she asked with a penetrating look.

'No, Mam, I'm not seeing Miles Walker.'

Megan's tone was so flat that her mother said no more. She was worried about Megan. There was something different about her in recent weeks, but she couldn't quite put her finger on what it was.

Chapter Twenty-five

Relief that the nightmare was over was uppermost in Megan's mind as she came out of the anaesthetic. Although she still felt woozy, the surroundings helped her to focus on her private soul searching. The cell-like room was completely characterless. White walls and paintwork, white bed, white painted bedside table. The narrow window was so high up that it was impossible to see anything except the sky. A nurse, also all in white, came in to check her pulse.

'Try and sleep,' she ordered. 'If you need anything use the bell,' she added, indicating a white button by the side of the bed-head.

Obediently, Megan closed her eyes. She had no intention of sleeping; she needed to think, to plan ahead. This really would be a turning point in her life, she resolved grimly. Never again would she let anyone take advantage of her, or exert as much power over her as Miles Walker had done.

She knew she had only herself to blame for letting her feelings for him transcend reason, blinding her to his behaviour. She had been far too eager to please, too ready to give in to his demands. His cavalier attitude when she had told him she was pregnant had finally broken the spell and made her realise how naive she had been.

She cringed inwardly. She had been so completely hoodwinked by his promise of marriage. She had trusted him implicitly, honouring her side of the bargain, telling no one, not even her parents.

Their interlude in Wales had been the ultimate triumph for Miles. It had proved his power over her, she thought bitterly. She had held out for so long, resisting his pleas that they should make love, ignoring his jests about her prudishness and his jeers when she still steadfastly refused to give in to his demands. It made her even more embittered that she had fallen for the oldest trick of all: an empty promise of marriage.

Tears stung as she relived the events of the bittersweet time they had spent together at Tynmorfa. The tender, whispered pledges, and the passion of their love-making. She had been so convinced that he felt the same way about her as she did about him.

No matter how she looked at it, Miles had behaved despicably, leading her on, winning her trust, while all the time he was planning to marry Carol Brocklehurst.

She slid her hands down underneath the crisp white sheets, gaining comfort from the feel of the flat outline of her barren stomach. She closed her eyes. Although there was nothing in the room to distract her thoughts, she wanted to shut out the world, to concentrate on what measures she must take if she was to start afresh.

She didn't intend to leave Walker's. To disappear would be making things far too easy for Miles. She wanted revenge and as long as she was working at Walker's the knowledge that he had made her pregnant would haunt him. It would be sweet vengeance! Even when he realised she'd had an abortion he would still worry in case she said anything to jeopardise his plans to marry Carol Brocklehurst.

Revenge, punishment, atonement: such thoughts were so alien to her that for a moment Megan wondered if she was still under the influence of the anaesthetic.

But so too were deception, lying, and subterfuge – and she had resorted to all of these, she reminded herself. Even over this weekend! Her mother's words when she had said she was going to Beddgelert rang in her ears.

'You must be mad! If that's really where you're going, of course, and not off seeing that Miles Walker.'

Although she'd emphatically denied the accusation, when she'd been saying goodbye as she left home, she knew that her mother was still suspicious.

She was grateful that her father neither cross-questioned her or tried to dissuade her from going. 'If you break down or have any problems, mind you phone home, *cariad*,' he counselled as he waved her off.

Problems! She wondered what he would do if she rang him now and said where she was, why she was there and what had just happened.

That was another difficulty. Her father would want to know why she was leaving and she didn't want to add to his worries.

She often wondered how he coped with her mother's vacillating moods. She seemed to alternate between long brooding silences and onslaughts of bitter accusations. There were times when she blamed him for Lynn's death because he had brought them back to Merseyside to live.

He bore these tirades with commendable fortitude, but Megan knew he took them to heart. He had grown quieter. His face was drawn and there was a myriad of tiny lines around his dark eyes that hadn't been there a year ago. At one time his great interest had been football but now he rarely went to a Saturday match.

The change in him was nothing compared with the alteration in her mother, of course. She was a totally different person from when they lived in Beddgelert. Her happy, sunny nature seemed to have gone for ever. The vacant, lost look that had been in her eyes when she'd sat week after week at Lynn's bedside had been replaced by a hard, cold stare.

She was distrustful of everyone and Megan often felt saddened by her attitude. More than once she'd been tempted to leave home, but couldn't bring herself to let her father cope alone.

But what of the future . . . her future?

Megan moved uneasily in the bed. Her aching body was a sharp reminder that her days of innocence were over. From now on she intended to guard against heartbreak. She would not allow herself to fall in love ever again.

Before she drifted into sleep she thought of Robert. She knew she owed him a lot and was grateful. Without his help she would never have had this second chance. Perhaps she should have married him when he had asked her, she thought wryly. He would make a wonderful husband. He was so sincere and dependable; so conventional and considerate. She would have been cherished and protected for the rest of her life. Even though she didn't love him, they were the best of friends and she enjoyed his company.

Poor Robert. He, too, was one of life's victims. His family had owned a dairy and it had been taken for granted that when he left school he would go into the business. He'd found delivering milk unexciting. The sight of the huge liners sailing down the Mersey, bound for unknown destinations, made him restless. He longed to travel, but his parents were opposed to the idea so he took matters into his own hands and ran away to sea.

'I knew if I tried to discuss it with them they would try to talk me out of it so I just packed my bags and left a note to say I'd gone. I picked a boat bound for South America, one that would take me halfway round the world, so that I couldn't change my mind if I felt homesick. We must have been somewhere in mid-Atlantic when my father died from a sudden heart attack. It was months before the news caught up with me and still longer before I could get back to Liverpool.'

His face had hardened at the memory and he was silent for so long that she'd had to prompt him to go on.

'My mother was devastated,' he told her. 'She couldn't run the dairy business single-handed and by the time I got back she'd acted on her solicitor's advice and sold up and moved to a house in New Brighton.

'I didn't go back to sea again. She never fully recovered from my father's death so I couldn't leave her on her own. It was a pity about the business but I was never really interested in it.'

'And that was when you went to work at Walker's,' prompted Megan.

'That was a stop gap, a bit like treading water. It gave me independence yet kept me at my mother's side. We could look after each other. When she died, shortly before you came to Merseyside, I fully intended going back to sea.'

'So why didn't you?'

'Various reasons,' Robert said with a wry smile.

When she left the nursing home next day, Megan still felt weak and slightly unsteady on her feet. The effort of walking to her car left her in a cold sweat.

She sat behind the wheel for ten minutes, waiting for her heart to stop thumping and her head to stop spinning, before she turned on the ignition. She wished she had agreed to Robert's suggestion that he should collect her.

'You look absolutely washed out,' her mother commented when she arrived home. 'I knew that journey was going to be too much for you!'

'Give me your keys and I'll get your case and garage the car,' her father offered.

'Did you have trouble with the car?' he asked as he came back into the house.

'No, it went fine. Why?'

'All the way to Beddgelert and back?'

Something in his voice made her look up. There was disbelief in his eyes and she looked away quickly, a guilty flush staining her cheeks. He didn't press the point, but his face tightened as he went out of the room.

A chill chased down her spine as she tried to work out why he suspected she was lying. He couldn't know where she had been. No one did . . . except Robert, and he wouldn't betray her. He had done everything possible to help keep her secret. He had not only booked her in under a false name, but had even taken the precaution of paying in advance, in cash.

Her mother might have voiced suspicions that she was going away with Miles Walker, but surely her father wouldn't take any notice? Not now that Miles' engagement to Carol Brocklehurst had been made public.

She longed to tell them the truth, but that would implicate Robert as well as denigrate her still further in her mother's eyes.

A bewildering profusion of doubts tormented her. In the end she could stand it no longer and said that as her head still ached she would have an early night.

Her entire body felt bruised and sore as she undressed and crawled into bed. Sleep eluded her.

Next morning, while she was driving to work, she suddenly realised why her father had asked if she'd had trouble with her car. His words as he'd waved her goodbye echoed in her ears. 'I've checked the oil and filled her up. There's enough petrol in the tank to take you to Beddgelert and back.'

When he'd put the car away he had obviously checked them both again, she thought grimly. It was second nature for him to do so; it was something he did automatically every time he took a lorry out on the road. Not only was the tank still almost full but the reading on the milometer showed less than thirty miles difference. Beddgelert and back was almost two hundred miles.

It was too late now to try to explain, she thought miserably. He knew she'd been lying. It was one more secret to be buried in her past! She seemed to be digging herself deeper and deeper into the morass, she thought unhappily.

By the time she reached the office she felt far from well and hoped she would have the will-power to cope not only with the day's work, but everything else that lay ahead. Being strong and resolute about the way she would treat Miles had been easy when she'd been half doped by anaesthetic.

Before going into the office she checked her appearance and frowned at her reflection. Dark circles made her brown eyes look too big for her face. The peach blouse she was wearing drained every vestige of colour from her cheeks.

She applied some more lipstick, but that seemed only to accentuate her pallor. She wished she had some rouge but it was something she never used. She ran her finger over the top of the lipstick and blended it onto her cheeks, then frowned at the result. It made her look more washed out than ever.

Megan hurried through the general office with

a brisk, bright greeting. Myra and Mavis were talking to Olive, all three bunched together at the reception desk. Mavis tried to attract her attention, but she didn't stop, she was in no mood for gossip.

In the sanctuary of her own office, she sat at her desk wondering how she was going to cope for the rest of the day, she felt so fragile. I should have said I had the flu and taken the day off, she thought exhaustedly as she picked up the white envelope that was propped prominently against her typewriter and opened it.

Inside was a deckle-edged invitation card. The silver-embossed words danced crazily in front of her eyes. She read them several times before they fully registered. Then, tight-lipped, her cheeks flaming, she slipped the card back into its envelope. That was one wedding she wouldn't be attending, she decided grimly.

Chapter Twenty-six

The entire staff had been invited to Miles' wedding and Megan listened in aloof silence as the other girls in the office chattered excitedly about the forthcoming event. As they discussed in minute detail the outfits they were planning to wear she felt almost at screaming pitch.

The office was to be closed for the day so she was kept busy rearranging deliveries or postponing them so that the staff who worked at the docks would also be able to take the day off.

'We're organising a collection to buy a wedding present for Miles. Do you want to chip in, Megan?' challenged Olive.

'Of course,' Megan told her, reaching into her handbag for her purse.

'You don't have to . . . not if you're buying him something special on your own,' Mavis told her pertly.

'I'll give the same as the rest of you,' Megan stated coolly. Inwardly she felt in turmoil, but she was determined to face the situation as dispassionately as possible.

After the way Miles had treated her she ought to be able to dismiss him from her thoughts completely, yet, no matter how hard she tried, she found that was impossible. Memories, fragmented moments of emotion, struck like lightning flashes leaving her vulnerable. He even invaded her dreams. She would waken from her nightmare with sweat rivering down her body and feeling as weak as if she'd endured some terrible illness. She wanted to run away, to hide in some dark, isolated corner where she could give way to her tears in private and no one would sympathise or criticise.

Each day was traumatic. Having to talk to Miles in the office, knowing that others were within earshot and could hear every word she uttered, made her tongue-tied. It sent her brain spinning so that she was bedevilled by a sense of her own inadequacy and weakness. The deepening despair she felt deadened all her faculties so that she was under a constant strain.

Even worse was when Mavis or Olive were actually in the room. Then she was conscious that they were watching Miles and her, registering the unspoken conflict between them. And she knew that afterwards they would discuss every syllable and every look that passed between them, and either pity her or laugh about her being another of his conquests.

Megan found the situation at home equally trying. There were interminable arguments between her parents as her father tried to persuade Kathy to overcome her resentment and accept the invitation to Miles Walker's wedding.

'Mr Walker is bound to notice if we're not there,' he said worriedly.

'Then you go. No one is stopping you,' snapped Kathy, her lips a tight, uncompromising line.

'You've been invited as well!'

'No one is going to worry whether I'm there or not,' commented Kathy acidly.

'They will. If you stay away the Walkers might take it as a personal slight.'

'Good! That's exactly what I intend it to be,' she told him with grim satisfaction.

'But we ought to go,' pleaded Watkin, running his hand through his hair, a look of distress darkening his face.

'Then go!'

'I want you with me, *cariad*. Come on, let's try and put the past behind us. Go out and buy a new hat, or a whole outfit, if you like. Megan will go with you.'

'Dress up and let them think we've forgiven their son for killing our daughter?' retorted Kathy scathingly.

Watkin shook his head sadly. 'Will I never get through to you, woman, that it was an accident!'

'He killed her!' Her eyes blazed angrily, colour stained her sagging cheeks.

'The roads were wet, the scooter skidded,' Watkin explained patiently.

Kathy stood up, walked over to the window and stood there staring out unseeingly.

'If we don't attend the wedding when we've been invited then my job could be on the line!'

'What's so special about being a lorry driver?'

'If I'm sacked, it mightn't be easy to find another job, the way things are at the moment.'

'Rubbish! I don't know why both you and Megan didn't leave Walker's right after our Lynn was killed. I don't know how you can bear to take that man's money.'

'Kathy, it was an accident,' repeated Watkin, wearily. He walked over to her and placed his hands on her shoulders. Gently he planted a kiss on her brow. She made no response but remained staring out of the window as though in a trance.

If only Kathy would accept the truth, he thought sadly. His heart ached for the way she was suffering but they couldn't bring Lynn back.

He tried asking Megan if she would talk to her mother and see if she could persuade her to change her mind, but Megan refused to intervene.

'Why don't you leave well alone,' she advised. 'Mam might seize the opportunity to speak to either Mr or Mrs Walker and cause an unpleasant scene.'

'Don't talk daft, girl,' he said angrily. Yet he knew there was a possibility of that happening, knowing Kathy's hatred towards Miles. If Miles had shot Lynn at point blank range she couldn't have thought him more responsible for her death.

'I'm not going and that's that,' Kathy declared the night before the wedding. 'You may work for the Walkers, but they don't own us.'

'I want us to be there,' he insisted. 'We've been given time off specifically so that we can attend the wedding.'

'Then go!' Kathy Williams screamed, her face distorted with rage. 'If you do don't come looking for me afterwards because I'll have gone to join our Lynn.'

Hands over her ears, Megan walked away from

the argument. She understood why her father thought they ought to attend the wedding, but she knew only too well that it was impossible to reason with her mother when she was in one of these moods.

'I've no time for Walker or his son,' Watkin said bitterly as he followed Megan out of the room. 'I'd like to see them both in hell for what they've done to my family. I don't intend giving them the satisfaction of knowing that, mind you. Even if I can't persuade your mam to go to the wedding, then I'll have to stay with her, but I still want you to be there,' he told Megan curtly. 'I know what that bastard meant to you . . . and I've a pretty good idea what you've been through and what was going on when you went away for the weekend recently.'

The knowing look in his dark eyes sent a shiver through her and an embarrassed flush stained her cheeks.

'No, Robert didn't tell me,' he said before she could question him. 'I worked it out for myself. We'll say no more about it but someday this family will get even with the Walkers, I'll promise you that.'

Megan bit down on her lower lip, too moved to speak.

'Go to the wedding, Megan,' he urged. 'Get all dressed up, girl. Do our family proud. Show that bugger Miles that you are not heartbroken on his account.'

She wanted to refuse, to dismiss the idea as ludicrous, but she realised how much it meant to her father.

'All right.'

She looked away quickly, disturbed by the gleam of satisfaction that flooded his face.

Her feelings for Miles remained like a raging torrent inside her head. Attending Miles' wedding would be the ultimate peak of endurance. To see him standing at the altar rails waiting for his bride; to endure the solemnity of the service; to watch as he and Carol Brocklehurst walked back up the aisle, arm in arm, legally man and wife, called for a strength she wasn't sure she possessed.

St Hilary's church was already packed when Megan arrived. Relatives of the Walkers and representatives from the leading shipping and haulage companies that operated from Liverpool docks filled the front rows.

Two rows in the centre of the church had been reserved for Walker's employees and as she and Robert took their seats Megan was aware that many eyes were on them.

She felt quietly confident, knowing she looked her best. Her cream coat over a blue and cream floral dress was pretty yet restrained. The blue hat, banded in cream, suited her colouring and struck just the right note of formality.

For a moment as they took their seats she felt her senses spinning and the congregation became a blur. She breathed deeply, clutching tightly hold of her cream handbag, in an effort to stop herself shaking. Then gradually her heart stopped pounding and she was able to take stock of who was present.

She quickly spotted Mavis, resplendent in a

vivid yellow dress and matching hat, sitting next to Olive. She'd heard them discussing the details of what they would be wearing so many times over the past weeks that it was like seeing the rerun of a technicolour film.

Mr Newbold, wearing a grey suit, was sitting in the same row accompanied by a stout middle-aged lady in flamboyant pink whom she assumed must be his wife.

Simon Gregson and Bob Donovan, the two shipping clerks, were sitting together and as they nudged one another and stared at her and Robert she gritted her teeth, knowing there would be plenty of gossip about them being together.

Then she caught sight of Miles in his flawlessly cut morning suit; he had never looked more handsome. He seemed completely at ease and Megan wondered what he was thinking as he waited for Carol Brocklehurst to arrive.

How could he be so poised and self-possessed knowing the many lives he had wrecked? Had he wiped from his mind how he had two-timed her, flirted with Lynn at the Stork Club and the circumstances that had caused Lynn's death.

She shivered. If he could put all that behind him and live only for today then perhaps he really was the monster her mother claimed him to be.

As the music changed, signalling the bride's arrival, she watched in growing anguish as Miles and his best man took their places at the altar steps. Her world rocked as if the past was closing round her, a dark curtain shutting off any chance of happiness.

As Miles half turned, and she saw the welcoming smile on his face as he watched his bride approach, Megan felt her heart would break. For weeks now she had steeled herself to hate him, to despise him, to resent the way he had used her as an object for his lust and then discarded her when she needed him most. Yet deep down she knew that his effect on her emotions was as powerful as ever.

She hated her own weakness in still loving a man who had shown so clearly that he had no respect whatsoever for her and who sought her company for one reason only. A man who could discard her without a second thought when he no longer needed her.

With a supreme effort, Megan brought her thoughts back to the present and forced herself to concentrate on what was happening around her as Carol Brocklehurst came down the aisle on her father's arm.

As they passed by, the sheer blanket of whiteness that filled her vision made Megan catch her breath. For a terrifying second, it was as if she was back in the hospital where everything, walls, ceiling, bedding and furniture, had all been stark white.

When Robert's hand reached out and took hers, squeezing it reassuringly, it was almost her undoing.

She glanced sideways, studying Robert's profile and the firm set of his broad shoulders. He was kind and gentle; good-looking in a rugged sort of way, and she knew he loved her deeply. So why hadn't she accepted his offer of marriage?

As she returned the pressure of his hand she felt like a traitor to her own feelings, to her family, and most of all to Robert. Was she making him endure the same emotional trauma as Miles had made her suffer? she wondered guiltily.

Perhaps it was time she stopped turning to him whenever she was in trouble. Maybe she ought to break the tenuous thread of friendship that kept him at her side and leave him free to find the happiness he deserved, she thought sadly as she struggled to focus her attention on the service.

It was like some terrible, endless dream listening to Miles and Carol Brocklehurst exchanging their vows. Then came the interminable wait while the bride and groom, and close family, adjourned to the vestry to sign the register.

She felt a surge of relief when the service was over and the newlyweds headed the procession that began to move slowly down the aisle. It would be the start of a new life for her, too, she vowed. From now on, she really would put Miles right out of her mind. Forget the past completely; forget all that he had meant to her.

As they drew level with the pew where she stood alongside Robert, Miles stared straight at her. Shocked and mesmerised, she was conscious that Robert's hand had grasped her arm tightly as she stiffened. With a sharp intake of breath she managed to hold her head high. Inwardly she prayed that no one else had noticed the way Miles had looked at her.

At the reception, she forced herself to chat

casually to Mavis and Olive. Mr Newbold, looking far less authoritative away from his books and ledgers, introduced his wife to them all.

She felt utterly lost when Robert momentarily left her side in order to collect some food. She longed to leave, but knew that it would be noticed if she did. Her father's plea that she didn't let Miles know how much he'd broken her heart and wrecked her life kept her resolutely talking and smiling.

When the announcement was made that the bridal pair were about to leave on their honeymoon, she made no attempt to join the laughing crowd making for the front door to wave them off.

'Come on,' Robert urged. 'You've played your part too well not to take the final curtain.'

She looked up at him, startled. She'd been congratulating herself on how convincingly she had been behaving. That Robert had realised that it was merely an act filled her with chagrin. Numbly, she stood by his side on the driveway, well back from all the well-wishers clustered round Miles' car, everyone laughing and joking as they tied an assortment of good luck tokens to the bumper.

Carol came out onto the drive on her own. She looked stunning in a pale green dress and jacket that complemented her vivid auburn hair. Envy and jealousy brought a lump to Megan's throat.

'Lost him already, Carol!'

'You'll have to watch him!'

'We all know what Miles is like . . .'

Laughter and wisecracks came from all sides.

Carol looked nervous as she settled herself in the passenger seat of the car and wound down the window so that she could reply to the banter.

Megan felt a hand on her shoulder and her heart raced as she turned and saw it was Miles. There was an inscrutable look on his face and for what seemed eternity they stood there staring at each other. She wanted to speak, to say something so cutting that it would sear into his heart, but her mind was blank.

Without saying a word, his lips brushed her cheek.

For a moment she thought she had imagined it, but the enraged look on Robert's face told her she was not dreaming.

As Miles took his place behind the wheel of his car she saw the bewilderment on Carol's face. She looked away quickly, knowing that everyone else must have seen what had happened and found Mrs Walker's gimlet gaze, livid with hate, directed at her.

Heart thudding, her face burning, she reached for Robert's hand. This time, he remained unresponsive.

As Miles started the engine and pulled away down the drive, the crowd shouting good advice and good luck, Robert freed his hand from her grasp.

'We're leaving,' he said sharply. Tight-lipped, he strode towards his parked car. Abjectly, Megan slid into the passenger seat, staring straight ahead as Robert manoeuvred out into the road.

Neither of them spoke on the drive home. When

he stopped outside her house, Robert left the engine running. He sat with both hands still on the wheel, not looking at her. He made no attempt to open the door for her, but sat staring fixedly in front of him, waiting for her to get out.

Megan didn't know what to do or say. 'Aren't you coming in?' she asked as she fumbled with the catch.

'No!' His tone was clipped, cold and decisive.

'Please! They will be expecting you. My dad is probably waiting to hear all about the wedding,' she persisted.

'In that case I'm sure you will be better on your own, then you can tell him as much as you want him to know and no more,' he said with studied irony.

'Robert, it wasn't my fault. You saw what happened. I couldn't stop him . . .' She placed her hand on his arm in a pleading gesture, silently beseeching him to understand.

He shook her hand away, irritably, as if she were a fly or a speck of dust. 'No more acting, Megan . . . not with me,' he exclaimed, revving the engine impatiently.

As she closed the car door he pulled away, savagely crashing the gears, leaving her standing in the roadway.

'Isn't Robert coming in?'

'No, he thought it better not to do so.' Quickly she blinked away her tears as her father met her in the doorway.

'I'm glad in a way,' he told her in a conspiratorial whisper. 'It might be better if you didn't say anything about the wedding . . . Your mam is still very upset.'

'Don't worry, I don't want to talk about it. I have a terrible headache so I'm going straight up to my room! Goodnight.'

Chapter Twenty-seven

While Miles was on his honeymoon, Megan found that work became a palliative. She felt more relaxed and no longer dreaded going into Mr Walker's office to take dictation. When Miles had been in the room she'd found it very difficult to concentrate, knowing that he was watching her from beneath lowered eyes.

Her relationship with Mr Walker also underwent a subtle change. Although he was considerate to work for she had always been intimidated by him. She admired his business acumen and high standards. In her first week as his secretary she had been dismayed by the number of times she had been asked to retype a letter because it contained an error or he detected that she had made a correction. Only perfection was acceptable.

'Look at it this way, Megan,' he explained when he had seen she was almost in tears. 'In the shipping business, we handle commodities on behalf of other people that are worth many thousands of pounds. If we can't take the trouble to send them a correctly typed letter, or invoice, then how can they be confident that we will safeguard their goods and interests?'

As she came to know Mr Walker and his methods better, Megan realised that this meticulous attention to detail was the cornerstone on which Walker's Shipping Company had been built up over the years.

Miles relied more on personality than efficiency. After making him a director, his father was proud of his son's flair for carrying off big deals and bringing in new business. Now, in Miles' absence, he was shocked beyond belief when he discovered the slipshod way the paperwork connected with these deals had been handled.

He took Megan into his confidence and a new rapport developed between them as they tried to sort out the muddles Miles had created. Mr Walker discussed each transaction with her in great detail and she found herself playing a far more decisive role.

Mr Walker was still far from well and the strain of Miles' wedding seemed to have taken its toll of his strength. He tired easily and often arrived late or left the office just after lunch. Without Miles there to deputise for him, Megan found more and more responsibility seemed to be falling on her shoulders.

In many ways, she felt she was replacing Miles. This feeling increased even more towards the end of the first week when Mr Walker asked her if she would drive him to Manchester.

'My meeting tomorrow with The Docks and Harbour Board is very important so I want to arrive feeling fresh and I still find driving something of a strain,' he explained.

'Of course,' she agreed willingly. 'I'm not sure you will find my car all that comfortable, though!'

She smiled apologetically. 'It may seem rather cramped after . . .'

'We'll be going in my car,' he interrupted.

'You mean in your Rolls!' she exclaimed in astonishment. 'It's rather a responsibility,' she demurred. 'Supposing I had a bump . . .'

'It's fully insured,' he told her curtly. 'Give it a try. If you find it's too much for you then next time I'll make other arrangements.'

Before she left work that evening, Mr Walker asked her if she would like to familiarise herself with the controls of the car she was going to have to drive next day.

The gleaming blue Silver Cloud, with its personalised number plate MW 100, was in sleek, showroom condition. To Megan it seemed as big as a bus. Nervously, she sat behind the wheel, conscious of the luxurious softness of the upholstered seats. The instrument panel looked so complicated that she felt alarmed.

She listened attentively as Mr Walker explained the driving mechanism and instrument layout. When he switched on the ignition, the powerful purr of the engine made her realise the enormity of what she was undertaking in agreeing to drive it.

'Right then, Megan. How about trying it out?' He smiled encouragingly.

She made one false start because she was so nervous. That mistake corrected she found driving the gleaming monster was simplicity itself. She went home that night looking forward to their trip to Manchester.

The car behaved beautifully when they set out next morning. The swift acceleration made her nervous at first, but the ease of steering, and the instant positive response when she braked, soon restored her confidence. She found driving it exhilarating. Even nosing through city traffic was less traumatic in the Rolls than it would have been in her own small car.

When they returned to the office later in the day, Mr Walker's compliments on her driving ability brought a flush to her cheeks.

'Perhaps it responded so well to your touch because it carries your initials on the number plate,' he commented jocularly.

'I enjoyed driving it,' she told him. 'Sheer magic!'

'So you won't mind acting as my chauffeur again if I need you?' he commented, a twinkle in his keen blue eyes.

'I would consider it a pleasure,' she assured him.

When she told her father about it he was so proud of her skill that he relayed the episode to Robert the next time he came to the house.

Robert was far from pleased. 'He employs over a dozen professional drivers so why not use one of them if he needs a chauffeur?'

'He's probably afraid the rest of you will go on strike if he does,' Megan flared. She felt annoyed, Robert's criticism was ruining what had been such an enjoyable experience.

There had been a rift between them ever since Miles' wedding. Robert's anger over Miles kissing her before he'd left on his honeymoon had deepened. Whenever they met he was curt and unfriendly, going out of his way to criticise or make scathing remarks, until she wished he'd stop coming to the house at all. Surely he saw enough of her father when they were at work? If he wanted to meet him in the evening for a drink then why couldn't they meet at a pub? she thought angrily.

As she was leaving the office the following Monday evening, Mr Walker called her back.

'Megan, do you think you could drive me to North Wales tomorrow? I have to collect some papers that I left behind when I was staying there over the weekend.'

She agreed nervously, although longing to refuse. Mostyn was the last place she wanted to visit again. It would be embarrassing meeting Sybil Jones, but she had no excuse ready.

Next morning, knowing what lay ahead, only will-power and her determination to forget the past gave her the courage to go to work at all.

'We take the main Chester road as far as Queensferry,' Mr Walker told her as he spread out a road map on his desk and indicated the point they were making for and the route he wanted her to follow. 'After we cross into Wales I'll direct you.'

She nodded, afraid to speak in case she said something that divulged the fact that she had been there before and knew every inch of the route they would be taking.

Once she was behind the wheel, the need to concentrate and the sheer joy of driving the Rolls helped to put all other thoughts out of her mind.

The car responded to her slightest touch, its six-cylinder, automatic gearbox tuned to perfection.

It was a perfect early autumn day. The ride was so smooth that the scenery seemed to flow past the window, alternating between green open spaces and ribbons of houses. Once they reached Queensferry and were over the border into Wales, Megan felt exhilarated. With the River Dee flowing into the Irish Sea on one side and the Halkyn mountain rising up against the blue sky on the other, she felt as if she was flying as she pressed her foot down on the accelerator and the car cruised at high speed.

When they reached Holywell, Mr Walker suggested stopping for coffee at the Bell Hotel. Afterwards, he took her to see St Winefride's Well from which the small town took its name.

'At one time it was said to be the largest spring in the country,' he told her. 'The water never freezes, no matter how low the temperature may drop. The legend behind it is that, in the seventh century, Caradoc, son of the local chieftain, was in love with a young girl called Winefride. When he tried to force her hand she fled, but Caradoc gave chase and when he caught up with her cut off her head with his sword. Where her head fell a spring of water burst from the ground and, at the same time, the ground opened and engulfed Caradoc.'

'What a strange story,' Megan murmured. Even though the sun glinted warmly, Megan felt a chill run through her and she was relieved when they moved away.

At Mostyn, as she turned into the narrow sandy lane that led to Tynmorfa, every detail of her previous visit, the idyllic weekend when she had believed Miles to be as much in love with her as she was with him, flooded her mind.

'Goodness! I intended to direct you from Mostyn,' Mr Walker exclaimed in surprise as they pulled up outside his house. 'How on earth did you manage to find this place?'

'I . . . I know the area,' she stuttered in confusion, conscious of her silly gaffe. 'I used to live in North Wales, you know,' she added lamely.

'It wasn't around this area, though, was it? I thought your home was at Beddgelert?' he added, puzzled. 'Still, never mind, you've got us here safely. Come on in.'

As she followed his portly figure towards the door, Jason came bounding out, his raucous bark shattering the tranquillity around them. Ignoring Mr Walker he bounded straight towards Megan.

'Stand perfectly still, Megan, he won't hurt you,' Mr Walker cautioned. Before he had finished speaking the huge Doberman had flung himself on Megan, snuffling and licking her hand in a frenzied greeting.

'Great heavens! Whatever's come over the animal?' he muttered. 'I've never seen him behave in such a friendly way towards a stranger before.'

Megan remained silent, not knowing what to say. Then her heart pounded when the door opened and she saw Sybil Jones standing there.

'I've prepared lunch as you ordered, sir,' she greeted him. 'Would you and Mrs Walker like me to serve it right away?' As she looked past him and saw Megan her mouth dropped in surprise.

'Mrs Walker hasn't come with me today. This is my secretary, Megan Williams. Miles is still on honeymoon so Megan has chauffeured me here because my doctor still doesn't feel I'm fit enough to drive myself.'

Sybil Jones nodded politely, but her eyes narrowed speculatively, and Megan prayed she wouldn't be indiscreet and say they had met before.

'That was a lovely meal, thank you,' Megan murmured politely, forcing herself to meet the other woman's eyes when she finally brought in their coffee.

'Thank you, Miss Williams.' Sybil Jones' dark eyes were unfathomable as they met Megan's.

Megan looked away quickly, relieved they would soon be leaving.

She felt trapped by the web of deceit she had so inadvertently woven and wondered where and when it would ever end. Maybe it was her guilty conscience, she thought unhappily. Mr Walker had not seemed convinced by her explanation as to how she had found the place so easily, and he had certainly been mystified by Jason's reaction.

Over the next few days they were so busy with other problems that Megan was able to push the Tynmorfa incident to the back of her mind. Occasionally, when she looked up and found Mr Walker's shrewd gaze fixed on her, Megan would momentarily feel a flicker of concern. Then he would ask about one of the half-completed deals which Miles had been handling, and the moment would pass.

By the time Miles returned to the office, all the deals he had instigated had been consolidated and all the schedules had been trimmed and pruned so that everything was running like clockwork.

'I'm most appreciative of all the sterling work you've been doing, Megan,' Mr Walker told her as she completed the filing on the Friday night and tidied her desk before leaving for home.

'I've enjoyed the challenge,' she told him with a brief smile.

'I thought maybe you had. I've noticed how well you rise to difficult occasions. That's why I've decided to give you a new challenge.'

'Oh?' She frowned, mystified, waiting for him to explain further.

'Miles will be back at his desk on Monday. You've seen for yourself the mess he can get into so I want you to act as his assistant. Let me finish!' He held up his hand as she was about to interrupt. 'There will be a secretary to attend to letters, filing and routine work, leaving you free to handle the new deals or contracts as they are instigated.'

'How will Miles feel about such an arrangement?'

'Relieved, I should imagine. Miles has a flair for bringing in new business, but if it is left to him to organise the servicing of these new accounts we will end up in chaos. I know you can handle that side of things very efficiently. So, do you accept?'

She imagined how delighted her father would be when she told him the news. Then her spirits sank as conflicting thoughts rushed through her mind. Her mother wouldn't approve; nor, for that matter, would Robert Field. There'd be gossip around the office, too. Above all, would she be able to stand the strain of working so closely with Miles? she wondered.

'It's a challenge,' Mr Walker repeated, watching her keenly, 'but one I am quite confident you can handle.'

The sharp directness of his blue eyes brought the blood rushing to her cheeks. For a moment she wasn't sure whether he was referring to the work or her relationship with Miles.

Squaring her slim shoulders she met his shrewd gaze. 'Thank you, Mr Walker, I accept.' This was her chance to prove that Miles no longer meant anything to her and that she was in control of her own destiny, she told herself.

Chapter Twenty-eight

When Miles first heard about Megan's new status he felt extremely nettled that, in his absence, she had gained such a foothold and that his father regarded her abilities so highly. Tight-lipped, he riffled through his files and ledgers, frowning heavily, hoping to spot some inaccuracy. The neat preciseness of the entries fuelled his resentment even further, but he knew better than to show how he felt.

It had taken a lot of patience and persuasion to convince his father that he was experienced enough to be made a director and he had no intention of jeopardising his newly acquired power.

When his father summoned them both to his office and told him that, from now on, Megan would be acting as his personal assistant, he accepted the situation with outward charm that hid his deep resentment. Inwardly, he was fuming.

Throughout the meeting, Megan remained courteous, though cool, which unnerved him. He felt suspicious about her motives when she ignored his smiles and pleasantries and turned a deaf ear to his quips. She even looked different, he thought uneasily. She was wearing a smart grey suit and crisp white blouse and her hair was in a new style that made her look very sophisticated.

In the weeks that followed, the change in Megan disturbed him greatly. She was so confident and efficient. She ignored his outbursts of temper, even his sarcasm and irritability.

He was forced to agree with his father that she was an asset and to admit that the enthusiasm he felt when he first met a new client soon faded. He found working out schedules, checking references, and all the more mundane aspects of opening a new account, tedious.

Megan was extremely conscientious about such details. Her secretarial experience helped her to deal with all the paperwork in a methodical manner.

Mr Walker was delighted with her progress. In the past, he had suspected that there was some sort of relationship between Miles and Megan and it gave him considerable satisfaction to see how she was putting her career first and keeping Miles at a distance.

Miles' marriage had brought rich rewards to Walker's Shipping Company. They now acted as agents for most of the cargoes transported by the Brocklehurst Line. Their success was further enhanced when Mr Brocklehurst's associates also began to use them as shipping and forwarding agents.

Such rapid expansion made it necessary to take on more office staff. Myra Thornton became Mr Walker's secretary. A more experienced secretary, who could keep up with the mountain of correspondence generated by Megan and Miles, was also appointed.

Another large dockside warehouse was leased

to cope with the increased volume of cargo they were handling. Additional lorries were bought and they took on a number of new drivers.

Megan welcomed the constant pressure. Her mother was still grieving. It was impossible to divert her thoughts from what had happened to Lynn. She remained deeply depressed, shedding tears at the slightest reminder of the accident. Listless and unhappy, she grumbled incessantly and was completely uninterested in what was going on around her.

It was ironic, Megan thought, that now she could afford to take her mother out and about, and buy her new clothes, or anything else she fancied, shopping sprees had lost their appeal. Her mother neither cared about what she wore nor what she ate. She never shopped for food and rarely cooked a meal, leaving it to Megan, or Watkin, to do both.

Robert seemed to be the only one who could persuade Kathy to take any notice of what was going on outside her own four walls. Occasionally, he would persuade her to go out and would take her to King's Parade promenade where she would sit, staring at the sea, lost in her own dream world.

She had completely lost all interest in their home. The house in Belgrave Street, which she had been so proud of when they had first moved in, and described as a 'little palace', was no longer of any importance. Had Megan not cleaned it the place would have been unlivable in.

'You shouldn't be doing this, Megan,' Robert commented when he dropped in unexpectedly one

Sunday morning and found her scrubbing the kitchen floor.

'If I don't do it, then who else will?'

'I pay a woman to keep my place clean, and to do my shopping so that there's food to hand when I want to make a meal,' he told her.

'But it's my mam's job to do all that!' She frowned.

'It *was*. She doesn't seem to be able to cope at the moment, though, does she?' he pointed out. 'Get someone in to help out until she is better and well enough to take over again. She's on her own far too much. If you had a woman coming in each day there would be someone around the place for her to talk to.'

Robert was right, Megan admitted reluctantly and felt annoyed that she hadn't thought of it herself. When she discussed it with her father, he looked as taken aback as she had been.

'Do you think she would stand for having a stranger about the place . . . messing around in her kitchen and so on?' He frowned.

'You could ask her.'

'No.' He shook his head dubiously. 'I think it might be better coming from you. She might think I was criticising her for the way she's been neglecting everything lately.'

'She'd certainly resent it if I said anything,' Megan argued. 'She would probably think I was complaining because I'm having to help out.'

For days neither of them could think of the right approach. Then the answer came to Megan in a flash. The person to suggest it to her was Robert.

Robert not only persuaded Kathy that it was a splendid idea that someone should come in three mornings a week but he also found the ideal person for the job.

Mrs Brown, a perky little widow in her early sixties, was more than happy to have the chance of earning some extra money to eke out her pension. She reminded Megan of a chirpy robin. She was just five foot tall with a large bust and spindly legs. Her small dark eyes were like two polished buttons shining brightly above her red cheeks.

She was a hard worker and within a few days it was easy to see the improvements. There was a general air of freshness throughout the house. The furniture was dusted and polished; the windows sparkled.

In a very short time, Kathy was going out with Vi Brown. At first it was only as far as the local shops in Liscard Village. Gradually, a more adventurous routine was established. On the days Vi came, she and Kathy would spend the morning doing the chores together and then, after lunch, go across to Liverpool to do some shopping.

It made life easier for Watkin as well as Megan. He no longer had a strained, haggard look. He now had time to sit down in the evening and read the *Liverpool Echo* and he even began going out again for a drink with Robert. Megan, too, found she could relax when she came home from work and at the weekends had time to go shopping for herself, instead of for groceries to last them through the coming week.

It was all so idyllic that she knew it couldn't

last. Three months later, Mrs Brown dropped her bombshell by giving in her notice.

'I'm leaving Wallasey to go and live with my married daughter in Yorkshire,' she told Megan.

'I'm sorry to hear that. We'll all miss you. It's wonderful to see how much happier my mother has been having you as a friend.'

Kathy Williams seemed less perturbed by the change than Megan or Watkin. At first she seemed to be able to retain her new standards. She kept the house clean, went to the local shops and had a meal ready and waiting for them each evening.

Instinctively, though, Megan knew all was not well. Some evenings when she came home her mother was in high spirits and exceptionally talkative. At other times she would be withdrawn and seemed morose and depressed. Megan put her mother's erratic moods down to the fact that she was missing Vi Brown.

'Why don't you join a club or something and make some new friends, Mam?' she suggested.

'Leave me alone. I don't tell you what to do,' her mother snapped.

When she mentioned it to her father he brushed the matter to one side. 'You're just looking for trouble,' he protested. 'Give it time and she'll adjust. She's missing having Vi Brown around the place.'

'She needs to get out and meet people,' persisted Megan. 'Why don't you take her out, Dad? Take her to the pictures or out for a drink. I tell you what, why don't all three of us go out next Saturday night?'

'Splendid idea, and Robert could come along as well,' Watkin agreed, his face brightening.

'Robert?' She frowned. 'I imagine he has something better to do with his time.'

'If he has then I'm sure he'll cancel it for the chance of an evening out with you,' her father told her.

Megan bit her lip, refusing to comment. She thought she had made it quite clear to both Robert and her father that her career was all that mattered to her these days and she didn't think of Robert in that way.

Kathy seemed to be inordinately pleased by the idea of going out for a drink on Saturday night. She spent hours upstairs getting ready and came down wearing a dress Megan hadn't seen her in before.

'Come on,' urged Watkin. 'Robert will have given us up.'

Robert was waiting for them in the lounge bar of the Nelson. It was quite crowded but he had managed to keep seats for them near the window. As they settled down with their drinks, Megan was relieved to find that Robert was devoting most of his attention to Kathy.

Company was what her mother needed, Megan decided as she watched the way her mother's eyes were shining and the rapt attention she was paying to what Robert was saying.

As the evening wore on, however, Megan became increasingly concerned as her mother grew more and more voluble. Heads turned to look at them as every few minutes her laugh shrilled out.

'Perhaps we'd better be going, Megan,' Watkin muttered. 'I think your mam has had a drink too many.'

'She's only had two gin and tonics,' protested Robert. 'She can't be drunk on that!'

When they stood up to leave, Kathy proved him to be wrong. She swayed and stumbled, knocking into chairs and tables as they helped her outside. Once in the fresh air she became much worse. Her legs seemed to buckle beneath her and it took Robert and Watkin all their time to hold her upright. She was giggling helplessly as they helped her into the car.

When they reached Belgrave Street, Robert and Watkin supported Kathy indoors. She struggled and protested as they half carried, half dragged her upstairs. Then she collapsed on the bed, giggling inanely, before passing out.

'Why don't you go downstairs and make some coffee, Robert, while I help my dad to get her into bed,' suggested Megan.

'We'll just take off her shoes and cover her over to keep her warm,' Megan said when they were on their own.

'We'd better take her dress off as well,' fussed Watkin. 'It's a new one and she'll be upset if it gets all creased.'

It was a struggle, but eventually they managed it and Megan made her mother as comfortable as she could on the bed.

'You go on downstairs and I'll hang up her clothes and make sure she is OK,' Megan told her father. As she opened the wardrobe to hang up her mother's dress, Megan stared in disbelief. It seemed to be full of bottles. She took them out and lined them up. There were dozens of vodka bottles. Some of them had dregs in the bottom but most of them were completely drained. Hidden behind a pile of shoes she discovered even more bottles . . . full ones.

She was still kneeling on the floor, stunned by her discovery and trying to work out how long her mother had been a secret drinker, when her father came back upstairs.

'*Good God!* What's happening here, then?' His eyes narrowed as he looked from the bottles to Megan and back again. 'How long has this been going on?'

'I don't know.' She sat back on her heels, shaking her head. 'I have no idea at all.'

'She must have been drinking even before we went out tonight. That's why two gin and tonics sent her over the top!'

'It accounts for her moods. Sometimes she's on cloud nine. At other times she's so depressed that she doesn't even give you the time of day.'

He ran a hand through his dark hair in exasperation. 'I thought that was because she was still upset about what happened to young Lynn.'

'What are we going to do?'

'Let her sleep it off, I suppose. There's nothing else we can do.'

'I mean in the future, Dad?' She looked up at him, pleading with him to take control of the situation.

'I don't know, I just don't know,' he answered grimly.

Megan put her arms around him. 'Don't worry, we'll see it through,' she whispered as she hugged him. Even as she spoke she felt she could take no more. Her new job was so demanding that she felt drained, and now this added burden was just too much.

'We'd better go downstairs, Robert will be wondering what's happening,' Watkin said dully.

It was Robert who suggested a specialised clinic.

'Wouldn't that be terribly expensive, Robert?' Watkin frowned.

'Don't worry about that, Dad, I'll pay,' Megan said quickly.

'I don't want your money, girl,' he snapped. 'She's my wife. I'll pay whatever it costs.'

'She's also my mother,' Megan reminded him quietly.

'Settle it between you some other time,' Robert told them. 'I think she should go into one of these places as soon as possible. I'll make some enquiries?'

He's doing it again, Megan thought angrily, biting her lip to keep from saying anything. She knew he was only trying to help, but she wished it wasn't always Robert who found the answer to their problems.

A week later, Kathy Williams was undergoing a course of treatment in a special clinic near Maghull.

'My mother's on holiday,' Megan told neighbours when they remarked that they hadn't seen her about.

The house seemed empty without her, and, once again, Megan used work as a palliative. On the nights she visited her mother, rather than journey home to Wallasey and then have to go back again to Liverpool, Megan stayed late at the office.

Her late stint three nights a week had been going on for over a fortnight when Miles walked into the office unexpectedly.

'Heavens! I . . . I thought it was a burglar,' she gasped.

'What is there here worth stealing . . . except you?' he asked, putting an arm round her shoulders. 'You're not giving me the brush off, are you?' he muttered as she shrugged free. His hand caught at her chin, forcing her face up until he was looking into her eyes. Before she realised his intention his mouth was on hers, his lips demanding.

Angrily, she fought him off, her eyes blazing.

'Leave me alone, Miles. Get out of here . . . out of my life!'

'You seem to forget this is my company and I'm the one who gives the orders,' he retorted in a surly voice. 'No one, certainly not you, tells me to get out of my own office.'

'In that case, I'll be the one to leave.' With icy calm, although she was shaking and her knees felt like jelly, Megan picked up her coat and handbag.

'You needn't come back again,' he snarled. 'It won't do you any good to go running to my father tomorrow, either. I'll make sure he hears my side of the story tonight!' he added furiously.

With an effort she retained her composure, although her heart was pounding and she felt sick. His shouted threats that he would ruin her reputation and make quite sure she would never get another job in Liverpool rang in her ears as she hurried out of the building.

Miles' face, distorted with rage, haunted her as she went to visit her mother. As she remembered the ugly twist to his mouth and the callous look in his eyes, she wondered how she had ever considered him handsome or thought she'd been in love with him.

He was right about one thing, though: there was no longer any place for her at Walker's. The strain was too much; she wouldn't be going back.

Once she had made that decision, Megan felt almost calm. It was as if she had freed herself from bondage. Miles no longer had any hold over her, she told herself. Tonight had proved that the feelings she had once had for him really were dead.

Chapter Twenty-nine

Megan's heart sank as she turned into Belgrave Street the Sunday she brought her mother home and saw a familiar Rolls Royce parked outside their house.

As she pulled up in front of it and stepped out of her own car, Mr Walker lowered the window of the Rolls and called out curtly, 'Megan, I need to talk to you. I want to know what is going on. Miles tells me you've left.'

'Yes . . . that's right . . . I have.'

'You can't just walk out, Megan! Not without some kind of explanation,' Mr Walker exclaimed angrily.

'I am sure Miles has already given you one,' she retorted sharply.

'He has. Miles said there was some sort of dispute over the way the accounts were being handled and that you lost your temper and told him you were leaving. Is that true?'

Megan shrugged her shoulders dismissively. It was the sort of face-saving lie she would expect Miles to make.

'Well, Megan, is it?' He tugged the points of his waistcoat assertively.

'I'll leave you to draw your own conclusions.'

They stared angrily at each other for several

seconds. She was conscious that his face had become florid and his breathing laboured.

'It doesn't really matter what the argument was about.' He sighed impatiently. 'What I really want to know is when can we expect you back in the office?'

'I'm not coming back,' she told him firmly. 'And I really can't talk about it now, Mr Walker. I've just collected my mother from hospital, I can't leave her sitting in my car any longer.'

'I realise you must have a great deal on your mind at the moment,' he conceded, 'but do give it some thought. If Miles was at fault, or you decide you can't go on working with him, then we'll make whatever changes are necessary. You are the one person I can depend on, Megan. The firm needs you and it would be a pity to waste all your expertise.'

'I'm afraid I have nothing further to say,' she told him as she walked round to open the passenger door of her own car and help her mother out.

Tight-lipped, Megan assisted her mother inside the house and closed the front door. She stood there with her back pressed against it, breathing hard, trying to regain her composure as she heard the Rolls purr into life and drive away.

'What was all that about?' demanded her father coming into the hallway. 'Walker coming here himself! He said you hadn't been into the office all week! Don't you think it is time you told me what is going on, Megan?' he insisted as he took Kathy's arm and led her through into the living room.

'I will, Dad . . . later. Right now Mam needs a cup of tea and she doesn't want to be worried by silly things like this.'

Later that evening, after Kathy had been settled for the night, Megan told her father the whole story.

'Now do you understand why I'm not going back, Dad?'

'Of course I do.' He sighed deeply. 'I have a feeling that's not the end of the matter, though. Something tells me there's more trouble brewing.'

'What do you mean?'

He stared at her in exasperation. 'Mark my words, Miles Walker is bound to do something to get his own back.'

Megan hoped her father was being unduly pessimistic. She didn't think that there was very much that Miles could do since she was no longer at the office.

She pushed the entire matter to the back of her mind and concentrated on nursing her mother back to full health. The treatment at the clinic had been highly beneficial. Kathy was now eating and sleeping well, and even putting on a little weight. Her cheeks had regained some of their former roundness and her grey eyes had lost their dull, apathetic look.

Megan had helped her sort through her wardrobe and to smarten herself up. She eventually managed to persuade her to go to the hairdressers and, as a result, she was almost looking like her old self again.

She had changed considerably, though. She was quieter, more withdrawn, as if she'd moved into a realm of her own. She spent a lot of time out in the garden, sitting there lost in thought. She didn't even question why Megan was at home all day.

When neighbours stopped to talk, Kathy chatted readily enough, but she would never ask them in for a cup of tea, or visit them, no matter how often they invited her to do so. ·

Megan wished she would. She couldn't stay at home for ever. Even though her dad was earning good money, she preferred to be independent and wanted to start looking for a new job as soon as possible. She was afraid, though, that once she left her mother on her own all day she might slip back into the morass of despair she had been in before. She might even start drinking again, although she had neither taken a drink, nor asked for one, since she had returned home from the clinic.

A month later, when Megan thought it was safe for her to start looking for work, the next blow fell.

She was putting the finishing touches to the evening meal, and listening for her father's key in the lock, when Robert arrived. Megan thought he looked upset about something, but her immediate concern was how she could stretch the meal so that it would be enough for four people instead of three.

As she went through into the kitchen to put another plate to warm, Robert followed her. 'I've bad news, Megan,' he said, closing the door and standing with his back against it.

'Oh?' She turned to look at him, alarm in her deep brown eyes. Robert was still in his working clothes, which meant he must have come straight from the docks without going home to get changed.

'Miles has had your father arrested.'

'He has done *what*?' she gasped, her voice shrill.

'Ssh! We don't want your mother to know! Leastwise, not yet.'

'But why has he been arrested . . . what for . . . ?' She shook her head in bewilderment.

'There was a fire last night at the Walkers' home in Wales,' Robert told her grimly. 'Miles Walker has accused your father of being responsible.'

'What utter rubbish.' Megan laughed. 'Dad was here all evening.'

'The police say that *Plaid Cymru* is responsible and Miles claimed that he suspected Watkin of being a member. Even if he can't prove that your father actually set fire to their place, Miles will still accuse him of having persuaded his *Plaid Cymru* friends to carry it out.'

'This is outrageous! He's never been involved in any politics.' Megan slammed shut the oven door and whipped off her apron as she spoke. 'I'm going to see Miles Walker right now . . . and his father . . . and the police.'

'No! Wait, Megan.' Robert barred her way. 'There's nothing to be gained from losing your temper or upsetting your mother.'

'So how are we going to explain why my dad hasn't come home for his meal this evening?'

'I'll tell her he's out on a job and will be away overnight. Tomorrow, if they don't release him, we may have to tell her the truth. Take it step by step, we don't want to upset her more than is necessary.'

'And in the meantime my dad has to spend the night in a police cell!' Megan fumed.

'Megan.' He seized her shoulders, looking directly into her eyes. 'We both know he's innocent, but we won't convince the police of that by flying off the handle. We've got to think it through carefully, decide the right approach and above all keep calm.'

'And say nothing to my mother until we know what is happening unless it is absolutely necessary.'

'Exactly! We musn't let her see the evening paper, there's a piece in there about it. And tomorrow, of course, it may be in some of the daily papers.'

'We?'

'Yes, Megan, we. Your father has been a good friend to me and I shall stand by him no matter what happens.'

Megan returned Robert's steady gaze for a long moment. Then, with a sigh that shuddered through her, she collapsed against him, burying her head against his broad chest.

He held her close, stroking her dark hair, murmuring words of comfort. He had never felt so full of anger towards anyone as he did towards Miles Walker. He was prepared to accept that Lynn's death had been an accident, something that could happen to anyone. It was what Miles had done to Megan that he found so unforgivable. To promise marriage knowing he intended to marry someone else, to turn from her when she was pregnant and desperately needed his support, were both despicable acts in Robert's eyes.

He knew he was probably prejudiced because of his own feelings for Megan. The thought of Megan as his wife was still a dream he indulged in from time to time. Whenever he did, he ended up feeling bitter because she had turned down his offer of marriage and resentful that she could love a rogue like Miles Walker but have no time for him.

If only she had accepted his offer of marriage, he thought morosely. If she had, then you'd have been lumbered with Miles Walker's little bastard, and how would you have felt then? he asked himself scornfully. But even that would have been bearable if Megan had been his, he told himself.

He had helped her then and he was determined to help her again now. Perhaps one day she would recognise the fact that she couldn't manage without him.

Megan spent a sleepless night planning what she would do next. When she took her mother's breakfast up to her, Megan suggested she might like to have a lie-in.

'I have to go out,' she told her. 'I may not be back until around four o'clock. Shall I ask Mrs Pinter from next door to pop in around lunchtime?'

'Certainly not! Why should I want to see Mrs Pinter? You go and do what you have to, don't worry about me. What time did you say your dad would be home?'

'I didn't . . . Robert wasn't sure what time he would be back. Anyway, don't worry. I'll be home before him . . . I expect. There's some cold meat so make yourself a sandwich at lunchtime.'

When she reached the office in Old Hall Street, Megan gave only the briefest of greetings to Olive and Mavis. Myra Thornton tried to stop her but she brushed her to one side without any explanation and walked straight through to Mr Walker's office with Myra following on her heels.

Miles and his father were both there. Mr Walker was sitting in his high-backed leather chair, his hands resting on the polished walnut desk in front of him. He was in earnest conversation with Miles, who was sitting facing him. Miles was chewing his lower lip as he listened to what his father was saying.

Neither of them noticed the intrusion until Myra Thornton burst out apologetically, 'I'm sorry, Mr Walker. I know you said you were not to be interrupted, but Megan wouldn't listen. She pushed past me and . . .'

'That's all right, Myra. Please leave us.' Martin Walker's voice was curt, and he was frowning as he looked up.

'So, can we take it that you have come back to work, Megan?' he asked abruptly.

'No! I've come to demand an explanation for what has happened to my father.'

'Your father?' Martin Walker frowned. 'I've no idea what you're talking about.'

'Don't try and evade the issue,' she snapped angrily. 'You must know that he has been arrested and charged with setting fire to your house in Wales.'

Bewildered, Mr Walker turned to Miles. 'Is this true? You said the police had apprehended someone, but you never mentioned any name. Why wasn't I told who it was?'

'I thought it was better if you weren't worried by the details at the moment,' Miles said evasively. 'If he was found guilty then of course you would have been told all about it.'

'What the hell are you going on about, Miles? Surely the police don't detain someone unless they have pretty sound evidence?'

'Oh, they have,' Megan said contemptuously. 'Miles has made sure of that. It's hard to believe that he can take personal spite to such lengths,' she added bitterly.

'I don't understand. What do you mean, Megan?'

'Since you are bound to find out, I would prefer to be the one to tell you,' Megan said in an icy tone. 'Miles and I were lovers for quite a long time. He promised to marry me as soon as he was made a director of the company.'

'Marry you!'

Martin Walker looked bewildered as he glanced from his son to Megan and he was taken aback by the hatred that gleamed in both their eyes.

'You wondered why I was able to find my way to Tynmorfa the day you asked me to drive you there, and why Jason was so friendly towards me. Well . . . it was because I had been there before . . . with Miles,' Megan went on relentlessly. 'After he married Carol Brocklehurst, I refused to have anything more to do with him, and this is his revenge.'

'Is this true, Miles?'

'It's all lies!' Miles exploded angrily. His blue eyes were icy, his mouth twisted in a sneer.

'There's not much more,' Megan said bitterly. 'I don't hold Miles responsible for my sister's death, neither does my father. That was an accident. I do hold him responsible for two-timing us both. Lynn knew him as Flash and she was as much in love with him as I was,' she added bitterly.

'Good God! What has been going on? Miles . . .' The words ended in a gasping, choking sound.

Megan watched in dismay as the red flush ebbed from Mr Walker's florid face. A vein on his temple throbbed, his eyes bulged and his breathing became laboured. A convulsive shudder shook his body as he collapsed across the desk.

Miles stood transfixed.

'Help me!' Megan gasped as she struggled to loosen Mr Walker's tie. 'Tell Olive to send for an ambulance.'

His hand trembling, Miles picked up the phone, his eyes fixed on his father.

'Is he going to be all right?' he asked hoarsely.

'I . . . I'm not sure . . .' Her voice dropped to a whisper as she looked up at Miles. 'I can't feel his pulse!'

Chapter Thirty

Trying to keep the news from Kathy Williams that Watkin had been arrested was impossible. Although Megan had hidden the *Liverpool Echo* that evening, she was still feeling so upset over the way Martin Walker had collapsed and died that she completely forgot about it the next day.

Megan felt devastated when she saw her mother pick up the paper and moved swiftly to take it away, but her mother grabbed her arm and stopped her.

'Leave it!'

There was a fanatical gleam in Kathy's grey eyes as she sat on the edge of her chair, mouth open, reading the report.

Megan's spirits sank. 'Mam . . . let me explain . . .'

'Explain! You mean fob me off with more lies, don't you?' Kathy exclaimed bitterly.

'No, of course not! I only want to tell you the truth about what's happened.'

'Don't bother. I know more than you give me credit for, my girl. You and your dad hoodwinked me after our Lynn was killed. All that talk about it being an accident! The pair of you sticking up for that Miles Walker, when all the time you knew he was responsible. I couldn't stand any more of it, that's why I began drinking.'

'Mam. Please!' Megan knelt beside her mother's chair, a hand on her knee.

'I know I've been a burden to you all.' Kathy sighed heavily. 'None of you understand!' She rocked to and fro, her face contorted with distress. 'I'm to blame for Lynn's death. I knew all about this Flash and I knew she was seeing him. I should have put my foot down. Or else told your dad to have a talk to her and stop her going out with him.'

'It probably wouldn't have made any difference,' Megan murmured.

'I had my suspicions that he was no good. The fact that he refused to come and meet any of us should have put me on my guard but I did nothing about it.'

'It's all in the past, Mam . . .'

'At least she didn't bring any other worries home to our doorstep. I know you didn't either,' she went on garrulously, 'but if you hadn't gone ahead and done what you did then we might have had that to deal with, as well.'

'Mam . . .' Megan let out a long low breath of distress. 'I didn't think you had any idea . . . I . . .'

'No, you think your old mam is a bit simple. You're a cut above her with your education, fine job and smart clothes. I've got eyes in my head; I know the signs. I should do. I got caught myself when I was about your age.'

'Mam, please . . . don't go on like this.'

'You didn't know that, did you? A one-night stand and he sailed off next day. I was lucky, I suppose, because he came back in time to marry me before you were born. But that's all in the past, I don't want to talk about it.'

Megan remained silent, astounded by her mother's outburst.

'They probably thought that setting fire to Walker's place was Watkin's way of paying them back for their son killing our Lynn,' mused Kathy.

'Dad didn't do it, Mam! He was sitting here with us the night their place was set on fire.'

'And who is going to believe that?' snapped Kathy, her eyes glinting angrily. 'The police are looking for a scapegoat and he's got plenty of reasons for carrying out such a crime. Walker's son killed one of our daughters and turned the other one into a whore.'

'Mam!' White-lipped and shaken, Megan drew back as if she had been struck. Her mother was suddenly a stranger. She couldn't believe she was hearing aright.

'I'll make us some tea,' her mother said, rising from her chair. 'You look as though you could do with something stronger, but I don't suppose there's any drink in the house.'

'No . . . there isn't . . . and you know why.'

'Of course, I do,' her mother retorted. 'Can't trust your own mam, can you?' She gave a raucous laugh. 'Funny, isn't it, you preaching to me about how I should behave. Making me feel guilty!'

'Mam, I haven't meant to.' Megan's voice reflected the anguish she was feeling.

'Rubbish! You always have. Right from when you were small you would look at me with those big dark eyes, just like your dad's, and make me feel guilty whenever I enjoyed myself.'

'Mam, I'll make the tea. You sit still, you're not well . . . you're in a state of shock . . .' Megan stood up and tried to press her mother back into her chair, but Kathy shook her hand away.

'I'm as well as I'll ever be and I think you are the one who has had the shock this time. You're like your dad, Megan. You can't bear for people to know you have any weaknesses. Always so well behaved, saying the right thing and doing what is expected of you. Paragons of virtue, the pair of you! Lynn wasn't like that. She enjoyed life and liked a good laugh. I never needed to hide anything from her. I wonder what your dad would say if I told him about you having an abortion?'

'He knows. I've already told him,' Megan said shakily.

For a moment Kathy stared at her in disbelief. Then she threw back her head and laughed hysterically. 'In that case, he probably did set fire to Walker's place,' she crowed.

It was three days before Watkin was brought before a magistrate. Three endless days for Megan, tortured by her mother's revelations and accusations as well as filled with concern over her father's well-being.

It was almost as though their roles were reversed. Kathy was the one who cooked and tidied around. Megan stayed slumped in a chair trying to decide what to do for the best.

'Sitting there staring into space isn't going to do any good. Go and find yourself a job. You might need some money to pay your dad's fine,' Kathy told her cynically. 'If he gets sent down then you'll be the bread-winner, remember.'

'Dad's innocent. You know that! We can prove he was right here.'

'I've already told you that our word won't carry very much weight!'

'How can you be so complacent about it? I don't think you really care.' Megan rounded on her mother furiously.

'I'm just facing facts. When they learn how you were carrying on with Miles Walker until he decided to dump you, they'll put it all down to revenge.'

'Dad wasn't anywhere near there that night. He was with Robert all day, making a delivery in Doncaster, and he came straight home after work. Robert's the one person who can prove Dad is innocent.'

'Poor dab! Playing on his feelings as usual, are you?' her mother taunted. 'The only time he ever hears from you is when you are in trouble. Use him, don't you.'

'I'll do anything to see that my dad is set free,' affirmed Megan vehemently.

In face of the cast-iron alibi from Robert, the case against Watkin was dropped. Megan's relief was tempered by her father's bitterness.

'Well, there's one good thing come out of all this,' Kathy commented later that evening after Robert had gone home and the three of them were on their own.

'And what's that?' Watkin frowned. His dark eyes were puzzled.

'We've finally finished with the Walkers,' she declared triumphantly. 'You won't be going back there to work and our Megan won't be working there, either. So that's the end of it.'

'Plenty of other jobs about, Dad,' Megan told him in an over-bright voice when he said nothing. 'I wonder which of us will get fixed up first, eh?'

'I don't know. Better start looking, I suppose.' He tried to match the optimism in her voice as he reached out for the *Echo* and turned to the 'Situations Vacant' pages.

Kathy's eyes narrowed as she watched them, a satisfied smirk on her mouth.

Finding work took time. There were plenty of driving jobs advertised, but after the first two or three interviews Watkin found that the moment he gave his name, and stated that he had been at Walker's, interest in his application vanished.

'Don't contact us again, we'll get in touch with you if we need you,' became such a standard response that he grew disheartened and embittered.

'Robert will probably give you a reference . . . if Megan asks him,' jibed Kathy.

'That'll do!' Angrily, Watkin turned away, his hands balled into two tight fists to control his feelings.

He had still not grown used to the change in Kathy. In some ways it had been easier when she had been in the depths of despair and speaking to no one, he thought irritably. Now she was as touchy as a wild cat and with claws to match. Everything he said or did brought a verbal attack that shattered his nerves. And it wasn't directed only at him. Megan was getting the sharp end of her tongue as well.

'Why are you getting on at the girl so much?' he asked when they were on their own. 'She's got enough on her plate as it is.'

'Has she? More intrigues, more things she's kept hidden from me, you mean,' sneered Kathy. 'You are as bad as one other with your dark secrets.'

'She didn't want to worry you,' he protested.

'Only because she couldn't bear for anyone to see her in a bad light,' Kathy said contemptuously. 'She pulled the wool over your eyes and no mistake! Letting you think she was the good little girl, the studious one, out to better herself,' she taunted. 'And all the time she was carrying on with that Miles Walker. Well, she got her just deserts there and no mistake, now, didn't she!'

'That will do, woman!' Watkin's voice thundered out in anger.

'Always dressing to kill, flaunting her airs and graces, too good for the likes of me and Lynn. Always telling poor little Lynn off for enjoying herself. Looked down on her because she worked in a café. She couldn't help it if she had no brains. Took after me, did our Lynn. She was pretty, though, and liked a laugh and a good time. There's enough misery guts like you and Megan in the world, blighting everyone's life . . .'

'Will you pipe down!' Watkin's roar brought Megan hurrying through from the kitchen to see what was wrong.

'What's the matter now?' She looked from one

to the other, perplexed. She was not used to her parents quarrelling in this way. Usually, her father ignored Kathy's petty nagging.

'I was telling your dad what a dark horse you are,' Kathy said slyly. 'You quiet, studious types, always with your nose in a book, are all the same.'

'I don't think there is very much you can tell Dad that he doesn't already know,' Megan told her quietly. 'Why don't you leave him alone? He's worried enough at the moment about not getting a job . . .' She stopped, frightened by the menacing look on her mother's face.

For a moment it seemed that her mother was about to strike her. Then, with a sharp cry, Kathy crumpled onto the floor, convulsive sobs racking her body.

'Ring for the doctor, Megan!' Watkin ordered as he knelt down beside his wife and cradled her in his arms, stroking her hair, murmuring words of comfort.

The doctor diagnosed Kathy's collapse as being caused by depression, brought on by feelings of guilt, ill-health and severe shock. 'In the normal way I would recommend she was treated in a hospital,' he told them. 'In this instance, I think Mrs Williams needs to have her family around her. Nursing her won't be easy. She'll have spells when she is extremely lucid, and may say things you find hard to take. There will be other times when you will find it impossible to communicate with her, she will be so withdrawn. She will need expert counselling, which I can arrange. Most of all, though, she is going to need constant supervision. Will you be able to manage that?'

'Yes. We will both be at home for the next few weeks,' Megan said quickly, looking across at her father.

'Megan's right, Doctor,' agreed Watkin dourly. 'We'll be here to look after her.'

'Good! I'll call in every two or three days.' He handed Watkin a prescription. 'These tablets will help to calm her. If you have any further problems get in touch with me.'

When he reached the door he paused and looked at them both from over the top of his glasses. 'She may say a lot of things you find very hurtful, things dredged up from the past that you may have thought long forgotten. Cleansing the mind is all part of the therapy. It can provide clues as to the problem that has caused her present condition. Try not to let it upset you too much, I don't want any more cases of depression.'

'Perhaps we should have had her taken into hospital,' Watkin Williams muttered after the doctor had left.

'Nonsense, Dad. We can look after her. She's better off at home.'

'I hope you're right. I feel it's too much to expect of you, though, Megan. I . . . I don't want you hurt again.'

'I won't be, I promise you.' Gently she kissed his cheek. 'Over the last few days we've found out what Mam thinks about both of us. I don't think there are any more skeletons left hidden in the cupboard,' she added ruefully.

'Let's hope you're right.' He sighed deeply and

Megan's heart ached to see how thin and ill he looked.

'We'll have Mam back on her feet in no time,' she vowed cheerfully. 'Everything will work out all right, you'll see. It's going to be a new start all round,' she promised confidently.

Chapter Thirty-one

'Something wrong?' asked Watkin as Megan came back into the sitting room looking white and shaken. 'Who was that on the phone?'

'A Mr Ramton. He's the Walkers' solicitor.'

Watkin frowned. 'What did he want? They're not still trying to prosecute me over the fire, are they?'

'No, no, Dad, it's nothing to do with that.' Megan shook her head emphatically.

'Well, what is it, then? More trouble? You look like you've seen a ghost.'

'A cloud not a ghost!' She gave a wry laugh. 'Mr Ramton says that Mr Walker has left me his Silver Cloud.'

'You mean his Rolls Royce!' Her father stared at her in disbelief. 'What on earth made him do that?'

'I don't know!' She pushed her hair back from her forehead in a bewildered way. 'He did once remark that my initials were on the number plate. He made a sort of joke about it when I was driving him to Wales. They were his initials, too, of course,' she added quickly.

'And Miles Walker's!' her father reminded her. 'That car is a status symbol! I've often heard men down at the docks say how proud old Walker was of it. He even had his own special parking spot with the registration number written in white paint on the ground to make sure no other car was left there by mistake.'

'The only other person permitted to drive the Rolls was Miles, and he wasn't allowed behind the wheel all that often,' murmured Megan. 'So why has he left it to me?'

'Someone once told me that, when he first had it, old Walker would hire a taxi if it was raining rather than get the Rolls wet. I can't see Miles letting you get away with this one,' mused Watkin, shaking his head.

Miles wasted no time in phoning Megan about the Rolls. 'You don't intend accepting it, I hope?' he said abruptly.

'Why ever not? It would be ungrateful to turn it down.'

'Cut the nonsense, Megan. That car is our company status symbol and I intend to keep it. Anyway, what would you do with an expensive car like that? You couldn't possibly afford to keep it on the road. It drinks petrol!'

'I must keep it . . . it's a gift . . . from your father,' she reminded him.

'Have you any idea what it costs to have it serviced?' he went on relentlessly.

'Not yet. I haven't gone into such details.'

'It would take at least three months' wages . . . that's if you were working. Look,' he snapped angrily, 'I'm willing to buy it back from you. I'll pay the full market value for it.'

'I don't intend to sell it.'

'Megan, it belongs to the company . . .'

'It did. It doesn't now,' she pointed out determinedly.

'I can see it's pointless trying to discuss this with you,' Miles snapped. 'Think about it and phone me when you are ready to sell. I'll wait a week and if you haven't contacted me by then I'll take you to court. I want that car and I intend to have it . . . one way or the other. If I have to go to court, I'll make sure the whole world knows exactly what sort of person you are. After I've told them about our affair, they'll be able to put two and two together. They'll realise how you made up to my father and tricked him into leaving you the Rolls.'

'You would lie in court to get your own way?'

His cynical laugh still echoed in her ears long after she had slammed the receiver down.

The more Megan thought about it the more frightened she became that Miles might carry out his threat. It was not the loss of the Rolls that worried her, but that the slur on her character would have a devastating effect on her mother.

The feelings she had once held for Miles were now completely dead. She felt so nervy and edgy, though, that it took her all her time not to lose patience with her mother or snap at her father. Finally, she was in such a quandary about what to do that in sheer desperation she turned to Robert, feeling that he was the only person whose advice she could trust.

They met in the lounge bar at The Nelson. His momentary look of surprise when she told him she had been left the Rolls was replaced by a frown when she told him how Miles had reacted.

317

'I don't know what to do.' She sighed heavily. 'It's a wonderful car, but I suppose Miles is quite right, I can't afford to run it.' She gave a bitter laugh. 'I haven't even got a job at the moment.'

'If you don't let him have the Rolls he will take you to court, you know,' warned Robert. 'What's more, he'll certainly carry out his threat to try and blacken your character.'

'You think he would go that far, even though it would reflect on him?'

'It's different for a man. Nice girls don't sleep around.'

'What do you mean by sleep around?' exploded Megan. 'There has only ever been Miles.'

'I know that, but try convincing other people. The way Miles will tell the story he'll make it sound quite different.'

'You believe me, though, Robert?'

'Of course I do!' As their eyes met, he looked away quickly. 'Another drink?' As if to break the spell, he stood up and picked up their empty glasses.

As she watched Robert walk over to the bar she thought what a wonderful friend he was. No matter what problem she had, he was always willing to help her to solve it. And invariably she found herself taking his advice because it was so sound.

The fact that he seemed to think Miles would not only be prepared to go to court over the car, but that he would be willing to make public every detail of their relationship, worried her more than she cared to admit.

'Apart from how much it might distress your

318

mother, Miles' revelations could seriously affect your career prospects, you know,' Robert commented when he returned with their drinks. 'Once the story has been plastered over the *Liverpool Echo*, and possibly in some of the national dailies, your new boss will think you fair game! If you disappoint him then you'll probably be out on your neck pretty quick.'

'You mean someone might hire me because of that rather than because I'm a competent secretary!' she exclaimed, colour staining her cheeks.

'It's still a man's world, Megan.'

'And women play right into their hands,' Megan said bitterly. 'They mollycoddle them at home and pander to them at work. Being a secretary is a cross between being a wife and being a nanny.'

'Always playing the support role, but never the boss!' Robert laughed grimly.

Megan sat bolt upright. Never the boss! Why not be the boss? she asked herself. Why not have a company of her own? She had plenty of knowledge about import and export, organising freight, storing cargo and dealing with customs regulations.

She turned to Robert, her eyes bright with excitement. He listened in thoughtful silence. By the time she stopped expounding her plans he seemed to be almost as enthusiastic as she was. When she paused for breath, he began enlarging on the ideas she had already put forward.

'You'll have to clear up this mess with Miles Walker first, though,' Robert reminded her. 'I'd approach him face to face and try to come to some sort of amicable arrangement, if that is possible. He's offered to buy the Rolls, so that could provide you with some capital to start your business,' he pointed out. 'Would you like me to speak to him for you, Megan?'

'No!' She placed her hand on his arm to soften the forcefulness of her reply. 'It's something I've got to do myself,' she explained.

'You'd better have the Rolls valued before you go to see him so that you ask the right price for it.'

'I've got an even better idea,' she said thoughtfully. 'I'll ask him to swop the Rolls for one of the lorries!'

Miles smirked with pleasure when Megan presented herself at his office next day.

'I've come to talk terms,' she said stiffly.

'I'm glad you've come to your senses. The old man must have been out of his mind when he put that in his will,' Miles said dismissively.

'Yes, as you said it is one of the company's status symbols. Especially with its personalised number plates!'

'So you're prepared to hand it back.'

'Oh, no! It's not going to be quite that simple, Miles,' she told him coolly.

His eyes narrowed and his mouth tightened. 'You mean you want the market price,' he sneered as he pulled out a cheque book and unscrewed the top of his fountain pen.

'There's no need for that.' Megan held up her hand before Miles could start to write. 'I want to do a deal. I'll give you back the Rolls in exchange for two of your lorries. I'll take the new Commer and the Bedford . . .'

'Sod that!' he exploded. 'Do you know how much they cost? They're the newest ones in our fleet.'

'Well, I don't want the old clapped out ones, now, do I?' She smiled sweetly.

'Why do you want lorries in exchange for the Rolls anyway?' Miles asked in amazement. 'You must be mad!'

She stood up and began to move towards the door. 'That's the deal or I keep the Rolls.'

'Why do you want the lorries?'

Megan's eyes narrowed and for a moment she thought of ignoring his question. 'I'm starting up in business for myself,' she told him and her voice cracked like a whip in the silence.

Miles' lip curled and he stared at her in disbelief. He was sure she was bluffing, but as their eyes locked he saw how determined she was.

'You'll never succeed, you know,' he said scathingly. 'You're taking on a great deal more than you can cope with, Megan. They won't give you the time of day down at the docks. No reputable company will entrust their cargoes to a woman.'

'Really! You mean it's a man's world? They're happy enough to let a woman type the invoices, fill in all the forms and organise everything from the office.'

The scorn in her voice startled him. He had never thought of it like that before and grudgingly he had to admit to himself that she was right.

'I suppose you are going to try and pinch all our best customers,' he sneered.

'I hadn't thought of doing so, but it is quite a

good idea,' Megan countered as she moved back towards his desk. 'Are we agreed, then? You'll give me the two lorries in settlement for the Rolls.'

'Not those two. There's a Morris and a Ford you can have instead.'

'They're ready for the scrap yard and you know it. The Morris was involved in a smash the year I joined the company and it's been a problem ever since.'

The deadlock seemed unsurpassable. For another twenty minutes they argued. Megan stuck to her ground. Where once she would have given way to male authority, now she was like a tiger fighting for its share of the kill. She refused to give an inch. It had to be the two vehicles she had stipulated and reluctantly Miles recognised this. Grudgingly, he gave in to her demands.

'Whew!' His old grin was back and for a moment Megan felt her heart thundering. Miles' devastating charm, and animal magnetism, still had its effect on her. Then she steeled her mind, remembering the past and all the heartache he had already cost her.

'Are we clear on all these points?' she persisted, frowning down at the notebook in which she had listed the details of their transaction.

'I'm not sure!' He held out his hand. 'Let me check it and make sure that you haven't made any mistakes.'

With an inscrutable look she passed the notebook over to him, smiling to herself as she saw his puzzled frown as he stared uncomprehendingly at the shorthand hieroglyphics written there. He looked up at her questioningly, but she returned his gaze blankly.

Silently, Miles passed the notebook back to her and without a word she dropped it into her handbag. He found himself comparing her with his wife. A feeling of discontent swept through him. Memories of the ripe softness of Megan's body, the sweetness of her lips, her compliant surrender as they'd consummated their love, filled his mind. It was never like that with Carol. She made love as if bestowing some tremendous favour.

He had found married life disappointing in other respects, too. Megan not only had a body made for loving, but she had a needle-sharp mind that he had found equally stimulating.

His father had recognised Megan's business acumen and now she was no longer in the office Miles realised more and more how great an asset she had been. He wanted her back but it looked as if he had left it too late to ask her.

'Right. I'm glad that's settled,' Megan told him. 'You have the necessary papers drawn up and I'll ask my solicitor to contact Mr Ramton. I'll arrange for the lorries to be collected as soon as the legal formalities are completed,' she said briskly. 'I shall expect them to be in clean condition and intact,' she added as a parting shot. 'No removing spares, or any other tricks. Remember, I know everything about those vehicles.'

Before he could reply she had gone, closing the door firmly behind her.

Chapter Thirty-two

Megan had never worked so hard in her life, yet at night, although she was dropping with fatigue and every bone in her body was aching, sleep eluded her.

Long after she was in bed her mind was a jumbled merry-go-round of all the things she had done that day and tasks that still needed her attention. Even when she finally dozed off she would dream about work.

It often amazed her that problems which had seemed insurmountable when she went to bed had a logical solution by the next morning.

Robert was wonderfully supportive. Without his help and guidance, Megan was sure she would never have managed to get her haulage business started. He constantly suggested shortcuts, or ways of doing things, that she just wouldn't have considered.

It had been Robert who had found a one-room shed with a phone that they were able to rent as a temporary office on the dockside. He'd given it a coat of paint and then bought a second-hand desk, two sturdy straight-back chairs, a typewriter and a filing cabinet to furnish it. He'd even painted her name in black letters on a piece of white board and nailed it to the door.

'There you are, now you're in business,' he told her. 'You can start writing around, offering your services to some of the local companies.'

'I've already prepared a publicity letter; I only needed an address for replies. I didn't think it would sound businesslike to have them sent to me at home.'

'The best of luck, then. It may take a while before you get any response,' he warned. 'Half of them won't even bother to reply.'

Waiting for work to come in was the hardest part, but Robert boosted her morale whenever it seemed to be sagging.

When she told her father that she had swapped the Rolls for two lorries, he had looked at her blankly.

'What did you do a thing like that for?' he asked in a puzzled tone.

'So that we would have vehicles to drive! I'm going to start my own haulage business with you in charge of the transport side of things,' she told him excitedly.

'I can only drive one lorry at a time so why do you need two?' he muttered, staring at her in bemusement. 'You won't be able to afford to pay a driver, girl.'

'I'm driving the other one!'

Her father had scoffed, railed, ridiculed, but she had stuck to her guns. Robert had backed her and insisted on taking her out for a meal.

'Put your glad rags on, kiddo,' he ordered, 'we're going to celebrate in style. I'm going to take you to the Adelphi for a nosh.'

'The Adelphi! Will they let lorry drivers in there?' she teased.

'No one will know when you're dressed up, and I won't let on if you don't.' Robert grinned.

The dining room at the Adelphi Hotel was the most magnificent room Megan had ever been in. Its mirrored walls reflected the tables that were spread with gleaming white napery, glittering crystal, sparkling cutlery and pretty flower arrangements as well as the elegantly dressed people sitting at them.

It was all so imposing that Megan felt self-conscious and wondered if her simple, knee-skimming pink dress with its scoop neckline was really smart enough for the occasion.

It was so much easier for men. Robert was wearing a three-piece navy blue suit and had merely substituted a black bow tie for his usual striped one, and yet he looked as correctly dressed as any other man in the room.

Even better than a great many of them, she thought as she admired the square set of his broad shoulders. He was so powerfully built that it wasn't until he stood alongside other men, and his shock of light-brown hair was way above their heads, that it became apparent that he was over six foot tall.

He was quite a remarkable person, she thought fondly as she listened to him ordering their meal. Quietly confident, he wasn't in the least daunted by the waiter's supercilious manner.

They were halfway through the first course before Megan relaxed enough to look around and take stock of people sitting at nearby tables. When she did, she was taken aback as she met the gaze of Stanley Martingale, one of Walker's most valued customers.

She returned his nod of recognition with a smile, but felt disconcerted when she saw him rise and make his way over to their table.

'I'm sorry to disturb your meal, Miss Williams,' he murmured after she'd introduced him to Robert, 'but I wondered if anything was wrong with Miles Walker. I've been trying to get in touch with him all week and he hasn't returned any of my calls and . . .'

'I'm sorry, Mr Martingale, but I can't help you,' Megan interrupted. 'I don't work there any more.'

'Really! They'll certainly miss you!' His shrewd green eyes narrowed under their bushy grey brows. 'I can offer you a job, Megan, if you need one.'

'That's very kind of you but I've gone into business on my own account,' she blurted out, her colour rising.

'You have! Let me guess . . . hairdressing . . . a beauty salon . . . one of these new secretarial agencies. Send me the details and I'll put the word around . . .'

'It's nothing like that. I've started my own haulage business.' His startled expression made her smile. 'So if you need anything moving . . .'

'Well, I do! That's why I've been trying to contact Miles. I've got a consignment due in first thing tomorrow on the *Marie Louise*, one of the Magda Line boats . . .'

'And you want it moving right away?'

'That's right! I haven't any storage space available in my warehouses so I want it taken straight off the boat and up to Newcastle. Could you handle a job like that?'

'Certainly. I'll collect the papers from your office first thing in the morning,' she told him crisply.

'Dammit, you mean it!' Laughter convulsed him, making him cough and splutter as he shook his head from side to side, staring at her in disbelief.

'Don't you mean it, Mr Martingale?' asked Megan stiffly, her cheeks scarlet.

'By God, I do. Let's shake on it.' He extended his hand and pumped hers energetically. 'It's good to do business with you. Enjoy your meal.'

Stanley Martingale was still shaking with laughter as he went back to his table. Minutes later he sent a waiter over to their table with a bottle of champagne.

Delighted by the turn of events, Megan clinked glasses with Robert in a toast. 'To the success of my very first order,' she murmured, then turned and raised her glass in Mr Martingale's direction.

Although Robert was pleased for her, he was more than a little irritated by its timing. It spoiled the evening as far as he was concerned. He had chosen the Adelphi because it was the finest hotel in Liverpool and he had felt it would be the perfect setting in which, once again, to ask Megan to marry him.

Now, after Stanley Martingale's interruption, it didn't seem to be the right moment to do so . . . not if he wanted his proposal to be taken seriously.

He remembered the first time he had seen her,

not long after the Williams family had arrived in Liverpool. She had been so shy, her elfin face so serious, and the soft lilt in her voice so captivating that he had felt unexpectedly protective towards her. Her demure aloofness had intrigued him.

She'd changed since then, both in character and appearance. Her dark hair was no longer caught back behind her ears, but sculpted to her head in a style that framed her cheeks. The wispy tendrils over her ears and forehead emphasised her long lashes and dark eyebrows, imparting a gamin look, especially when she was wearing her working outfit of a jacket and trousers.

The elegant dress she was wearing for their outing, a sheath of glowing pink, skimmed her body in a figure-flattering way. A single strand of pearls added a touch of sophistication.

His hand went to the pocket of his jacket, feeling the small square box secreted there, longing to slide the ring that nestled inside it onto her slim finger.

When he had first heard the rumours linking Megan's name with that of Miles Walker, he had been incensed. For the first time in his life he had known what it was to be jealous. He had debated whether or not to warn her that Miles was a philanderer, but hesitated in case by doing so he put his own friendship with her on the line.

Providing a shoulder for Megan to weep on when she learned that Miles was to marry Carol Brocklehurst had not been easy. It became an even greater torment on learning that she was pregnant with Miles' child. His offer then to marry her had not been made lightly. He would have been prepared to accept the child if by doing so he stood a chance of winning her love.

That was all in the past, he reminded himself.

Now, sitting across the table from her, watching her dark eyes glow with excitement at securing such a sizeable order for her new business venture, his spirits sank and he deplored his own diffidence. If he asked her now she might think it was because of her business success.

The moment the thought crossed his mind he rejected it. He knew her too well ever to believe she would think that. His hand went once more to his pocket, fingering the little box hidden there. Should he do as he had planned and pop the question as the climax to their meal?

What if she should refuse? He didn't want to contemplate that, not for a moment. Yet, if she did, he would be more than ready to agree she should have time to think it over. He'd even planned for such an eventuality by making arrangements to go on a walking holiday so that she wouldn't feel pressurised into giving him an immediate answer.

He withdrew his hand from his pocket. The question and the ring must wait. It would be far better if he went on holiday as he intended, and asked her when he came home.

Chapter Thirty-three

Watkin Williams was apprehensive when Megan told him she would be transporting incoming cargo for Stanley Martingale.

'You do know he is one of Walker's main customers?' he cautioned.

'Of course I do! I worked in the office long enough to know every customer they had, didn't I?' she retorted sharply.

'Well, is it right, girl? Poaching like this, I mean.'

'I'm not poaching.' Her eyes flashed as she defended herself. 'He came to me, I didn't approach him.'

'From what you said, Martingale simply asked you if you knew why Miles Walker wasn't returning his calls.'

'And I told him I didn't know because I wasn't working at Walker's any more.'

'Ah well.' He shrugged. 'If, as they say, "all is fair in love and war", then I suppose the same thing applies in business as well.'

With Robert, they planned the best method of unloading the *Marie Louise*, and which of the lorries to load first, how long the trip would take and the most suitable route.

'Megan, are you sure you'll be able to drive . . . ?' Watkin asked apprehensively.

'Look, Dad, let's get it straight once and for all. I'm in charge and I drive whenever there's enough work for two lorries,' she insisted. 'Right?'

'That's the worst of having a woman boss,' lamented Watkin. 'They always get the better of you,' he added with an indulgent smile.

'Well, at least you know where you stand!' Robert laughed. 'I hope things go smoothly. I'm off tomorrow on a walking holiday in North Wales. Shall I say "hello" to Beddgelert for you?'

'You can certainly do that, boyo!' enthused Watkin, his eyes lighting up. 'I wish I was going with you.'

'Oh, Dad!'

'Only joking, girl,' he said quickly, seeing the expression of dismay on Megan's face. 'This job is much more important.'

'You do miss the mountains, though . . . and so do I,' she added wistfully.

'We'll go back to Beddgelert again, some day. You make a fortune for us, and then we can retire back there. In the meantime, we can always look across to Wales from King's Parade, and see the mountains outlined against the skyline, and know they are still there waiting for us.'

Megan and her father left home just before seven next day. The morning was grey and raw. Megan turned up her collar and pulled on thick gloves, trying not to let her father see that she was already shivering with the cold.

When they arrived at the docks, Watkin went to check over the lorries and to make sure they were filled up with fuel, that the tyre pressures were right, and that there were adequate ropes and tarpaulins for their loads. Megan went to find the captain of the *Marie Louise*.

Captain Johann Ingers was a short, blond Dutchman with huge shoulders and massive muscles. His light blue eyes narrowed as he surveyed the slim, dark-haired girl with her serious manner and light lilting voice who had come on board to claim the cargo he had brought from Amsterdam.

'Is it not to go into a warehouse here on the dockside?' he asked in surprise.

'No. We are transporting it straight to Newcastle.'

'You have papers authorising collection?'

'Not yet. I still have to collect them.'

'No papers, no cargo.' He shrugged dismissively, his massive shoulders heaving.

'I'll have them when I bring my lorries alongside at nine o'clock, so be ready to unload,' she told him curtly.

Leaving him still bemused, Megan went to collect the documents from Martingale's office, then headed for the bay where the two lorries were parked.

A grey mist swirled over the Mersey, cutting down visibility and lending an eerie mystery to the noisy, busy quayside as the day's work began. Gulls circled overhead, winged scavengers screaming raucously as they swooped onto the dockside in search of food.

When Megan found her father, he was white faced and shaking. 'What's wrong, Dad?' she asked anxiously. 'Are you ill?'

'I'm all right. It's the lorries! They've been sabotaged. Some bastard has taken a pickaxe to the fuel tanks on both of them! Can't you smell it, girl? Look on the ground, there's diesel everywhere!'

'Who on earth would do a thing like that? Could it be kids messing about?'

'Don't talk so bloody daft! It's someone out to get us, someone who knew about that load and was making sure we didn't take it.'

They stared at each other, dark eyes locked in consternation.

'That's it, then, Megan. You'll just have to go and phone Martingale and explain what's happened.'

'I can't do that! If we let Stanley Martingale down over this consignment then there'll never be any more work from him,' Megan exclaimed, aghast.

'True!' Watkin rubbed the back of his neck. 'And, not only that, but word that we are unreliable will spread through the docks in a flash.'

'And they'll say it's because a woman was running the firm,' she muttered grimly.

'That's defeatist talk, Megan!'

'I know, Dad. Forget I said it, I was thinking aloud. So what do we do now?'

'We certainly can't repair either of the lorries in time to pick up the cargo from the *Marie Louise*.'

'No, I can see that! So what else do you suggest?'

'If only we knew someone who would hire us a couple of lorries . . .' He stopped and once again their eyes locked.

'Robert would know someone,' they both exclaimed together.

'I'll go and phone him . . . I won't be a minute.'

'Hold on, haven't you forgotten something? He's away on holiday.'

'Of course!' She nodded. 'He's gone to Wales, how could I forget!' She passed a hand through her short hair in a gesture of despair, feeling utterly deflated.

Things had been going so well up until now. Too well, she thought morosely. Robert finding her an office on the dockside; Miles agreeing to her deal to exchange the Rolls for two lorries; and then landing a really worthwhile order. It had all gone so smoothly and now, suddenly, all their plans were in ruins.

Yet she couldn't just give up, she told herself. It meant letting too many people down. She'd told Captain Ingers that she'd be returning to unload at nine o'clock, so she must find a solution before then.

She checked the time on her watch. It was half-past eight, that gave her half an hour. Half-past eight! Her mind raced. Robert hadn't said when he was setting out. Perhaps it still wasn't too late.

'I'm going to try to get in touch with Robert, there's still a chance that he hasn't left home yet,' she called over her shoulder to her father as she sprinted down the quayside.

Her heart was hammering, the raw mist choking her by the time she'd reached her office. She rubbed the back of her hand across her eyes.

'Please be there, Robert, please do something to help,' she prayed out loud as she rang his number.

Robert hadn't left home. He had just finished

his breakfast and was stowing his back-pack and walking boots into his car when the phone rang.

For a moment he debated whether to go back indoors and answer it or not. It was probably a wrong number, he decided. He couldn't think of anyone who would be phoning him that early in the morning. Unless it was Megan.

The moment the thought came into his mind he rushed to pick up the receiver, afraid she might ring off thinking he had already gone.

He listened attentively as Megan explained what had happened to their lorries, his mind focusing on what he could do to help.

'Shall I call you back in about an hour?' she asked.

'No. Stay by your lorries. I'll meet you there.'

Holiday forgotten, he phoned around and within an hour he was driving to the dockside in an enormous articulated lorry. Megan's expression of relief when she saw him more than compensated for his own change of plans.

'Come on, let's get loaded,' he ordered. 'I'll tell you the details while we work.'

Two hours later, the cargo from the *Marie Louise* had been transferred onto the articulated lorry.

'Let's get the tarpaulin covers over it and secure them and then we'll take a break,' Megan told them.

Five minutes later the three of them were sitting at a table in one of the dockside cafés, warming their hands on mugs of steaming tea.

'I'll drive this lot up to Newcastle while your father sees about repairing your lorries,' Robert said, draining his mug and standing up.

'Hold on, I thought you were off to Wales on holiday?'

'That can wait for a day. The important thing now is to make this delivery on time and get your lorries back in action,' Robert told them.

'Perhaps I should come with you,' Watkin suggested. 'You can't unload on your own.'

'I'll find someone the other end to give a hand,' Robert assured him. 'It might cost a couple of quid but it leaves you free to get your lorries back on the road.'

It was almost midday before Megan managed to get to her desk. She spent most of the morning trying to locate the spares her father needed. When she finally unlocked her office door the phone was ringing.

'I was beginning to think you'd given me the wrong number,' an angry voice told her when she picked up the receiver. 'I've tried to phone you twice before this morning.'

'I'm sorry. We've had some technical trouble at the dockside. How can I help you?'

'I want a consignment of china collecting from Stoke-on-Trent and loaded onto the *San Francisco* by tomorrow night.'

'Rather short notice, isn't it?' Megan frowned as she noted down the details.

'It wouldn't have been if your phone had been manned. I tried to get you at nine o'clock this morning.'

'Yes, well, as I explained . . .'

'All the papers are in order, but they will have to be cleared your end. I'll give them to your driver.

What time will he be here? It's Shyfords in Victoria Road, Hanley. Tell him to ask for me, Bill Spencer.'

'Right. Ten o'clock tomorrow morning, Mr Spencer.'

'That's cutting it fine,' grumbled Bill Spencer. 'The crates have to be loaded onto your lorry and secured, you know.'

'All right. Let's make it nine o' clock then.'

'Is that the best you can do?'

'I'm afraid so.' To be there that early would mean her father would have to leave home before six and she didn't intend making it any harder for him. As it was, she was keeping her fingers crossed that they would have a lorry repaired in time.

After recording all the relevant details, Megan picked up the pile of post which still lay in the doorway and began sorting through it.

She had sent out a publicity letter over a week ago to some twenty leading Liverpool companies and these were the first replies she had received. She scanned them quickly. One stated they were already well serviced and had no intention of making any changes, but three others were interested. One asked her to phone with a quotation for collecting cargo from a ship due to dock at Liverpool the next day.

Ten minutes later she had phoned and secured the order. Delighted, she noted down the instructions to collect a consignment of raw cotton and then transport it to mills in Rawtenstall.

As she entered the details onto the movement sheet pinned on the wall, she was elated to see there were now two bookings for the next day.

Her jubilation vanished as she remembered the lorries might not be ready in time. She had a moment's panic. Suddenly, the enormity of the commitment she'd taken on hit her like a blow between the eyes. She wondered if it was all going to be more than she could cope with after all. She hadn't anticipated quite such instant success because Robert had warned her that she must expect it to take several weeks before she had any enquiries, and even longer before they were followed up by firm orders.

She pushed her momentary doubts from her mind and concentrated on finding dockers to help with unloading the ship and reloading the cargo onto the lorries. As she filled in the relevant forms, checked over the documents and prepared bills of lading and invoices ready for the next day, her spirits soared. If things went on like this she would be paying her way in next to no time, she thought triumphantly, so what was she worrying about?

By the time Robert returned from Newcastle, Megan was dazed with fatigue yet jubilant. She'd organised a work force and her father had both lorries in working order.

'So what are your plans for tomorrow, then?' Robert frowned, studying the movement sheet. 'You've got both lorries booked out, I see.'

'My dad will drive one and I'll take the other.'

'And what will happen about the office?'

She frowned. 'I'll just have to shut the door. I never thought we'd be this busy quite so quickly. I'll have to find someone to work in the office, I suppose.'

'Why not hire a driver?'

'A girl for the office won't cost a quarter what a driver is going to demand.'

'It's not the answer,' Robert told her firmly. 'You are the best person to be running the office. It's your business. You know what terms you are prepared to quote and you can make snap decisions when there are any special conditions or someone needs advice.'

'Yes, you're probably right.' She nodded. 'I hope one day things will be as well organised as that. For the moment, though, I shall have to pitch in and drive whenever it's necessary.'

'Look, Megan, I can drive one of the lorries tomorrow.'

'Nonsense, Robert.' She gave him a grateful smile. 'It would upset all your holiday plans.'

'That doesn't matter. I was going on a walking holiday, remember. I hadn't booked in anywhere.'

'Maybe not, but I can't let you make a sacrifice like that.' Touched by his generosity, her hand went out to rest momentarily on his arm.

'Rubbish!' His voice was gruff. 'That's settled, then. I'll have a word with Watkin, shall I?'

'Would you? I did say he was to be in charge of transport and don't want him to think I'm making decisions behind his back.'

For the rest of the week, the pattern seemed to repeat itself. Several more of the firms Megan had written to also contacted her, requesting a collection or delivery to be made right away.

'It can't possibly go on like this, but it is a wonderful start,' she enthused as they left the office at midday on Saturday. 'I really don't know how we would have coped if you hadn't been on hand, Robert,' she told him gratefully.

'It's a shame about your holiday, though. The weather has been exceptionally good this week,' added Watkin.

Robert shrugged dismissively. 'I wasn't all that keen on going anyway . . . not on my own.'

'Perhaps we could all have a day out tomorrow. What about a run out into the Wirral for lunch?'

'That sounds an excellent idea,' Watkin agreed.

Robert met them at the Parkgate Hotel and Megan felt it was almost as if the clock had been turned back and they were once more a happy family as they sat down to lunch.

'Shall we all go for a walk when we've finished our coffee?' she suggested at the end of their meal.

Watkin frowned. 'I think it might be better if I took your mother straight home, Megan,' he said. 'You come back with Robert, then if you want to stop off for a walk you can.'

As Megan noticed her mother's flushed face and sparkling eyes, her heart sank. The glass of sherry, together with the wine they'd drunk with their meal, had certainly affected her. It brought memories of her mother's drinking bout after Lynn had died rushing back.

Chapter Thirty-four

When Robert returned to work at Walker's the following Monday morning, he found everyone eager to tell him that Mr Miles wanted to see him in his office the moment he arrived.

'Reckon it's about you driving a lorry for Megan Williams last week,' one of the men commented.

'Oh! And which of you has been tittle-tattling?' asked Robert, looking round at the huddle of drivers.

'Surely you never thought you could keep it secret? The news spread like wildfire.' Barney Wilson grinned.

'What I do in my own time is my business,' Robert stated. He knew Barney was a troublemaker but, for all that, he didn't intend to let his comments go unchallenged.

'Not when you go against the boss,' retorted Barney.

'What do you mean?'

'You don't know, do you? You really don't know!' Barney chortled, his lips drawn back from his irregular teeth in a wolfish grin. 'It was on Mr Miles' orders that Megan Williams' lorries were busted up.'

There were muttered warnings from the rest of the men but they came too late. Incensed by what

342

he had heard, Robert grabbed Barney by the shoulders, shaking him like a dog.

'What did you say?' he growled, his light blue eyes gleaming like chips of ice.

'Give over!' Barney protested, trying to wriggle free. 'It wasn't me that carried out his orders.'

With a smothered oath, Robert flung the man from him, turned on his heel and strode out of the warehouse. Ten minutes later he was storming into the company's offices in Old Hall Street.

Miles looked up in astonishment when Robert burst into his office unannounced, then his face paled as he saw the anger burning in Robert's eyes.

'Ah! You got my message that I wanted to speak to you before you started work this morning,' he blustered.

'Yes! And I also heard that you arranged for Megan Williams' lorries to be sabotaged,' Robert snarled. 'So, what have you to say about that?'

Their eyes locked. Miles was the first to look away and, before he could answer, Robert leaned across the wide mahogany desk and seized him by the shirt front, hauling him to his feet.

The commotion as Miles tried to free himself from Robert's grasp brought Mr Newbold, as well as the girls from the general office, crowding into the doorway.

The anger went out of Robert as suddenly as it had flared. As his grip relaxed, and Miles fell back into his chair, shaking and dishevelled, the crowd melted. Avoiding each other's eyes, they scurried back to their desks.

343

'Get out of here before I have you arrested for assault,' Miles choked as he straightened his clothing.

'I very much doubt if you'll do that!' Robert told him contemptuously. 'There's a small question of sabotage to be dealt with. Don't try to deny it,' he snapped as Miles was about to interrupt. 'The man who heard you giving your orders told me about it in front of a dozen or more witnesses.'

'The fellow must be lying,' blustered Miles, 'I don't know what you are talking about.'

'You're despicable!' Robert's lip curled as he spat the words across the desk.

Full of contempt for the man who had caused Megan and her family so much pain and heartache, Robert moved towards the door, hands clenched tightly at his side. More than anything he wanted to teach Miles a lesson. It was too late now, the moment had passed, but he wished that he'd given him the hiding he deserved while he'd had the opportunity.

'You're sacked, Field. And don't think anyone else will take you on as a driver,' Miles called after him. 'I'll make sure that no one on Merseyside will give you a job of any sort.'

Robert paused, his bulk framed in the doorway. The contrast between them was marked. Miles, supercilious and brash; Robert, mature and self-assured. The scorn in Robert's eyes as their gaze levelled spoke volumes. Miles seemed to shrink within his sharp-cut suit.

'Be careful about what you say or do,' Robert warned. 'There are a lot of people who would derive great pleasure from seeing you get your come-uppance . . . and I'm their man!'

'You've left Walker's!' Megan stared in disbelief at Robert.

'That's right.' Now that it had actually happened he felt on top of the world; free; his own man at last.

Miles Walker's threats that he would never work again on Merseyside were so much hot air that they didn't bother him in the least. There was always a need for qualified drivers with his sort of experience. He might even go to sea again. Perhaps a few months apart and Megan might miss him and then . . .

He brought his wandering thoughts back to the present, knowing that going back to sea was the very last thing that he wanted to do. Being able to see Megan was as much part of his life as breathing or eating.

He wanted her so badly that it was like a continual throbbing ache inside him. The days when he didn't see her were filled with a sense of unease, an irrational sense of impending disaster, a feeling that she might need him and he wouldn't be there to help.

She looked at him shrewdly. 'Did driving for me have anything to do with you losing your job?'

He shrugged. 'Indirectly, yes. It was Miles who had your lorries sabotaged.'

'I thought it might have been!'

'We'd have a job to prove it was him, of course,

he's made sure of that; but Barney Wilson let it slip. I tackled Miles about it and . . .'

'And he denied it and sacked you in the same breath,' Megan finished contemptuously.

'Something like that.'

'So what will you do now? I'd give you a job but I'm not sure we can afford anyone . . . not yet. Unless you're interested in part-time work?' she suggested tentatively.

He shook his head. He wasn't sure it would work if he felt under an obligation to her.

As if reading his mind, she grinned. 'You don't fancy me as your boss, is that it? Well, what about this for an idea. You provide your own lorry and work for me on a self-employed basis.'

He looked at her and frowned.

'It will still be my company and my father will still be in overall charge of the transport arrangements,' she pointed out.

'We could certainly give it a try,' he agreed cautiously. 'It might take me a while to get the right sort of vehicle, though.'

'Fair enough! Until you do you could drive one of ours and leave me free to organise the office side of things.'

It took Robert a fortnight to find a suitable lorry and another week to have it fully serviced. While he was driving one of her lorries, Megan insisted that he received a percentage of the net profit on each load he transported, the same as he would if he was freelancing.

'I don't really know how I am going cope when you aren't here to help out with our lorries,' she

346

confided. I still haven't been able to find anyone suitable to work in the office.'

'I still think you should hire a driver and run the office yourself,' he told her. 'You can't beat personal service. People hate having to deal with an office junior. All these promises that someone will phone you back are no good. They want a quotation immediately and to be able to fix up when the load will be moved. Otherwise they simply go elsewhere.'

'You could be right,' she agreed. 'I had no idea I would be so busy. And there's so much paperwork to get through!' She indicated the dockets and forms piled up all over the desk. 'When I was at Walker's the work was split up between so many people that I had no idea how time consuming all this form-filling and invoicing could be when you have to do it single-handed,' she admitted.

The morning Robert drove up in his own lorry, Megan was as excited as he was. 'I should have brought in a bottle of champagne so that we could have had a launching ceremony,' she teased.

'You didn't?' Robert pretended to look disappointed. 'In that case, we had better go out tonight and celebrate.'

'You're on! The Nelson at half-past eight? I know my dad will join us and I'll try to persuade Mam to come along as well.'

Robert bit his lip, not wanting to upset the rapport between them, but a family gathering wasn't quite the sort of celebration he'd had in mind.

* * *

347

In the months that followed, they were so busy, working flat out, that they had little time to think of anything else. The weather had turned wet and foggy and everything seemed to take twice as long. Ships were held up at the Bar because even with tugs to guide them it was too murky for them to make their way upriver.

In the run-up to Christmas, Megan was bombarded by calls from firms who wanted goods collecting before they closed down for the holiday, or who were waiting for deliveries and were worried in case there were any hold-ups.

'You'd think the world was coming to an end, the fuss some people make about a bank holiday,' she grumbled as she handed a sheaf of papers to Robert. 'All this mad rush and then the week after Christmas we'll be sitting around twiddling our thumbs for days on end.'

'How about coming to the Tower with me on New Year's Eve?' he suggested to try to cheer her up.

'Yes, OK. Provided we are not still here working,' she accepted rather ungraciously.

'We have to get this lot cleared before Christmas,' he reminded her. 'There won't be a lot happening then for about ten days, you've just said so yourself.'

'You're right, of course,' she admitted. 'Thanks, I'd love to come. What's on? A dance?'

'A Grand Ball, no less. It is New Year's Eve!'

'Yes, and I remember the first time you took me there! Lynn was furious because Dad wouldn't let her come as well.' Her eyes misted over with tears as she bent over her papers, and Robert cursed himself for his clumsiness in stirring up such painful memories.

'So will you come?' he asked softly.

'I'll look forward to it.' She looked up and smiled.

Robert spent Christmas Day with them the same as he had done ever since they had come to live on Merseyside. This year, however, their celebrations were quieter, more subdued. Although no one mentioned Lynn, they were all acutely aware of her absence.

Megan cooked the meal. Kathy Williams tried desperately to be as bright as her flowered dress and to hide the fact she had been crying. As she watched her mother laying the table, Megan grew alarmed at the way she kept topping up her glass with wine.

'Make sure that Mam doesn't have too much to drink, Dad,' she whispered worriedly. 'We don't want her back in hospital.'

Megan's warning came too late. By the time Christmas dinner was served, her mother was already so befuddled that Megan persuaded her to lie down until teatime.

'I'll stay here and make sure she doesn't have any more to drink,' promised Watkin. 'Why don't you two go for a walk?'

'A brisk walk along the prom at New Brighton will do us both good,' Robert agreed.

It was crisp and cold with a blood-red sunset low over the sea by the time they reached King's Parade. As protection against the gale force wind, Megan was muffled up in a warm coat, a matching close-fitting hat, and the fur-lined gloves Robert had bought her for Christmas.

'I'm frozen in spite of all the layers I'm wearing.' Megan shivered as they strode along the promenade, their faces stinging from the lash of wind and waves.

'If you've had enough then why don't we go back to my place and have a hot drink before I run you home?' Robert suggested.

'Do you know, it's the first time I've ever been here,' Megan commented as, shortly afterwards, she walked into his living room and looked round with interest while Robert stirred the banked-up fire into life.

'I haven't made many changes since my mother died,' Robert told her as he drew the heavy velvet curtains. From a side table, he picked up a photograph of himself as a small boy and passed it to her with a smile before he went through to the kitchen to make their drink.

The hot coffee, laced with whisky, revived them both. Relaxed, Megan curled up on the settee with a sigh of contentment.

'I find it hard to believe sometimes that everything is turning out so well.' She sighed softly.

He smiled, deliberating, marshalling his emotions. He wondered if she still only thought of him as a friend, someone to turn to when she needed advice or whether the time was right to voice his feelings and ask her to marry him. He savoured the moment, playing over in his mind the spiel he had rehearsed so often, but her next words shattered his complacency.

'I never dreamed I would have so many customers so soon. I expected it to be an uphill
struggle, but the work has poured in and we've
plenty of bookings for the New Year, too. Are you
happy about the way things are going?'

'Business-wise, yes, but . . .'

'You think you've done the right thing, then, in
buying your own lorry and joining us?'

He sighed. 'A lot of the men who still work for
Walker's are green with envy,' he told her. 'Half
of them wish they were self-employed, too. It's not
just finding the work but having someone at the
back of you to look after all the paperwork that's
so important. It's what stops most of them from
going on their own.'

'If they have their own lorry they're welcome
to come along on a freelance basis,' Megan told
him. 'I'd take care of all the paperwork, but they
would have to understand that I'm in charge and
I allocate the loads.'

'It's a great idea and I know several of them
who would jump at it, but it would mean more
work for you,' he warned.

'They'll be responsible for maintaining their own
lorry, I'll simply contract out to them. It's the
quickest way I know of expanding until I can afford
to buy more lorries and employ my own drivers.'

'And is that what you really want from life,
Megan?' asked Robert softly. 'To build up a successful business?'

'Yes, and I intend to do it.' As she turned to face
him, her face glowed in the firelight and her brown
eyes shone with enthusiasm.

Robert longed to take her in his arms, kiss her as a woman ought to be kissed, not the chaste peck on the cheek or brow that he usually gave her. Once again, though, he sensed it wasn't the right time. Her enthusiasm for her business enterprise stymied him. He was quite sure nothing would distract her from her plans; certainly not the prospect of marrying him.

Chapter Thirty-five

1930 started with an avalanche of work. Christmas Day having fallen on a Wednesday, there had been no movement of shipping at all during the rest of the week. With New Year's Day also a bank holiday most companies had decided not to start work until the following Monday, the 6th of January.

When Megan arrived at her makeshift office at eight o'clock on the first Monday in January, she found a pile of letters waiting for her attention. She was busy sorting through them when Robert and her father came in to let her know that their lorries were loaded and they were about to leave.

Watkin was travelling eastwards to the Pennines and Robert north towards Scotland, so both men were concerned by the weather forecast and the snow-laden skies.

'Further inland, it's probably already snowing,' warned Robert. 'The salt in the air keeps Merseyside pretty free of snow. I'll try and phone in and let you know if everything is OK, but don't wait around for me to get back, Megan. I'll see you tomorrow morning.'

'What about you, Dad?' she asked anxiously. 'Do you want me to come with you?'

'No, you stay here. Judging by that pile on your desk you've got enough to do as it is. Apart from that,' he added when he saw she was about to argue with him, 'if you came with me and we couldn't get back, it would mean your mam would be left all on her own overnight.'

After he'd left, Megan tackled the estimates waiting for her attention. Her spirits soared at the number of new customers. At midday, she was clearing a space on her desk so that she could eat her sandwiches when she was interrupted by a tall young man with red, fuzzy hair, asking for Robert.

'I'm afraid he's not here at the moment. Can I help?'

'It's you really I came to see, Miss. My name's George Willis, but everyone calls me Sandy on account of me red hair. Robert said you might take me on.'

Megan frowned. 'You do understand that it would be on a freelance basis and that you'd have to supply your own lorry and keep it serviced? The arrangement would be that I would pay you a percentage on deliveries.'

'Yeah, I know. Robert explained it all. Smashing idea. I'm planning on getting wed and my girl-friend's old man said he'd draw out all his sav-ings and fix me up with a lorry if you'd agree to take me on. So what about it? I can start right away . . . as soon as I get hold of a lorry.'

Megan was impressed by his eagerness. 'There's a freighter in Canning Dock carrying pig-iron for delivery to Shotton. If I let you use one of my lor-ries, can you load up and deliver before five today?'

'That's great! You're a real corker! Sorry, Miss,

no disrespect meant.' His face turned the same shade as his hair with embarrassment.

As she handed over keys and dockets, Megan wondered if she was doing the right thing. He looked honest enough, but she knew nothing about him except his name. If Robert had told him to come for a job he must be OK, she reasoned as she went back into the office and phoned through to Shotton to tell them the pig-iron was on its way.

'I'm sending a new driver so do you think you could let me know as soon as you've taken delivery,' she asked before she replaced the receiver.

She tried not to think about Sandy Willis for the rest of the afternoon, but as five o'clock approached she became edgy and she was more than relieved when the call came through to say the load had arrived.

In the next few months she took on two more freelance drivers: Jock MacDonald, a dour Scotsman who said very little but was a steady, reliable worker; and Fred Greenford, a back-slapping jovial character whose idea of a good time was going for a 'bevvy' or a 'nosh'.

Megan was kept so busy that she knew she would have to take on someone to help in the office. Robert agreed with her wholeheartedly. 'You can't go on for ever working ten hours a day or you'll crack up,' he told her. 'You didn't even get away for a holiday in the summer.'

'Neither did you!'

'Only because you kept us all working so hard that I couldn't take any time off.' He grinned.

'Am I really such a slave driver?'

355

'You certainly expect everyone to have the same energy and enthusiasm as you have. Your father looks worn out . . . He didn't get a break either!'

'He will next year, I promise. My New Year's resolution is to send him and Mam off on a holiday.'

'Is that your only resolution?' he asked softly.

'For the moment . . . except to treat you better. I might even consider letting you have a few days off to go on that walking holiday you put off for my benefit,' she promised.

He drew in his breath sharply. 'And would you come with me?' he asked, looking straight at her.

She picked up her desk diary. 'Was there any particular date you wanted, Robert?' she asked, struggling to keep her voice level.

He shrugged. 'Forget it! Let's get on with running the business . . . that's what really matters to you, isn't it?'

'Yes, at the moment it is,' Megan said, ignoring his jibe. 'I'm worried about what effect the Wall Street Crash in America last October is going to have on shipping. It's causing consternation throughout the world so it's bound to make a difference to our business.'

In that, Megan was right. Lifestyles changed overnight. The dockers were dismayed because the shipping on both sides of the Mersey, south and north, and the river itself, seemed to come to a standstill. Ships lay at anchor right out to the Bar as the Port of Liverpool ground to a halt. Cargo boats jammed Gladstone, Canning, Canada and all the other docks.

When she had first started her own company,

the men on the quayside were full of admiration for her pluck in setting herself up in business. Now, the very same men suddenly seemed to turn against her because she was doling out work in as fair a way as she could instead of letting them adopt a 'first come first to get the job' system.

'Wouldn't fancy having a woman boss,' one of them told Sandy Willis.

'Yer talking daft, whacker! It's no different to having a man,' defended Sandy loyally.

'Hen-pecked, that's what you lot are. Working for a woman, having to do whatever she says.'

'What the hell you on about?' growled Jock, his massive fist curling and uncurling with anger. 'We're partners, we pull together as a team, which is more than you bloody lot do. Megan doesn't give us orders, not in the way you mean.'

'Bet she creams off all the best jobs for her old man and her fancy man, Robert Field,' taunted the docker.

Contact between Jock's fist and the speaker's jaw cut short any further observations. The scuffle that followed brought the police onto the scene. They didn't press charges. There were far too many hot-headed squabbles for them to take them seriously, unless someone was badly hurt.

As the months merged into one another, Megan found it increasingly difficult to keep her drivers busy. She shared the loads out on a strict rota basis, but even so none of them wanted to look for employment elsewhere.

'You've spoiled us, Megan,' laughed Sandy. 'We're used to big pay packets so the sort of wages we'd get working as a driver for anyone else would seem like chicken feed.'

'Yes, that's probably true,' she agreed, 'but it only applies when there is work coming in.'

'Most of us have a bit put by to fall back on the weeks when it doesn't,' affirmed Fred. 'Got to be prepared to take the rough with the smooth, you know,' he added philosophically. 'That's what you told us when we joined you and so far you've always kept to your word.'

Jock MacDonald was the one who was really worried. He had a wife and three children and only one wage packet coming into the house and no savings to fall back on. He said very little but his dour look and taciturn manner told their own story.

When, after two weeks of no movement, a single lorry was needed to carry a load to South Wales, his dismay was obvious to everyone when he realised that he was second on the list.

'I've promised to take me Judy out tonight,' Sandy groaned when Megan allocated the job to him. 'Do you think Jock would do the run instead of me?'

'You'd better ask him.' She looked across at Jock quizzically, although she knew full well that he would jump at the chance. She also suspected that Sandy had dreamed up the excuse so that Jock could have the work.

'Will things ever get back to normal?' she said with a sigh when Robert called into her office later that morning.

'At the moment they're getting worse. There's

another crisis looming, this time over Sterling,' he told her gloomily.

She walked over to the door and stood there staring out. It was a hot, sultry July day and the tiny office was like an oven.

'Why don't you take advantage of the fact that trade is slow and take a break from it all?' suggested Robert, his gaze taking in the weariness etched on Megan's face and the lassitude of her manner.

'I can't afford to,' Megan told him with a pathetic shrug. 'You can bet your life if I closed the office, even for a few days, we'd miss out on some important orders,' she added in a strained, querulous voice.

'You don't have to close it. Things are pretty slack at the moment, you said so yourself, so why not let your father run things here while you have a holiday before you have a breakdown?' he went on, pressing home his advantage.

The silent motion of her head showed her acceptance of his suggestion.

'Let's both have a week off. I never did get my walking holiday in Wales,' he added cautiously. 'I quite fancy the idea of taking it right now, while the hot weather holds, so why don't you come along with me, Megan?'

For a moment he was sure she was going to refuse. He held his breath as she walked back to her desk and flicked through the booking diary.

'Nothing . . . we haven't a single booking for the next two weeks!' She walked over to the movement chart pinned up on the wall. 'Blanks . . . nothing but blanks.'

'So it's the right time to take a holiday,' urged Robert. 'Your father will be here. It would be a boost for his ego to know you trusted him enough to leave him in charge.'

Chapter Thirty-six

As they set out for Wales, Megan's mind was full of the problems she was leaving behind. She wasn't at all confident that her father could cope with running the office while she was away and look after her mother at the same time.

Perhaps they should have been the ones to be going on holiday, not me, she thought guiltily, knowing how depressed her mother was. If only she would go out more, or even invite some of the neighbours in now and again for a cup of tea, I'm sure she'd be a lot happier, Megan mused.

She was at a loss to understand how her mother did spend her day. Often when she got home at night the breakfast dishes would still be on the draining board and the beds unmade. Sometimes there was food in the house, sometimes not.

Her mother had no set routine for any of the household chores, and Megan found a great deal of her own time taken up at weekends with the washing, ironing and general cleaning.

Remembering how organised things had been when Vi Brown had been helping out, both she and her father had suggested several times that they should get someone in to do the housework, but her mother refused even to consider the idea.

Robert concentrated on the road ahead. He had

been more than delighted that Megan had agreed to come away on holiday, but he was afraid to attach too much importance on what it meant in regard to their relationship.

Everything had been done on the spur of the moment. There had been no time to talk things through. He had simply checked over his car and packed some clothes, anxious to make a start before Megan could change her mind.

They would only be away for five days since Megan had insisted that they must be back home by the weekend so that she could pay the drivers herself. He hadn't argued. Five days on their own was more than he had hoped for and could provide the opportunity he needed.

He found the uncertainty of not knowing whether Megan cared for him or not unbearable and was determined before the holiday was over to settle the question once and for all. If there was absolutely no hope of her ever marrying him, it might be best if he went back to sea and tried to forget all that she meant to him.

As they crossed into Wales at Queensferry, Megan closed her eyes in an attempt to ignore the surrounding countryside and its past associations with the Walkers. It was some time before she realised that Robert had taken a different route, one that took them south through Ruthin to join the A5.

The sheer relief of discovering they wouldn't be going anywhere near Mostyn or Holywell helped her to unwind. By the time they stopped for lunch at Betws-y-Coed, her face had lost its tense, strained look and she had started to enjoy herself.

The picturesque little town nestling among tree-clad hills was packed with holiday-makers. They thronged the cafés and browsed in the countless gift shops that lined the main street, giving the place a carnival atmosphere.

'Perhaps we should drive on and see if we can find a pub on the outskirts of the town,' Robert suggested.

'It's one o'clock, we must eat soon, I'm starving,' Megan protested. 'Anyway,' she said with a smile, 'I like it here.'

'It's a pretty spot, I'll grant you that,' Robert agreed.

They lunched rather splendidly at the Gwyndyr Hotel. 'Shall we have a walk round before we get back into the car?' suggested Robert when they were finally ready to leave. 'I haven't eaten such a big meal at midday for years.'

As they emerged once more into the main street, the July sun was beating down, enveloping them in a shower of golden warmth as they strolled along, replete and content.

'The name of this bridge is *Pont-y-Pair* which means "the bridge of the Cauldron",' Megan told him as they paused entranced by the miniature cataract that formed as water fell onto the jagged rocks on the river bed.

'The local beauty spot, is it?'

'One of them. Swallow Falls is much more impressive. Do you want to go there? We could walk, it's only about two miles.'

'In this heat!' Robert's eyebrows went up in mock alarm.

363

'No, you're probably right,' she agreed with a laugh. 'We're not all that far from Beddgelert so shall we drive on then and stay there overnight?'

Megan was on familiar ground now and her pleasure and excitement increased. To her, the sky was more blue, the grass greener, the air more sweet.

When they reached Beddgelert, she insisted that they should sit for a while on the old stone bridge that spanned the river while she pointed out landmarks she remembered so well.

'Separate rooms or are we sharing?' Robert questioned when they finally decided it was time they arranged some accommodation.

'Robert, I'm surprised you should even ask such a question!'

The annoyance in her voice startled him and he silently cursed himself for his flippancy.

The moment she had made her cutting response, Megan regretted doing so. Why on earth hadn't she treated it as a joke instead of taking offence and snapping his head off? she thought guiltily. Her mother was right, she did treat Robert badly. No one could have been a more devoted friend. While she had been building up the business he had almost become her alter ego; someone she depended on for advice, and who could be relied on to boost her morale when things seemed to be going wrong.

Yet he had never once tried to usurp her authority, or claim any of the glory when things turned out well. He had backed her all the way, solid and reliable; a shoulder to lean on, the force behind her every move.

He was so resourceful that she wondered why he had never started his own business instead of using his talents to promote hers.

When she introduced Robert to Jennie Jones and Gwyneth Evans and saw the admiration in their eyes, her face flushed with pride. She studied Robert's strong, serious profile, seeing him as other people must do. Mid-thirties, good-looking with a strong square jaw and firm mouth, clear-eyed and powerfully built: she felt proud he was her friend.

She found herself remembering back to when she'd first arrived on Merseyside, and the way Robert had consistently brought her small gifts. He'd never failed to buy her lavish presents at Christmas and on her birthday, and countless times he had taken her out for a meal or dancing. She even found herself contemplating how different her life might have been had she married him.

That evening, as they lingered over their meal, talking about the day's happenings, Megan was suddenly aware of his physical presence. When their hands touched as Robert passed her another glass of wine she pulled back quickly, aware of a tingling sense of excitement. It unsettled her.

After his silly joke, Robert had decided to play it cool and keep his distance. For all that he was enjoying her company and he too felt acutely aware of their physical proximity. The opportunity to have her complete attention without her parents, one of the drivers, or the shrill of the telephone bell interrupting them was a bonus in itself.

For the entire five days of their holiday the weather was superbly warm and sunny and they explored the surrounding countryside as avidly as any tourists.

Robert had visited Wales many times before on walking holidays. He had enjoyed the challenge of the mountains, felt awed by their grandeur, but Megan knew all the mountains by name, as if they were old friends. He found her fierce proprietorial pride the day they climbed Moel Hebog very touching.

She took him to all her other favourite haunts and even right to the mist-clad top of Snowdon, where cotton wool clouds swirled all around them. They explored half-hidden *cwms*, sat beside tranquil blue lakes, sunbathed on the sandy shores at Porthmadog, and visited the centuries old castles at Harlech, Conway and Caernarvon.

Meeting her childhood friends, especially Ifan Jenkins, he could see why she had been attracted to Miles Walker. They were such complete opposites. Ifan was slow and shy; a gentle, easy-going giant, diffident of manner and purpose. In contrast, Miles must have seemed a sophisticated man-of-the-world with his glib tongue and devil-may-care manner.

Learning about Megan's upbringing helped Robert to understand her better. He liked Jennie and Gwyneth well enough, but Megan had outgrown them in the intervening years. Their naive outlook on life reminded him of Megan when he had first known her. Yet he was sure that if either of them had been suddenly dropped into the heart of Liverpool, or any other big city, they wouldn't have coped nearly as well as Megan had done.

The first time Megan kissed him goodnight of her own volition he was tempted to crush her to him, but ingrained caution held him back although his healthy physical craving, submerged for so long, ached to assert itself.

Later, alone in his room, at the other side of the hotel to hers, with only two days of their holiday left, he wished he'd taken advantage of such an opportunity to declare his love and ask her to marry him.

There's no need to rush things. This holiday is just the cornerstone for what's to follow, he told himself. From now on their relationship would be on a new footing; they were closer than they'd ever been.

'Have you enjoyed our holiday?' Robert asked as they sat in the Saracen's Head having a drink on their last evening. His hand went out and covered hers and his blue eyes took on a smoky look as he tried to control the passion building inside him.

'It's been wonderful!'

Their lips met in a light soft encounter that became a deep passionate kiss. He felt her stiffen in his arms. Then with a barely audible sigh she freed herself from his embrace and moved away.

'There's such a magical quality about this place I feel bewitched by it,' she said unsteadily. 'It's hard to believe that by this time tomorrow we'll be in the normal world again and back in Liverpool with a thousand and one problems demanding our attention.'

Chapter Thirty-seven

'Your mother is drinking again!' Her father's greeting the moment she walked in the door brought Megan back to reality with a jolt.

'Are you sure? I made quite certain there was no alcohol in the house before I left, not even any cider or cooking sherry.'

'Then she's obviously been out and bought some.'

'You found it?'

'Yes. Vodka this time! It was hidden in the back of her wardrobe. She'd been moody for a couple of days and I thought she was missing you. Then, on Thursday, I found her asleep in the armchair when I came home. When I tried to waken her, I realised she was out cold. Until then I hadn't suspected anything.'

'With vodka there's no tell-tale smell.'

'What are we going to do?' He shook his head wearily. 'Do you think we should get her back into a clinic?'

'Must we?' A shiver went through Megan at the memory of the trauma there had been last time. 'Couldn't we give it a week or two and see how she goes on? It might have been because she felt lonely. Were you working late while I was away?'

'No, not really. It's been quiet and I made sure I got back in good time.'

Megan watched her mother over the next few days and was forced to admit that her father was right about the drinking. Even though he'd taken away the bottle of vodka he'd found and tried to reason with Kathy, she was still drinking.

Megan couldn't understand where she was getting it. She searched all the cupboards, the wardrobes and every possible spot, looking for the source of supply. She found it quite by accident. The bottle was small and flat and her mother had hidden it behind a row of books on the shelves beside the fireplace.

'Grudge me my little bit of pleasure, do you?' Kathy Williams scowled when faced with the evidence.

'Of course not,' Megan told her. 'We would much rather you drank openly, though . . . and in moderation. We don't want you back into the clinic for more treatment,' she added as her mother looked at her in disbelief.

'I'll be careful, Megan!' Tears spilled down Kathy's cheeks. 'It bucks me up, and helps me get through the day,' she explained with a weak smile.

'We'll have to keep an eye on her,' Megan warned her father later. 'While we are out at work and she is on her own, she gets bored and lonely and that's when she turns to the bottle.'

'I sometimes wonder if she finds living on Merseyside something of a disappointment.' Watkin sighed. 'Yet when we lived in Wales all she could think about was getting back to Liverpool.'

'So many things have gone wrong for her since we've been here,' Megan said thoughtfully. 'And

369

all the old friends she was so looking forward to meeting up with seem to have moved away.'

'You could have a point there! What do you propose we should do about it?'

'Move back to Wales, I suppose. No, not to Beddgelert,' she said quickly as she saw her father was about to protest. 'I know she found it far too quiet there. No, I thought somewhere like Rhyl, where there would be plenty for her to see and do. Would you like me to make some enquiries?'

The following Saturday, Megan set off to house-hunt on their behalf. The first estate agent she visited was able to offer her a selection of three bungalows available to rent. She viewed them all but the one in Russet Gardens was, without a doubt, the most desirable.

It was only a short distance from both the shopping centre and the promenade. The living room was well decorated and there were two other rooms as well as a light, airy kitchen which overlooked the prettily laid out garden.

Her mind made up, she made the agent an offer. He accepted it without demur. The owners had already left the district and were anxious to rent.

Hugely pleased with her morning's work, Megan went back to take another look at the property. Leaving her car parked in the driveway she walked from the bungalow to the promenade to make sure it would not be too far for her mother whenever she felt like a stroll.

The three-mile stretch of coastline offered an impressive view of distant mountain ranges dominated by Carnedd Llewellyn, the second highest mountain in Wales. After checking out the local shops, Megan took the coast road home, confident that her mother would be much happier living there than on Merseyside.

As she drove through Mostyn, she instinctively deviated from the main route and took the road that led to Tynmorfa. When the white bungalow the Joneses lived in came in sight she decided she'd seen enough. It was pointless reviving memories long since dead, she told herself.

Too late she remembered there was nowhere in the lane where she could turn round, which meant either backing all the way to the main road or driving on as far as the Walkers' house.

As she manoeuvred the car into their gateway, a huge black Doberman came skittering down the gravel drive, barking furiously.

'Jason!' Impulsively, Megan opened the car door as the huge dog came rushing towards her.

'Heavens! There's a surprise seeing you again. Megan, isn't it?'

'Mrs Jones!' Megan stopped patting the dog and looked up, startled.

'It's been a long time since you were down here. Come on in and I'll make you a cup of tea.'

'I'd love to stop, but I'm on my way home from Rhyl, and I'm already late.'

'Funny way to come from Rhyl.' Sybil Jones smiled. 'Come on,' she insisted, 'a couple more minutes won't make that much difference. I can tell you all the news then.' Her beady brown eyes glistened. 'There's a crowd of weirdos living up there now,' she added, nodding towards the Walkers' house. 'Friends of Miles, most of them. All living in together like animals. Men, women, children all sharing everything, even the bedrooms! None of them do any work. Miles gives them money. They get by on that, and what they can forage from the garden . . . and their dole money.'

'How many did you say there were?'

'Twenty or more. They have wild parties when Miles is here,' she added disapprovingly. 'They're on drugs, of course, and it wouldn't surprise me if they gave stuff to the youngsters as well,' she added darkly. 'There's some right shindigs, I can tell you.'

'Don't the police know?'

'Our local bobby does, but he says what they do in their own place is their own business. They're not causing a public nuisance, not tucked away up here. We don't want to make a fuss since our home goes with the job, but there's some right goings-on, I can tell you! Some of the men frighten me silly when I pass them in the lane. Oh, you've no idea what it's like. It's enough to make his father turn in his grave. Mrs Walker never comes here at all these days. We'll walk up to the house and you can see for yourself . . .'

'No . . . no thanks!'

'Miles comes and stays here most weekends. He's probably up there now, though I haven't seen his car drive up the lane today.'

The thought that she might encounter Miles made Megan even more anxious to get away and as soon as she left Tynmorfa she pushed the matter

to the back of her mind. There were more important things to think about than Miles and his weird
friends.

She decided to let her father pick the right moment
to explain to her mother about the move and to
take her to see the bungalow.

Kathy didn't enthuse about the idea, but neither did she object.

'I hope your mother's going to show a bit more
interest when it's time to start packing,' mused
Watkin. 'She didn't even seem to care whether our
furniture would fit into the bungalow or not.'

'Why don't you buy everything new, Dad?'
Megan suggested. 'That way, leaving Liverpool
will give Mam a fresh start. It would be a chance
to help her put aside her memories of Lynn.'

'Everything new? That would cost a fortune!
What would we do with all the carpets and curtains and furniture we've got now?'

'I shall still be living here so it's a case of either
you buy new, or I do. And I think it would be
better if you were the ones to start afresh.'

'There's stupid I am.' He laughed. 'I forgot you
wouldn't be coming to Rhyl with us. Surely, you
won't want to stay on here in this house? Not all
on your own, girl! Why not give up this place.
You can afford to rent one of those posh flats
they've built at New Brighton. You know, Portland
Court. All nice and modern, right on the prom
with lovely sea views and everything.'

'We'll see,' promised Megan. 'Let's take things
a step at a time. This place will do me for the

373

moment and give you a chance to make sure Mam likes living in Rhyl. You might even want to come back here, you know.'

'I don't think so, not now that I've seen Russet Place,' he assured her. 'It's a lovely spot, and so handy for everything. Your mam is bound to love it there once she's settled in.'

'Well, let's hope so,' agreed Megan, 'because I was thinking that we could open a depot there and you could run it.'

'Do you think you are going to be all right living here on your own, then?' he asked anxiously.

'Of course I will be. Robert's always on hand if I have any problems.'

'Yes!' Her father raised his eyebrows. 'I was hoping that perhaps you . . .'

'Stop it, Dad!' Frowning, Megan cut him short. 'We agreed a long time ago that you wouldn't try any matchmaking. Remember?'

'But Megan you can't go on making him wait for ever!'

'Wait for what? I haven't promised him anything, have I?'

'Come on, girl, you know what I mean. The man is in love with you. He's been crazy about you ever since the first time I brought him home. All these years he's waited so patiently, giving up his time and his ambitions, so as to devote himself to your interests. You must see it.'

'We're just good friends,' she affirmed stubbornly.

'He wants to marry you, Megan! And if you don't make your mind up, then one of these days you'll find you've left it too late. Robert will have packed his bags and gone!'

'Megan, can you meet me for lunch at the Rendezvous Restaurant? It's urgent.'

It was so unlike Robert to make such a request that Megan was on tenterhooks for the rest of the morning as she puzzled over what he wanted to see her about. It had to be something very important, she decided. Otherwise he would have waited until he came into the office with the bills of lading and any other documentation that had amassed during the course of the day.

At one o'clock, she locked the office door and set off for Hackins Hey. Robert had already arrived and had ordered omelettes for them both.

'Your message sounded very ominous, is there something wrong?' she asked as she sat down.

'Well,' he lowered his voice and leaned across the table until their heads were almost touching, 'there's a rumour going round that Walkers are about to go bankrupt!'

'Oh, poor Miles!'

Robert stared at her in silence, shaking his head in disbelief. He had just told her what he thought to be the greatest piece of news he'd heard in years, expecting her to be overjoyed, and all she could do was murmur 'Poor Miles'. As far as he was concerned, Miles Walker was simply getting all he deserved.

'Is there anything we can do to help?'

'I would have thought help was the last thing you'd have in mind,' he retorted cuttingly. 'I expected you to be over the moon that he was on his way out.'

'Is that why you told me?' Her eyes were inscrutable as they levelled with his.

'No, it's not!' His jaw jutted aggressively. 'I did think we could benefit, though. Their fleet of lorries, the warehouse and a hundred and one other things will go under the hammer. We could use them . . . that is, if you still want to expand, of course.'

His jibe wiped the sentimentality from her mind. Robert was right. This could be their golden opportunity. Walker's main warehouse in Canning Dock was one of the best on the quayside. If they owned that . . .

She let her thoughts drift for a moment, remembering the first time she'd ever gone there. She had been curious to see where her father worked. Miles and one of the other shipping clerks had been there checking a consignment. She recalled how hurt she had been because Miles had ignored her.

'Yes, you're right,' she agreed, bringing her attention back to Robert. 'There will be some rich pickings. Can you get hold of an inventory?'

'By the time that is drawn up and circulated it might be too late. If there is anything you specifically want it might be better to act now . . .'

'Go and see Miles personally, you mean?'

'Exactly.'

She pushed her half-eaten omelette away and stood up. 'I must get back.' She laid her hand briefly on Robert's arm. 'Thanks for letting me know.'

'Don't leave it too long. It's not official yet but,

once it is, it won't be possible to do any private deals,' Robert reminded her as they parted outside the restaurant.

Megan went straight to Old Hall Street. It seemed strange to be walking into the building again. There were new faces in the general office. The girl on the reception desk repeated her name to make sure she had it correctly before phoning through to Miles.

'He'll see you right away. I'll show you the way.'

'There's no need, I know where his office is,' Megan told her.

Miles was at the door to greet her. They assessed each other in silence. Megan was shocked at the change in him. He was skeletal thin, his face sunken, and there were dark rings beneath his eyes. He didn't offer to shake hands, merely indicated a chair.

'I understand your company is in trouble,' Megan stated, coming straight to the point of her visit.

He scowled. 'Do you believe all the dockside gossip you hear?' he asked bitterly.

'I've come to make you a proposition,' she told him. 'I'm interested in your warehouse at Canning Dock. If you are not yet in the hands of the official receiver I thought we might be able to do a private deal.'

'You don't pull your punches, do you!' His eyes narrowed. 'How soon could you complete?'

'As long as it takes to write out a cheque . . . providing the price is reasonable.'

'I don't want a cheque. I must have cash.'

'You and Carol making a fresh start?'

His mouth twisted into a sneer. 'No, she won't be coming. It's been over with Carol for a long time. I knew I had made a mistake in marrying her even before we came back off our honeymoon!'

He assessed Megan's smart appearance. 'Obviously your business has survived the slump.'

'Yes, that's why I need another warehouse.'

'Then you've got yourself one.'

'You haven't stated a price.'

'Whatever you think it's worth. I'm getting out of the shipping business and going abroad.'

'Leaving everything behind . . . even the house at Tynmorfa? I met Sybil Jones not long ago and . . .'

'I'm selling it.' He stood up and came round to her side of the desk. Placing a hand under her chin, he tipped her face back forcing her to look at him. The burning, haunted look in his eyes frightened her. 'Why don't you come with me, Megan?'

'No!' A shiver went through her as she pulled away.

He gave a contemptuous laugh. 'Of course, I forgot. You're an entrepreneur these days, making quite a name for yourself.' He sighed. 'I should have married you, Megan. If only my father hadn't stopped me. Short-sighted of him really, because obviously he recognised your flare for business. He couldn't resist the one thing he'd set his heart on, though, the combined wealth of the Walkers and the Brocklehursts. Now I've succeeded in ruining it all. I'm glad you will be getting the warehouse, it's one

378

less acquisition my wife and father-in-law can claim.'

Megan wasn't sure whether to believe him or not. It didn't matter now; in some ways she'd had a lucky escape. Robert was twice the man he was.

'We haven't settled anything yet. You haven't named your price, Miles.'

'Whatever you think is fair. You know its value. Bring the cash here tomorrow, I'll be waiting,' he said as she stood up to leave. 'Here's the documentation,' he added as he handed her a sheaf of papers.

'I would much rather he'd fixed the price,' Megan frowned when she told Robert about the proposed deal.

'That would be too straightforward for Miles Walker,' Robert sneered.

'Yes, I'm not at all sure that I'm doing the right thing in going on with this.' Megan sighed.

'You'll do it anyway, since you think it's a way of helping him out,' he commented grimly. 'Make sure that the papers he's handed over are in order, or you could find you've parted with the cash and he's scarpered leaving you with egg on your face.'

'Robert, how dare you say such a thing! You certainly believe in kicking a man when he's down,' she added scathingly.

'You really ought to settle by cheque or credit transfer not by cash,' her solicitor advised when she called at his office the following morning to collect the transfer documents she had asked him to check over.

Megan nodded but said nothing as she took

them from him. Silently, she stowed them away in her briefcase alongside the bulky package she had already collected from the bank.

A tight smile played around Miles' mouth as he took the package from her and dropped it into a leather holdall by the side of his chair.

'Aren't you going to check what's in there? It might be old newspapers cut up,' Megan said with a ghost of a smile.

'I trust you! Are you sure you won't change your mind and come with me, Megan?' His voice was pleading, as if the chasm that had grown between them had been miraculously breached.

'No Miles, my life is here,' she said firmly.

'That was what I expected you to say, but I needed to be sure.' He held out his hand. 'I'll never forget you, Megan. And thanks for the money, you won't regret that either.' He drew her towards him so that their bodies were touching. He bent his head, his lips rested on hers, but she felt no flicker of emotion . . . nothing.

She walked out of Old Hall Street knowing it was the end of an era. She went straight to Canning Dock, eager to inspect her new acquisition, planning in her mind how she would use the additional warehouse space.

For several minutes she stood on the quayside, admiring the vastness of the building and finding it hard to believe it was now hers. Then she slipped the key Miles had given her into the lock and went inside.

The first thing she noticed was that it wasn't empty. Puzzled, she lifted the light grey sheeting from the massive bulk in the centre of the ware-house, then caught her breath in astonishment. The Silver Cloud Rolls Royce, with its person-alised number plates, MW 100 gleamed at her from under the covers.

On the windscreen was an envelope with her name on the outside. Her hand was trembling as she opened it.

MEGAN
IT WAS ALWAYS MEANT TO BE YOURS
THE KEYS ARE IN THE IGNITION
MILES

Chapter Thirty-eight

Their new warehouse at Canning Dock proved invaluable. Megan's haulage business was suddenly in a different category now that the effects of the slump were beginning to ease. Dockers and seamen, like everyone else, were keen to recoup their losses.

Robert became more involved with the administration and spent less and less time out on the road, so she installed two large desks, one for her and one for him.

'I think it's time everyone realised how much we've grown,' insisted Megan.

He looked puzzled. 'I'm not sure I quite follow.'

'Carefully designed publicity. I want all our vehicles to be in the same colours. A company livery, not a hotchpotch of odd lorries like it is now.'

'Mmm! You have a point there, I suppose.'

'Can't you see it, Robert?' Her eyes sparkled with enthusiasm. 'Our entire fleet all carrying the company name. A name that will be recognised not only here in Liverpool but right across the country . . .'

'Hey! Steady on. Our drivers are only small-time chaps, operating with one lorry apiece.'

'That's how it stands at the moment, but it can change.' She tapped on the desk with her pen. 'Why can't each of them employ a driver and operate a second lorry? Most of them have taken on a mate to help with loading and unloading. Now, if they were offered a slightly higher percentage on each load, don't you think they would be prepared to operate a second lorry and hire another driver?'

'I suppose some of them would be interested,' he admitted. 'Most of us are keen to increase the size of our wage packet.'

'Exactly!' Her face glowed. 'The storage capacity is available, we have an ever-growing network of contacts, so all we need is extra lorries.'

'Well, why don't you buy more vehicles yourself?'

'No.' She shook her head. 'It would tie up too much of my capital and slow down expansion in other areas. What is even more important, it would cut down on individual involvement. As it is, fiddling and pilferage are non-existent because each man is personally responsible for what he carries.'

'It's an interesting idea,' he admitted cautiously, 'but I'm not sure if any of them will be able to afford a second lorry.'

'They can! I've already made enquiries. It will be possible for them to buy a vehicle on hire-purchase if we vouch for them. We will also tell them that all the lorries must be in a specified colour and carry the company name in silver lettering on a deep blue background.'

He gave a nod of approval. 'That sounds good!'

'I'm glad you're in agreement. I was also wondering, since you are becoming more and more involved with the administration . . . I'm planning to open a new depot in Rhyl, or somewhere close by, and to put Dad in charge of it, so if you would like to come into the office on a full-time basis . . . as general manager?'

'I could be persuaded.' He grinned. 'What's the deal?'

'Basic salary plus a percentage of the overall takings?'

'That sounds tempting.' He scribbled down some figures on the pad in front of him, nodding in satisfaction.

'What are you going to do if I'm in the office all the time, holiday abroad in the sun?'

Robert regretted his words the moment he uttered them. Megan quivered with anger. Her face hardened, and when she answered her voice was icy and distant.

'I shall still retain overall control of the business,' she said stiffly.

'Yes, of course. That was meant as a joke.' He sighed. 'You intend to go on expanding?' he asked cautiously.

'Most definitely. And not just with road haulage. I have other ideas . . .' She hesitated as if she was about to impart some exciting news. Then she shrugged and looked away.

Robert held his breath waiting for her to go on. When she did, her voice had its old, natural warmth and he dared to hope.

'About this position of general manager, Robert. I was counting on you taking it,' she said confidently. 'No one else could do it as well as you! Anyway,' she said with a grin, 'I wouldn't want anyone else working alongside me.'

Megan wasted no time in putting her new plans into action. She talked to the drivers and explained the scheme to each of them individually. They were all enthusiastic and promised their full support.

'It means a lot more work and far greater responsibility,' she warned.

'I don't mind that if it means more money in my pay packet,' Jock told her sombrely.

'It's a grand idea,' Fred agreed, his eyes shining with enthusiasm.

'It couldn't have come at a better time,' Sandy told her. 'I'm going to be a dad in a few months' time,' he confided, 'and that means Patsy will be giving up her job so the chance for me to earn more is wonderful news, I can tell you.'

With Robert's help, the project went ahead smoothly. He even agreed with her that they should launch the extended fleet publicly by throwing a party for all their customers.

'We could hold it in the Canning Dock Warehouse the first week in September,' Robert suggested. 'Leave it any later in the year and all the decent weather will be gone. You don't want customers freezing to death as they stand around on the quayside admiring our new fleet!'

When the great day finally dawned, Megan found the months of preparation, and attention to detail, paying off. Every tiny piece of the jigsaw fell smoothly into place. Even the weather was on their side, a clear and balmy day with barely a ripple on the Mersey.

The warehouse was decked out with bunting in

deep blue and silver. The fleet of twenty lorries was parked in front of the warehouse. As Megan had stipulated, they were all painted light blue and carried a silver logo depicting a huge globe of the world emblazoned with the letters MW in dark blue.

The drivers all wore dark-blue denim trousers and light-blue denim jackets with a smaller version of the logo emblazoned in silver on the breast pocket.

Megan, wearing a crisp silver-grey suit and a blue silk blouse, felt nervous but very proud as she stood beside the bonnet of the Silver Cloud Rolls that was also parked outside the warehouse.

In her carefully worded speech, she thanked workers and customers alike for their confidence and support. Then she invited everyone to enjoy the food and drink laid out inside the warehouse.

It was a tremendous celebration and Megan was aware of the pride in her father's voice as he talked to people.

As she sipped restrainedly at a glass of champagne, Kathy Williams looked years younger than when she'd lived in Wallasey, and the relaxed happiness on her mother's face added to Megan's joy.

With words of praise from all sides ringing in her ears, Megan went to find Robert, eager to see his reaction. She found him standing alone, and was shocked at how miserable he looked. She had expected him to be as happy as she was. After all, he had been part of the enterprise since the very beginning. He wasn't a mere cog, he was its mainspring!

'What on earth is wrong?'

'Nothing!'

'Come off it, Robert!' Anger made her speak sharply. 'We've known each other far too long for me to believe that.'

'Anti-climax, I suppose.'

'Why? Everything is going like clockwork. You are the only one, apart from my dad, who's been involved in the project right from the very beginning. I might never have succeeded without your help.' She touched his arm. 'I am extremely grateful.'

'I haven't done it to earn your gratitude! I've done it because of what I feel for you, what I've always felt for you ever since the first moment I walked into your home. You still don't understand, do you, Megan? I love you!'

'Robert . . .'

'Let me finish!' The anger in his voice silenced her. 'At one time, when it was only Miles I was up against, I really believed that one day you would recognise him for what he was and when you did I would have a chance. I love you so deeply that whenever you've turned to me for help I've been eager to do anything you asked.'

'But Robert . . .'

'No, please let me finish. I've watched you build up this business from absolutely nothing and admired every step you've taken. I can't imagine anyone else being willing to trade in a Rolls Royce for a lorry, or,' his face twisted into a wry smile, 'have that same Rolls Royce handed back as a gift.' He shook his head in bewilderment. 'I suppose even Miles wanted to see justice done in the end

. . . That's the sort of effect you have on people, Megan.'

He thrust his hands deep in his pockets as he turned and surveyed the impressive line-up of lorries, the bunting-draped warehouse and the laughing, happy groups of people standing around.

'Miles was a formidable opponent,' he went on, 'but at least he was only a man.' He waved a hand expressively. 'Against this set-up I don't stand a chance!'

'But Robert . . .'

'Let's be realistic, Megan. Would you give up being a successful business woman in order to marry me?'

'No, Robert. I wouldn't give up my career for marriage.'

'Well, at least I know where I stand,' he muttered bitterly. 'Thank you for being honest.'

'It's the answer you expected!'

'Yes, but not the one I wanted to hear!'

Surely Robert must know that he had picked the wrong moment for a discussion of this sort, Megan thought exasperatedly. She wanted to tell him how much he meant to her, but the words that formed in her head sounded trite, as if she was saying them simply to pacify him.

'Half the time you don't even know I exist,' he said mockingly.

'That's not true, Robert . . . and you know it.' Anger made her choke.

'Then give up all this and marry me.'

Megan bristled. It wasn't a plea or a proposal, it was an order. No one, not even Robert, was

going to give her orders, or take away her independence, she vowed.

'Is that your answer . . . silence?'

'I could never knuckle down to being bossed
around by anyone else, not even my husband,' she
added scathingly, 'and well you know it!'

'Did I ask for that?'

'It must be what you expect, otherwise why
order me to give all this up and marry you?'

'So that's your answer; your final decision!' He
turned away abruptly.

The thought of Robert walking out of her life
for ever sent shock waves through her. Deep in
her heart she'd known for years how Robert felt
about her, ever since her first Christmas in
Liverpool. Lynn had told her, so had her mother
and father. Robert was the one person she could
always turn to in an emergency. Strong, reliable,
and wise he had never failed her.

As he turned back to look at her and their gaze
held, a thousand unspoken messages of love and
desire spanned the void between them.

'Robert!' She moved towards him, her hands
outstretched. As he reached out and took them her
heart began to beat faster. His grip tightened as he
drew her into his arms, holding her so close she
could hardly breathe, crushing her crisp silver-grey
suit into a myriad of creases.

She could feel the powerful beat of his heart
against her breasts. His muscled thighs, as they
pressed against her own, were like rocks; a
strangely satisfying feeling. She looked up into his
strong face with a faint sigh of happiness. Her

hands went round his neck, pulling his head down until their lips met in a tender kiss that deepened into one of hungry passion.

For Megan it was no ordinary kiss: it was a pledge of commitment. Placing her hands flat against his shoulders she pulled free, her cheeks flushed.

'Sorry!' His face darkened as he let his hands drop limply to his sides. 'Hoping that you would give up all you've worked for really was a stupid dream!' he muttered.

'Can I say something?' she asked quietly.

'Go on!' His eyes were inscrutable, his mouth a tight line, his square jaw tipped forward as if ready to receive a blow.

'I wouldn't consider a takeover, Robert . . . but I could be interested in a partnership. That's if you find such a proposal acceptable,' she added, her eyes twinkling.

He stared, uncomprehendingly for a moment. Then his frown changed to a broad smile.

'Yes, that would be acceptable,' he breathed. 'I'm overwhelmed. Hard to believe, but I find it acceptable all right!' He took her into his arms again, caressing her face with his lips, whispering endearments that sent her pulses racing.

'The party's breaking up we'd better be getting back,' she murmured. 'Shall we tell them?'

'I think everyone's had enough excitement for one day!' His mouth claimed hers again in a long, lingering kiss that left her dizzy. 'Anyway, it's much too precious a moment to share with everyone else,' he murmured.

Chapter Thirty-nine

People looked in surprise as a Silver Cloud Rolls Royce turned into the cemetery and was driven sedately along the wide gravel path before coming to a stop.

Heads turned in astonishment as a bride, looking almost ethereal in her white satin dress, her gossamer-fine lace veil billowing in the light breeze, stepped out. Escorted by a handsome broad-shouldered man in morning dress she picked her way daintily over the grass towards a grave guarded by a beautiful white marble statue of a sweet-faced angel holding a musical instrument.

Megan and Robert stood holding hands in silent contemplation for a moment, until they were joined by Watkin and Kathy.

'I wish you could have been my bridesmaid, Lynn,' Megan said softly as she laid her bridal bouquet of spring flowers on her sister's grave.

Gently, she kissed her mother's cheek, then, with Robert's arm circling her waist protectively, she walked back to the car.

Watkin and Kathy remained at Lynn's graveside a moment longer while Kathy tried to compose herself. She was still dabbing the tears from her eyes when they reached the car and headed for the Hotel Victoria to join the wedding guests who were waiting there for them all, ready to celebrate.